Turning Points

A NOVEL

A.B. Arnold

Quintessence

GOLDEN, COLORADO

FIRST EDITION

The characters and events in this book
are fictitious. Any similarity to real persons,
living or dead, is coincidental and not
intended by the author.

Arnold, A.B.
Turning Points: a novel / by A.B. Arnold
-Ist ed.
p.   cm.
ISBN-13   978 – 0 – 6151 – 6579 – 0 (softcover ed.)
ISBN-10   0 – 615 – 16579 – 6
Library of Congress PCN
LCCN 2007938104
1. Self-realization.   2. Family and Relationships
3. Friendship   4. Poetry   5. Grief   I Title

10   9   8   7   6   5   4   3   2

Published by Quintessence, Golden, Colorado USA
Book Design by Quintessence Studio

Distributed by Lulu
www.lulu.com/quintessence
Printed in the United States of America

For my mother, my 'sisters' and for Ruthie

Warm thanks to my husband Stephen who encouraged me to see this labor of love through to final completion. I extend my gratitude to all my pre-readers and in-process supporters for their suggestions and assistance. Finally, a special thank you to my editor Rich Hecht.

You know the feeling...
You're forgetting something
Spinning round and round
Wanting to understand
Trying to remember

You know the feeling...
Nothing
Can conjure that
Distant memory which
Never clarifies
Never confronts you

You know the feeling...
Days drawn to eternity
You're lost, devoted to fulfill
This silent, driving force
Calling You

Calling you home

One

WEDNESDAY, APRIL 2

I think how a person holds their newspaper tells you what kind of person they are," Wendy surmised. She fumbled to tear open sugar packets without sending crystals flying out over their table.

"Why would you think that?" Kelly often humored her best friend's whimsical thought processes. Her coffee, which was hot, was all she cared about. It had to spur on her creative inspiration for the day. "I mean, what difference does it make?" she queried, realizing when Wendy didn't immediately launch into her hypothesis, she should at least be encouraging.

"Well, think about it, a newspaper's totally a pain to look cool with at these puny tables…"

Kelly's thoughts wandered as Wendy chattered on. She sipped her coffee intermittently.

"So don't you think it's true?" Wendy prompted a conclusion.

"What?" Kelly gazed haplessly around the café realizing she had zoned out on her friend's voice. Mornings come too early, she thought; did Wendy have to be so chipper? "Sorry. Tell it to me again."

"Just look around. That woman over there," Wendy nudged toward the back of the café. "The flyers are falling out, the entire paper's spread out all over her table, she can't even put her drink down. She is one-handedly out of control."

"So what? You figure her life's a mess?" Perhaps that's the kind of conclusion Wendy's looking to draw here. Kelly's conclusion was that people come to coffee shops to drink coffee and read.

Wendy analyzed another victim. "That loner over there, he's not reading anything." Fresh newspapers were stacked on the counter near his table. "He's probably paranoid," Wendy's eyes narrowed and shifted.

"He's probably meditating. Leave him alone!" Kelly ordered under her breath. "I have to get going. Deadline day and no less than three meetings crammed in my schedule."

As Kelly reached for her knapsack, Wendy launched another hushed attack; she was on a roll. "I've seen that guy before. Check out his newspaper, Kelly."

She saw a man in the far corner by the window. The section he read was folded in quarters, within comfortable grasp. The unread sections were nested aside on his table. He had room for his coffee cup and one free hand besides. A Fader's Café denizen, he comfortably reclined in his chair with one leg resting over the other; as far as she could tell, he didn't notice their glances. Good. But he must have heard Wendy giggle as she sized him up as an obsessive-compulsive neat freak, and a creature of severe habit. This is a café; everyone here is a creature of severe habit, Kelly thought to herself. She hurriedly gathered her belongings and quickly kissed her friend out of apologetic sympathy, rather than as a goodbye gesture.

Kelly didn't have spare time to promote Wendy's notions. Perhaps she should have cut her morning practice short at the rink, in an effort to be more on top of her day. Days like this you need to snatch early, Kelly thought, or else they just progressively slip away, and out of your calendar control. As she walked briskly past the Dalhousie University campus gates to arrive at her office at Graphix Alive, she couldn't remember finishing her refill, or which sidewalk trash canister the to-go cup found.

Mornings for her had to start early if she was to stick to her plan of fitting in three morning practices before work each week. Most Dal Arena ice sessions conflicted with her work schedule and those that didn't were congested with school kids; weekend sessions were like open house at the zoo. It was enough that she coached during the Saturday mayhem from nine to noon every week. It was her schedule and she needed to stick to it. The average unmotivated person would pull the covers overhead and beg for five more minutes.

She unlocked her office door at eight-fifteen. In her private washroom at the back of her office, she opened the closet where she kept her suits and accessories for work. She felt like blue today, so she selected the navy pantsuit with brushed gold buttons and hung it on the hook on the back of the door. Her pale-gold knit tank shirt was still under dry cleaner plastic, and today she remembered to remove the tag. Behind a closed door she morphed from athlete to professional graphic artist, accented with heeled shoes and jewelry, and her hair loosely clipped up; anyone would assume she had come straight from home.

She stowed her packed lunch in the mini-fridge and put a pot of fresh coffee on for her clients and her colleagues Linda and Paul, a married couple who co-owned Graphix Alive. Paul, the senior graphic artist, earned a fine arts degree in graphic design and Linda looked after everything that kept Graphix Alive breathing: front-line personnel, the accountant, the organizer and doer of everything required, expected and unexpected. Their ten-year old business grew from the ground. By year four, they hired Kelly, coincident with relocating to the renovated Mansard Victorian; Graphix Alive grew into more personnel, better lighting and a larger work environment that looked upbeat. It was a place that formed a strong visual impression, the assurance of their success; it was the nature of the business. And where do all these clients come from, Kelly wondered as she surveyed her appointment book. Their current contract obligations included glossy packages for AirTech Industries, oversize four-color panel advertisements for a local clothing outfitter, brochures and stationery for several small businesses, along with the continuous stream of projects from local advertising firms. These days, Kelly sensed the need for another hiring round. The aroma of Kona blend drip coffee began to swirl around her, and she was momentarily comforted.

They say it's a small world. If it weren't for Wendy, Kelly wouldn't have this job, one among many reasons she owed a lifelong debt to her. She didn't consider herself an artist and this wasn't her dream job. More like a nightmare on a merry-go-round, it was a continuous whirl of deadlines and the eyestrain from the computer kept her perpetually dizzy. But she was organized, adept and gifted enough to do what Paul required: to help develop and collate preliminary and secondary designs and copy layouts, take over midrange planning and design, until the firm and the client converged on a common vision within budget. Paul knew that clients appreciated Kelly's productivity, patience and perseverance, as well as her attractive package that combined a professional look with her skill; she was the ideal representative in a contract's formative stages. She had an innate sense of palette, pattern and proportion. Although Kelly held no degree in her so-called field of expertise, only she perceived the detriment. At age twenty-one, Kelly came to Paul Jameson via enthusiastic recommendation from Wendy's father, Arthur Kaine. At that time, Kelly was employed at Kaine, Marshall and MacLeod, one of the Maritime's pre-eminent advertising firms, not because she wanted to be in advertising, but because she needed a self-supporting income. Arthur immediately made a place for Kelly when Wendy, as his employee and more importantly as his daughter, approached him in desperation for her best friend's plight. In the year and a half Kelly worked at KM&M, support staff trained her in desktop publishing; and with corporate sponsorship, she earned an official diploma by correspondence. To an outsider, it may have been a validation of her ability; it wasn't even something she wanted to hang on her office wall. But that piece of paper was a springboard to a career that Kelly could embark upon. Six years ago, Paul needed a copy artist more than anything else. Contracting Arthur's corporation for Graphix Alive advertising requirements, while symbiotically servicing KM&M's whole host of graphics needs, Arthur used his connections when he sensed it was time for Kelly to move on.

Wendy knew unflinchingly upon graduating high school that she would work for her father, and not because family and friends assumed she would. She loved the glitzy world of advertising, and the doors it could fling open for her. She was a self-admitted shopaholic, the very living example of female consumerism that every retailer subsisted upon. When it came to buying, Wendy was Everywoman. Representatively, she was the banner motivation for advertisers far and near, and she intuitively understood why various advertising campaigns either hit or missed their mark. She had the knack for landing both sides of the consumer coin; she was KM&M's corporate asset while she earned her credentials in advertising, and the retail market's asset while spending her father's money. In any case, she had a brilliant mind for conceiving effective campaigns, and anyone who suggested she was spending unearned money of daddy's would be taken to task.

The name Wendy and the description "impulsive" were synonymous. From the first day of kindergarten, Wendy took a liking to Kelly instantly; perhaps she had found her willing and suitable sidekick. Predictable, shy and impressionable, Kelly was nervously captivated by Wendy's outgoing spontaneity, and bewitched by her daring almost brazen approach to life. Like an acquired taste, Kelly learned to love Wendy's sense of fairness, freedom, spirit, and enthusiasm, and to a lesser degree, her devilishness. As children, whenever Wendy wormed her way into trouble, Kelly instinctively worked her out of it. Both girls grew up without siblings, so they proceeded through the topsy-turvy journey of life as sisters. And just like sisters can be, they were as different as black and white. The same age, with their birthdays separated by a month, Kelly was born under the sign of Capricorn and Wendy under Aquarius; earth versus air, loyal versus carefree, practical versus adventurous.

Kelly, an energetic, brown-eyed girl of average height, slender yet solidly built, ignored comments her entire adolescence that she was too tall to be a skater. Her figure held a slim architectural strength. Wendy was forever jealous of her bone structure, especially her cover model jaw line and cheekbones. Kelly never understood her unfounded jealousy, remarking on many occasions that Wendy was the one with classic fine features: she was petite, with porcelain complexion, chestnut brown hair and green eyes; she was blessed with a delicate Celtic contrast. Wendy hated being likened to a northern pixie, so she abandoned the familiar tailored bob hairstyle, and opted for a short, textured and highlighted look that looked fashionably unkempt; people wouldn't think pixie now. Kelly only would chop her longer locks if it meant curbing five minutes off her morning routine.

They say opposites attract. Discipline always came easily for Kelly and it was a dividing line of their polarized personalities. Both girls thrived on intellectual challenge and found clever ways to work around their differences. Most discussions ended in stalemate following nothing less than a heated discussion. For twenty-two years, Wendy tirelessly attempted to lure Kelly away from her irresistible compulsion to be angelically good, testing her moral principles at every bend. Conversely, Kelly diligently tried to tame Wendy's wilder ways and make her see the more far-reaching consequences of her heedless actions, mostly when it came to men.

Knowing the background, each had made inroads of influence on the other and if it weren't for the faintest sense of progress in either direction, both women might have called it quits years ago. Together, they appeared as the perfect complement to each other; that's what their parents always said, anyway. Others just wondered what they had in common that they remained friends all these years.

The evening wind had a bite and she felt her cheeks reddening. April in Halifax could still hold cruel touches of winter. As she made her way home to her second-level flat of the Old Victorian on the corner of Walton and Larch Streets, the weight of her treasured custom skates in her knapsack felt unusually heavy. She prayed she wasn't coming down with the flu. A restful evening with the company of lemon tea beckoned her. She didn't bring any work home with her this time, a bad habit she was now in the long, drawn-out process of quitting. Still, there were times when exceptions had to be made, and luckily, this week wasn't one of them. She hated the term workaholic, knowing full well it applied to her. She had her own reasons to feel quietly proud, on several fronts her life was improving. She was taking control as her doctor had advised her, even if it wasn't obvious to the rest of the world.

Her fingers felt numb from the cold as she slipped the key in the door of the Old Victorian. Since the tragedy over nine years ago, she called this one-room flat home. For an eighteen-year old back then, it was affordable, cozy, and placed her in close company with other tenants, mostly students, and Mrs. Wiles, their landlady. She often remembered Mrs. Wiles' kindness her first couple of years here. Instinctively, she checked on her every now and then, to ask her how things were and make polite chitchat. To both of them, it meant much more than small talk.

Kelly's long and narrow second-floor flat offered all the condensed comforts of home. The kitchen and living area was highlighted by a front bay window facing Larch Street, and another on the south side between the kitchen table and the fridge. Whitewashed built-in shelving around the Larch Street bay window-seat extended around the corner to the kitchen table. Toward the back of the flat were her bedroom and a small bathroom. Her antique three-quarter double bed was against the back wall under a small window. She was lucky to find sheets for that bed anymore. Her antique oval-mirror dresser stood next to the bathroom door. In the center of the flat, oddly enough, was the kitchen, consisting of a serviceable island that housed kitchen cupboards, drawers, a three-burner stovetop and a one-basin sink. Across, the fridge was on the left side of the bay window and her toaster and microwave oven sat on the window ledge. This little kitchen had the benefit of summer evening sunbeams, but the warped wood casement windows were drafty in winter. Standing at the sink, she could gaze upon a poster of San Francisco's Japanese Garden hanging upon the back of her door. Its green open stillness offset the occasional mild claustrophobia. To the left of the door was her ivory muslin sofa, plump with colorful print cushions. She simply couldn't imagine anyone else fitting in here. Even the company of a forcibly confined cat would be too much guilt for her to bear. She harshly reprimanded herself for the books strewn across the sofa and the bills piled on her tiny coffee table. A place this small has to be kept completely in order, there's nowhere to escape clutter should it get out of hand, she kept chiding herself as she tidied up, while her supper heated in the oven. How many days of her life had she tortured herself with this useless chatter in her mind? The objective at hand was to just clean up, without mental barrage. The last item she picked up to put away was her journal, a simple leather-bound book, with gold-deckled pages and a satin ribbon. As she pressed it to her, her eyes surveyed her four walls in the dull evening light. The impressionist art prints softening the high plaster walls seemed to slow the blood rush. Monet's Bridge over a Pool of Water Lilies hung above her sofa. Van Gogh's Sunflowers and Cypresses flanked the wide archway to her bedroom. Above her bed was Monet's Four Trees. Thank God for art. Thank God for music. She set Debussy's Suite Bergamasque to play in her stereo. Her mind settled then began to float. Music had the power to lift her, to send her soul where it longed to be. Her mind led her in sweeping curves and effortless turns. Standing motionless, she experienced the sensation of lightness, just like when she skated. The intruding call of the oven buzzer broke the peace of her mesmerized state.

FRIDAY, APRIL 4

Faders Café buzzed with the usual morning congestion and the counter line-up was nearly to the door. Kelly was grateful she made it in before the rain.

"Hey, where were you last night? I called." Wendy dashed parentally.

"What time did you call?"

"It was after eight, I think...don't tell me you were out on a date." Wendy should have been a lawyer. She knew never to ask a question she didn't already know the answer to.

Wendy's tone of voice that accompanied any comment relating to Kelly's social life was growing too familiar. "And what if I were, there's no point in telling you, you wouldn't believe me anyway." Setting her coffee and orange-cranberry muffin down, she carefully tucked her knapsack under her chair. "I was just out on the back deck getting some fresh air. The sky cleared up enough to see the stars. I can't wait for summer." She longed to see her favorite summer constellation, Cygnus, the Swan.

Sensing a lighter mood, Wendy began to tell her about the new man in her life. This one was different, she claimed yet again.

Kelly knew Wendy's last two boyfriend catastrophes had been clients who undoubtedly became haplessly charmed by the woman who may as well have promised them the billboard moon. "He better not be another client, I hope you've learned your lessons. It's bad enough you found yourself in a situation where you had to pass the file to your colleague and then with this last guy, the contract fell through altogether. Not good for business." Kelly picked at cranberries baked to the muffin paper.

Since high school, Wendy hadn't floundered single more than a month or two at a time in fruitless pursuit of the indefinable. A series of hasty, bad choices born of desperate measures accurately described Wendy's love life. There were some potential winners but Wendy never stuck it out long enough with any of them. For her, if the magic wasn't there, it wasn't going to appear out of thin air.

"Someone else at work introduced me to him. His name is Franklin. Not Frank," she emphasized, "Franklin. He's going through a divorce right now." Wendy continued, "He's looking to put together a spread for a charity campaign and our firm is defraying some of the costs by volunteering our services. The client file isn't mine."

"Divorce?" Kelly honed in.

"Umm, yeah. He's in his forties, and he was married for eleven years. We're meeting for lunch and you'll be happy to know it's not a business lunch."

"Alert. Man on rebound."

Wendy knew where Kelly was headed. In mere seconds, she would bring up Jimmy who was newly divorced when Wendy began dating him. The fact that Jimmy had married a woman he had been dating for two months - at a Christmas party - was the reliable example. A local Justice of the Peace, who happened to be another party guest, performed the impromptu ceremony. Wendy came to realize shortly after she began seeing Jimmy that it was a match made in hell. "Hey, at least I'm still trying," Wendy insisted pointedly.

She had stopped enquiring with any sincerity into Kelly's social life over a year ago; Wendy opted for one-liner sarcastic jabs instead. Kelly had long surpassed her limit of patience when it came to being asked. Like clockwork, Wendy would unsubtly offer to set Kelly up, since she seemed to be having so much trouble finding someone on her own. She went on as though Kelly were a forsaken humanitarian cause society needed to contend with. And predictably, Kelly flatly refused. What reason did she have to believe that Wendy's choice of a prize date would amount to anything worthwhile, when she couldn't secure herself with any of her own choices? There was no point in asking a drowning person how to swim.

The cold rain Halifax was known for continued to fall, providing a steady stream of dampened sniffling morning customers, and both women were relieved they had brought their umbrellas.

May 5

Freedom

Without, will I walk deeper into darkness?
Such a curious stillness that shares
A wicked sense of security with me.
Time be the ocean of ice,
Ascend me into Light,
Illumine my road to freedom.

A path of unity and duality,
With visionary glimmer and glint,
Steely sharpness carves my direction.
The journey that had no beginning,
Can never end,
The dance that sweeps me into Light.

Re-emergence began when my blades touched the ice for the first time in seven
years.
There is an inexplicable cold comfort in remaining attached to sorrow - a
strongly binding one.

The soul cannot live or love …
broken, by depression,
caged, by limitations
fearful, of its own nature or existence.

There can be no freedom if one does not know oppression.

In those times of despair and suffering, my faith brought me to a place where
I had to confess all of my ungratefulness - that I had been left with many
blessings…Yet, I was thankful for none of them.

I am preparing to break free.

June 18

My father and I used to love to lie on the grass in the backyard and just ponder the stars on summer nights. We were not astronomers…we were dreamers. The permanence of the night sky helps me endure this immense emptiness in my heart.

Stars,
Sleep on black velvet
Surround me
Sparkle, precious gems of night
Sigh and fill my sight…

Tiny pinpoints of light,
Tossed a thousand thousand years ago.
Tender peace and security near
True strength than safeties we hold dear.

My spirit travels galaxies
Sonorous, nebulous, diaphanous
Longing lifts me to the skies
Could heavenly light shine from my eyes?

August 14

I just re-read Frost's The Road less Traveled…Love in my heart, reading this poem, I miss my mother. In her youth, she framed it, and hung it in the kitchen, so all those older and younger would know

Timeless Cherishment.

My Mother

A Resistance Original
She hated her piano lessons
Crotchety Major General
Slayer of her symphonies
Mom finally went AWOL.

Why do people force their ways upon others? Is it because it's all they know?

I remember being in tears after my first novice divisional competition, when Alex and I had competed two dances. Certain influential people there said I was too tall to be an ice dancer, and I was too young at the time to know that those comments were weighted. Mom wouldn't let me allow biased, narrow-minded viewpoints to thwart or limit my pursuit of life. When I feel the energy for pushing through life draining from my veins, remembering mom's indomitable purpose of seeking truth, within one's own realm, reaffirms me.

I've never walked the "traveled" road either. Wendy wanted me to attack life, the way she did. Wendy was the road trip rover who wanted company in the passenger's seat, not because she needed a navigator.

High School Hassles - Wendy was constantly warning me that if I didn't eventually give in to Christopher's wants, he would leave me and move on to a wildflower more ready and willing to bloom, that all guys were that way and it didn't necessarily have anything to do with love. Looking back, my first love, like Wendy's, was never meant to be, nothing what I had imagined it would be, never the way I understood it to be.

So I walked the lonely road
Of dreams pointed true north
Directions we know to follow
Others we have to let go.

January 23

Wendy didn't show up this morning, again. I have an hour to write – I refuse to go in early to work although I'm officially swamped. I promised Dr. Lake to change my old workaholic tendencies. Too many contracts for this time of year, and clearly not enough inspiration – all my work is starting to look the same ..stale and short on creativity. Spells death in this business.

It feels good to write here at the cafe – a change of routine, a different host of sights, smells and sounds. Why have I never taken the opportunity to write here before? It's not that I don't like my flat, it's home…

I see several familiar faces among ones I've never seen before. You would think that coming to the same place just about every day for I don't know how many years, you'd recognize everyone by now. Maybe everyone else is brave enough to move on, to explore and discover new places.

For a homebody like me, old habits are hard to break. I know Dr. Lake is right - she has been right from the beginning. I'm glad I listened to her and got back on the ice. It amazes me that my body didn't forget everything and that I didn't break my leg my first time back. So bad habits can be broken. My body feels strong, agile and light again - the intense re-training was worth it - and my mind has something else besides work to think about, I only wish it were enough to bribe the ever-elusive creative muse. I just don't know why I'm in a creative rut right now. Why am I so blocked?

Cindy just dropped a tray of glasses - nearly all of them broke, judging by the sound of things. Everyone else here looks just as startled as I feel. It gave a few of us a reason to smile for a moment — probably a shared relief that we didn't do it. My heart is still in palpitations, though. I wonder if there will ever be a time that the sound of breaking glass won't affect me this way.

Two

Perhaps it really does take the better part of a decade to recover to the point that the world could look at her and think she was normal. But when Kelly did try to picture her life from an external perspective, she saw an ordinary woman making it from day to day. Maybe it was all a figment of her imagination, no more than memories of a nightmare.

It was turning out to be much harder to live as though nothing had happened. She hadn't really been following Dr. Lake's advice. At certain crossroads, Wendy warned her with purely the best intentions: if she let people know, especially in her father's cold corporate environment, it would backfire; they would use it against her. People could sense the weaker ones, and knew how to find their sore spots and keep them down. It was Darwinism, plain and simple. Under Wendy's protective wing and watchful eye, Kelly rejoined the world of the living. She rarely strayed from the assigned path and went through the expected motions; she had no choice when she proved she couldn't do it alone. If she were to survive, her life had to become a scrupulously choreographed dance performance, with Wendy both leading and adjudicating.

Where would she be without Wendy? The question permanently hovered in her subconscious, occasionally falling to the forefront of her mind. Wendy's family took her in after the tragedy and helped her back on her feet after her dependent innocence was so catastrophically stolen in an instant, at the age of seventeen. Only she remained, and for years following, it made no difference that she did.

Arthur and Marilyn Kaine were the nearest to parents that Kelly would know following the death of her mother and father, Bridget and Ian Pearson. Together with Wendy, they became her family. The Kaines willingly oversaw the legal issues and the incessant estate and probate matters from moment one. They sought her opinions and invited professional recommendations before making financial decisions. They gave her as much financial independence as was deemed appropriate by the estate's financial planners, as the Pearsons' wills had designated. Wendy's parents made certain that her inherited investments continued to be diversified and well managed so she could draw an interest income in the future. Jointly, they had made a decision to sell the Pearson family home and the property's equity, once liquidated, was also invested in Kelly's name.

She never imagined her life to end up this way, despite her eternal gratefulness to the Kaine family for all they had done for her. Her sheltered youth prevented her from knowing what to realistically expect. Now, she was back on her feet, as firmly planted as she could be. She had come further than anyone would have guessed. But even now, she dared not stray, and not because she might appear ungrateful or irresponsible. Currently, her life was completely within her control, observation and measure. Learning enough over the years about investing, Kelly was able to relieve the Arthur and Marilyn of their financial management obligations. They knew she would always be careful. She knew she could call on them for advice at any time. Regardless how mundane it felt, she relied on the inherent safety of her rooted position and her routine. She didn't want to be intimidated by the uncalculated risks that used to confront her at every turn. She refused to return to those dark woods again. She prayed daily that she be out of the woods.

Dr. Karen Lake requested assignment to the teenage girl immediately, having come to know of her case from the County. Once Dr. Lake's department ascertained Kelly would be under the legal guardianship of Arthur and Marilyn Kaine until she reached the age of eighteen, the next step was psychological evaluation and treatment. This was the mandatory procedure following any suicide attempt. Without question, the four years following her parents' death were the most precarious. Karen Lake was part of the team responsible for Kelly's being alive today. She worked with the Kaines to provide Kelly with a successful transition into her forced, terrifying, new existence; they had to ensure she would stay alive and she wouldn't again use prescription medication or any other means to physically undo herself.

Kelly had to return to Dr. Lake after a two-year absence from therapy to treat the recurring and acutely frightening battles associated with her chronic form of anxiety that shared symptoms with post-traumatic stress disorder. The only explanation that Dr. Lake could offer the twenty-four year old, who was now able to manage the basics of daily life, was that any stressful change in her lifestyle had the potential to meet with negative symptomatic consequences. Dr. Lake assessed her life routine in detail and offered suggestions for improvement that didn't rely solely on medication changes. Inside the sphere of Kelly's world, no one besides the Kaines knew of her tragic past and her valiant struggle to live beyond it except her colleagues Linda and Paul. Kelly shared only partial information with them three years ago; she classified her personal history on a need to know basis. They came to know when Dr. Lake advised Kelly that it would be in her best interest to take on one small project that her boss would give her, a task she would be responsible for from conception through to completion. Clearly, there was no way that her work situation could improve without Paul's knowing a partial reason that summoned his participation. Without seeing the full picture of her frightening past, he nevertheless took to the current task with both concern and warmth and never once wanted Kelly to feel weakened or lost in her position as his associate since that time. It never would have occurred to him that a prescribed gesture of his confidence in her to foster her autonomy could make such a radical improvement in Kelly's self-esteem. In any case, while it was a manageable step for him, it was an enormous step for Kelly to tell him even a fraction of her truth.

Reevaluating time management and life balance, thanks to Karen Lake, Kelly dug her skates out of her closet and invited her single greatest passion back into her life. Dr. Lake was adamant she needed to have the physical connection, not just to her childhood, but also with her own body. Engaging again in an activity that Kelly once enjoyed, one she could internalize and focus her mind upon, would further her progress toward positive self-awareness. Rather than living so separately from her external world and her community, hiding as it were, Dr. Lake prompted her to consider coaching again. She would get out to meet people, work with children, and share her expertise.

SATURDAY APRIL 5

They planned to take in a matinée after Kelly finished coaching. She came in from a foggy drizzle to find a message from Wendy on her answering machine indicating that plans had suddenly changed and she needed to postpone theirs for a day. It was her routine that when things didn't go as planned, Kelly reached for her journal. Her current volume was the last of seven identical dark brown, leather-bound books. She averaged one book in just over a year, but she tended to do most of her writing in fits and spurts over the past decade, coinciding with those times she was in the most danger psychologically, those periods when she felt the bottom falling out again.

SUNDAY APRIL 6

"So how did your lunch go with Frank-lin?" Kelly caught herself just in time. "Two medium popcorn and a large Sprite," she motioned to the concession attendant. "We'll share the Sprite," she nodded to Wendy.

"Pretty good, I think. He's better looking than I remembered him being. Have I ever dated anyone that old?" Wendy asked furtively. She didn't want any of the other moviegoers to grab wind of her social agenda.

"Wendy, since when has age mattered to you? You've dated guys five years younger, seven years older…. one would think you were non-discriminating."

"I prefer non-judgmental."

"How about not judgmental enough!"

They both laughed. As they maneuvered their way through clustered crowds in the Cineplex lobby, Kelly piped up, "I suppose you have a matching theory on what you can tell about people by what they order at a theater?" The discourse between them hadn't been so light and humorous in ages, they both thought simultaneously.

Wendy, recognizing the healthy mockery, began part two of her social profile thesis right on cue, "Of course, there are your standard popcorn people, narrow-minded conformists you might guess, but I think they come to theatres because they're addicted to the aroma of fresh-popped kernels and fake butter... then, on the other hand, you have the mammoth-size chocolate bar people. Closet megalomaniacs."

"Let me guess, they're addicted too..." Kelly interjected.

"You got it." They both were elated at how elementary it all was. If only everything in life could be this obvious.

"So did he talk to you about his divorce?"

"A bit. I asked. I know, how bold of me. He told me they were married for eleven years. He found out about eight years ago that she was having an affair, and when he confronted her with it, she told him she had been having affairs for years. Now whether that was true or she said it to spite him, I don't know. He believed her. He told me that his work sends him out of town a fair bit, it's always been that way. So if she got lonely, what could he do?"

"Kids?"

"He has a son, about ten or so."

Kelly tried to shun speculation that Franklin might not even be the boy's biological father. "If she was so lonely, why didn't she say something to him? They could have done something to stay married. He could have stayed home more. In the end, it's the kids who lose out." Kelly wondered how sane people could so easily abandon basic common sense, conditional on the initial assumption of sanity.

"Maybe it was just easier to move on to someone else."

Kelly earnestly hoped that comment wasn't a reflection of Wendy's own philosophy, as she suspected it might be. It was only a matter of time until Wendy would meet the consequences of her actions face to face. She called her on it, "Do you think that's a legitimate answer?"

"I'm not saying it's not an answer. Maybe she didn't connect with him and she did with someone else."

"Or," Kelly juxtaposed acridly, "she didn't try hard enough. They didn't try hard enough. There's a kid involved. Why do people keep making excuses, choosing the easy way out thinking they'll come out ahead? People are so weak to begin with and then wonder what went wrong. Human intelligence has evolved to this?"

Wendy's expression blanked out. Kelly did not want to pursue it any further. She realized she had made her point. Once again, their time together had degraded to emotional mudslinging.

No one should have to settle, for anything, Kelly thought. People can't be pigeonholed according to popcorn or newspapers. It's not black and white; yet, everyone jokes about it because they desperately want it to be, so everything would make sense. People settle all the time, in their careers, in their relationships, in nearly every decision plaguing average life. Kelly lay awake in her bed. Like a well-worn tape, the same plethora of thoughts afflicted her and it would be yet another night of raging insomnia. For a well-established issue of disagreement between them, why was she still so disturbed? She wavered; maybe Wendy was on the right track. She wasn't settling, that's for sure and she touted her acceptance of the facts - they were both at an age where finding a single, unattached man worth having was a miniscule probability. She had demonstrated time and time again her ability to widen her playing field to keep pace with the times. Heaven knows, Wendy was not going to live out the rest of her life single, not if she had the starring role. Kelly examined the possibility that Wendy knew exactly the type of man she was looking for, and that she would find him, eventually. Kelly then questioned why she self-righteously insinuated that a divorcing couple she'd never met hadn't done enough to keep their marriage together. A list of brazen assumptions, and none with confirmation…the entire line of thinking led her to question whether her avoidance of intimate relationships was the same kind of copout excuse, although along a different distressing vein.

In those hours that she lay awake, she watched how the dim light of the streetlamps through leafless trees portrayed jagged, angry faces on her walls. Her bed sheets un-tucked with each toss and every turn. She analyzed every aspect of her relationship with Wendy, years of shared events and history between them. She sensed the claustrophobia closing around her again. She darted out of bed and tried to pace her heart rate back down; she was certain the creaky floorboards of her flat would wake Mrs. Wiles below her. She switched on the small shelf lamp by the window-seat, picked up her journal and opened it to the first fresh page past her last entry. Her pen galloped line by line, and she kept writing until the words exhausted themselves. Heavy, burning teardrops exploded from within her and caused the trails of ink to run and melt into each other like watercolor.

MONDAY, APRIL 14

The Monday morning arena experience was unlike any other. While night's cloak barely lingered over waking homes, Kelly switched on the rink lights to illumine the icy perfection that awaited her blades. Between mid-May and late-September, a frosty mist occasionally settled above the blue-tinged surface, causing a surface softening that subtly sparkled like glitter. It was only the last week of April, maybe it meant summer would come early this year. Monday dawn sessions are always empty, even the arena employees are difficult to locate at that hour, but she knows they're around. She luxuriated in the silent bite of her blade run like a hot knife through butter, hearing only the suggestion of an edge rip as she stroked with both grace and power. The slower and more complete the blade stroke the better, she thought. She knew how to perfectly balance her weight over her blades and the sensitivity of her knees and ankles constantly adjusted for silence, never sacrificing muscle power. With absolute ease and grace, almost as if in slow motion, she turned from forward to backward stroking, aiming for the same liberating movement. For her, nothing in life could come close to this frictionless sensation of uninhibited freedom and perpetual motion, the silence broken only by the wind past her ears. One day, she might have enough courage to skate a free program in a Club show, one that she conceived and choreographed. Kelly had the capability to visualize complex connecting steps to exacting detail and it was good for her to imagine a life beyond her limits.

Since Wendy started seeing Franklin, she rarely made it to Faders for morning coffee with Kelly. Opting to tack extra time onto her lunch break, Wendy met Franklin for lunch on as many weekdays as their schedules would allow since Franklin spent weekends with his son. Kelly suspected they were becoming too quickly serious about each other. Life with Wendy was an uncontrollable roller-coaster ride and Kelly secretly hoped that Franklin would not be the next in the littering long line of Wendy's dumped lovers, especially if he was a good man, and more importantly, if he was good to her. People get divorced all the time and Kelly knew she needed to relax about it. Wendy spoke highly of him but hadn't introduced Franklin to her as yet, presumably taking her best shot to not jinx a potentially good thing. Kelly had always met Wendy's prospects but for some reason this was unfolding differently. She reminded herself again that she would no longer question her best friend's judgment and instead would think only positive thoughts for Wendy and her new relationship.

Dressed head to toe in black, Kelly wore a long-sleeved bodysuit, a zipped cropped sweater under her warm-up jacket and Adidas track pants; for some reason, on ice or off, black was just the color of choice for skaters. Even her ponytail band was black. Bouncing into Faders, she made a quick survey of the seating, spied a few familiar faces, and decided to grab one of two free tables. She chose the one bathed in sunlight. She removed her jacket and hung it on the back of the chair and promptly slung her knapsack over her right shoulder and headed for the order counter. Her usual order, 'medium coffee, half regular, half decaf, in a hot mug for here' gave her enough caffeine surge to launch her neural system but not leave her feeling wretched especially if she hadn't slept well. She intended to write in her journal this morning, eager to sort out the enlightenments that most recently came to her, minor but positive nonetheless. She could feel a change occupy her, pointing her in the direction of personal liberty and peace. She credited herself for adopting a new sense of independence in the past week, an opportunity founded upon Wendy's refocused energies. Granted, they weren't talking as often, compared to times when Wendy was effusive with infatuation. Yet, Kelly felt secure recalling the more cheerfully affirming talks they did have recently. The break from each other was doing them good.

Hot coffee in hand, she carefully made her way toward the cream and sugar stand. Her knapsack was bulky, and when she had to readjust it upon her right shoulder; she was concerned about absentmindedly knocking someone over with it. At least with Wendy's company, she could leave her bag at the table. Pouring cream and grabbing a stir-stick, she turned around holding her coffee in her right hand. She was caught by surprise when her knapsack forcefully struck an unknown stationary obstacle and slid like dead weight off her shoulder, pulling her coffee mug down to the floor with it. In an instant, she knew she had unintentionally clobbered another customer with ten pounds of figure skates and paraphernalia. She quickly lifted her knapsack out of the coffee puddle that began to flow along the café's slanted old wooden floor. Thankfully, the nylon bag protected her skates from the creamed coffee that dripped from her knapsack. Kelly searched frantically for the napkin dispenser and as her gaze left the minor calamity, a wad of napkins appeared in front of her; it was the hand of the person she clobbered. Before she could look to him, while still drying off the dripping bag, an apology fluttered and fled from her lips.

He stopped her mid-sentence by placing his hand on her shoulder, "Hey, it was my fault, I bumped into you. I am really sorry."

"No, it was my fault." Her voice quivered in embarrassment looking for a place to set her knapsack down. "I swung around and I shouldn't have, not so fast anyway. Oh my gosh, I'm so sorry, did I spill coffee over you?"

"Observe," he held open his arms in display, "no spillage. But it did get all over you," he frowned.

She saw it had splashed over the lower half of her right pant leg. Less coffee on her skates then, she sighed. Another handful of napkins would do it, and Cindy had left a stack of fresh napkins on the stand after she mopped the floor. Small café, amazing service, she thought.

Returning to her sun-warmed table, she tried to collect herself. She felt terrible. It wasn't the end of the world, just an embarrassing accident. She looked out the patio window and yearned for summertime when the patio tables would be set up and everyone could bask in the sunshine, even if the temperatures weren't Hawaiian. When her eyes returned to her table, another dark green mug of hot coffee had miraculously appeared in front of her. Whoever did this was stealthy, she thought. She rose up in her chair and looked around. The gentleman victim of her skate bag attack approached her table holding the cream carafe.

"Half decaf, right?" He handed her the cream and a stir-stick.

With a dazed voice, she answered, "Yeah, how'd you know?" It was at that moment she recognized him, the quarter-folded neat-freak newspaper guy.

"Where's your friend today?" he asked innocently.

Oh God, she thought, he knew; he must have known all along, even though he never looked up that day! She was going to kill Wendy with her skate blades at first opportunity. She looked down to stir her coffee, "Um, I don't know where she is today…" There was no covering this one up. Her shyness instinct was kicking in strongly and she wanted to bolt. She had even forgotten to breathe.

He sensed it was time to take his leave. "Hey, enjoy your coffee, sorry again."

Just as quickly as he had appeared, he was gone. She desperately wished her coffee mug were big enough for her to crawl into. How did he know she took it half decaf? Cindy must have told him.

WEDNESDAY, APRIL 16

Kelly never got her opportunity to do bodily damage with her skate blades before her next visit to Faders. At the door, she felt faint and thought twice about going in. What if she spills her coffee on someone else this time? These must be the kinds of thoughts that afflict all worrywarts of the world, Kelly imagined. She drew in a deep breath of cool morning air and prayed for mercy. She was third in line, and many tables were vacant. She scanned the blackboard for the day's specials even though she never ordered gimmick-of-the-day drinks. When her turn came, she asked Cindy for a cinnamon-hazelnut latte, the second item listed. Caught off-guard, Cindy had already begun to serve up Kelly's usual, so she dumped the drip coffee out and began to prepare her half decaf latte.

"Taking the plunge?" a voice asked. He had come in just after her.

"Uh huh," she smiled. Far more relaxed than on her last visit, she glanced in his direction and confided, "After what happened Monday, I decided it was high time for a change." Before he had a chance to respond, she charged, "I'm really sorry about what happened, and I never got a chance to say thanks for the replacement coffee. Thank you." She looked at him directly. He was tall with chocolate brown eyes, his medium ash brown hair slightly wind-blown.

He got Cindy's attention when she presented Kelly's drink, "Large coffee, black, please." Then he responded to Kelly, "You're welcome."

Kelly's hand intercepted, "Cindy, that's on me, please." It was the least she could do for someone who had been kind to her.

He noticed her garnet ring on her left hand as she took back her change.

They chose the table in the corner. "Little things can make your day," he said as they set their drinks down and got settled. He extended his hand for an introduction, "I'm Rick."

Her hand met his. "Kelly." His hand was warm from the coffee cup.

"Is your friend planning on showing up today?"

Most guys decided sooner rather than later they had a thing for Wendy and Kelly was not surprised that he asked about her again. "My friend, Wendy, has stood me up on more than one occasion. Now we have no standing arrangement," she smiled, "we get along much better this way."

"Sounds like a good friendship to me." It was not a manufactured compliment on his part, but a well-observed fact. He had noticed the long-time pair on many occasions and was not ready to admit to one of them right away that he found them genuinely entertaining, like comfort TV re-runs. Over so many days, he could see their friendship wasn't a constant all-out trial at every turn and if he didn't know better, he might think they hated every moment of it. Like rival litigators who relished trying cases against each other, each of them was under the other's skin, for better or worse.

He pegged Wendy's career pretty closely, guessing her to be a fashion retail representative, a far closer mark than he hit for Kelly. She chuckled when he guessed her to be a ballet student. It was a fine supposition, he argued, her posture was near perfect at all times combined with the effortless way she moved, even when she stirred her coffee. She surveyed her post-arena attire, okay, she conceded, given what he had to work with. She confessed to him her amazement that someone would think her a student, at her age, and if she could make real money as a dance instructor, she might actually give it a shot. She knew she would enjoy it more than graphic design. She hesitated to venture a guess as to his vocation, but she had to, in order to humor him and keep the game going. She had never taken time to study him the way he had obviously analyzed them; she was at a disadvantage. She suddenly remembered Wendy's newspaper theory and how his was folded neatly and logically. She took a long look at him, dressed in a pressed shirt with the sleeves partly rolled, and semi-casual trousers. She guessed him to be a mathematician or a computer systems analyst. He raised his eyebrows, smiled and sipped his coffee.

"Well? Am I way off?" she asked eagerly.

"Not as far off as you might think." He wanted to keep up the suspense.

"Actuary?" she asked.

"Nope, getting colder," he stated.

She was fresh out of guesses.

"Give up? Advanced Materials Engineering."

Engineering certainly involved math, so she felt quietly satisfied. Wendy and her newspapers, she was right after all. "Advanced, like space age materials?"

"Excellent guess. Kind of, but I don't build rockets, or bombs." He felt obligated to dispel the stereotypical mad scientist cliché.

She could handle the disappointment.

He worked in the Engineering Complex off the main campus, which was in the opposite direction than Graphix Alive. He thanked her for her company and they casually agreed that they would see each other next time. Whenever that might be, she prayed, let it not involve dripping coffee.

April 5

Passamaquoddy Indian Poem - Traditional

…

For we are the stars. For we sing.
For we sing with our light.
For we are birds made of fire.
For we spread our wings over the sky.
Our light is a voice.
We cut a road for the soul
For its journey through death.

…

Their death imploded me like crushing forces of abysmal depths. In my nightmares, I relive that horrific night as though I was in the car with them, watching the oncoming headlights growing, filling and blinding my sight, feeling the jarring, hearing the thunderous crash, the wailing of twisting metal, the hailing of window glass from all directions…. until all I perceive is black silence.

I plummet helplessly, indefinitely through the void…

Only I remain, I am the broken shards of glass.

Life shades of mundane gray, innocent voices, random comments, familiar images stir what lays lost in the abyss that used to be my heart. They conjure the strangest forms of comfort…so many memories, if I allowed myself to remember them all, would drown me and wash me away. Conscious barriers that I have built provide some emotional protection while unconscious ones cause me unidentifiable distress. I am suddenly reminded of the faded image fantasies that I so passionately clutched upon in my innocence – what I wanted my life to be like, and who I wanted to be.

April 7

       loyalty

ultimately, who are we to each other
that we are destined for our living days
to question the actions and desires of the other
to silently judge the choices and decisions
that each is sure she never would have made
are we forced, so helplessly tied to each other
do i really know you
or are you just another figment
of my imagination,
like the nightmares, have you become
the destination of my own projected fears
wrapped up in a tidy package I call you

do you know me
is yours a genuine love
and respect for me
for who i truly am
or have you just felt sorry for me
like the abandoned pet you had to take in
so it wouldn't die shamefully on your doorstep
i nearly did die on your doorstep
from that moment forward
you unwittingly became responsible for me
and i became forever trapped and bound to you
is this where we must remain

Insidious Interference

You stop seeing the person you love for who she really is, and see instead your own wants and needs for her. Living my life through Wendy's experience meant innate safety, like a rare species living captive but protected under glass. She knows everything I have been through, more than anyone knows, more than she should have to bear. Wendy grabs life by the horns. I watch. My life became a vicarious lie – any interest for excitement filled through her close encounters. I hide. I find seclusion from walls, within and without, fiction is safer than living your own intrigue, romance or action-drama.

Before it presumes to be written,
Before it can be read,
It needs to be lived.

What keeps people together? Convenience, shame, or mistaking years of togetherness for reliable comfort… maybe a manipulative power that comes from detailed knowledge of someone's life? When is it time to move on? What constitutes undivided loyalty to another and when did we cross the line beyond it, and to our own detriment?

I fear I am the cement that has weighted her feet while she wills to stay afloat. From the day it happened, she has felt obligated to stand sentry for my heart, and she has, loyally, for all these years. The guilt of this burden is becoming unbearable because my sense of loyalty to her has malformed into pressure of a non-repayable debt. My sense of loyalty to myself has perforated. Her loyalty to me is no longer a wanted act of dutiful protection. What used to be our friendship has undergone a twisted metamorphosis at its very core, and has become a mutated relationship of sickening faith-driven dependency.

Three

THURSDAY, APRIL 24

On the early mornings they met up at Faders, Kelly received an intro to materials science. Dalhousie University's materials testing lab, where Dr. Richard Hutchinson worked, was partially subsidized by a private corporate grant, which it was lucky to win in today's competitive market. Rick was in charge of his lab's contribution toward a consortium-based project responsible for testing and characterizing new materials called composites that would have potential applications in modern hybrid and fuel cell vehicles and other advanced industry applications. Where and how the materials would be used was not his business; however, characterizing their physical properties was. The ways their strengths varied under changes in load and temperature, and how they behaved under exposure to a host of other elements were the types of experiments the lab conducted. In many cases, results of the research led the group of scientists to re-develop better materials. Rick earned a doctorate in Materials Engineering a year ago and this job was part of his post-doctoral research, a handy step before solidifying a career position in industry.

A wonderful change of pace, Kelly appreciated learning about aspects of an industry she knew little about. Rick communicated clearly and articulately to her. Occasionally, she got hung up on his industry's impressive lingo, a foreign language to her. Her initial reaction was to play along, but when she halted him for explanations and definitions, he never gave her the feeling she had just asked a stupid question.

Rick wanted her to tell him about graphic design, and she did her best to sound knowledgeable. She listed software applications and described to him methods of four-color lithography, font styling, color balance and the benefits of offset printing. All the while, he reclined comfortably in his chair with one leg resting on the other, and Kelly noticed how those dark chocolate eyes never left her. Maybe it took a scientific type to be captivated by what she did for a living. Wendy only seemed interested if it dealt with her firm's ad layouts. His interest withstanding, Kelly nattered on. In the end, she actually fascinated herself.

What impressed her more over the many days was how easy it was for them to talk, given they had nothing in common. In her life, she had never stepped outside the Canadian border and within the last decade, he had traveled to the Andes to try his hand at mountain climbing, visited Australia for a month where he learned to scuba-dive, and hiked a week-long foot safari to the top of Mount Kenya. She loved to watch his face light up whenever she initiated him to tell more of his world travels. She wanted to know what he learned of the people of such distant lands. He tried to explain to her about how his strange connection with Andean music had lured him to Peru; and oddly, how he witnessed influences of African rhythms in the music of an isolated mountainside village. There, an elder taught him to play the charango, a type of lute that was made from the shell of an armadillo. The broad scope of his experience aside, inevitably, Kelly found herself able to relax in his company; she had met someone even-tempered and good-natured who seemed genuinely interested in her. His comments to her were kind, encouraging, and not once did she ever feel slighted for the questions she asked. Discussions sometimes digressed toward Wendy. Kelly didn't want to make Wendy's life and wild ways a prime topic of conversation without her there to defend herself. So she concentrated on their twenty-two year history as best friends instead and felt it within good judgment to share with him funny stories from their childhood. She opened with the time Wendy fell out of the McLaren's backyard tree house. The Pearson's next-door neighbors' son, Christopher, had been a long-time friend of theirs and attended school with them from grade two to high school graduation. Chris and his father had spent their first summer on Laurel Street building the arbor-fort and it wasn't even three days' christened when they had to rush Wendy to the hospital to set a broken forearm. Befitting her dramatic inclinations, Wendy brandished a stick in fierce protection of the fort from imaginary attackers. She lost her balance from the platform and plunged over the railing, nearly ten feet to the ground. It was a wonder that just her spirit didn't break along with her arm. Chris' mother was distraught; without delay, his father doubled the height and thickness of the railing surrounding the platform. No child was going to tumble from that tree house onto their back lawn ever again.

Rick relayed a similar story from his childhood, recalling the day when he and his younger brother, Kevin, were doubling on Rick's new bicycle. Their parents instituted a no double riding law after the last series of stitches and bandages. Disregarding it, they flew down the hill fantastical until Rick had to unexpectedly swerve around a fallen tree branch. Kevin panicked and lost his balance, the whole system lost equilibrium and they both came hurtling down, scraping along several feet of pavement. It was the worst case of road rash their mother had treated, and to this day Kevin's deviated septum reminded them all of it. The brothers were grounded, no bike riding, with Rick's punishment outlasting Kevin's by two weeks, since he was older and supposed to be in charge.

"Is Kevin still bitter?" she asked, wondering if brothers were anything like sisters when it came to unforgotten wounds.

"Nah, we laugh about most of it. You miss it when you don't have it."

Kelly didn't respond.

"Hey, I know what I wanted to ask you, before I forget," Rick said as he snapped his fingers, "they're bringing in a jazz trio this weekend, here at the Café. Would you have time to meet here. . .?"

"Saturday?"

"Eight o'clock says the poster."

"Eight it is, then."

It had been years since Christopher McLaren's name had come up in conversation. Wendy rarely brought his name up, she was careful not to. Chris was the only boy Kelly ever dated, the only one she wanted to date. When others asked to cut in, she politely declined. Having been neighbors and fast friends since age seven, no one was surprised they ended up an item. Even their parents amicably discussed plans for a summer wedding after Chris and Kelly completed their undergraduate degrees. Christopher planned to leave home after graduating high school to attend McGill University's Law program. They intended to maintain a long-distance relationship during those years, and their parents were supportive. He departed for Montreal only months after the raging drunk driver snatched Kelly's parents from her life. Kelly knew it was over. Everything was over. His academic plan notwithstanding, Chris couldn't handle the state she was in, and it would have been unfair to have expected him at the age of eighteen to know how. It wasn't her fault, nor was it his, and he couldn't turn down a four-year scholarship. Kelly never would have wanted him to abandon his dream and stay home, even if it would have been enough reason for her to live.

It was just too much to take. A person simply wasn't designed to handle that kind of devastating loss all at once, at such a young age. Wendy feared the worst for her best friend's broken heart and battered life. Could a girl ever realistically heal from this? She did her best to encourage Kelly to go out once in a while, even just for a casual date, if not for a serious relationship. She understood every time Kelly refused. All she could do was pray for the day to come when her friend would be able to live once more, free from the fear of being hopelessly abandoned again.

SATURDAY, APRIL 26

Kelly ran in from the hall to answer her phone. "Where are you?" Kelly asked, raising her voice, sensing Wendy couldn't hear her, "Are you on your cell phone?"

"Yeah, I'm flying a kite!!" Wendy's voice sang audibly.

"What??" It was a statement that didn't need clarification.

"I'm with Franklin and his son and we're at the park testing out Timothey's new kite his dad got him for his birthday! I just had to call you. It's beautiful out! You need to get out here and do this with us," she encouraged breathlessly.

"Oh my gosh, you don't give much notice. I don't think I can, I have laundry going and I have to see it through. You know how Mrs. Wiles gets when we leave wet laundry in the washer."

By this time, Wendy had stopped chasing the kite tail, in an effort to better concentrate on the crackling voice coming through her cell phone.

"And then I have to go out this evening…" Kelly continued.

"Go out where?" Wendy's breath returned just in time to interrupt.

"I was just going to tell you, to Faders, there's a jazz trio scheduled to play tonight and I promised someone I would meet him there."

"Meet who?"

"No one you know, not yet, anyway. Don't panic, just a friend." She knew Wendy wouldn't interrupt her from here on in. "We met about a week ago, we collided actually, it was a mess, but that's another story. He's a regular, his name's Rick and he's an engineer."

"Engineer? He drives a train?"

"Definitely not."

"How old is he? Is he married? What does he look like?" Wendy went through the standard list.

"I don't know how old he is, older, I don't know. He's not married. At least I don't think he is. I never asked." She realized she was starting to sound like someone she knew all too well. She then justified, "He wasn't wearing a ring."

"A lot of married men don't." Wendy spoke from first-hand experience.

"Look, I'm pretty sure he's not married, besides, I'll find out tonight so we can both rest, okay?" The line was starting to crackle again, so they said a quick goodbye, planning to have breakfast together Sunday morning.

The night was clear, still and unseasonably warm. She was dressed in low-rise jeans, heeled shoes and a pale green jersey. Her hair was clipped up casually. As she rounded the corner onto Coburg Road, the lights from Faders' bay windows cast a welcoming glow on the sidewalk ahead. She could hear the din of a crowd, applause and joyous music. A veritable spring celebration, she thought, what a great idea to get out and hear some soul-inspired music. Even if her new friend were to bail out at the last minute, she intended to enjoy her outing.

Faders' main door was open to the sidewalk; the music and activity spilled out onto the patio space. It was the most crowded Faders had ever been inside. The jazz trio included a keyboardist, an upright bassist and a female vocalist. Looking around, the place looked more alive than ever, a far stretch from the morning and afternoon pace their regular customers had come to expect. She didn't see Rick. She scanned the crowd again; there was no sign of him. Perhaps he was in the back section, which she couldn't see in direct line of sight from the crowd in the doorway. She cleverly stepped outside onto the patio, walked a few paces and peered inside from the bay window. She turned and rested her back against the wood-paneled wall. Her watch read ten past eight pm. She had arrived late. Maybe he was here and then he left. She turned to look in again. The trio had begun a new piece, much slower and moodier and just her style. She could skate to this, no problem...she instinctively began to move, hips rounding and rolling in sultry rumba fashion with swaying shoulder movements to complement. It was the kind of music that begged a body to dance, she thanked herself for choosing the freedom of the out of doors rather than inside, which was quickly becoming bottleneck congestion.

"That's why I thought you were a dancer. You are."

She turned in surprise as he just appeared out of thin air, yet again. "Hey! I thought you might have left." She stood perfectly still.

"Hey! I thought I'd be too late and you'd have left. Glad to see that isn't the case. Do you want to get a drink?" He motioned indoors.

The decision was made, iced drinks. Kelly danced with the music, "Sorry, I just can't stay still when there's music around," she began. "Actually, I dance when there isn't any music. Wendy finds it royally embarrassing."

"Dancing to your imagination, it's a talent to be blessed with. People should dance if they want to."

They were just as amused to watch others enjoying themselves. Two sets of The Motion Trio's music covered the spectrum from Latin rhythm to soft jazz; some were cover tunes, others original. Oh, what it would be like to own such a repertoire, they joked wishfully to each other. Mutually, they agreed it was time for some fresh air so they took a walk up to Spring Garden Road.

"I hope they plan this kind of thing again." Kelly said with delight.

"In which case, we'll come back."

Agreed, unless he was married. It had been on her mind all day. Fearing no other chance, she had to ask and now. "Question for you," Kelly quipped.

Rick stopped walking. He raised his eyebrows, at the ready.

She waited for other pedestrians to pass by. "Not that this matters to a friendship," she waved her hands softly, "maybe it does, and it should, if you are…I'm not sure….you're not married by any chance, are you?" There. She did it. Now she would wait.

"Never been. You?"

"No, definitely not."

That was settled. Wendy could sleep now. So could she.

SUNDAY, APRIL 27

The incessant buzz of her doorbell announced Wendy's arrival loud and clear. Kelly glided down the main staircase, unlocked the front door and let Wendy in to the front vestibule. Wendy handed a large brown bag filled with fresh bagels, cream cheese and fruit into Kelly's waiting arms. The two of them made their way up the stairs, straining to contain their grins and giggles. Once safely in her flat, it would be a battle over who would go first.

Kelly respectfully deferred to Wendy and wanted to know how meeting Franklin's son went. Clearly her relationship with him was progressing further than she thought. Was it too soon for Wendy to be meeting his son? Did the boy feel insecure? The two women talked circles around it, but as far as the kite-flying day went, Timothey was a wonderful kid who seemed to like Wendy. He decided she was his new friend who had come along for the day beneficially as his playmate, not as his father's. Wendy continued to speak well of Franklin, his values as a father, and as a person, and she relayed openly his painful experience in his failed marriage, at least to the extent that Franklin had shared with her. As Kelly had already predicted, Wendy suspected that Franklin might not be looking for a new romantic relationship, but rather was in deep need of a caring heart, someone he could call an intimate friend.

Hours passed with long conversation accompanied by strawberries, melon, bagels and bottomless cups of Earl Grey tea. When was the last time she and Wendy had spent a Sunday this way? Wendy was tickled to learn that Kelly's new engineer friend Rick was the neat-freak newspaper guy. She wanted to know every detail, each nuance and sentence spoken between them. Kelly tried to recount as much as she could remember. Satisfied enough that Rick wasn't married, Wendy pressed Kelly for her innermost impressions, desperately wanting her to spill. Did she really like him? Was she attracted to him? Did she think he was attracted to her? Kelly refused to answer claiming that these were not issues tabled for discussion. Yes, they obviously must like each other enough if they're happy to talk every time they meet. They both love good music. She told Wendy to relax. As it stood, he knew nothing about her; they knew nothing about each other. That was it. That was enough.

TUESDAY, APRIL 29

Morning was bright and cool with no rain in the forecast. Sleekly dressed in straight-cut black dress pants with a matching long-sleeved suit jacket, she reached for her fitted leather topcoat. Selected locks of her hair were loosely pinned up, leaving the majority of her shoulder-length mane free to just be. She rarely gave her hair that much liberty. With the comfortable lightness of only her wallet and lunch in her knapsack this morning, she headed out the door.

She arrived at Faders in time to meet Wendy and she was looking forward to the occasion. Between her working overtime to meet deadlines, and seeing Franklin over lunch when she could, Wendy had assured Kelly that she would try to pop in during the week in hopes of meeting Rick. Kelly walked in to find Wendy already there, seated at their favorite table with her French roast steaming. The two women began to chat spiritedly about their day to come. Within moments, it occurred to Kelly to look around for Rick, whom she had neglected to locate in her preoccupation with Wendy. Looking toward the order counter, she saw him standing in line. Good timing, she thought.

"Just a second." Kelly interrupted Wendy while she was elucidating her most recent ad layout. "Hold that thought." In a flash, she grabbed her wallet and snuck in the lineup next to Rick.

"Good morning," Kelly sang to him, her voice light and relaxed.

Now here was a sight for sore eyes, Rick thought. "Yes, it is. Good morning to you." His hands were in the pockets of his leather coat. Her bright eyes, congenial smile and the sharp visual contrast of her highlighted hair, against the blue-black of her sleek suit-jacket was easy for anyone to take at seven forty-five in the morning. He could be convinced to search out a need, any need, for services from Graphix Alive. "You should wear your hair down more often."

"Oh. I'll keep that in mind," she half-laughed. "Wendy's here this morning. She wants to meet you."

Introductions happened as Wendy and Rick shook hands across the table and appropriately commented that they had seen each other here before. Kelly bowed out of much of the morning's conversation to allow Rick and Wendy to get to know each other. Wendy was her usual charming self, filled with intelligent, effervescent conversation. Rick was suitably entertained by her chatty presence, and with pleasure, he answered the two questions she did ask him. Kelly checked the time and announced her departure. When Rick suggested that he walk her to work, she pleasantly declined and counter-offered that he stay and talk with Wendy.

"So you two have been friends since you were kids?" he opened.

"Yeah, we're like sisters. We fight like sisters too, but most of the time we manage, so it's pretty real." Wendy confessed, "We're as different as you can get and we don't see eye to eye many times, but we're lucky to have each other. We need each other. I look out for her."

"She needs to be looked out for?"

"Well, you don't know her. Let's just put it this way, her radius is pretty...um... limited." Wendy commented cryptically. "I mean, she's shy, I guess you'd say."

"She doesn't strike me as so shy. Not like you." He grinned. Choosing to let it remain there, Rick stood up to leave for work, thanked Wendy for the company and said he looked forward to next time.

WEDNESDAY, APRIL 30

The following morning, Rick did walk Kelly to work in the opposite direction from the Engineering Complex. He told himself that even workaholics need a change, every bit as much as coffee, and this was a welcomed one. Kelly relinquished her knapsack to his left shoulder upon his offer, surely a sign of growing trust, as they talked.

"You lug this haul around with you everywhere?" Rick was amazed at her indisputable strength assuming this was the culprit of the collision weeks ago.

"Yeah, most days. You'll never guess what's in there," she teased.

His interest was piqued; cinder blocks had crossed his mind, although he wasn't going to venture a guess if she wasn't planning on delivering. His mother had taught him very early on that it wasn't polite to ask a lady's age or what she carried in her purse. "Haven't gotta clue, but I can tell you, whatever it is digs into your back if you don't carry it just right."

She laughed, "You're right." They stopped on the sidewalk and she lifted the knapsack off his shoulder and set it down on a mortar-capped cobblestone wall. She unzipped the flap, and very much like a magician would a rabbit, she pulled out her right skate. The blade had a black terry cloth 'soaker' cloaking it, which she removed so he could inspect it.

"Holy heck, woman." He held the skate weighing approximately four pounds and ran his index finger along the length of the blade, careful not to press too hard. He remembered from his youth how sharp skate blades can be. A story for another morning, he thought. It read MK England with the word Dance etched near the middle. Rick admired the workmanship that went into the boot and the architectural side honing of the narrow blade. She was absolutely right, he never would have guessed. "So you're not just a dancer, you're a skater."

"Correction…try to be."

"I'd love to see you skate sometime."

"No," she abruptly replied.

"Okay then," he quickly retracted.

"That came out wrong, sorry. There's not much to see, anyway."

Perhaps this was the shyness Wendy had mentioned. "I doubt that. How long have you been skating?"

They began walking again once she fitted the skate back in the knapsack. "Since I was a kid, about eight or so. I tested and competed until seventeen and…" she paused, "then I quit." She hesitated again. "I only just got back into it three years ago."

"You must have done really well. So why'd you quit?" It was a natural question to ask, however, it met with increased hesitation and a noticeable drop in spirit.

"Just too much going on. It was more than I could handle."

Judiciously ending the conversation then and there, Rick saw Kelly into the foyer of Graphix Alive. Spying a square post-it note pad on Linda's unattended desk, he scribbled his home and lab phone numbers and with comedic panache, stuck it ceremoniously on her arm. "Call me." His tone befitted his gesture.

"Okay," she nodded as she plucked the sticky yellow square from her jacket.

SATURDAY, MAY 3

There was only dead silence. She awoke with a start, her hands in powered fists clutching her bed sheet. Her heart was seismic beneath her flesh, it pounded as though it would burst right through. Her face and her hair at the temples were soaked with tears and she could still hear herself screaming. It always took her a minute or so to re-establish herself. She was in her bed, in her flat, on Larch Street. Wiping the tears from her eyes and gasping for breath, it had happened again.

She sat up and planted her feet firmly on the bedside rug. She worked her toes into its pile until sensation returned. She concentrated on the whirring sound of a lone car, muffled through her bay windows, as it sped past the Old Victorian. Within moments, she was walking around, feeling and hearing the floors creak in the all right places. She knew sleep would elude her now, as it always did.

Hours passed. In the early morning dark quiet, she held her right skate near to her heart. Her hands caressed its sturdy curvature, as the tips of her fingers discriminated each stitch in the welts and seams. Tears streamed down her cheeks and blurred her sight. She looked upon the framed photograph of herself with her mother and father, lit only by Larch Street's sodium rose glow. They were all so young, having lived a lifetime ago, having died a lifetime ago.

There was nowhere for her to hide.

April 30

There are times when I don't know my own heart's needs or motivations, but for these journals. Truth seeps through the fortification I have built - the barriers have weakened over time. Many writers have professed that the act of writing transcends us - that truth emerges from a higher place, from somewhere other than ourselves. Dr. Lake has encouraged me to write so I can know who I am. One day I may uncover the strength to end this torment.

May 3

Blackness

Blackness will find me yet again.
Nowhere can I hide,
As lark sings morning's light,
It knows its time has come.

Blackness knows my secret places.
Its cold heaviness
Descends upon me,
Like a sodden blanket.
I wait out the night, I pray for the Light,
To envelop me, to surround me
Lift me, keep me afloat,
Long enough to find breath.

Ten years long, in twenty days,
You are gone again,
Leaving me, solitary
In Blackness of sight.

There are times I feel you,
Clasping my tiny hands,
Guiding me through the emptiness.
There are times I want you
To call me, to take me to you.
Carry me to your Otherworld,
Free me from the shackles
Of this Netherworld.

Reaching forever upward,
My distant angel swan
Swims your sky,
I long to touch your souls.

Am I still your child?
Do you still watch over me?
I am still your child.
I am only your child,
Watch over me as I wander
Paths of fruitless search
One day to stumble upon
Light I long to meet.

I will never be okay. I go through the motions of daily existence - perpetually shunning the void in my heart. It took years for Dr. Lake and Wendy's family to be convinced that the suicidal tendency within me was gone. For their sakes, I let them know their efforts had not been in vain. The temptation of suicide will never be fully vanquished. I have grown so grievously reliant on its promise. It sustains me by desensitizing the substance of my soul to loving or needful attachment in this world. I dare not say anything to anyone, but this demon that stalks me cannot be ignored. It roars. It must be appeased for I fail to manage it.

I am a coward, suffering a profound lack of faith as to why my parents were taken. They would want me to live the life they gave me. Cruel fate, I am forced to do it alone, without them, without their guidance, without their comfort, without their love. I am obliged to live my years out of duty. When can I join them? I fear I will tire of this fight waiting for that time to arrive.

Four

FRIDAY, MAY 9

W endy," he called to her.
She heard something through the music flooding from her headphones and when she looked up, she saw Rick peering at her holding a cup of coffee. Wendy removed her headphones and closed her work file. "Oh, it's the doctor. Well, not that kind of doctor," she commented parenthetically. "What's up in Materials-Ville?"

"Nothing worth getting into. Have you seen Kelly?" He was edgy.

"When? Today? No, not yet," she frowned.

"I haven't seen her all week. It's possible I might have missed her one of these mornings, but usually she's around, right?"

"Yes, she is, one thing you can always rely on Kelly for is her routine," Wendy responded dryly.

"Have you talked to her lately? She's not sick or anything?"

"Look, I've been swamped and no, I haven't talked to her all week. She hasn't called me. But then again, I haven't called her either." She stopped to ponder. "What day is it?" She checked the date on her cell phone. "The ninth. Uh oh."

"Uh oh, what? An appointment or something?"

"Does she talk to you? Has she talked to you?" Wendy interrogated.

"Not lately. What do you mean?" Rick sat down next to her, unable to figure her out.

In the quick press of three buttons, the line connected. It rang until her machine answered. "Kelly, call me. Cell." She set the phone down and declared, "I don't think she's home." She tried her work number and Linda answered dutifully that Kelly was in her office, but busy on the other line. Wendy thanked her and let it go. "She's at work. She's fine. Happy now?"

The two of them sat silently, staring at each other. Rick wondered whether there was any reason to worry, because if there weren't, he was at a loss as to why he was worried. She talks, of course she talks, he reverted to Wendy's last question.

"How much has she told you?" Wendy wryly continued her interrogation.

"About what?" This exchange was far too vague for his scientific mindset.

"About her. I mean, do you talk about personal stuff or just small-talk stuff?"

He considered the specificity of her question, then responded, "We talk about everyday stuff, nothing out of the ordinary." He paused again then offered, "But there have been a few times I've said certain things and she kind of fades out, like she doesn't want to go there. I never thought about it too much, that if she didn't feel like talking, it's okay, I respect that."

"Good. You have no right to pry. Everybody has stuff they don't want to get into, let it go, don't worry about it." Wendy tried to sound reassuring.

Rick found her evasive. He headed off to work leaving Wendy with the instruction to let Kelly know that he asked about her.

At five-thirty pm, Kelly's forehead was cracking open with throbbing pain from the effective combination of several sleepless nights and a charging locomotive schedule. Spring pollen made it worse. All she wanted was to survive the month of May; however she lived through it, she wouldn't complain. Many files were piled on her computer desk and that's just where they would stay until Monday as she was in no shape to entertain any homework. All week, her skates had stayed home but there was no way around tomorrow morning as she had students to coach. Maybe the ice time would do her good. Her office line lit up and Linda informed her that a gentleman was there to see her. As she opened her office door, she heard Rick's voice thank Linda at her desk.

She stood at her open door. "Oh, wow," was all she could think of to say at first. "Hi. What are you doing here?" Kelly attempted a greeting.

"Hi." Rick returned nervously. "I know it's late, and I don't have an appointment..."

"Oh come on." She waved formality off and led him into her office.

"I'm here on official business, actually," he continued, "I'm prepared to be a paying customer, but if the job's too small, I understand."

"What are you talking about?" Kelly asked blankly. She didn't even realize she sounded impatient.

"A logo, for a business card...I'll need one eventually, and you're the perfect one to do it, if you have time...you haven't been around, so I guess you're busy..." his eyes darted in various directions around her office. "No rush...you know what, forget about it."

Discomfiture not being his normal cloth, she tried to put him at ease. She offered him a seat and he perched himself on the edge of the sofa. "Sorry how that sounded, no job's too small, I'd be happy to do it, and as for paying, let's come up with some ideas you like first before talking currency." She pulled a narrow-width binder from her shelf that held several sample of logos and cards that their firm and she, in particular, had designed.

He flipped through it quickly. "These are great. Anything like these would do," he declared indiscriminately.

"Let's work a timeline, when do you want to have the samples?"

"You know what, I haven't thought that far ahead." Looking directly at her, he asked impulsively, "Are you okay?"

"I'm fine." She shrugged her left shoulder, "Why?"

"I haven't seen you in a while. You look tired."

She huffed, "I am tired. And don't start calling me baggy eyes."

It was the first real smile he'd seen since he walked in.

She tidied up her office, vanished behind the bathroom door and changed into casual cottons and sneakers, popped two aspirins and dug out her knapsack from the closet. He was taking her to dinner; she was too drained to refuse.

He could see she hadn't been sleeping well; at the very least, he'd make sure she ate. He was unaware of her depression. He hadn't seen her since the post-it note; she never did call.

She was too weary to process his myriad dinner suggestions; she expressed her worry that she'd be terrible company for a Friday evening. They decided on pizza and a quiet evening.

Rick's favorite pizzeria, Tony's across from The Commons, was not far from his place. He drove as she sat in silence. He didn't want to bombard her with chit-chat and hoped that by the time she ate, she might feel more alive. Arriving in the underground garage of his high-rise building, they took the elevator up to the tenth floor of Oakton Gate Tower. His building was about a fifteen-minute walk from her place, she estimated. Her headache was starting to yield. The aroma of freshly baked pizza permeated the elevator. Kelly leaned back on the elevator wall and rested her head on Rick's shoulder. Its sudden deceleration awoke her from her brief rest. His apartment was number ten-fifteen, easy enough to remember, she thought, should she ever be invited back. It occurred to her to make an effort to be social.

Upon unlocking the door, without a second's delay, they were greeted by a small voice that meowed twice. Stepping inside, careful to not let the little shorthaired ginger feline out into the hall, Rick helped Kelly off with her jacket, while Rudy, as Rick called him, purred noisily and rubbed figure eights around Kelly's ankles.

"We call those 'ochos' in Tango-speak." She bent down to pick Rudy up and get a good look at his adorable face. He had a small patch of white on his nose and three black dots around his nostrils. "Shall we Tango, you and I?"

Rick could see she was feeling better already; she was dancing with his cat. Rudy undoubtedly was enamored with his new dance partner.

"You didn't tell me you had a cat," her voice sang.

"And clearly I don't need to ask whether you like cats." He called her from the kitchen, "Come have some pizza." He had taken out plates and a handful of napkins. "Wine?"

"Definitely not." Her decision was firm until the glorious crimson hue radiated from his glass. She thought again, "Okay, just a tiny bit. Two sips worth, that's all. Hopefully those aspirins won't notice."

"If you're lucky, they will."

They carried their plates and wine glasses to the living room and set them down on the light oak coffee table. Kelly plopped down on the taupe carpet and rested her back against the sofa. She sighed in relief. Rick sat on the floor next to her. As she sipped her wine and picked at her pizza, she was happy to see there were mushrooms and olives. It was the first time she felt like eating anything all week.

Her eyes scanned around his place as she nibbled. Rick's home, a one-bedroom apartment, was well laid-out. Compared to her compressed surroundings, his apartment felt giant-sized. There was a combined living room and dining room space, and a walk-through galley style kitchen with full size appliances. One entry to the kitchen was from the dining room, the other from the hall that led straight back to where she assumed the bedroom and bathroom were. The oak dining table for four matched the coffee table and end tables. In the living room was an earthy sage green sofa with a matching armchair with large cushions. Directly in front of her, a series of bookcases flanked a central entertainment cabinet. Spanning the length of the wall, they were filled with tomes, CD's, fascinating pieces of native sculptural art, physics-style mobiles, a component stereo system and a television. Along the left wall was a patio door framed with heavy dark green drapes that led to the balcony, and along the right wall was a computer desk lost under stacks of papers. There were modern art prints on the walls. No question, this was a fantastic apartment and it looked lived in; so much for obsessive-compulsive neat freak.

They discussed their mutual workaholic tendencies and Kelly admitted she was proactively working to change her habits. And yes, it was difficult to control at times, especially when workloads became unmanageable, like this week.

"I figured it must have gotten crazy, when I didn't see you all week at the café, and I hadn't heard from you. I was hoping you'd call."

"Sorry. I would have, eventually."

"Hmm." Rick's terse response indicated how unconvincing she sounded.

She turned to him and rested her elbow on the sofa, "I'm glad you came by the office seeing as I couldn't get my act together enough to get to Faders. Thank you. This is just what I needed."

Rudy came and curled up on her lap as though she belonged to him. Kelly guessed she would be another potentially sympathetic figure to press for food and affection. Rick watched her stroke the fine fur around Rudy's forehead, her face appeared drawn and there was a distant sadness in her eyes that he had never really noticed in all their meetings at the café. He realized that maybe he'd never really looked at her, for as much as he had seen her. She began to talk about how hellish her week had been at work. He listened closely, hoping she might indicate what else was really going on with her, if anything. But she said nothing specific. Rick had no intention of pushing her to satisfy his own curiosity, even if it meant that his concerns would not be allayed.

They spent the rest of the evening discussing their varied tastes in music. Kelly curled up on the carpet in front of the oak shelves that held Rick's CD's, numbering well over a hundred. Many discs had been taken out so she could study the leaflets and she was convinced she had struck a gold mine as she perused his collection. There were titles and artists she had never heard of, like Africa Kundara, and fusions of international music, like Spanish Celtic. Celts were in Spain? Remarkable, she thought. Rick encouraged her to borrow whatever she wanted, and her imagination spun in all the excitement of endless creative possibilities. New music always met with unexpected joy. Priority one was to find music to skate to, pieces that flowed with texture and rhythm. She could up her chances of surviving the insomnia-ridden nights yet to come by being carried to spiritual realms that only music held the hall pass for. She spoke of her frequent bouts of insomnia with a tinge of twisted humor, probably a result of her fatigue.

"Have you ever talked to a doctor about why you suffer from insomnia?" He knew occasional sleeplessness was common, however, hers seemed to be more serious.

"Oh yes, it's one of many afflictions on my list." She shook her head with dismal disappointment. Her medical chart still contained far too many issues for a person her age. "Sometimes medication works, but not always because insomnia just catches you by surprise, and you just can't get to sleep once it hits."

They listed all the things they could think of to encourage a good night's rest, none of which were new to Kelly: hot milk, deep breathing, reading, soft music, counting backwards from ninety-seven by fours, taking a long evening walk to soak in some fresh air, while not soaking in sugar or caffeine in the evenings. As far as soaking was concerned, the only thing she admitted not being able to do that her doctor suggested was indulging in a warm bath. She didn't have a bathtub, only a shower stall. Warm showers weren't much of a substitute.

"Worrying about it never helps, either," Rick reminded.

"Tell me about it. If someone invents a mute button to be able to turn the neurosis off, sign me up." Kelly said that while controlling her ruminating tendencies helped, she felt the real problem at its source involved recurring nightmares. They intruded unannounced and were almost always the cause of a stolen sleep. "My doctor has been trying to help me deal with them, and I keep journals, I have been for years. I'm not sure it's really helping though."

"What kind of nightmares? Do you remember the details? I never remember my dreams."

"Oh no, I remember them, in precise detail. They've been recurring for so long, they're pretty much the same kind, same style, same intense feelings, it's like watching the same horror re-run over and over again." She shifted in her place. "Anyway, I don't want to even talk about it. My life is jinxed enough. Be warned, you might want to keep your distance."

"I don't believe that for a minute." With his hand cupped firmly around the back of her neck, he whispered his conclusion in her ear, "No wonder you can't sleep." He got up from the living room floor to crawl upon the sofa in time for a Friday night slouch. "You know, there was a time when insomnia wrecked my life."

His sympathetic statement redirected her attention away from the Pink Floyd Live double CD set she was studying, and hoping to borrow from him.

Rick continued, "It bugged me for a year or two, off and on. Then it eventually went away. Maybe people go through cycles and it's just something you have to live with, until you get through it, especially if you don't know the root cause of it."

"So you didn't know why you had insomnia," she concluded.

"I didn't say that."

They had reached a stalemate. Neither of them wanted to delve deeper. Their quiet evening together drew to a close as Kelly had overshot her fatigue level. Even the cat had retreated to the darkened bedroom for the night. Rick offered to take her home, and with a handful of his CD's, she gladly accepted the ride.

SUNDAY, MAY 11

Kelly dragged her feet in returning Wendy's multiple phone messages that had accumulated since Friday. Having spent the morning coaching, she chose to sleep the rest of Saturday away. When sleep came, she didn't refuse. Wendy had no choice but to limit her calls of concern because the machine was no longer answering. Kelly had unplugged her phone. A decade of experience with Kelly prepped Wendy for times like these. It was the month of May and Kelly's recurrent depression was right on schedule and with it came Wendy's concern; she had learned to moderate her reaction, she needed to. When Kelly rang her back, Wendy ran through the normal battery of questions: Was she eating? Were the nightmares keeping her up? Was there anything she could do for her? Kelly answered flatly, bewildered that Wendy still cared after all these years. In the end, there was nothing that Wendy could say or do that would make any difference. Kelly knew her friend had been growing increasingly tired of this, and of her. She didn't want to burden Wendy with one more ounce of trouble since apathy had long been knocking at Wendy's door. It had been ten years and there would still be tens more.

With maple buds blossoming, the day was bright and clear. Kelly took the opportunity to repot her indoor plants that barely survived the long winter on her drafty window ledges. Sustaining life in any form would surely lift her spirits, so she gathered her gardening supplies from the Wiles' storage cellar, and carried them up to the back deck. In her housecleaning garb, she began her spring task. The bagged earth felt cool and crumbly through her fingers but a bit too dry to the touch. She moistened it and waited for the water to be absorbed before transferring the plants into their new container beds.

"Great day to not be indoors!" a voice called up to her from the Walton Street sidewalk.

Kelly leaned over the deck railing to confirm it really was Rick's voice she thought she recognized. "Hey! What brings you round these parts?"

He neglected to answer her question. "I thought that was you up there, but I wasn't sure." He was out for a run, clad in very springtime attire, a tan T-shirt, black shorts and running shoes.

"Wow. You belong in a Nike ad." Wendy's career influence on Kelly was apparent. "I'm repotting these sorry excuses for houseplants. Come on up."

In five nimble steps, skipping three stairs at a time, he was there. "Nike would have to fire me." He held up his foot for her to check the logo - Reebok. Noticing fine crystals of mica from the soil on her cheek, he enquired, "You just about done?"

"More or less, why?"

"You busy after this?" They may as well have been playing the game of questions.

"Why are you asking?" It was getting funny. She began to giggle.

"Wanna go for a run?"

"Where?" Kelly persisted, as did her laughter.

Deadpan, he began to enunciate and draw out his question, which further prodded her giggles. "Where would you like to go?"

She was going to put an end to this nonsense. "Anywhere," she answered with leaden intonation. She motioned to him to pick up the leftover soil and the tools, as she had grabbed her plants. "I'll need a minute to change."

He didn't actually enter her flat, but took the opportunity to survey her compact surroundings from his vantage point as he leaned against the door casement, the door rested ajar on his right arm.

"Come on in," Kelly insisted. She rooted through her dresser. It had been an age since she went running. Was she too tired to run? Too late now, she had already agreed to join him. Finally and with conviction, she pulled out a gray, cropped v-neck shirt and black track pants out of her drawer. She slipped into the bathroom then came out dressed for running with her hair more securely tied back. She was working sunscreen into her cheeks and forearms. "Need SPF?"

"Thanks, I'm good." He was impressed that she didn't insist on wearing make-up. Did she even wear make-up? He couldn't remember, which led him to conclude that if so, she didn't overdo it, unlike some women. They headed out.

Birds were chirping; it was too beautiful a day to be indoors, and Kelly thought it a happy coincidence that he was in the neighborhood. She was secretly relieved that she had slept away a dark, drizzly day instead of this one.

They maintained a slow, comfortable pace that allowed them to talk as they made their way to Point Pleasant Park, the city's favored recreational spot. With an abundance of inland wooded and coastal gravel trails, it was within spitting distance of downtown that made visitors feel they had left city limits and stepped back through the doorways of time and into nature. Situated on the protruding point of a small peninsula that jutted out into the harbor, the entire park was legislated a site of historical significance. Scattered throughout its boundaries were military treasures, surrounded by natural woodlands; the chances were favorable of stumbling upon an abandoned munitions bunker or storage facility whose walls were still partially buried. Higher tower views that once allowed for full visibility of the open harbor approach were situated closer to the coastal trails and were protected by stone walls and surrounding moats. All of these sites were popular with families, where children could play make-believe. In the summertime, the university drama department presented Shakespeare's comedies, histories and tragedies in these ingeniously adapted theatrical settings.

"The air here really is different than anywhere else in the city," Rick allowed his lungs to fully expand with appreciation as they rested atop a wall of an old bunker.

"It is," she agreed. "You're right, you don't experience this fragrance anywhere else. It is unique. Brine and pine." Her breathing naturally slowed. It had been a pleasantly relaxing jaunt to Point Pleasant and she wondered why she had stopped jogging.

They walked by an old bunker and found themselves meandering for a sensuous diversion amidst the trees, rocks and loosely scattered brush. The woodlands were carpeted in a humus sheath of crispy brown pine needles, the earthy floor snapped and succumbed as they stepped around roots and granite rocks. They heard warning calls and the rushed scampering of chipmunks. The occasional cry of a crow broke the imperceptible backdrop of the ocean's wave breaks. Kelly's fingers caressed rough tree bark as she strolled, and ground moss glistened like emeralds in the dappled sunlight that filtered in through the leaves. Down a wooded hill, alongside a gurgling brook, they walked in silence cherishing nature's peace, until they met a peripheral coastal trail. Set high above the seashore, an escarpment of tall birches and conifers partially obscured the view of the water, and sheltered them from the full effect of the onshore breeze. It felt noticeably cooler here.

"You look rested today," Rick casually mentioned as they walked, "a world better than Friday." He noticed how good she looked in general, fit and in fine form.

"So you can't call me baggy eyes," Kelly grinned. "I finally slept better Friday night, thank you. I caught up the rest on Saturday. No nightmares, thank goodness."

"That's all we ask." Rick took her left hand and guided her off the trail, toward a path that only he seemed to distinguish, and they began to descend the steep escarpment.

"Where are you going?" Kelly grabbed a tree trunk to secure her stead. "It's more than a hundred feet to the bottom!"

"Don't worry, give me your hand and just scale it sideways. It's easy."

Within minutes, they descended to the seashore. Kelly marveled as she looked far up to the trail. She turned to take in the shore's breathtaking vista. The waves sparkled in the sunlight, rippling from the cool, salty onshore breeze that entered the Northwest Arm. Rick sat on a large rock shelf that nature had granted to accommodate the one of a kind view the city boasted.

"Come here often?" Kelly smiled, as she gazed upon what she observed to be a perfect picture, but she didn't have her camera. You couldn't ask for a better subject or a more ideal setting, she thought.

"Funny you should ask."

His smile made her aware of herself. She scrambled up the rocks and seated herself cross-legged just below where he was. They both faced the inlet, soaking in the sun, listening to the rhythm of the lapping seawater.

He bent down and put his hand on her shoulder. He spoke softly from just behind her ear as he pointed to a place across the Arm, "See that place?"

"I see some houses nestled in the trees…"

"Exactly. See the one I mean?"

"The white one with the windows?"

"Yep. I'm going to buy that place."

"Really, when?" she turned quickly to him. She looked back to the awesome vantage point of the property in the distance and imagined the incredible view of the inlet it would hold with all its windows.

"I don't know. Haven't thought that far ahead."

She began to understand. "Is it even on the market?"

"Who knows?" He explained to her that every time he visits Point Pleasant, he ends up in this very spot…he looks at his dream house…his mind wanders to lands beyond the ocean…he ponders life. He'd never seen anyone else down here, no one in their right mind would scale that escarpment, and it was for that reason alone he kept coming back here and always would, until he didn't need to anymore.

Kelly realized that Rick had never been to the white house with the windows, and he had never seen it from the inside. He didn't even know how to get there from here or which side road it was on. For inexplicable reasons, he loved that house, its would-be view, and it didn't matter what it looked like inside, it was perfect for him no matter what.

"Are you saving up for it?"

"You know it." He smiled. "As much as you can plan that far ahead. The future can be a hard thing to predict."

"Hmm. That's why I never think about it."

"You never think about it?"

"Well, I have to be able to plan a week ahead, a month ahead, everyone has to. But I really don't think too much beyond that. I don't even think I can, now that you mention it." Kelly was perturbed and confused by her own reflective analysis.

Her statement confused him because it didn't seem to fit her nature. For a self-proclaimed worrywart suffering from insomnia, Rick wondered, how could she claim to not be able to think about her future? The two concepts seemed incongruous. He protested, "Do you know what exactly is worrying you, if you say it's not your future?"

He had discovered a flaw in her foundational logic and this beset her; he could see right through her. She knew all along he was too smart for her.

"You're intriguing, Kelly."

Her imagination bounced to Wendy's concept of intrigue, the much sought after, highly intangible entity in her line of work. In every advertisement layout, intrigue was the very essence to capture and emote, whether the advertiser was selling a luxury automobile or designer perfume. She knew Rick wasn't comparing her to cars or fragrances. "I know, none of my jigsaw pieces fit quite right," she responded defensively.

"That's not what I'm saying." He maintained a gentle tone.

Her gaze ventured somewhere beyond the open sea. She had faded out again.

"A woman I dated once caused me several sleepless nights," he tried to amuse her with a lilt.

"Yeah? For good reasons, I hope." Kelly's eyes squinted in the sunlight as hers met his. He had brought her back.

"Hell, no. I wish." He fixed his sights upon a ketch in the distance making its way back into the inlet. "She scared the crap out of me."

"You don't strike me as the easily scared type. She must have been quite the woman."

"She had ideas of her own when it came to romance, let's just put it that way."

"Enough said."

May 7

Enervation

lost breath my fate — heart wrenched in grief - can't stand up straight
all that remains - a hung-out mind, - a strung-out heart - a wrung-out soul,
a phantasmic - whole affliction - of deadened sense - while all the world
whirls, swirls about - separate without .   .   .   .   me.

May 10

Satisfaction

I don't believe in reinvention.
Nor in tweaking with perfection
Mystic souls though long since passed,
Contemplated well enough my claims,
And then surpassed.

Validated by the written word, there rests common ground in each of us.
Wilde, Dickinson, Blake, Rilke and Cummings, how then are we
strangers in time and space to each other? For we all have looked upon the
same stars ...

May 11

My eyes fell once again upon 'I hide myself within my flower' in Emily
Dickinson's 1924 Anthology one sleepless night just shortly after I met
Rick. I feel I have met a person who sees me. Not through me. I am
troubled. It happened again today, but this time, I was strangely content to
be this flower, his flower.

Five

MONDAY, MAY 12

S eated on the edge of her bed, Kelly held the little yellow square notepaper. She watched her clock strike ten pm. She pried her fingers from the sticky part of the paper. Only her bedside lamp lit her flat. Her heart rate spent the evening accelerating, now it was over one hundred eight. She had stretched and done deep breath meditations earlier, but as the night wore on, her pulse kept climbing. Reading didn't help bring it back down, neither did the Mark Knopfler instrumental CD she borrowed from Rick.

These were the precursors of her nightmares. She was terrified to get into bed and switch off the lamp.

TUESDAY, MAY 13

"You were out on Sunday when I called." Wendy spoke authoritatively.

"You didn't leave a message that you called." Kelly was certain that Wendy was starting up again, like a parent checking in on the hour. She didn't need this over her lunch break, let alone over the phone.

"No, I didn't bother. Don't tell me you were out stargazing in broad daylight."

"Very funny. It was a gorgeous day, I went for a jog and spent the afternoon at the park."

This little piece of news awakened Wendy's curiosity, since Kelly had stopped jogging a couple of years ago. "And you decided to do this out of the blue? When was the last time you went jogging?" Her tone reflected a rhetorical statement, rather than a legitimate question.

"Exactly. It had been one day too long, and that's why I went."

They dangled in uncomfortable silence until Wendy offered Kelly an invitation to the Mercury Club on Saturday night. Her new favorite alternative underground band, a local group called the Phish Experience, would be playing. With her many acquaintances, Kelly figured, wasn't there anyone else that she could manipulate into going? Kelly had witnessed the Phish Experience when they debuted, and it was one time too many. She had secretly promised herself that if Wendy ever asked her again, she would find an excuse not to go. The group's sound fit into no enjoyable category yet Kelly reluctantly agreed to give them another shot because she was unable to manufacture prior plans on the spot. She was tired. Her head felt like a brick. She took a breath. There was still time.

Why she neglected to tell Wendy earlier that she had gone jogging with Rick escaped her. It also dawned on her that she hadn't told her about last Friday evening at his place either. There was no point with nothing to tell. In her mind, she could hear Wendy's voice lecturing her: how she was making a big mistake, that it was dangerous for her to be spending time alone with a man she knew nothing about, who knew nothing about her. He only wanted one thing. She was safer on her own. **And if he were to know he would drop you like a hot rock…how soon you forget**… The demon Agramon's voice distorted from Wendy's until it succeeded in taking over. **No one wants you… no man would ever want you…** Agramon continued to brutally assault her and Kelly couldn't make it stop.

The darkness that pervaded her flat had enveloped her soul. It was slowly constricting her. Kelly was huddled in fetal position on her sofa, suffocating the cushion trapped in her arms. She remained there for several minutes struggling to breathe, until she felt the tightness in her chest subside. She gave in. The voice subsided. Agramon was sated. It was nine-thirty pm. She was finally alone again.

She needed to remember their touch, their loving voices. Her heart remembered them but her mind could not. She felt empty, physically and spiritually. It had been ten years. Maybe they had been gone too long now. And she had succeeded in forgetting. Maybe now, it was too late to call them back in her memory. She got up and switched on the hanging lamp over the bistro table by the kitchen bay window. She took out her favorite peach blossom teacup and put a kettle on the stovetop. As she waited for the water to boil, she walked to her music shelf, where the silver framed photograph stood.

She looked upon her mother, Bridget, vivaciously attractive at forty-five. Kelly prayed she would take on her mother's looks, particularly as she would age. At fifty-one, her father, Ian, looked a casually distinguished man. There was such a sense of brightness to them with Kelly at the picnic table in their back yard next to her mother, and her father standing behind them. She was sixteen. She remembered the day Christopher took the photo. Her parents had planned a barbecue celebration for Kelly, Wendy and Christopher, upon completion of grade eleven. It was the party that began their summer, the last summer they would spend together, the last summer she would enjoy with her mother and father.

As steam blew through the whistle, she caressed the photo glass and choked her tears back. Chamomile tea with honey was a suggestion for the list they forgot to mention. This silly, ephemeral thought cheered her for a moment. His eyes smile the same way her father's used to. Setting her teacup on the little end table, she curled back up on her sofa and fluffed the cushion she had unwittingly crushed. The kitchen globe lamp cast a warm, diffuse glow through the golden stained glass shade. The hot tea calmed the edge off her nerves.

The little yellow square notepaper was stuck at an odd angle on her phone receiver. She must have carried it from her bedroom the previous night when she began to write. She lifted it off and studied his handwriting. His printing was legible with slight forward slant. She could see from the pattern of his strokes that he hardly lifted the pen away from the paper when he wrote causing subtle ties to join individual letters. She reached for the phone receiver and dialed his number, and if he weren't home, she wouldn't leave a message. She didn't want to bother him. On the third ring, he picked up.

"Hello." His voice had an immediately comforting quality.

"Hi. It's me."

"Hey, it has to be." There was a pause. "So says the caller ID."

"Oh. So I guess you have my number now."

"Only if you want me to. I can have a very short memory when required."

She took a long breath. "I would have called sooner," she began, "but I guess I just didn't feel I'd be good phone company...I'm not sure I could be." She spoke softly.

"Nonsense. How're you doing, Kel?"

"Oh, okay. No. Not okay..." She tried to smile to cover her words, "I'm not calling at a bad time, am I? Because if I am, I'll let you go. Never mind..." She was beginning to stammer. She sounded agitated.

She could never intrude, he thought. "Nothing's going on here. Just reading a paper published by our competition. Rudy wants to play and I'm trying to tell him that now's not the time." His voice reflected the current battle for attention, "Rudy, quit it. Sorry, he's attacking my ankle." He started to laugh, as he picked up the cat to thwart his clawing antics. "Come here, cat! He wants his catnip mouse," he informed her.

"This goes on every night?"

"Yeah, basically. He gets a second wind right about now and he'll go nuts for a little while then settle down." Rick fidgeted on his couch, looking for Rudy's furry toy mouse that no longer had a tail.

"Catnip's not going to settle him down, what are you thinking?"

Both he and Rudy searched between the cushions - that's where it usually ended up. "Found it. It's his favorite toy. It's so old, there isn't even any catnip left in it, I don't think. Actually, there's barely any fluff left, now that I look at it."

Kelly smiled as she imagined Rudy's feline frolic and his teeth-worn mouse; she didn't notice her heart rate coming down.

He heard her sigh. "So, Kel, tell me. How come you're not doing okay?" he asked gently.

"We forgot chamomile tea. We need to add that one to the list."

"We'll do. Did you sleep last night?"

"Don't worry, I'm doing fine, really."

"Look, either way, you can say so. What's up?"

There was silence on the line. He was listening.

"The nightmares are back, in full force, it seems. Something's weird, Rick, they're getting to me even when I'm awake."

"While you're at work?" He grew concerned.

"No, I'm busy enough during the day, between skating, work, with all the usual stuff as long as I'm busy, I seem to be okay. But it's afterwards. Like now, in the evenings....when it's quiet." She stopped. A chill caught her so she lay down on her sofa and pulled the throw blanket folded on top of the sofa over her; he waited for her to continue. "I can't sleep. I'm afraid to." Her voice began to break.

"Scratch chamomile off the list?"

"Yes."

He could tell she was in tears. "Well, good that you called then. If you can't sleep, then we'll talk, for as long as it takes, until you sleep. Shouldn't be hard. I'll read you a section of this high-temperature materials testing paper, that'll do the trick, God knows, it does for me."

Her encumbered heart lightened. She had met someone who could make her laugh, even when there didn't seem to be anything to be happy about.

"How's Wendy?"

"Wendy's the way she is... Wendy. Fine, bouncing reactively through her life. She wants me to go to some stupid concert with her on Saturday night. I'm getting a migraine just thinking about it."

"Does she know about the insomnia, the nightmares?"

"Oh yes, more than she wants to." Kelly hesitated. "Old news. I don't even bring it up anymore...there's nothing she can do. There's nothing anyone can do."

"Whatever this is, it really has got you. What's eating you?"

"Everything." She whispered despondently with a summative catchall.

"You fresh out of hope?"

"I'm beyond hope," she stated matter-of-factly as she buried her heavy head further into the fluff of the cushions, "I'm beyond help."

"Nah, I don't think so," Rick slurred, "you haven't passed the fail-safe point yet, I can tell. Do your parents know what you're going through?"

"I wonder." That was all she said about that. "Do me a favor. Talk to me. Tell me something. Anything."

"What do you wanna know?"

"Anything. Whatever you want to tell me." She wanted to listen to the sound of his voice. The phone didn't do him justice. She pictured him on his couch, with his feet up on the coffee table, with Rudy bouncing and wriggling around him.

"Well," he thought, "okay. Here goes nothing. I grew up in Hampton, population a whopping eleven hundred, in the sticks, about five hours' drive away. My dad worked at the bank and my mom was the very typical housewife and mother, the best. She kept us in line, as much as she could. Bad combination when you have sons growing up in a small town, boys with too much time and nothing to do. Dad was kind of like the figurehead, this lording presence, he pushed his opinions around, tough as an old boot. Mom used him as the trump card when we got out of hand, and it worked for a while, then it stopped. Kevin was more of a slacker, he still is in some ways. Let's just say he's far more easy-going than I am."

Kelly wondered how that could even be possible.

"He used to play in a band with his buddies from school, and they used to practice in the basement sometimes, much to my mother's chagrin, and dad just let him do it. Kev was failing math, barely passing English, I had to tutor him, but dad never really locked horns with him like he did with me, and over far less I might add."

"Hmm. Why was that?"

"I guess dad just didn't have high expectations for Kev, he never did. He saw him for who he thought he was. I never saw him as 'beyond hope', he was just a kid, irresponsible and out for a good time. That's what mattered to him, his friends, his music and people having fun. To be fair, he wasn't an academic. I barely was."

"I don't buy that for a minute." Kelly smiled.

"It's true. Stuff didn't come easy for me, like for some of my friends. Take Mike for instance."

"Mike? You've never mentioned Mike."

"Mike Hartfort. He's to me like Wendy is to you."

"Oh. I hope you get along better than we do."

"Most of the time. Pushy bastard know-it-all. We try to play squash every week on Wednesday nights. He's a doctor, general practice, internal medicine. His life unfolded pretty naturally, he knew how to work. He rode the straight and narrow, all the time, like a beacon. If you ever got lost, you just had to look to Mike, and he'd set you straight. This guy's brutally honest and totally confrontational. My guess was he had to adjust his bedside manner if he was going to have to tell people how long they have left to live. He's an amazing doctor, very dedicated."

"So you say you were 'barely an academic'?" Kelly redirected back to her point of interest.

"And that's being generous. Strangely enough, it seemed the harder I tried, the more I managed to disappoint my dad. Maybe it just proved that no matter what, I'd never cut it. It just got to the point where I didn't care anymore, you couldn't do anything to please him. So I gave up, at least during high school. I got the grades I needed, but never made it high enough on the honor roll for dear ol' dad. But it was enough to get me into university and the floundering just continued from there.

"Bachelor of Engineering?" she guessed.

"Nope. First, undeclared major. Second, Diploma in Engineering, then Bachelor of Engineering, minor in physics."

"Barely an academic, eh? Right."

"I had to work for it. A lot of students coasted and still came out ahead of me."

"So what then? Was it enough for your dad?"

"What do you think?" Rick challenged. "There were other issues in the way, which just kept the wall up," he paused, "always issues in the way."

"Even now?"

"It doesn't matter. Old news." He changed the subject, "Kevin graduated high school, and got a degree in Commerce, but he works in a pro-sound store here, selling amps, guitars, keyboards and all that stuff. The shop loves him, because he can demo anything for anyone at any time. For a supposed slacker, he knows his stuff, makes a good sell." His tone grew light and humorous.

"Cool. So, does he get along with your dad?"

"Yeah, more or less. It's easier when you don't live at home, when you're far away."

Her heart sank as she heard his words. "How often do you get home?"

"A couple times a year, usually at Christmas."

"That's all?"

"That's enough."

Kelly could scarcely remember Christmas with her family. Some memories felt like yesterday, while others felt forever away.

"I'm not boring you to sleep, am I? Lemme dig out that paper..."

"Keep going. So after you got your degree, did you do your Ph.D. after that?"

"Not exactly. I had to do a Masters first. I had planned to do it, but...."

"Change of plans?"

"Hmm...Yep. I moved to Mississauga and got a job in industry, with McDonnell Douglas. I worked there for three years, until I was twenty-five or so. Then, I came here, worked full-on for five, nearly six years straight, got the pieces of paper that stated I was certifiable, useful to modern society, then I started the post-doc work I'm doing now. End of story."

"End of story." Kelly's eyes felt heavy; perhaps she would sleep now. She felt the most relaxed she had in days.

They talked for a few more minutes about the activities of their week thus far and the days to come. Rick informed her that he would be out of town for three days to conduct a series of experiments in Montreal at the National Research labs. He asked her if she could look after Rudy while he was gone, and if not, he would ask Mike. She was happy to accommodate. They would discuss it over coffee in the morning before he left.

WEDNESDAY, MAY 14

Kelly listlessly leafed through the newspaper's entertainment section, scanning the ads to see whether the Phish Experience concert was still scheduled to take place this Saturday. Sure enough, 'Mercury Club proudly presents for a one-night only return engagement: the Phish Experience.' She loved the name, too bad she didn't feel the same way about their music, if she ventured to call it that.

Floating at eye level in front of her, his hand held a binder ring with three keys dangling from it. "Good Morning," Rick greeted her in her ear from behind her.

Kelly's eyes darted in surprise as she looked up to him. "Hi. Thank you." She energetically snatched the keys and dropped them in her knapsack pocket.

"One's for the main door, the small one's for the mailbox and the other's for the condo."

"It's a condo?" she tossed her head, impressed that apartments could graduate status to condominiums, just like that. "Forgive me."

"It's an apartment when you rent it," he professed, "it's a condo when you earn equity on it." He sat down ready for the stirring morning challenge with Kelly, seeing as Wendy wasn't around.

"So don't tell me you had to buy your parking spot," she remarked.

"Got a good deal." He smiled at her then retrieved a folded letter from his leather coat pocket and gave it to her, "This is where I'll be, hotel number, lab number," pointing to the respective listings on the page. "Rudy eats a rounded scoop full of kitty kibble twice a day, I feed him in the morning and in the evening, and here's the number for the vet, which you won't need and here's the number for the building manager, which you also won't need. At least I hope not..." He gave her the look. "What's in the paper that's so interesting?"

"That concert I told you about, here it is." Kelly positioned her index finger on the Mercury Club ad. "One thing you need to know about Wendy, her taste in music matches her nature, slightly off-the-curve," she stated dryly.

"Hey, I've heard of them. Great name, Phish Experience. My brother knows those guys. He's probably setting up their equipment and doing their sound check."

Kelly raised her eyebrows, baffled by seemingly random connections.

"Anyway, I should get back home and finish packing. I just came out to pick up some stuff at the lab to take with me. You're sure you don't mind? .... You can check in on Rudy tonight and one more thing – make yourself at home." Rick purposely poked her arm as got up from the café table. "I'll be in touch with you later tonight, and thank you for this."

"Don't thank me now." Kelly swatted his jacket.

"Friday." He jiggled her ponytail as he brushed by her on his way out the door.

She reached out to swat him again but he got away, "Friday."

It was past seven pm by the time Kelly reached Rick's condo. She first stopped by her flat to drop off her things and grab a quick bite for supper; a grilled cheese sandwich was both fast and filling. She remembered to fish out Rick's keys from the pocket of her knapsack before heading out to Oakton Gate, condo number ten-fifteen. She would jog to and from, only on well-lit streets since it was already dark.

As she fiddled the key into the deadbolt lock, holding Rick's mail, she could hear Rudy's little voice excited that his food supply would be presently replenished. Expecting the cat to be disappointed that the body entering the doorway was not Rick's, Kelly was flattered that Rudy responded as warmly to her as he did the other night. She hung the keys on the key hook, and immediately swept Rudy up and rubbed him around the ears. She had never heard a cat purr so passionately. She could feel the soothing vibration throughout his little body. "Have you been all alone?" she questioned his amber saucer eyes. "You must be hungry, yes, I know."

She set Rudy upon the floor and he trotted impatiently behind her with his ringed tail held high like a question mark, chirping, as she headed in the direction of the kitchen. She found the kitty kibble on the kitchen counter; Rudy's dish was on the floor by the wall near the oven. Deftly tap dancing to avoid orange paws under foot, she began to fill the dish as Rick instructed, and she hadn't finished pouring it in before Rudy delved into it. A few kibbles bounced off his head onto the floor. Kelly giggled, listening to him purr as he ate, and every so often, he chirped his pleasure. Next to the bag of kibble stood a piece of paper, folded like a tent. It had her name on it.

Thank you. Make yourself at home. I mean it.
I'll call you here (or at your place) at ten.
R
PS: Please check my phone messages.

Kelly checked her watch to see it was nearly seven-thirty.

With Rudy joyfully occupied with supper, Kelly switched on the lights in the condo and took the opportunity to have a closer look around. She studied each item of native sculpture on his living room shelves, picking up each souvenir and feeling its weight. Three looked to be carved stone, of native Indian origin, shaped into animals, which likely were representations of spirit guides: the wolf, the bear and the eagle. Others were carved wood and looked to be of African origin. The last two were cut obsidian, black volcanic glass containing minute flecks of gold that shone in the light. She had no idea where these would have come from; they also looked tribal. She set two of the physics mobiles, crafted in chromed metal, into motion. One was a series of five balls that swung and bounced back and forth off each other. Conservation of momentum, she remembered from high school physics. The other gyroscopic mobile demonstrated rotational momentum. Fundamental laws of science aside, they were mesmerizing to watch.

Rudy had finished his supper and was seated on the telephone table behind the sofa, licking his paws. "Someone else who appreciates the benefits of discipline," Kelly remarked as she tickled Rudy behind his ears. Her eyes glanced to see that the answering machine light wasn't flashing. She continued down the hall past the telephone table. On her left, just past the kitchen was the bathroom. She flipped on the light switch and peeked in. The washer and dryer were tucked behind bi-fold doors on one side of the bathroom. On the counter was a large folded white towel, and another tent-style note. Kelly lifted up the paper to reveal a small bottle of Lavender bath oil. She smiled as she read the note,

> *Lavender. Add that to the list.*
> *Take your Dr.'s advice.*
> *R*

She laughed out loud, had he done this especially for her? She pushed the bath curtain aside and gave the idea of a deliciously warm lavender soak serious consideration for a few moments. It was far too appealing to not take the opportunity. Maybe tomorrow, she would think about it.

Continuing down the hall, past the linen closet, she switched on the light to the bedroom that lit a standing floor lamp in the opposite corner of the room. A large window opposite the door offered a bird's eye view of the southwestern part of the city. She could see the urban lights twinkling in the distance. Kelly surveyed the room which was more than spacious enough for the bed, and the matching mission-style pine night tables and dresser that had iron accents. An abstract, low relief, pressed metal wall sculpture hung over the bed. By the window was a small curio table. Rudy announced his presence with a cheerfully inflected meow as he entered the room. He sprung upon the bed and took his place in the very center of it, to continue his bath regimen, vertically outstretching his hind leg through to the tips of his four toes. The bedcover was printed in chalky mute colors including the same sage green as in the living room as well as touches of black. Rudy's swirling orange and cream fur made an artistic contrast to the background color scheme. Kelly flopped on the bed and began to play with him, fiddling with his paws and interrupting his routine. Congenially obliging for the first few seconds, Rudy then revealed his claws to her hands. Kelly took the hint. She sat up on the edge of the bed. The mattress was comfortable as she pressed her palms into its cushy pillow-top surface.

Upon the dresser stood a series of framed photographs. She walked over to look at them. The first photo was an eight by ten of his parents. She smiled, catching herself in a sigh. She could see how much he looked like his dad, but he had features from his mom as well, especially her eyebrows and cheeks. Next was a five by seven of Rick and Kevin, possibly taken when they were in college or high school. His younger brother was just as good looking, but in his own way, his features looked predominantly like his mother's. The third photo, taken around the same time, was of Rick and a woman that Kelly surmised was his sister. Rick never mentioned a sister. Whoever she was, she looked lovely, with deep, piercing eyes and long, wavy, chestnut hair. Kelly couldn't understand the tidal draw she felt to this picture. Unable to resist, she picked it up to get a better look at it. A small slip of paper slid out the bottom from between the frame and the backing. Kelly immediately fumbled to slip it back inside the frame. She hadn't looked any closer than her initial glance, and didn't want to. She was forced to remove the backing from the photograph in order to replace the clipping. Having done so, nervously, she placed the photo back on the dresser where she found it. She turned off the light and darted out of the room. Her heart galloped. Agramon launched into full scolding tirade: **That's what you get for snooping, for being where you have no business to**

be…for being where you're not wanted. That was it. She was going to grab the keys and get out.

As she unlocked the deadbolt, the phone rang. By the second ring, it occurred to her that she should answer it and take a message, as Rick had requested. She ran to the telephone table and grabbed the receiver just before the machine engaged. "Hello?" she gasped.

"Oh, hello… I must have dialed the wrong number, I'm sorry," said a woman's voice on the other end.

"Um, no, maybe not, who are you looking for?" Kelly thought quickly.

"I'm trying to reach Richard…Hutchinson," the woman qualified.

"Oh, you have the right number, but he's out of town. May I take a message?"

"Yes, this is his mother," she announced sweetly, and unsurely. "To whom am I speaking?"

"Oh, hello, Mrs. Hutchinson. I'm Kelly. I'm a friend, well, a neighbor, actually, of Rick's. He's asked me to look after his cat while he's away."

"Kelly, how wonderful! Why isn't Mike looking after the cat?"

"Mike? Gosh, I don't know. He's a doctor, right?"

"Yes, good point, dear. He's probably tied up with being on call, patients and all that."

"Yes, I suppose." There was a brief moment of silence until Kelly remembered, "Oh, you know what, Rick said he would check in later this evening, I'll be sure to tell him you called. He's supposed to be back later on Friday."

"That would be good, dear. Richard's lucky to have such a nice, sweet friend…-ly neighbor," she commented tentatively, but in a very motherly way.

"No problem at all, it was good to talk with you, Mrs. Hutchinson." Kelly smiled as she hung up the phone then headed back to her flat.

Her phone rang around ten o'clock, just as she expected. Kelly reached for the receiver on her nightstand. "Hello there, you." She took the chance.

"Hey there, yourself. I tried you at home but there was no answer, so I figured you'd come back."

"Indeed, I had. Your mother called," she announced the first item on the evening's conversation agenda.

"Of course she did. When?"

"Just past eight or so, right as I was leaving. She didn't know you were out of town, so I told her you'd be back on Friday."

"She knew I was going out of town. I told her."

"She said she didn't know…well, no, actually, she never said that. You know what, I don't know."

"Let me guess. She asked who you were?" Rick sounded like he was smiling.

"Mmm, yes, who was I, where was Mike and probably, even though she didn't come right out and ask, what was a strange girl doing in her son's condo?"

"So you two had a lovely chat, I see." He waited then asked, "Did you make yourself at home?"

"Tried not to. It was hard. But I played with Rudy."

"You didn't find what I left for you?" he asked disappointedly.

"Yes, I did." Kelly perked up. "Lavender, it's perfect."

"Did you try it?"

"Not yet."

"You'll actually need to try it, make sure it works before we put it on the list."

"I will."

"When?"

Kelly flustered, "I don't know."

"You really should take opportunities when they're available to you, Kel."

They gently sparred back and forth until Kelly relented. She agreed to have a wonderfully long bath tomorrow evening, and she would make doubly sure Rudy didn't fall in the tub, as Rick notified her of his cat's odd predisposition to keeping company on the tub ledge.

"So, it sounds like you talk to your mom fairly often."

"Yeah, she usually calls me once a week and I call home about that often too. We talk about nothing, most of the time. Just details, how the day went, that sort of stuff. Sometimes about Kevin, if he's in a jam."

"Just the comfort of hearing the other person's voice."

"Exactly."

"Does she bug you that you're not married?"

"You know it," he laughed, "she gets on these kicks every now and then. She worries that my lifetime companion will be my cat. You know what's weird is that she never bugs Kevin."

"Wendy's mom bugs her all the time. Every new guy she dates for longer than a month, her mom's wondering if it's time to book the church, call the florist. Her list is done, she's ready to go. All they need is a viable groom and she'll take it from there."

"Clearly, Wendy's mom is more than one step ahead of mine. I guess I should shut up and stop complaining. Do you get bugged by your folks?"

Kelly responded in a monotone, "I never date, so marriage isn't an issue."

"What? So who's been beating all the guys away with a stick? You hired out a Hell's Angel?"

"You had to wait until you were a thousand miles away to ask me about my love life? What guys specifically would you be referring to? All the ones lined up at my door? Sorry, wrong address, try over at Wendy's place."

"Forgive me, I didn't mean to pry, but hey, you started it. I'm still agog that you say you don't date. It's gotta be by choice, because I refuse to believe it's by circumstance."

"Choice," she answered definitively.

"Hmm. There are a lot of jerks out there, you know."

"That's what I've been told."

"And you've crossed paths with more than your share of them?"

"Nope. Wendy has and that's enough. For me, there was only one. He left me. The end."

"Let's find him. I'll kick his ass," Rick offered. "How long ago?"

"Ten years," she whispered.

"Are you saying you haven't dated in ten years?" He was floored.

"You're the one with the Ph.D., you do the math." Kelly retorted, hoping sarcasm would dispel her embarrassment.

"Wow, you got me beat by three whole years. Flat-out, you win."

That was something she was not expecting to hear. "You mean to tell me you haven't dated in seven years?"

"Closer to eight, actually, sorry. Not seriously, no. And it's not the kind of thing one eagerly broadcasts."

"What's your excuse?"

"Work, and in a field that doesn't offer scads of she-types to select from."

"So, you haven't dated by circumstance," Kelly concluded.

"No comment."

"Who was the last woman you dated seriously?"

"Don't go there."

"Why not?"

His voice suddenly quieted, "The woman I proposed to."

Kelly paused. Then, sheepishly, she probed, "I thought you said you were never married."

"The wedding never happened."

Kelly had serious misgivings about asking him any more questions.

May 12

Disobedient Grief.

Egotistical and Tyrannical
You rule with Fear

Agramon

Should nightmare sneak in
And grab hold of me,
To strangle life's breath
from my body once again.
You, monster, will not spare me.
You lurk, my past, You wait.

If only sleep could be the masquerade,
Worn, then doffed, like a dream,
I could rest.
But hollow fortitude
Shielded safe by solitude
Cracks, then finally, breaks.

You lurk, my future, You wait

I'm the only twenty-seven year old I know still afraid of the dark - not a darkened room - but the blackness when I close my eyes - so frightened to sleep, heaven forbid to dream.

Swirling in the snare
Solitude's promise: Safety
Silently breeds fear.

Companionship feels so foreign to me, it paralyzes me when all I want is for someone to grab my hand and pull me out of this downward spiral. Why am I so terrified to accept the gift of companionship from anyone? Why do I repudiate the nagging, throbbing, painful desire to allow myself one who might understand? Because every human soul I have loved, entrusted my heart to and depended upon has abandoned me.

To forge companionship fearlessly — how weary I have grown of the gossamer fantasy. There is nothing worthy left to give, for it has all been taken from me.

May 14

Water Under Bridge

Wretched histories,
We are told we must move on,
Forgiveness is lost.

From our tragic pasts,
We are told to just let go,
Suppression is forced.

Beyond our loves lost,
We are told never look back,
Masked by avoidance.

Water, nature's way,
Misery flows on, we run,
We hide, hearts stagnate.

Within still waters,
Rests my foundational peace,
Sleeps this deep silence.

May 15

Road Trip

Murky waters of grief
Soul of sandstone
Promises of Oases
That never arrive...
Daddy, are we there yet?

Six

THURSDAY, MAY 15

Wendy walked into Kelly's office carrying a bulging file folder, and dropped it onto the table. "It's all in here. God help us all." Wendy huffed as she relinquished her burden.

"Are the digitals in there too?"

"Yes, and the prelim layouts, copy, photos, negatives, everything. They want proposals by next Friday. Happy designing."

Kelly shoved the bundle aside, her mind unable to process the imminent due dates. She had stopped by the market near Rick's place after she fed Rudy his breakfast. She began to lay out lunch for the two of them, "I picked up lunch for us this morning, all your favorites: Southwest black bean salad, pita bread and hummus, extra spicy."

"I think it's a fine combination, eclectic, like us." Wendy scraped some hummus off the container lid to sample it.

As they ate, Wendy talked openly about the progress, or lack thereof, on the Franklin front. "He's royally messed up," she mumbled through her black bean salad. "I think he's far more fragile than he lets on. He doesn't talk about anything else except his relationship failures, his wife's betrayal, the divorce, how it's affecting Timothey. Talk about baggage."

"Everyone has baggage, Wendy." Kelly was sympathetic to this man's plight, "Divorce is serious, can be damaging, especially to a kid. Nobody escapes divorce unscathed, no matter how old you are or how much experience you have."

"Too much baggage for me. He may as well be the CEO of Samsonite. I've had it." Wendy stated in frustration, "He's a nice guy, but he's so damn serious about everything. I'll be honest, it's a downer to be around him. Why can't he just zip it?"

Kelly listened to the callous comments blank-faced. Wendy's brutal honesty had always affected Kelly very deeply. In two decades, she had experienced Wendy's nature to its core, and she had viewed her full spectrum of behavior. She had witnessed it all, from her profound sense of loyalty all the way to her distinct lack of empathy. "So, you're not going to see him anymore?" She didn't know why she bothered to ask.

"I've said this before, I'll say it again. In the end, men only want one thing. And until they get it, they'll suck you dry for every ounce of life you have."

"Where is this coming from? Why do you always say that? Not everyone is out to get you." Kelly's heated reaction rebutted Wendy's coldness.

"Where is it coming from? Where the hell have you been? Or have you not been paying attention?" Wendy's anger was beginning to spill over.

She needed to regain control of this conversation, "Look, Wendy," she set her lunch plate down, "I've been right here, all along. I've watched you bounce through life, from man to man, like a pinball machine. Why do it myself when I've lived it all through you? This emotional roller coaster you're on is too much, Wendy. If your life is too much for me, it has to be too much for you. Goddammit."

Wendy quieted and set her plate down across from Kelly's and leaned back in her chair.

"You have to find another way to go through life. You can't keep building people up then selfishly dumping them because their lives don't fit your ideal. This way, you'll always be on the lookout for something more, and never happy with what you have." Kelly knew the last thing Wendy wanted was a lecture, though she sorely needed one. There was nothing in life that Wendy feared more than being alone. Perhaps bearing witness to Kelly's life only amplified her fear and desperation. Since they were eighteen, Kelly had been enduring life alone, day after day. Undeniably, she was a living example of Wendy's worst nightmare, and always within her sight for reminder. To Kelly, it made sense: Wendy's harsh dissatisfaction, her cold indifference, overall and not just in regard to Franklin. Wendy's mounting bitterness and negativity from her own repeated relationship failures had been invariably rubbing off on her in recent years. Countless times, Wendy had reminded her that in the end, because of her situation, Kelly was better off single…all the good ones were already snagged by women who were luckier, or maybe just more manipulative…she was safer relying on number one. Kelly heard Wendy's voice in her mind more than her own these days. Her lifelong protectiveness was endearing, at least it was in the beginning, but she felt stifled now. It had grown too penetrating; now the judgmental voice seems to have adopted a life of its own.

Kelly prudently skirted around the prickly topic of men. Astute in her decision, she chose not to mention the fact that Rick went out of town and she was looking after his cat until tomorrow. Wendy would find a problem with it, as with anything that fell into the out-of-bounds-for-Kelly category.

Instead, they turned their attention to Saturday's plans. Kelly planned to renege, but thoughtfully changed her mind in light of the tedious lunchtime conversation. Wendy insisted that Kelly come to her place for a lasagna dinner before heading to the Mercury Club. Kelly offered to bring Tira Misu for dessert; somehow, she would try to have a good time.

Rudy sat upon the tub ledge like a little loaf of gingerbread, crouched on all fours with his eyes dreamily half-closed. Lavender redolence filled the bathroom and Kelly luxuriated in the warmth, sensuous froth. Even though she hadn't skated today, every muscle in her body was thankful for this gift. She brought in a pair of candlesticks from the dining room table; the subtle flicker of the flames cast a tranquil light that danced with the shadows on the walls in an affectionate pas-de-deux. For this sole therapeutic luxury, she considered vacating Mrs. Wiles' flat for a real apartment.

Kelly came out to find Rudy in his rightful place in front of his dish eagerly awaiting her arrival. He began to tango around her ankles until she fed him. She ate black bean salad and hummus leftovers slowly while a Baroque guitar collection of Andrés Segovia played in the background. She remembered her parents' love of Segovia and decided she needed to make a trip to the music store. Her thoughts vacillated between dysfunctions in her relationship with her best friend, and her new friend's marriage that never took place years ago. By nine-thirty pm, Kelly had taken a long look through the new Kaine design project and finished her stretching. Rick's living room offered abundant space for movement, another luxury that made Kelly rethink her cramped flat. The phone rang and she crawled onto the sofa to answer the phone behind it, "Hello?" She smiled and settled herself into the cushions when she heard Rick's voice. Rudy took the opportunity to engage her in a late evening game of fetch with his haggard, tail-less mouse.

"Hey there," he greeted, "I tried you first at your place this time, you're a hard one to predict."

"Hey, I made you a promise and I kept it. Are you going to get after me about that?"

"No, definitely not. How was it?"

"Relaxing, thank you. I made sure Rudy didn't fall in."

Rick talked spiritedly about the progress of the experiments then complained about the numerous teleconference meetings. Kelly talked about her day and how Rudy was doing. "We're playing with his catnip mouse. Did you know your cat could fetch? I'm amazed!"

"Yep, that's what he does. He'll practically bring it right back to you, but then, like the feline power assertion control freak he is, he'll drop it a foot and a half away from you then wait for you to get it and throw it again. He won't ever bring it right to your hand. He lets you know you work for him." Rick described Rudy's behavior like a practiced pet psychologist.

"So, closet passive-aggressive." She waited through a brief pause in the conversation and then asked him, "How did you sleep last night?"

"Hey. That's my line."

"Yeah, too bad. It's mine now."

"I never sleep that well away from home. I don't like hotel rooms. How did you sleep?" It was his turn to ask.

"Same. I'm sorry you didn't have a good night."

"No need to worry about it, it happens."

"I only asked because I think our conversation last night went in a direction that it shouldn't have because of me. It was my fault."

"You know you're in trouble when you have to start censoring the natural flow of conversations, especially if it gets to be a habit."

"It's called being thoughtful," she clarified.

"It's called being real."

"Shouldn't it be a combination of both?"

"Agreed," Rick conceded. "I think the art of conversation seems to be lost in this age. I believe it is an art. You're responsible for its development, but you also have to respond to the infinite possibilities when it decides to go off-trail."

"Interesting philosophy," she responded with enthusiasm, "I can't say I ever thought of it that way. But that makes sense. When you block conversation, or try to control it, you're limiting the creation of the art that becomes your relationship."

"Some artists will tell you when you block creative departures, it stops being art and becomes no better than an exercise."

Kelly thought of her various edge-technique exercises and compulsory dances. "The purpose of exercise is for disciplined practice, but you're right, art is meant to be for true self-expression, more than the sum of its parts."

They rested in the silence that was their mutual understanding. Kelly felt strangely peaceful. After a moment, Kelly opened, "You know, I have to go to that concert with Wendy on Saturday night…"

"You still don't want to go?"

"I'm not sure. I don't think the concert is the issue. She assumes so much." She began to voice her true feelings, "I just don't feel like having to justify things all the time."

"Why, is Wendy expecting you to justify yourself? You don't have to explain anything."

"Easy for you to say. I bet Mike doesn't bug you about everything in your life."

"Only the stuff I deserve to be bugged about. Like when I'm being a jackass. He tells me I'm just as stubborn as my dad."

"Tell me you're a Taurus and I'll scream."

"What are the dates for Taurus? My birthday is May second."

"Good Lord, that explains it. Astrology says you're supposed to be bullheaded, it's the classic Taurus trait."

"The letter L if I know, I'll take your word for it. Astrology could very well be a load of crock, but it does give me the convenient excuse I've been looking for all these years, thanks." He laughed, "It doesn't explain my dad, though."

"Happy belated birthday, by the way."

"Thanks. And not another word about it."

Kelly laughed that he wouldn't give her an opportunity to make an age-related wisecrack. "I don't know how, but maybe Wendy and I are just too wrapped up - more than we need to be," Kelly continued, "I guess that happens after twenty-two years, you stop really seeing a person and you base everything off of your own assumptions of who they are. You start to forget who you are, where your opinions end and the other person's begins."

"Maybe you're more alike than you are different. Did that ever occur to you?"

She was willing to re-explore this wheel-welled road. "I think she sees things in me that she doesn't like, about who I am, who I've become. In some ways it scares her, like she recognizes herself. I'm sure the opposite is true too, that I see things in her that maybe have to do more with me than her. There's just so much we can't seem to talk about anymore. All we do is push each other's buttons and pour salt in wounds. Forget speaking in tongues, I just realized I'm stuck on metaphors."

"Too many mirrors, not enough smoke," Rick jested.

"Oh my gosh!" she laughed aloud, "Can I use that? That's excellent. We're like a magician's illusion trick that confuses the mind."

"I'll hang out my shingle, like Lucy. Five cents, please." His humor had a way of lightening her outlook on their dysfunctions. Kelly paused to further consider her situation. "Can I tell you something?"

"Sure, shoot," he encouraged, "that'll be another five cents by the way."

"I have real reasons as to why I don't date. Fear mostly, for the purposes of self-preservation. I look at Wendy's life, I see where her choices have gotten her. I don't want it."

"There's nothing wrong with that. A person should do what's right for them, what makes them happy. There's something to be said for learning from other folks' mistakes. There has to be meaning in how you live, and if it isn't there, you owe it to yourself to find it. I will say one thing to you, though. Self-preservation is mandatory, Kel, never sacrifice the truth of who you are. So don't let fear be the limitation for anything, it just takes hold and lords a power over you. When you're locked by fear, you can't ever reach that point of true self-expression."

She listened carefully and knew where he was going, and she just wasn't ready to go there.

"Question for you. Wendy said something along the lines that you operated within a limited radius and that she looks out for you. What did she mean by that?"

When would Wendy have had an opportunity to say anything about her to him...only that morning at Faders, she deduced. She then speculated what else she could have said to him. "Well, she's obviously told you exactly what she means. My radius is limited. She's clearly demonstrated over the years that she's the woman of the world and I'm not. Simple as that."

"Too easy. That says nothing as to why she says she has to look out for you. You gave her that job?"

"She's decided on how the world works and she's taken it upon herself to protect me from it."

"And what have you decided about the way the world works?"

"That she might very well be right. I don't know actually." She was beginning to feel badgered.

"I think you're old enough to make up your own mind. You should be prepared to find out for yourself. Why are you living your life based on her conclusions, choices you said yourself you wouldn't choose?"

"What I've been forced to learn over the last decade is more hell than anyone should have to know. I can draw my own conclusions, from my own experience. I've had to," she emphasized defensively. "Wendy sees me as loaded down with more baggage than anyone in their right mind would willingly adopt, and she's right about that. No one wants to take on that much crap," she answered bitterly.

"Hey, slow down. This isn't an attack," he reminded her forcefully, "this isn't an attack." His voice released.

She was on the verge of tears.

"Listen, Kel, you're right. When you love people, and they've influenced you, you do change. They change you. You can't avoid it. You do start to become like each other, for better or worse. But what you can't do is ever lose yourself to another person. Never let what they want out of life define who you are and what you want. Smoke and mirrors. It's the worst damage you can do to yourself, telling yourself that you aren't worthy enough to be your own person. You send a message to the other person that you're up for sale." Rick's voice returned to that comforting quality that she found calming.

Through her silent tears, she whispered, "She believes I'm too fragile to handle the world on my own. She's right, it's something I haven't really done, I refused to earlier on and now, it's become the status quo. She hates me for it, and that she has to look out for me."

He wished he had all the pieces to her puzzle. "Sometimes, circumstances put you in a position where you feel helpless. I know what that's like, but it's temporary. It takes time to rebuild, but if you know where you want to go, it's a start, no matter how long it takes to get there. But you have to commit, to stick to the process of rebuilding and re-strengthening. Good friends to keep you company along the way help too."

"Wendy's trying. She really is. Even though she means well, I don't think it's helping me." Kelly's thoughts were starting to clear. "And obviously I haven't been helping her either."

"What she might not realize is sometimes the best intentions still have a way of influencing badly. Which brings me back to why you have to be your own person, so you'll know what's helping and what isn't. You won't see yourself as fragile or dependent, and you won't resent the other person, either. If you don't need to be looked out for, or you don't want to be looked out for, then tell her that. There's a lot to be said for standing up for yourself."

"The voice of experience..." she wondered aloud.

"The sad voice of experience. I didn't stand up for myself when I should have. The longer you let these things go, the harder it gets to make your stand later on. And before you know it, you're locked in a pattern that you never intended to be in."

"You're referring to your dad?"

"In some cases, yes. In others, you find out the hard way that it's too late, and you can't do anything about it, except live with it. That's the worst, especially when you discover that you can't live with it, and it weighs you down like an albatross."

"Rime of the Ancient Mariner, exactly." Kelly related.

"Mistakes aren't worth squat if you don't learn from them. And if you're anywhere near as stubborn as I am, you'll know that it isn't so easy to face it for what it is and move on. It's easier to make a zillion excuses."

"An issue of timing? Waiting for all the planets to align?" she kidded.

"Something like that."

"An issue of ego?" she pushed.

"Something like that."

It was getting late into the night and Kelly had an early morning ahead. Even artists must learn when to let their creation rest, when to consider it complete, if only for the time being.

FRIDAY, MAY 16

It was another one of those days that managed to steal away from her. The new Kaine project was paramount priority and would occupy the entire upcoming week. There was simply no putting it off, despite the other contracts in progress that still needed their fair share.

Kelly felt tired virtually all the time from the depression and the more frequent anxiety attacks which weren't showing signs of letting up. She stole a few minutes between tasks to call Dr. Lake for advice about increasing her medication for the panic symptoms. During what extended to a lengthy phone consultation, Dr. Lake advised her to keep to her schedule as much as she could, to maintain balance in her days, and to do things she enjoyed doing, not only what needed doing. She advised Kelly that any dosage changes in her panic medication would take time, possibly upwards of thirty days to notice. Dr. Lake was fully aware that Kelly was within one week of facing the tenth anniversary of her parents' death, and she encouraged her to call if she needed to come in and she would re-arrange her schedule to fit her in. In closing, Dr. Lake reminded Kelly that in the event of a panic attack, to remember her breathing techniques and to remind herself that she was safe, perfectly safe, and so were her parents.

She stopped by the market on the way back to Rick's place. She told him she would put together something simple for supper, knowing he'd be tired when he got home. Rick was thankful and thought it a great idea, if it wasn't too much trouble for her; they would spend the evening together. Remembering that Rick's fridge was well stocked with fresh vegetables and there was rice in his cupboard, she picked up chicken at the market as she planned to make a casserole. It was a favorite recipe of her mom's, simple and delicious and very much in the comfort food category. Little things like this kept her in touch with herself, her former life, the happy times, even if it meant her emotions might swell uncontrollably as she diced celery and sliced mushrooms. It was just the way it had been for so long. She felt fragile and worn. Life had transformed into a delicate balancing act: moving through daily life, working to concentrate on the present, versus straining to maintain who she was and the life she came from, and struggling to preserve memories that receded further and further away as days became years. This sensitive balance lurched into a constant tug of war: living like a recluse in the here and now or living secluded in her past.

As she tidied up the kitchen, Kelly heard the sound of a key in the deadbolt. He was home. "Perfect timing, Doctor," she called out when he entered the door.

"Hey there, you," he responded as he unloaded his luggage in front of the coat closet. The aroma of baked chicken filled his condo. Rudy trotted from the kitchen to greet him. The luggage conveniently blocked his path to the partially open door. He picked his cat up and they rubbed foreheads like true companions. "Hi, Rudy. Were you a good cat for Kel?" He spied her leaning against the kitchen archway, drying her hands with a tea towel. She was wearing khaki drawstring pants and a navy blue tank shirt, and her hair was loosely clipped up. The cat really may have caught his tongue for an instant. "Now you are definitely a sight for sore eyes."

"Hope you're hungry, supper should be ready in a few minutes."

"Great, you really didn't have to go through so much trouble." He hung his leather coat up in the closet, while Rudy sniffed at his luggage with cautious interest.

"No trouble. Time tested recipe, I can do it with my eyes closed."

"And one hand tied behind your back?"

"Yep. You must be tired. How was the rest of the trip?"

"Pretty standard fare. More experiments lined up for here and for there later on. Better busy than bored, I always say." He wandered into the kitchen to see the production. "We know what gift was behind door number one. So what lovely prize is behind door number two?"

"Hey," she swatted him with the tea towel before he touched the oven door, "you'll see when it's ready." Kelly began to open cupboard doors at random.

"Wine glasses?" he predicted.

"Yes."

"Over here, on this side of the kitchen, behind door number three, we have a lovely set of goblets for our lucky contestant." Taking out two glasses, he asked, "Red or white?"

"White today, I think."

He opened the fridge. "I see you didn't drink yourself into oblivion while I was gone."

"I was reserving it for this coming hell week, hope you don't mind." She frowned at the thought of the misery to come.

"I'll remember to pick up extra then." He wrapped his arm around her neck and pulled her into him.

"Get the hard stuff," she added as she patted his back.

"Do I have time for a shower before dinner?"

"Your house."

She was in the process of dishing out casserole when he reappeared in the kitchen smiling, "Smells like lavender in there." He had changed into track pants and a t-shirt, and his hair was still wet. "Oooh. That looks good." He eyed her creation. "Secret family recipe?"

"Yes. It's worth millions to the Pearson family." She handed him a plate and they gave the idea of sitting at the dining table like civilized folks a flash of consideration and unanimously agreed upon the Friday night favored location, the couch. Rick's mail lay in a pile on the coffee table. As he sifted through it, he tasted Kelly's culinary creation, "Mmm, you're right, this is worth millions."

They were barely seated two minutes when the phone rang. "It's your mom," Kelly grinned.

"Funny. The only woman I can count on to call me." He picked up the phone from the table behind him.

Kelly picked through her casserole as she nibbled slowly. Rudy was on the floor by her feet, his nostrils and whiskers twitching at the glorious scent of chicken and creamy sage. His tail flicked and swayed in delight. His facial expression conveyed the look of immeasurable confidence in her; his glistening golden eyes beckoned the essence of unfailing generosity of humankind. She was listening to Rick's side of the conversation.

"…Can I call you back?…. This amazing chicken thing my friend made…. Yeah…." Rick's voice inflected as information was systematically extracted out of him; all along, he remained good-natured with his mother. Periodically, he would look at Kelly, smile then nod his head in embarrassed disbelief.

Meanwhile, Rudy's glowing saucer pupils stared at her with undivided loyalty, ready for a sample of chicken. She looked down at her plate for a fitting morsel then drew in a deep breath as Rick's lighthearted banter with his mother pressed on.

"…Oh, I don't know, about a month or so… about five-six, blond-ish," he fiddled with her hair clip as he attempted to determine the natural color of her hair, "Oh yes. Very," he drawled. There was a pause.

Kelly's eyes shifted suspiciously in his direction until they met his. She then handed Rudy more chicken, which he gleefully devoured without even slowing to chew it.

Rick worked to close the chat. "I'll call you tomorrow… Yeah… Okay. Say hi to dad….Bye." He returned the receiver to its cradle and resumed his supper.

"Does she want Wendy's mom's phone number?" Kelly offered sarcastically.

"I think so. We'll let the two of them discuss their mutual guilt-afflictions and neuroses in between florist price comparisons and wedding planner appointments. She's impressed that you cook," he relayed with raised eyebrows, "she also told me to apologize to you for the other night."

"What about the other night? There's nothing to apologize for."

"She said she might have come across kind of strange. She wasn't expecting someone to answer the phone." Rick had nearly cleaned his plate and there was no debate on second helpings.

"Naturally, that's nothing to be sorry for."

From the kitchen, she heard him say to her, "Mom said when she called the other night, you sounded just like my former fiancée on the phone. I think that's what freaked her out."

"Hmm. Really." How much like his former fiancée was she, Kelly wondered. They looked nothing alike, at least according to the photograph in his bedroom of him and the woman she assumed was her. Kelly gave no inclination that she wanted to pursue the matter.

"More wine?"

"One is more than enough, if you expect me to stay awake."

"More for your hell week, then." He re-corked the bottle and returned to his seat then fiddled with her ponytail again instead of eating. Rudy, atop the telephone table behind Kelly, took this as a signal to play with her gold hair clip as it shimmered in the lamplight.

She giggled loudly when she found herself afflicted by both of them pawing at her hair. "Excuse me, guys," Kelly rolled forward, "and we wonder where the cat learns it from." Kelly thumped Rick on his shoulder.

He recoiled, laughing. It was worth it. Rudy had landed on the couch next to her, upside down. Her gold clip was now out of her hair in his possession. As the cat mauled it, Rick suggested innocently, "You know, you should wear your hair down more often."

"So I've been told." Her droll reply was exactly as he anticipated.

They were in the kitchen when Rick began, "I knew both Mike and Rebecca in high school, but Rebecca and I didn't start dating until we were in university. We got engaged just before we graduated."

"How old were you?" Kelly asked. The evening's jovial tone had already begun to shift, Kelly noticed, perhaps his mother's comment on the phone instigated it.

"I was twenty-two and Rebecca was twenty-one. After graduation, we had moved to Ontario, for work. We were thinking of getting married in three years, she wanted a June wedding."

Rick would have been twenty-five by the time he married her, Kelly calculated. "Long engagement, planned for a reason?"

"Monetary."

"Understood." Kelly smiled.

"Life went on, time flew. The wedding date was approaching with a million details that I didn't have a clue about. Rebecca and her mom did all their planning for the ceremony and reception at home in Hampton, the guest list, seating arrangements, decorative details. The phone bills were hell. It was a crazy time, a lot going on, and everything mattered." Rick talked to Kelly as one would to a trusted friend. "The list seemed endless to me, and Rebecca kept insisting that it was all in the details, that every little nuance had to be just right. It was beyond me, I was no help and I'm sure I was more a pain in the ass. So it went. All was on schedule, the invitations had been sent out and everything was confirmed. Then one night, Rebecca was walking home from the bus stop. She was coming back from an evening class…"

She knew the wedding never happened. Kelly felt her breath beginning to grow shallow as he narrated his story like a documentary. She feared where the ending was going; her pulse had shot up just at the time she needed to listen to him. She knew it would get progressively more difficult for her to maintain equanimity. Her airways felt constricted. She felt herself breaking out into a heated sweat. Kelly tried to concentrate on the feeling of the warm sudsy water in the sink as she finished up the supper dishes, scared that she would be overtaken by uncontrollable panic.

His back was to her as he talked, "It happened in a crosswalk that she had crossed I don't know how many times in the few years we lived there. Some bastard driver, speeding like a bat out of hell, out of nowhere, hit her, just like that. He probably didn't even see her." His recollection of the host of painful memories caused him to become distressed, "He didn't even stop. There were no witnesses. I never had a chance to say goodbye to -" He stopped speaking when his voice broke apart.

Kelly suddenly went cold as a shock penetrated her bones. The image of the newspaper clipping falling out of the photograph frame flashed in her mind's eye: Cates, Rebecca Elise; age 24; died March 24th.

After a brief pause, he continued, "Within the blink of an eye, she was gone. Stolen. Her life had been obliterated in one second. By accident. And there was nothing anyone could do about it."

The sound of his voice grew faint and muffled, then started to Doppler-shift away into swirls of galaxies that rapidly expanded and closed in all at the same time. Kelly felt the kitchen floor sway beneath her feet. She caught herself against the counter. There was a stabbing pain in her heart as she gasped for breath. The wine glass she was rinsing slipped from her fingers. It crashed and shattered on the kitchen floor. The ominous sound resonated like an amplified explosion in her ears taking her to a place she feared to be.

Rick turned around to see her nearly doubled over the sink, "Hey, are you okay?" She couldn't speak. He helped her to the living room couch and brought her some water. He had no reason to think that a reaction of such gravity could have come as a direct result of hearing how Rebecca had died. He was shocked and astonished by the sudden onset of her condition, and he feared for her health. He checked her pulse; it was turbulent and racing according to his hasty estimation. "Are you okay?" he asked her again. "Can you breathe okay? God, you're white as a sheet."

A moment passed. She gasped. She was in no frame of mind to explain her tumultuous reaction. At a loss for words, with her hand covering her lips, "I'm so sorry... I'm so sorry... so sorry...." were the only words she could muster, and she kept repeating it, monotonously. Irrepressible tears began to fall and now Rick felt completely at a loss. His hand reluctantly left hers as he went on a frantic search for Kleenex. Bathroom tissue was the closest he could find. When he returned, Rudy was seated on her lap staring into her eyes; even the cat could sense how distraught she was. She stroked his fur slowly and rhythmically, as she killed time, waiting for Rudy's pet therapy to take effect.

"Are you okay? I am so sorry. I shouldn't have even brought this up, not without having warned you about how it ended." He wished he had just shut the hell up in the kitchen. He whispered to her as he held her, "I wasn't thinking."

She wanted to find a way to handle it, to support him, if she were to be the kind of friend to him that he'd been to her. As he held her against him, she sensed that he needed comfort and assurance more than she did at the moment. "It's okay. I'm all right." She summoned strength back into her voice, calling it back from the cosmos far away. Her tears had stopped flowing and she was able to breathe again.

"I don't even know why I brought this up..."

"If you need to talk, you need to let it out. Say what you need to say."

"No. There's no point. It was wrong of me...I shouldn't have..." He deliberately ceased speaking.

"Don't stop. Go on."

He sat in silence for a long moment. "I don't know. In many ways, I guess I had forgotten how horrible it all was. I hadn't really thought about that night in an age, until tonight," Rick admitted. "I shouldn't have brought it up, period. Some things are just better left in the past..."

She recalled what he had said to her the previous night about the fateful directing of conversation. "It sure seems that way. But you know, this can't live locked there, trust me, it won't die locked there, no matter how much you force it away." She felt his pain innately; it coursed through her veins. "Knowing that it wasn't your fault is only cold comfort. I am so sorry."

They sat quietly together in allegiance. She looked up at him wistfully, "Do I really sound like her?"

His eyes looked into hers. He didn't feel like talking anymore.

May 15

I see why we walk away from each other...but what initially draws us together, then binds us? The invisible tether?

The mind may have her agenda,
Just like the body,
But only the heart loves what it knows

The Intangible

Guilt is a heavy entity.
Its weight presses upon my heart
Only sheer moments from collapse.

May 17

     Trust

Should life's miseries by reason happen,
I want to sing its song.
In its truth I want not to wrong,
But in turn, bring your soul comfort.
For to bear the truth of your misery,
Your soul could console mine.

Were you to know eternal burdens
That mine is forced to bear,
Yours you may grieve to share.
By way of miracle might I fortify,
To burst beyond life's mystery
Then I shall know freedom.

Bereaved we be, lost innocence,
Left wandering in the night.
'Til lark's song kindles light,
But not alone must we aimlessly roam.
Heart in hand, your soul to keep
And carry with it my own.

Trust seeps to the surface sporadically, dendritically, portending the flood of truth…this surrendering announcement of my soul's volition, its vocation.

The panic attack I suffered earlier tonight in his presence was the worst I have ever experienced in a waking state. Usually, these post-trauma reactions torture me through nightmares, nocturnal ambush. Did his heartbreaking tale he entrusted to me trigger it, or was it his voice?

His voice…feels like essential nourishment to me that sates my starvation.

I have never seen my own nightmare reflected through anyone else's eyes. Please let this not be what tethers us… my grief-stricken bind to Wendy is destroying our friendship, our sisterhood.

My irresponsibility has caused me more remorse that I can abide. When it happened, I didn't care anymore, I could never have the future I wanted, the life I dreamed of - only an endless road, dry and dusty, receding to a lonely stark horizon. With no respite from the dull tired ache that would eventually become my lone permanent sensation.

I heard in his voice the same ache - loneliness.

Seven

SATURDAY, MAY 17

Recreational skate is now over, please clear the ice." The overhead announcement sent swarms of skaters young and old scrambling for the boards. Ozzie on the Zamboni waited to resurface to grant Kelly the precious ice time she craved before the next contract session. She rarely skated for anyone to have the pleasure to watch. With only the music in her mind, Kelly floated as though she painted a celestial portrait of falling stars on ice. Every one of her ballet-styled moves blended seamlessly into the next as her entire being danced in powerful silence, her hair and her dark blue chiffon skirt cascading and swirling as she skated. Ozzie smiled as he gazed upon her; she could make two minutes in a very long and mundane day seem like eternal bliss. As he rolled the behemoth onto the ice with its augers grinding, the horn honked twice signaling that her treasured time was now officially up. Kelly closed her dance with a heightened twirl that delicately fell to one knee, and slowed to a natural finish. In her final pose, on one knee, her body arched back as her arm reached for the sky. Ozzie called to her, "Always a class act, Miss Kelly."

She rose gracefully, smiled and took a melodious bow to him as he drove past her on the perimeter. As she exited the ice, she reached for her blade guards and wrap sweater. A little girl in skates left her mother's side and ran to her, enthusiastically flinging her arms around her waist. As Kelly warmly embraced the nine-year old now wrapped around her hips, she spied Rick up in the stands. She was surprised to see him inside the arena.

He came down when Kelly finished up her chat with the young skater and her mother. As they left, Kelly donned her sweater over her sleeveless navy bodysuit. Looking at her glistening forehead, Rick said, "You're popular around here."

Kelly smiled sweetly at him, waving her hand in shy denial. "I'm just me. How long have you been in here? I thought you were going to wait for me outside." She fiddled with the hair band that had come loose then pulled it out altogether.

The power of speech had suddenly abandoned him. He stole the hair band from her twiddling fingers.

She half-smiled, looking away from him out the arena doors. She returned her attention to him, in particular to his eyes, "Did you make it to work this morning?"

"Yep. For a while anyway, didn't get much done, just paperwork." Rick, apparently still dumbfounded by this discovery of her hidden magic, leaned against the cold iron railing. His eyes never left her.

They walked through the heavy double doors out of the ice rink and into the foyer. She caught him twiddling with her hair band. Seeing her for the first time in her skates, he remarked, "God, you're tall in those things."

"Up three and three-quarters," Kelly expertly quoted.

Rick reached his arm around her waist and gently pulled her into him, "I'm parked right out there," he pointed through the windows outside the arena "Ten minutes?"

"Nine if I push it." Her fingers casually slipped from his as she disappeared down the hallway.

He walked out to his car, unfolding his sunglasses as he exited the building. He'd have enough time to call Kevin at the pro-sound warehouse to see if he was planning to work the Phish Experience concert.

Kelly ambled toward him wearing her shades and a long-sleeved soccer jersey and track pants, holding a half-filled water bottle. Her face savored the scintillating warmth of sunshine. She saw him leaning against his dark green SUV, with one foot crossed over the other at the ankle. He was wearing a long-sleeved forest green polo shirt over beige jeans and hiking sneakers. "Ever been told you look like your car?" She patted him on his shoulder as she handed him her knapsack to stow in the rear hatch. "Thanks for picking me up," she stated warmly. "Do we know where we're going?"

"No. You want to drive?" Rick offered.

"Oh no! If you love your car, you should know not to offer it to me. I don't drive," she flashed her palms in bold refusal. "I got my license when I was sixteen but I haven't driven in forever. I wouldn't remember how."

"You really should learn again," he suggested for her independence.

"Who knows, maybe someday. Where are we going?"

"Anywhere you want to go."

"As long as it involves lunch."

Rick walked around the SUV to let her in first. Holding the door open as she climbed in, he leaned over the doorframe as she settled in and said, "Ever been told you look like an angel?" He shut the door and checked that it was secure. Once he was in, he handed her the purloined hair band.

They drove in silence down the south shore coastal road. Having the windows rolled down made it seem like summer had arrived early. Kelly was glad to have her hair band back, so that she could enjoy the ocean breeze more than her wind-blown locks would. The day was clear with only high, scattered clouds, the fluffy kind she loved that looked like cotton balls. The ocean waves crashed with white caps in the sunlight; she hadn't seen the ocean such a deep Prussian blue. The joys of having a car, she thought. Wendy had always been highly attached to her car from the day she learned to drive for the freedom it provided her. How utterly understandable: they weren't more than fifteen minutes out of the city, yet the rugged coastline experience made her feel worlds away from her snow globe existence. The air was salty and cool, the distinct scent of seaweed wafted as they drove. They pulled into a small gravel parking lot next to a sign that read 'Crescent Isle Beach'.

"Oh wow, we used to drive by here when I was a kid," Kelly pointed to the sign as they went by, "but we never stopped. I've never actually been here."

"Well, now you can say you have." He pointed out her lost seat belt receptacle as he unbuckled his. "This was one of the first places I discovered when I moved here."

From the rear hatch, he retrieved his knapsack and they walked aside the grassy dunes to a boardwalk. The long, windblown blades of grass in the sand led Kelly to question how they could flourish. A series of shallow steps led them onto the beach. Folks were seated on beach blankets, children were scattered around making sand forts, and others were engaged in ritual Sol worship. Further along the beach, older kids and their dogs were chasing Frisbees. Astonished, Kelly and Rick spotted a couple of hardy souls wading in the water, jumping the waves as they crested. They walked further down the toffee colored beach until Kelly could no longer smell suntan lotion. The wind was gentle on her face. She happily slipped her sneakers off so her toes could wriggle freely in the cool sand. From his knapsack, Rick pulled out a small beach blanket and a lunch of homemade roast turkey sandwiches.

"No wonder you didn't get much work done this morning, you were too busy preparing picnics," Her girlish know-it-all tone made her sound a little like Wendy.

"Priorities, honey." Rick handed her a sandwich.

They ate leisurely. Kelly wanted to reap every joy of the rare afternoon experience... the freshness, peace and stillness, because it will have felt all too fleeting when stuck inside a smoke-filled and very noisy Mercury Club later that evening.

Rick sat resting his arms upon his knees. Noticing that she really could sit in full-lotus position, he watched her sway with the breeze, as though to music. "Same music you just skated to?"

She spied him devilishly, "How did you know?" Then she flashed that high-voltage smile.

"I saw something today I'd never seen before."

"Do tell, Doctor."

He smiled at her title for him, "I saw you. In your element." He tousled her already windblown ponytail.

"Oh please." She shook her head incredulously as her face flushed. She took in several deep breaths trying to draw closer to her the place where the distant blue of the water met the fading blue of the sky.

"Seriously," he said, "more perfect than an angelfish dancing in tropical waters, one hundred percent natural. I don't think I've ever seen you so comfortable, anywhere."

She felt herself flush and managed to squeak out, "Unlike now." She looked down at her toes and brushed sand off them. "You weren't supposed to be watching, you were supposed to be waiting for me outside. Had I known you were there, Doctor, I might have landed on my nose," she looked back at him, "then you really would have been impressed."

He was amused by her bashful response, "All kinds of folks were watching. The you I saw on the ice was totally uninhibited, highly capable. Very far from helpless or what was your word, fragile?"

"Are we back to 'intriguing'?" She looked at him with narrowed eyes.

"Hell no. Not going there again," he joked as he gently shoved her.

Kelly thumped him in the ribs, "Helpless, fragile, and intriguing, I can make your life hell." She fell over as she turned to continue her assault.

He restrained her arms against any more of her girlish assaults, "Try, baby." She was half on her back with her knees partly up. He waited at the ready for another verbal jab. He was disappointed she had relented. "Want another sandwich?" he asked her as he stared her down.

As he hovered over her, she unexpectedly jabbed his side with her right knee and in a swift turn of the table, she now had the upper hand. Perched over him, she answered, "Yes, Doctor, I would."

As he lay on his back, he complimented, "Sharp moves, Pearson. You're strategically more cunning than I thought. I'll think twice before I underestimate you again."

While they shared another sandwich Kelly emphasized, "The ice is the only place I can go where my problems can't follow me."

"Saw it with my own eyes."

"The day they follow me in there is the day I know it's over for me."

She sounded so serious. He stroked the back of her neck, "Everyone needs to have that kind of place, or thing they passionately love to do, where problems have no choice but to sit in the back seat and shut up."

She relaxed against him as his arm reached around her, "For all the days I shunned skating from my life, I thank God every day for it now," she said with her face partly turned to him, as she watched three seagulls dash and play over the water. "So Doctor, what's your private passion? And don't you dare tell me that it's your work."

"Music. Guitar."

"Acoustic classical, by any chance?" She hypothesized from his CD collection.

"Yep, six string. But I've had this hankering to try electric."

"Fantastic." She reached for his hands. They were dexterously lean and strong. They would have to be. "How long have you been playing?"

"Since I was fourteen. Kept me out of trouble." He joked, "Well, only some of the time. Kevin plays electric bass and rhythm guitar. But my friend Mike's a cello guy – too classy for us."

"You seem to have a lot of music around you. That's important. Nobody really played in my house, grandpa played the fiddle right up until he died, bluegrass was his game. My mom played the piano, but she hated taking lessons and my dad played the trumpet in his school band, but neither of them really kept up with music past school. Wendy played the clarinet in junior high, which her image was happy to ditch in high school. Do your parents play?"

"Well, my mom sings in her church choir, she's loved doing choral stuff her whole life. Dad was never much into music, he was more bookish. Gets it from my grandfather."

"Fiction? Non-fiction?"

"Everything, literature, poetry, periodicals, you name it. If it's printed, he'll read it. If it's scribbled, he'll read it."

"I guess people weren't meant to thrive without their passions. I like writing, but I don't do it regularly enough. There are times when it feels like I haven't written when I really needed to, especially when I'm bogged down. Then I go back and see that I did manage to eke something out."

"Your journals?"

Kelly nodded. "Mmm…meant to record dreams and sort out thoughts and express feelings, therapeutic stuff."

"So, is that what they call stream of consciousness?"

"Yeah, it started out that way. It's nothing like that now. Well, maybe it still is. Things take on lives of their own with me, it seems."

"How do you mean?"

"Don't laugh."

"I won't, I promise," he began, "unless it's really ridiculous, then I can't guarantee my reaction."

"Smart ass. I've been writing poetry over the past couple of years."

"No kidding! Does it rhyme? Because you know, it's not poetry unless it rhymes. Can you tell I'm still stuck in grade four?" He boyishly wiggled her ear.

"You fool," she drew back, slapping his teasing hand. "Not always, it's more free form. I like to think of it as composing art with words, painting pictures with them. Rhyming isn't a necessary condition for conveying an image or a feeling."

"You're too highly evolved for me, I'm still crawling out of water onto land."

"On another note, one thing I've noticed is how time just passes when I'm skating."

"I know what you mean, I just go off into my own little world with my guitar and nothing else can get to me, not even Rudy. He usually goes off and hides somewhere. Doesn't say much for my talent, does it? If only we could find a way to concentrate on the good things that matter." He swept wisps of her hair away from her eyes and purposefully kissed her cheek to reinforce his point. "Potentially good news, chances are I'll see you tonight at that concert."

"Is your brother doing their sound-check?"

"Yeah, he's a roadie tonight, one of many dashed dreams of his. I told Kev I would meet him there, so he'll come out at some point mid-racket and find us."

Kelly laughed at his sardonic wit she loved since day one. "Good news indeed."

Wendy's cheerful horn called to her from Larch Street. Kelly was dressed in a black sleeveless halter-neck top, black jeans and a wide leather belt with a silver buckle. Her hair was up, loosely twisted and held in place with a spring-clip and she had selected a dark shade of lipstick. She grabbed her leather coat, wallet and the Tira Misu and headed down.

"Trés chic!" Wendy accentuated in a sultry voice. Her eyes grazed the rim of her sunglasses, "You should go to work looking like that, sends a message no one can deny."

Kelly hopped in Wendy's sporty red two-seater, "I think I was willing to declare summer officially here as of this afternoon, now if the nights would only cooperate and get a little warmer."

Wendy's apartment was a standard one-bedroom that featured a sunken living room. She had inherited the light maple European minimalist furniture from her parents' family room. Her place was comfortable and casual, decorated in Swedish colors of blue, yellow and white that reminded Kelly of her afternoon on the beach. Considerately, Wendy had gone through the trouble to tidy up for her visit. Normally, her dining table and living room were cluttered with just about everything imaginable from piled up mail to jewelry. Wendy had the irritating habit of never picking up after herself; however, the tornado had been miraculously conquered. And she managed to pick her up on time.

Their dinner conversation unfolded as Kelly anticipated. It commenced with how their week had overwhelmed them like a flashflood, how they both drowned in deadlines and fought overtime every step of the way. Over her delicious homemade lasagna and red wine, Wendy addressed more pressing matters to announce she had stopped seeing Franklin as of this past week. She was somewhat reconciled that this man she held hope for wasn't living up to her expectations. Resignation quickly gave way to frustrated indignation as she proceeded to discharge her emotional artillery at no particular target, but toward misanthropy in general. Her rant of resent surrounding her deteriorating love life, her family, her friends, her colleagues, outlasted their dinner.

Maybe she was bothered by Wendy's tone of voice, self-righteous and unforgiving. Or maybe it was the words she chose to express her feelings, whether purposely or inadvertently. Kelly was sure she was listening to Wendy's mother, Marilyn, particularly when Wendy struggled to justify her expectations as entirely realistic. From what Wendy had always said, her mother's world was exactly crafted, right to the outer circumference of her involvement and influence. It was the only way life made sense to her. Marilyn's upbringing was small town, parochial, protective and traditional. Friends and social matters were categorized and carefully managed, obligations were met, and she fully expected that favors granted were to be returned in kind in a timely fashion. Judgments of others were liberally handed down under the superficial impression of cautious concern. In the Kaine household, everything needed to have a sensible order and a rightful place. The brazen ways Wendy would forcefully insist her opinions about the shortcomings of others reminded Kelly very much of Marilyn.

As if fate had played its trump card, Marilyn's daughter came into the world to teach her there were more than a few ways to scale a fish, and her daughter's haphazard approach to life tested her at every turn. The relationship between Wendy and her mother was touchy, argumentative and often histrionic. Wendy was rebellious and challenging while Marilyn remained as insularly steadfast as she could. Despite her habitual condemnation of her mother's absurdly wide expectations and increasing narrow-mindedness, Wendy, deep within her heart, longed to be like her mother in one most crucial way: her mother married a solid, reliable man who vowed to take care of her and built for her a world of sustained congruence.

Kelly experienced the Kaine's family dynamics intimately, having lived with them for nearly a year as a second daughter. Over time, she observed both the destructive effects and the constructive influences of this combination of parenting. Marilyn Kaine was neither a weak nor submissive woman, however, her relationship with Arthur could be construed as socially conventional. Marilyn deferred to Arthur when it came to matters of finances and business and Arthur gave Marilyn her freedom in home matters. With only one daughter to bestow and focus their love and attention upon, Wendy grew up under keen eyes. Arthur tended to give Wendy her space given that she seemed to be constantly embroiled in melodramatic arguments with her mother. Her father was a strong developmental figure in her life, always aware of her progress, and rarely provoking. As a result, Wendy forged a more natural and relaxed style of communication with her father. When Arthur did choose to intercede in her life, Wendy paid attention.

Kelly was beginning to understand Wendy's capital motivation: she intended to find a man like her father, authoritative, reasonable and resilient. She would keep sifting through men until she found him or until she exhausted her precious vital resources in the search. As they loaded supper dishes into the dishwasher, Kelly enquired, "Did you and your mom have another fight?"

"We always fight." Depleted from her dinnertime tirade, Wendy's voice retreated, "The latest battles have been over Franklin. Mom doesn't want me to see him. At all."

"She wants you hold off until the divorce is final?"

"She says she doesn't want me involved with that kind of man." Wendy's insolent tone accurately reflected the nature of the arguments she had been having with her mother. "She's been growling at me for weeks now over this. I think it's because he has a kid."

"I know your mom is old-fashioned, she's always been that way. She's really adamant? Where's your dad on this?"

"In my mom's dream world, you're a virgin when you get married, that your husband is too, and you keep a home, have kids and live faithfully ever after till death do you part. Dad doesn't see what the big deal is. He keeps reminding mom that Franklin's legally separated from his wife, so it's not like I'm digging my claws in a happily married man. I'm not a home-wrecker."

"I guess he is still married, until they're officially divorced, if that's her issue," Kelly posited. "But, here's what I don't get. You say you're not seeing him anymore, and you've been talking like you want to have nothing to do with all his depressing baggage. What difference does it make what your mom thinks if you're not seeing him anymore? Why are you still fighting?" Kelly polished off the remaining red wine in her glass with determination and placed it carefully in the sink's sudsy hot water.

"God, I don't know Kelly! My mom's cracked. She bugs me everyday!" Wendy groaned in exasperation as she let her head fall back as if to get a better look at her ceiling.

"May I say something? Maybe you don't want to give up on Franklin just yet and that's why you're frustrated. There's nothing wrong with that. As for your mom, she has to live in this century, and if she doesn't, that's her lookout. You've got your dad's support, somewhat. For sure things with Franklin aren't going to resolve on the time scale you're thinking. He needs to rebuild his life, his heart, and that takes time. He has a kid. You have to give it time. I can say from experience that it's better not to go through it alone, not if you don't have to. It's not always about whether it blossoms into a love relationship. Maybe he needs you as a friend. Don't you want to be there for him?"

"It would be so much easier if it weren't so damn depressing. Every time he talks about his divorce, I feel like all relationships are doomed to failure, of course the banner exceptions being my parents and my grandparents. So why even bother."

"Hey," Kelly swatted her with the towel, "not all relationships are necessarily so miserable or that perfect. You're filtering. You're seeing things only at the ends and forgetting the middle. There's always middle ground. It really is all shades of gray. Even for your parents and grandparents, ask them, they'll tell you about times when it wasn't so wonderful, and times when...."

She stopped mid-stream and Wendy observed that her upbeat expression had just fallen away. Ahead of her own dialogue, Kelly foresaw the emotionally exigent path of her thought process. She needed a second to collect her thoughts. She looked away, closed her eyes, took a deep breath, and called upon the courage to press forward, for Wendy's sake. "My parents had their marital issues, right till the end. I don't know what about exactly, but they never had a chance to resolve them. Maybe they thought they'd have years left. I remember when I was younger I used to think my parents had a perfect marriage, a perfect life. It was all I wanted and I believed that Chris and I would have that. That it was destined for us and we would make it. I see now that my view of the world was filtered. Dreams get outdated, but they were still my dreams, even if they never came true." The initial strength in her voice had gradually dissipated, "It's not until you look back after time that things seem clearer. Maybe nothing is destined, other than what you make it to be."

"Look, I know no relationship is ideal, but you shouldn't stop dreaming. Then you stop living. And you end up settling for some selfish jackass because he was the next thing that happened along." Wendy was still fired up.

"Agreed, never settle on a jackass. But don't throw out a potential diamond in the rough without inspecting it first. Just be smart and patient and base your decisions on real things, not superficiality." Kelly's tone lightened, "Wendy, you make your own rules. Obviously your mom's rules never applied. For one thing, you haven't been a virgin for I don't know how many years."

Wendy smiled ruefully. "Yeah and look how far that's gotten me." Her expression saddened following her self-observation.

Kelly suspected her memories had rebounded to Carlo, her first lover whom Wendy confidently planned would be her husband for life. There had been several lovers since Carlo, but she had lost count, likely Wendy had too. Her friend's wan expression became vacant as she took out dessert plates. "I'll put some tea on," Kelly said quietly as she reached for the kettle. She decided she wouldn't speak anymore of what was on her mind. Inescapable heartbreak overcame her as well. She knew spending the rest of this evening in a public venue was a bad idea.

Only a half hour remained until they were scheduled to head out to the Mercury Club. In hopes of boosting morale, Kelly mentioned, "Hey, Rick's brother is going to be at the concert tonight, I believe he's doing their sound."

"Rick's brother is an audio guy?"

"I believe the correct term is audio engineer, and no," they both exclaimed together, "not the kind that drives a train!"

Kelly went on to explain, "He's not a certified audio engineer, he just does this kind of stuff. He's friends with the members of the Phish Experience. That's what Rick said. He said he might be there tonight too, he'll hang out with his brother at some point I suppose."

"So Doctor Rick's got a cool brother. You never told me that." Wendy was already impressed.

"Younger brother," Kelly qualified.

"Is he cute?"

"I don't know."

"How much younger?" Wendy raised her right eyebrow in curiosity.

"Haven't got a clue. Rick's thirty-three, thirty-four, so maybe his brother is around twenty-nine or thirty...I've never met him. Maybe we'll see him tonight and you can ask him yourself. Knowing you, you will," Kelly stated wryly.

"So, how is Rick, the Mad Scientist?"

"Mad," she reveled in the delectable creaminess of her Tira Misu, "he has a reputation to live up to, for the benefit of people like you."

"Seriously, what's going on with him?" Wendy did not hide her nosiness.

"Nothing. He's fine."

Kelly's terseness made her feel blown off. "He's fine. Well that just says everything," Wendy blustered. "Come on."

"What do you want me to tell you?" Kelly grew annoyed.

"Tell me something about him," she pressed, "about you two."

"Well, gosh, he's a nice guy, he's easy to talk to." Kelly knew Wendy would not be satisfied with her trite answer so she offered, "He was out of town for a couple of days and he asked me to look after his cat while he was gone."

"Do you think he's cute?" Wendy persisted in her irritating silliness.

"Extremely. Eyes to die for."

"You talking about Rick or his cat?"

"Ha. Ha." Kelly felt no desire to divulge anything. She had partly succeeded in easing the evening's tension. Entering into a discussion involving any man at this point would be sisterhood suicide. Wendy was teetering on the brink of a flustered fit, and Kelly very near an internal breakdown.

Wendy was downright sour that Kelly wouldn't spill about Rick. "You know, you've changed, and for the worse I might add. You're so secretive all of a sudden, even for you. I have no way to know whether there really is nothing to talk about as you say, or there's actually plenty to talk about and you just don't want to tell me." Exasperated that Kelly was withholding potentially salacious details, as her best friend, she felt she had a God-given right to be told. "Clearly, you've been seeing him. How come you never talk about him to me?" Wendy exclaimed with a bitter edge as they prepared to leave her apartment and head out to the concert.

"Wendy, I don't talk about him to anyone," Kelly began passively, hoping Wendy would calm down. "You know what, never mind," she concluded unenthusiastically. Kelly forecasted the remainder of the evening to be tiresome enough. The thought of having to tolerate deafening booming bass, high frequency distortion hiss and seizure-inducing flashing lights, topped off with clouds of hideous forms of smoke suddenly seemed insurmountable to her. She felt her energy drain, drop by drop. And her irritation mounted with every second of Wendy's mania.

"Why won't you talk to me? We're supposed to be best friends!" Wendy cried, "I tell you everything!"

"Yeah?" Kelly raised her voice to her own alarm, "Well there are times I wish you wouldn't! Thanks to years of your selfish insensitivity, I end up knowing way too much, a hell more than I want to know about you," her voice fell, and then finally broke, "the way you really feel." Bewildered, her reticent disappointment rebelled and continued to tumble uncontrollably from her lips, "I've listened to you, day in and day out. It hurts. I know what you really think, the worst of the world, of good people, and of me, and it makes me sick." Kelly withdrew when Wendy's dour eyes and stunned expression squarely faced her. They stood tense and silent in Wendy's foyer. Kelly massaged her left temple and labored to regain her composure, "Look, I'm sorry. I didn't mean for that to come out." One hand was on her creased brow, the other holding her wallet. "This is just not a good time right now."

"Okay, fine," she snapped. "Clearly, you said what you had to say, wonder why it took you so long." She grabbed her coat and tore obstinately out the door, "We're going to be late."

Kelly closed her eyes and tried to regain her breath as she pulled the door shut. She caught a tear before it streamed down her cheek.

The Mercury Club two-story nightspot featured lesser-known talent, placing a high priority on local artists. The dark, coffeehouse atmosphere attracted an eclectic clientele with a range of age and musical tastes. The Club's concert settings were small, hosting no more than two hundred on each level. Intimately arranged, the stage was at the same level as the bistro tables, which were small and decorated with simple hurricane style paraffin lamps. Dimly lit wrought iron sconces hung on the walls. Informal dinner, drinks and desserts were available and guests were expected to bus their own tables.

Neither of them had said a word to each other since leaving Wendy's apartment, until they were forced to scout for a table on the second floor where the concert was being held. The Phish Experience auditory assault was well underway and it was nearly impossible for her and Wendy to communicate without shouting at the top of their lungs. Even then, they misunderstood each other, so they resorted to a prehistoric version of sign language. They headed for a vacant table near the back; Kelly knew she couldn't get any further away from the rack-mounted speakers. The floor vibrated beneath her chair. She took a long look around the hall for Rick. Then she focused upon the mixing console and its operators, studying the faces of each of the three guys as best as she could in the intermittent flashing lights, while they tweaked knobs and fiddled with cables. She didn't recognize any of them as Kevin from the photo in Rick's bedroom. Wendy nodded at Kelly's charades to get drinks, so Kelly meandered to the bar and ordered two glasses of red wine. While waiting there, the bartender told her the band would take a break in just under an hour. Kelly took the opportunity to take the pair of Extra-Strength Aspirin tablets she wrapped in Kleenex and tucked in her wallet change purse.

Approximately two-thirds of the way into the band's first set, Kelly felt the warmth of his hand on her shoulder. She checked to see it really was Rick, who crouched down next to her chair. Her headache hadn't yielded, yet she smiled a hello. There was no point trying to talk over the blaring dissonance. Absorbed in the concert, Wendy didn't notice that he had arrived. Rick grabbed a vacant chair from a neighboring table, he then leaned into Kelly's ear and hollered, "How are you?"

She looked at him edgily. She closed her eyes and shook her head ever so imperceptibly. Rick offered her his hand and she squeezed it tightly.

"You look real unimpressed," he shouted again in her ear, then smiled.

She shouted back in his ear, "God, save me." Her eyes shifted to Wendy's direction, then back to Rick's. She knew she couldn't conceal her immediate distress from him. He looked past her at Wendy who appeared impervious on many levels, lost to the atmosphere, completely unresponsive, and wholly indifferent to their presence. Kelly just shrugged her shoulders, her facial expression screamed torture.

Rick stood up and led Kelly away from their table. Wendy did take notice; she watched them as they shuffled, hand in hand, between clusters of seated guests to the staircase landing on the opposite side of the concert hall. It wasn't necessarily any quieter there, but it was a brighter unoccupied space where they could try to talk. Rick leaned with his back against the wall as he pulled Kelly toward him. "It's very clear. You're so not okay," he shouted at mid volume. His hands took ownership of the small of her back.

"Gosh, what would make you think that?" She was relieved to just be in his presence. Resting her forehead on his chest, she slipped her arms around him, under his leather coat. His back was warm and her sleeveless arms enjoyed the benefit.

"You look stunning, by the way," he complimented in her ear as his fingers caressed her bare shoulders.

She had to stand on her toes to reach his ear, "Thanks, I feel like shit." She rarely swore. "How tall are you, anyway?"

"Six-two and shrinking. Too tall for you?" He lowered his head for her to make it easier.

"No, I'm too short. Problem solved with higher heeled shoes. Is Kevin here?"

"Yeah, somewhere, possibly back stage. Maybe he'll find us during intermission. I want you to meet him."

"I want that, if I survive long enough. Wendy wants to meet him, too." She hated screaming under any circumstances.

Rick cupped his hands around her ears and kissed her forehead, "We'll get out of here soon enough, alive, that's a promise. You should let Wendy know she owes you big-time for this."

Kelly rolled her eyes. "You don't know the half of it, Doctor." She glanced across the hall toward Wendy.

They stood talking at the top of the staircase until intermission. Wendy watched them the entire time from her table with her arms folded, her blood ready to boil over any second. The way Kelly smiled at him, talked to him, the way he held her seductively, the way she refused to talk to her about him, how Kelly lashed out at her earlier in the evening, this entire scenario was as transparent as glass. The house lights came up to signal the group's twenty-minute break. People left their seats, milled around, purchased drinks and food and the din of the crowd seemed hushed compared to the preceding hour. Kelly and Rick returned back to the table where Wendy was seated with the same expressionless look on her face.

"Can I get you a drink?" Rick offered.

Wendy shifted her eyes toward him and responded curtly, "No, thanks."

"Kel?" he offered again.

"No, thanks. Sit," she ordered him tensely.

When Kevin found him, the two brothers greeted each other in a laid-back manner and they shook hands amiably. Kevin was shorter than his brother, with darker hair. His features were not as sharply defined as Rick's, but Kelly knew Wendy well enough, she was taken by his back-alley, boyish look.

"I'll have to return in a minute or so, but I wanted to come over," Kevin spoke hurriedly, as he took in the view of two dazzling women seated at his brother's table. Eyeing Kelly, he asked Rick forwardly, "Aren't you going to introduce me?"

"Yeah, Wendy, Kelly, this is Kevin, my pain-in-the-ass little brother." Kevin tried to shake hands with Kelly first but Rick grabbed Kevin's neck in a headlock, removing all formality. Rick could tell Kevin considered Kelly a definite knockout.

It didn't take Kevin long to deduce that Wendy was the one Rick wasn't seeing. He went ahead and assumed she was fair game. "So, how are you enjoying the concert?" Kevin posed enthusiastically.

"Great! So you know these guys?" Wendy responded cordially, trying to work Kevin for a backstage pass.

"Yeah, I was around when they got together two years ago, they wanted me to play with them, but I was with another band at the time. We were doing different stuff. Phish Experience have gone in their own direction now, but I'm still friends with Jake, the bassist, and I know the other guys, too."

He and Wendy were granted no more than five minutes flirtation time, which they used effectively, when Kevin announced his departure in preparation for the second half. Kevin shook Wendy's hand, encouraging her to remain after the show, as he would take her to meet the band. He then extended his hand to Kelly's, "Really good to meet you, I'll be seeing you again for sure," he commented over-assertively as he nudged his big brother's arm for agreement.

"Get out of here. Go be useful." Rick laughed, shooing his kid brother away.

"I'll take this opportunity to visit the little girls' room." Kelly rose as she handed her wallet to Rick, "Hold this for me?" She whisked away, apprehensive to leave Wendy and Rick alone in such an awkward situation.

"So, how are you doing?" Rick asked Wendy congenially.

Wendy didn't answer right away, feigning the impression of a thoughtful delay, Wendy commenced, "You better watch it, you don't know anything about her."

"Excuse me?"

"I know what you're doing, you don't fool me." Wendy glared at him, "I can see right through you. You can't handle her. And she will not be taken advantage of." Her voice was steely and sharp.

Rick sat back in his chair, stupefied. He knew better than to respond to an unprovoked attack, especially in a public setting. If she were going to steal a scene, here and now, it would be a solo.

"You're in way over your head with her." Wendy grabbed her purse, and stood up to leave, verbally stabbing him as she left the table, "Back off, I mean it." Her tone was malicious. She then stormed off toward the bar.

The house lights had dimmed and Rick promptly left the concert hall. Kelly returned to find the table empty, with her only hers and Wendy's coats on their chairs. The Phish Experience began their second set and completed two songs before Wendy returned, a fresh drink in hand.

"Do you know where Rick went?" Kelly shouted worriedly.

"He left," Wendy said blankly.

He wouldn't have left without saying goodbye, she thought, and he had her wallet. She huffed as she looked around the concert hall. It took two panoramic passes before she spied him hovering at the top of the staircase, trying to get her attention. She got up and walked over to him.

"Hey, I came back and you were gone," she said with concern.

"Just went out for some fresh air. I need to get out of here," he admitted with a strained expression.

"Okay." Her concern hadn't left her; she looked deeply into his eyes.

"Come with me."

Without hesitation, she replied, "Let me get my coat. I'll let Wendy know I'm leaving," as she pointed in Wendy's direction at the back of the hall.

"I'll meet you outside." He darted down the stairs.

Kelly leaned over from behind Wendy and shouted, "I'm taking off. I've got a Manhattan headache."

"Fine," Wendy said as she shrugged her shoulders. "Are you taking a cab home?"

"Don't worry," she was already walking away.

She floated down the stairs, choreographically maneuvering around other concertgoers, without missing a beat in her glide. She pushed the windowless door and stepped out to the sidewalk. Cars were whizzing by, and several people huddled near the entrance smoking and talking. She lingered briefly in the environmental paradox on the sidewalk: the blanket of smoke that hung by the entrance doors outside was thicker than the clouds of it inside. She looked in both directions, up and down the sidewalk. Rick appeared as if from thin air, as he always did, and helped her with her coat.

"Thank you for rescuing me." She was finally able to speak at normal volume for the first time since arriving at the Mercury Club. She wormed her arm into the coat sleeve. "Have you got your car?"

"Yeah it's down here," he tilted his head in the direction of a parking lot around the back of the building. They began walking and then he stopped suddenly. He held her arm until she was forced to stop. Startled, she turned around to see what the hold-up was, only to discover the full-force of his arms as he pulled her to him. He kissed her with conviction having placed one hand securely on her cheek. When he was done, he kissed her again. She stood where he had stopped her, frozen. What just happened was not her imagination. Her mind reeled and her heart raced, it occurred to her that she needed to stand up on her own two feet as she was about to fall to the ground. "What on earth?" she asked in a stilted whisper.

Still touching her face, and with a hint of a smile he said, "Sorry. Long overdue. Too long." He breezed his fingers through his hair and scratched his head, "Your constitution simply amazes me, Kel." He took her hand, pulling her out of her spellbound inertia.

She wondered what he meant about her constitution. As far as she was concerned, her soul's foundation was cracked, certifiably porous. "Where are we going?"

"Where do you want to go?"

"Anywhere quiet, where there's no smoke," she stammered vaguely, "I need fresh air."

The night was cool without a trace of a breeze. Rick drove them to the waterfront and adeptly steered his SUV into a street-side space that to Kelly looked too small. "Wow. Where did you learn to drive? Remind me to take lessons there." She was impressed at his skillfulness, the kind that eluded her when she learned to drive eleven years earlier.

"Easy. Three rules. Once you know them, it always works. I'll teach you sometime."

They walked around the harbor front, alive with nightlife atmosphere; restaurants were filled, and music could be heard from all directions. The twinkling lights of the city reflected in the water; instinctively, they headed to the end of the pier, and sat upon a low wooden ledge between pier posts.

"Is your headache any better?"

"Yes. No surprise. I needed to get out of there every bit as much as you did."

"More, I think. How was your dinner with Wendy?"

"The Tira Misu was good."

"How was Wendy?" His pointed emphasis was comical.

"You know better than to ask me that," she bumped his knee with hers. "Not a banner evening." She turned to view a white double-decker yacht sailing into the harbor, likely back from a beautiful day trip outing.

"You two obviously had a fight, not the first and certainly not the last. She cares about you, in her own...debatable way," Rick lectured dryly. "She's just worried about you."

"She's always worrying about me, in between not giving a shit about me and wishing I'd just go away."

That was twice that night, Rick noticed. She was racked by something, and he was pretty sure he knew what it was. "Do you talk to her?"

"Yeah, and...?"

"I mean, do you talk to her... about me?" he qualified.

"About you?" Kelly asked quizzically. "No."

"So, you haven't said anything to her..." he fished again.

"About what? I have nothing to say to her about you, except I did tell her when she pressured me earlier that you were out of town until yesterday and you asked me to look after Rudy."

"I think she's worried you're drifting. Away from her."

"We are drifting!" she wailed. "We have been for a while, for years now. Did she say something to you?"

Rick shrugged his shoulders nonchalantly.

"What did she say?" Kelly became insistent, "Tell me."

"No. Nothing that matters, forget it."

"She told me you had left after intermission."

"Yeah? Wishful thinking on her part." Rick smiled.

"You know, I blew up at her tonight at dinner. And if she took it out on you, it does matter. I saw how cold she was to you all evening, don't think I didn't notice that."

"Do you think I'm in over my head with you?"

This tangential question just complicated her thought process more. She looked down and studied the weather worn wooden slats of the pier, trying to fathom the surreal fog of this conversation. "I don't know... yeah, probably. If you knew enough about me."

"Do you think you're in over your head with me?"

Her fog wasn't lifting. "You tell me. Remember, I'm the limited radius wallflower who doesn't know anything."

"She's worried about you, that's all." Rick was confident in his assessment. He leaned forward. "She's upset. She doesn't trust me and she's entitled, given that she doesn't know anything about me. She's worried I'll take advantage of you. She said that I know nothing about you, which incidentally, is true." He drummed his fingertips together, staring out at the calm water. "Partially true."

"Partially true." Kelly leaned forward to keep him company.

Rick turned to look at her, "I know what I need to know and that's why nothing she said really bugged me, so don't let it bother you."

"It hurts me. So much hurts me." She was supporting her head in her hands, her elbows dug into her knees.

"Look, I care what you think, not what she thinks."

"This is ridiculous, that's all." Kelly sat up and professed, "My life is such a God damn big deal to her, and she takes it upon herself to run it, say whatever she wants, but only when she feels like it, when she can pull herself away from her own dramas. You know, there's a reason I haven't dated anyone, haven't been with anyone, and they're my reasons. They're valid to me, even if they don't amount to a hill of beans to her or anyone else. That's fine," she emphasized, attempting to stay open-minded amidst her growing fury, "for ten years, she's pitied me, 'poor Kelly, all alone, everyone she's ever loved in her life has left her. She has no one except me, thank merciful God for me.'" She huffed, "Little wonder I'm so scared. If people have an ounce of sense, if they value their life, they should stay away. I'm clearly too dangerous to love or just plain cursed."

"Excuse me," Rick interrupted at speed, "wrong and again wrong. No such thing as cursed, or jinxed," Rick loudly argued in her defense. "Sorry, had to clear that up before you went any further. Keep talking," he encouraged swiftly.

She exhaled deeply like she was breathing hellfire. "So, now, here I am, ten years later to the day, basically, just praying I can find a way to survive until the end of next week. I need a miracle. That's all. Is that too much to ask?" Kelly burst out into vengeful tears, the kind that burned her eyes.

Rick reached out to her but she bounded up from the ledge and walked away from him. She was definitely racked, and he was now completely unsure of what it was that happened ten years to the day. Uncertain what to do, his instincts told him not to let her walk too far away. He would chase her if she ran.

She stopped about a hundred feet away. He sauntered in her direction, his hands in his pockets, giving her plenty of time and space to collect herself. Whatever this was, he realized he was in way over his head; there was no question about it. Maybe Wendy was right. As he approached her, she turned to him, but refused to look at him. He purposely bumped right into her, wrapped his arm around her neck and they kept walking along the marina.

"It's not too much to ask," Rick guaranteed her. "Miracles aside, I find myself praying to survive any given week on a regular basis." He made her laugh when she was trying incredibly hard not to, and that made her laugh even harder. "Take it from me, coffee helps, so does a stiff drink every now and then."

"You're an idiot," she exclaimed laughing.

"Yeah, go ahead, make my life hell. You offered ..."

They found a bench near a restaurant marina. All in rows, a forest of masts rocked gently in the moonlight. "So, is Kevin seeing anyone right now?"

"Couldn't tell you. I don't know, he was seeing some girl a while back, but he hasn't mentioned her in a while. So maybe not right now. Why?"

"I never warned him. I wonder if I should have."

"Too late now, probably." He smiled, envisioning his little brother hexed to helpless under Wendy's charms.

"This is all so embarrassing. It just figures, the first man that I really meet, the first man that I like, the first person it seems I could really talk to without being judged...the nerve of her. I have never, ever said or done anything like that to someone she cared about. It's just not my business."

"It's not her business, you're right. But, it's a little deal as far as this silly Saturday night goes." Rick aimed to shed light with a broader perspective. "But what I think isn't a little deal, where you're stuck, is the burning question we've addressed before. Where inside you does she end and you begin? Where and when do you draw the line?"

"Do we even have a line? We're enmeshed, it seems, and for worse."

"Okay, good place to start. You need a line when it comes to her, and once she crosses it, you have to say something. Things won't change if there are no decent boundaries, both ways."

"I did that tonight. And look what's happened. I'm just handling all this very, very badly, Rick. Not just tonight, years of this confusion. So much of my life has been lived through her, and I know I've permitted it, but her opinions have always mattered to me. I don't know why I care so much what she thinks. I don't want for her to think half the things she does, especially when she's way off base. I thought my opinions mattered to her." She sighed and reflected. "I don't make it a habit of talking about my problems to just anyone, certainly not about the one who's supposed to be my best friend, but I'm failing here, miserably."

"So what?"

"So what?? I can't just blow this off."

Sensing her dismay, he reissued, "What I meant was that everyone struggles with stuff like this, handling things in ways they wish they hadn't, you, me, the whole of humanity, so what?"

"Because it's the plight of human kind, so what?"

"We all screw up, we all have to deal with it, so what," Rick concluded with assurance. "Attitude, Kelly. Don't give up. Life's an open road."

His poetic reference rang a bell. "Robert Frost?"

"Walt Whitman."

May 17

Poetry is what I sift through on this road less traveled. Pages of books have been my travels . . . until recently when I ventured out, I stumbled upon fellow traveler, a comrade who is gentle, patient, receptive, and observant, with a roaming spirit that is securely ensconced within the warmth of his heart. I just finished reading Whitman's Song of the Open Road, and he wants me to read the works of Kahlil Gibran and Pablo Neruda also.

May 18

I still don't know what happened between Wendy and Rick last night during intermission. She selectively chooses what she says. His nonchalant evasiveness last night does nothing to protect me. Even though I had no desire to hear her voice after how she behaved, I had to call to let her know she crossed the line. I predicted she would defend her assumptions, paranoia and her misplaced parental authority - she did. She laid into me about my not consulting her, for foolishly trusting a man I didn't know, and that she could see as plain as day that he would have his way with me, that I had been charmed by him and was asking to be taken advantage of.

There is nothing here that I would ever consult her on.

Rick, as usual, hit the nail right on the head last night when he said she's just worried about me. Accepted, there's far more in this brewing cauldron beyond her worry we're drifting apart. Why does she need to protect me? I don't want her to, and I told her again this morning.

Does her driving compulsion to nanny to my life minister to her ego? Yes. She needs to be needed, and more importantly, she needs to be in charge (of anyone, anything!), just like her mother.

Entangled

opposing gaze across a mirror line
my eyes upon your visage
masked by swirling mists of time

opposing ends of a telephone line
my voice not from my soul
lost in the riddles of your rhyme

opposing hearts across a battle line
my fingers slip from grasp
thwarted from dreams sublime

opposing views of the finest line
my eyes upon your soul
for in reflection, I see mine

There used to be a time when Wendy and I reflected goodness in each other
— we mirrored widened possibilities for each other's growth, we illuminated
facets that remained shadowed by our own limited natures. How did we
become so entangled in each other? How did we let each of our
individualities be relegated to second place, allowing each other's fears to
fetter us?

Eight

SUNDAY, MAY 18

Kelly had never seen a southwestern omelet skillet-baked on the stovetop the way Rick made it. With white mushrooms, green shallots, red and yellow bell peppers, it was resplendent in color. While she chopped coriander leaves, Rick topped the rainbow creation with grated cheese

"Coffee?"

"Definitely. Doesn't have to be half decaf either."

"Didn't sleep again? Good lord, woman. High octane it is. What are you up to now, four nights?"

"Thanks for keeping count." She picked up the canister of coffee beans and inhaled its oily, rich aroma. "I'm starting to think that the longer you go without sleeping you can convince yourself you don't need to anymore. God, this smells wonderful."

"Have you talked to Wendy as yet today?" He didn't try to feign innocent concern.

"Uh huh." Her lips were pursed.

He didn't press it. "Kevin called me this morning and said he spent most of last night at an all-night coffee bar with her."

"Hmmph."

"He's quite taken with her."

"I'm surprised she didn't take him home, she has plenty of coffee there."

"Guess she got her backstage pass after all."

She guzzled her strong coffee then indulged in Rick's gourmet brunch complemented by whole-wheat toast. "I declare this omelet one of the seven wonders of modern cuisine."

"Wonder number two, my mom does this amazing thing with pork chops in this velvety smothering sauce. I can't reproduce it."

"How is your mom? Your dad?"

"Good. I'm willing to bet she'll be calling in the next hour or so."

"Great, I'll answer the phone again and weird her out," she giggled.

Rick laughed and added, "Yeah and while you're at it, tell her we can't talk right now. That'll really do her in. She may never call again."

"Oh, we wouldn't want that." It felt so good to laugh about nothing; if only her depression would pay attention, it might eventually take the hint like a bad houseguest and depart altogether.

After brunch, Kelly found herself absently staring out the patio door at the driving rain. Rick had asked how her parents were as they finished eating. She lied without thinking and said they were fine. Maybe it wasn't a lie – her parents were in heaven; certainly, they would be finer there than here. She held Rudy who was contently curled up in her arms, purring peacefully with his eyes half-closed as she rubbed his neck. Day seemed like evening. Sheets of rain pelted the windows rattled when the wind blustered. The condo felt unusually dark in the dreary gray-washed light until Rick switched on the table lamps when he came into the living room. She noticed him rooting through his video collection; within a minute they curled up on the couch to watch a comedy. Kelly remembered the last movie she'd seen with Wendy and it brought back more than she wanted to think about. This, on the other hand, was another appealing opportunity to laugh at nothing. Rudy snuggled himself between Kelly and Rick, the prime location of feline choice. Rudy enjoyed the restful warmth briefly until Rick displaced him in hopes of Kelly sidling up closer to him. Rudy, disappointed in his relegation to the cold end of the sofa, made it only as far as Kelly's lap on his second attempt. He rested his little striped head and closed his eyes for the afternoon cuddle. Within minutes, her hair clip was no longer in her hair, although his fingers certainly were.

He switched the TV off the instant the movie ended. She willingly remained enveloped by him. "Your mom never called," she pointed out as she looked up to him.

"Funny about that," Rick said looking down at her. He could have cared less at the moment. "Would you like some tea?"

Kelly followed him into the kitchen as he arrayed every flavor of tea he owned. She considered each one and decided upon Ceylon peach once she sniffed the package.

"It's imported from Sri Lanka."

"A man who cooks Food TV omelets and drinks Ceylon tea, now I really have seen it all. Where have you been all my life?"

"Hiding from crazy women."

Kelly couldn't suppress her seismic burst of laughter at his deadpan response, "Like the one who kept you up at night?"

"Oh Hell."

How could he keep a straight face, she wondered, she couldn't quell her impish giggle fit brought on by the lowbrow movie; perhaps the lack of sleep really was getting to her after all. "You have to spill."

"You mean about her wild suggestions?"

Kelly's giggles grew sillier.

"Apparently, if I had stuck around with her, she would have brought in more of her kind, had she had her way!"

"Penthouse delight! Where do you find these women?" She thwacked his shoulder.

"Bloody Hell," he recoiled laughing, "she found me. Target acquired. Locked on. Fire."

"Take it as a compliment."

"No way. She's the main reason I've been hiding ."

She stood behind him and wrapped her arms around his waist. When she rested her head on his back, she realized he smelled incredible. She remembered how good her dad smelled, and how she loved to be near him when he came home from work.

"Unfortunately, I can't always hide from her. She works in the Complex."

"Sounds like she has a complex."

"You tell her that," he suggested impatiently.

Her fit had sufficiently subsided and with resumed rationality, this was a conversation she had no business being involved in. "Stick to the Run and Hide strategy."

"Works for Rudy. What's your excuse?" He deftly came round and faced her once he set the tea.

She responded flatly, "I'm cursed, remember?"

"Oh yes, devilishly hexed," he humored her, "bullshit."

"At least I can say I've never had a swingin' lover who was into inclusive relationships. I'll admit it."

"Good, may you never." He waved his finger at her as though he were casting a spell.

They brought the tea to the living room and resumed their curl-up on the couch, as Rudy played with his mouse. Instinctively pawing and batting to animate it, he had to make the predator-prey struggle worth the effort. In a flash, he headed for the kitchen lair, mouse in jaws.

She sipped her tea. It tasted exquisite. "Did you ever tell your mom about this woman?" Her giggles returned.

"Are you nuts? Would you tell your mother…never mind, scrap that. Bad enough, my mom thought Rebecca was forward. Heck, Rebecca was old-fashioned by comparison. I only dated this crazy woman three times until I figured out she had no time to waste."

"So you didn't entertain her wild ways."

"Hey," he said emphatically, "I entertained nothing, except the nightmares that followed. Terrorized me for weeks."

The telephone rang. Kelly set out on a search for Rudy while Rick chatted with his mother. The cat had settled down in the bedroom for a power nap. She sat on the edge of the bed and watched him; she could tell he wasn't completely asleep, just resting his eyes. There was a hint of smile on his face, she thought. Rudy was fully aware of her presence and it would be only a matter of time before he could no longer resist and open his eyes. She goaded him by taking the tip of his tail and gently lifting it to his ear and delicately tickled the tiny hairs inside. His ear twitched reflexively, and he shook his head as he opened his eyes. Rudy instinctively rolled over as he grabbed at his tail, trying to bite it; the source of his irritation would not get away alive. He instantly twisted upright, ready to lunge. But the hand retracted. He sat up and began scratching behind his irritated ear. He then looked up at her and meowed, his little paws stepping tentatively up onto her lap as he chirped. She meowed back to him and lifted him up to her chest. When she reclined against the headboard, he settled in her arms and began to purr. The afternoon had descended into evening and the day's storm had let up to a fine drizzle.

Rick walked in. "There you are. My mom says hi."

"Hi, back."

He sat across from her on the foot of the bed. "Why are you hiding in here?"

"One thing you need to know, I'm always hiding," Kelly answered softly as she stroked Rudy's head.

"Well, your wanted poster isn't up, you have no need to hide." Rick slapped her foot playfully and invited her back to the living room. "Bring that savage lion with you." Rick commanded theatrically, like a jester in a Shakespearean court.

The complacent ball of orange fur napped peacefully in her arms. Kelly raised her eyebrows.

"Well, he's savage with me," Rick touted, "You just happen to have a calming effect on him." Rick's expression grew comically suspicious, he pointed his finger, eyebrow at the ready; he concluded with impeccable timing for dramatic flair, "Must be your feminine wiles. Ah."

Had he taken drama in school, she wondered, or was these droll performances natural? "Prithee tell, Sir Richard the Bold," Kelly played along as they headed for the living room, "why do you command his servitude? Do you think this savage beast would divulge any mystical secrets out of domestic loyalty?"

"Plenty, my fair, *hot* maiden," he spoke in an unusually low voice with a breathy highlight. "Plenty and most secretive. He has succeeded where I have repeatedly failed. He's captured your heart. Besides, the beastly creature knows where all my unpaired socks are."

Kelly's giggle fit had returned full force. Just then, Rudy wriggled out of Kelly's arms, exited stage right and retreat under the bed. "Now that you've said that, he's going to go hide your socks in a new place."

Rick shook his head in classic comic annoyance, "I'll never fathom what's in his pea-brain. God knows he'll never tell." Rick pulled out his guitar case from his closet. "The best kind of friend to have, incidentally."

"True. There's a lot I wouldn't tell my best friend."

"Wise, but brace for revolution once you discover that holding onto too many secrets burdens what otherwise might have been a light and happy soul," he waved his finger at her, smiling coyly.

"Voice of experience again?"

He transformed into Dr. Frankenstein's Igor and hobbled out of the bedroom, dragging dead weight with his right foot. "Yeees, master." They returned to the living room and he sat down on the couch and began tuning his classical guitar.

It looked to be a fine instrument. "Is it hand made?" She came and sat next to him to get a closer look at the woodwork and finish.

"As opposed to factory-mass-produced with recycled Popsicle sticks and shoestrings? Yes." He mumbled with the pretense of bitterness, "Cost me a fortune."

Just like her custom-built skates. "An investment in who you are is very much worth it in the long run." Her anticipation grew as he readied himself.

He played a Bach étude from memory as a warm up.

She picked up a pad of paper and a pencil from the telephone table and curled up in the armchair. Rudy brought Kelly his mouse for a game of fetch; she wrote in between passes. With each toss of the mouse, Rudy would set upon his chase to eventually pounce victoriously upon his catch. He would then roll upon the floor, continuing to maul his prey until he was certain it was truly dead – each time.

Rick played on through the evening until suppertime. Some of his repertoire was classical, but he also knew many folk melodies, and spent some time extemporizing his own creations. When she wasn't writing she watched his hands intently as they maneuvered with relaxed exactness. None of his creative work had been transcribed to paper; he played everything from memory, experimenting with different rhythms, patterns and intonation as he enjoyed the journey. His musical voice boasted nearly twenty years' experience, and Kelly wondered why he hadn't devoted his life to writing music. He had much within him that neither would nor could be spoken aloud; however, he had his music, his own way of connecting and reaching, more potently than words. Feeling as though she had ascended to the heavens, she listened on, delighted, riveted. She wrote the word heart. She wrote it again: He + Art. Awestruck by the ways his music emoted lyrically, she was captivated by her own response to his music.

The rain had finally stopped and a lingering mist shrouded the city. It was nearly ten o'clock by the time Rick brought Kelly back to the Old Victorian. She fiddled for her keys through the folded sheets of her evening's writing that she stuffed in her jacket pocket. She felt inept and clumsy. "How can I find the words to say thank you for today…" she began, "when I can't even find my keys in this stupid pocket. I just had them a second ago."

He felt the weight of her self-consciousness. "Friends don't have to say thanks for being friends."

"Yes, they do. Very much so."

"Hey, you put up with me. I should be thanking you." He took the keys from her hand and unlocked the deadbolt for her. They heard a door creak open one floor down.

"Mrs. Wiles," Kelly warned as she rolled her eyes, "perfect timing, as always. Shhh."

"Den Mother?"

As they stepped in her doorway into the pin-drop darkness of her flat, she reached past him to shut the door only to find that he had already done so. Now, she was completely surrounded by his arms. There was no reaching the light switch. Her heart skipped a beat before she reminded him of the time. He held her close. She tried to calmly breathe through what felt like her lungs seizing the moment he pulled her to him. She was afraid to be this close to anyone. His body summoned in her sensations she had refused to let herself feel. She wanted to halt the escalating panic, so she forced herself to accept his affection as perfectly permissible and natural. Much to her own surprise, her panic dissipated. She lingered in his arms as they leaned against her door in the silence of the night; miraculously, he could make seconds feel like hours. Her eyes closed, she concentrated on his heartbeat and felt the warmth of his back under his leather coat.

He hadn't completely ignored her precautious comment of the late hour. "Try and have a good week, I know you're not looking forward to it." He spoke softly as he removed her hair clip. His hands massaged the base of her neck.

"Pray that I make it to the end of the week, then maybe I'll really be free. It would be an absolute milestone, more than you could ever know."

"You'll make your milestone, and we'll celebrate. Save it up for me then."

Save it up? She was overflowing in trouble and she knew it, yet she didn't pull away from him. She needed to be released, but when she remembered his hands stroking the guitar strings, she feared what she wished for, her needs accrued to an unimaginable magnitude. Tossing away her wonted prudence, her hands reached around his neck and drew him to her.

The passion in her initiation pleasantly startled him to an immediate response. She could play the game of surprise as well as he could, he thought, as his lips savored hers.

They honed their concentration on each other until intense vertigo struck her. She prayed he wouldn't let her go too suddenly, or else she might drop straight to the floor from the tension that had been building all day, or from the fearful panic that suddenly decided to make its reappearance. Unable to discern the pain from the pleasure that flooded her, she pushed herself away from him, "I think you need to go," she tried to regain her breath as twinges of vital alarm fluttered through her belly, "I know you need to go."

He was sorry it was over so soon. "Mmm," he kissed her forehead, "already gone." He smiled at her as he handed her hair clip over, "And thank you for that." As she began to close the door behind him, he asked her, "You okay?"

"Fine, yeah." She pressed, "Go, now."

In the blink of her eye, he was gone. In mute darkness, her hands moved slowly, deliberately, as she locked the deadbolt and latched the safety chain. She turned from the door but couldn't move away. Leaning her back against it, she slid down until she couldn't sink any further. Her eyes focused on nothing in the dark. The panic was stalled, but her belly was knotted so tightly she was now unable to feel. She would have preferred to cry in this safety, but she was immobilized in the blanket of blackness by such curious stillness. Its wicked sense of security descended upon her.

TUESDAY, MAY 20

The first cancellation on the week's agenda was her skating. Everything else, save emergencies, lay in purgatory. The Kaine design project, now at peak momentum, swept through Graphix Alive like a tornado. Daylight hours were devoted to the ad campaign for Randall Brothers, a major men's clothing retailer that utilized the services of Kaine, Marshall and MacLeod. Lunch hours became meetings with Randall reps to select options and layouts, with take-out on the side. They would attend to other contracts after hours. It was going to be a hellishly long week.

Kelly scribbled Rick's wise words, "Better Busy than Bored" on a little pink square of notepaper, and she stabbed it centrally, with vengeful satisfaction, onto her bulletin board. She had come into work at six am; swamped in a quagmire of work, she checked her watch; it was six-thirty pm. Her neck felt stiff and tight, the killer frontal headache would arrive in momentarily. She sat up, stretched and massaged her forehead. Supper hour was upon her, but since she ignored the hunger pangs at lunch, her stomach just gave up signaling. She called it a day and needed the evening walk home.

As she sauntered past the campus gates, her head felt bludgeoned. Random half-thoughts began but she was at a loss to complete them. It irritated her, like having a conversation with a person with no short-term memory – an idea would be started but part way through, this person would forget to finish. Failing completion every time, her mind simply began each thought again, endlessly.

At home, she gazed absently into her fridge. She was either experiencing early senile dementia, or she was staring at the onset of a breakdown in the face. Her waning ray of optimism, that it had been too long since she had last eaten anything substantial, was that her blood sugar had hit rock bottom. Her door buzzer sounded. She traipsed down the main stairs to the front door of the Old Victorian. It was Rick. "What are you doing here?"

"What say, no cheery hello?" He sounded too merry to be begrudging.

"Cheery hello," Kelly responded wryly. "If you didn't bring liquor, then forget it."

"It's only Tuesday. You need it already?" He saw her lean against the door casement of the front vestibule, fading fast.

"Better without then, I haven't eaten in about eight hours."

"Well then," he commanded like a heroic leader, "let's fix that."

She felt herself being dragged up the main staircase as she trod step over step. Everything felt laborious. They stepped into her flat. "So now it's your turn to stare mindlessly into my fridge." They both leaned against her kitchen island studying the near empty the little white Frigidaire. "Have you eaten?" she asked him.

"No." He pulled out the last quarter loaf of whole wheat bread and a half-package of sliced deli chicken, "Grilled chicken sandwiches with cheese, onions and black olives. I win."

If she had the mental energy, she might have mustered a sardonic quip in response to his hodge-podge suggestion. "Whatever, Doctor Food TV."

He laughed at his new title, "Don't you know, anything with black olives is Euro gourmet, where have you been?" He decided at the last minute to dip it in a garlic-laced egg batter.

She watched his serendipitous hot sandwich creation come to life; the whole culinary event took no more than ten minutes. "Mmm. You should be on Food TV, more than those pretentious yahoos they have on right now," she said as she sampled his speedy work of wonder.

"Yep. We'll call it Desperate Fridge: Real Eating In Under Fifteen Minutes. People will watch that."

"Damn right they will," Kelly rallied. "We'll print cookbooks they can order, too. We'd make a fortune.... Well you would. How is it that you're here? Did I already ask you that?" Her mind jumped thought tracks.

"You did, I never did answer your question, did I? Called you earlier to invite you to dinner, but you weren't home. You weren't at work either."

"I must have been lost on the road in between."

"Came to see how you were doing."

"No, you came to make me Desperate Sandwiches, like that was part of your master plan. I'm as pathetic as they come, today. And as you have experienced first-hand, so is my kitchen."

Rick was glad to see she still had a sense of humor, as tired as she was. He suggested a brisk evening walk to the neighborhood park. They found a bench at one end of the pond where ducks had gathered, some already hunkered down for the night.

He saw how she sat with her arms wrapped around her knees, her heels propped upon the edge of the bench. She looked portably compact, folded up like a lawn chair.

They sat in silence. "Ever been in a rut you can't seem to get out of?"

"Sure, who hasn't? Work-related?"

"Life-related. Nothing about my life has really changed in the last, oh, decade."

"I've only known you for a month, so I can't really comment."

"Well, safe to say you basically have, except for being ten years older, not much has really changed. Not what I imagined for my life."

"And you said you never thought about your future. I say you must have if you feel you haven't lived up to your imagination. Was your plan to be big-city rich and famous?"

"I don't care about that. It's about who I am. I am making changes for the better, slowly, but..." she still didn't feel secure enough with him to finish her sentence.

"Don't stop there if you have more to say."

"It seems every time I try to break free, something pulls me back, like one step forward, but two back. I wasn't kidding when I said I'm in hiding."

"Sure you don't mean hibernation? That's natural."

"Hibernation means going underground for winter. I hide year-round. Perpetual hibernation."

"That's not true, otherwise how would I have met you?"

She felt stupid.

"What are you hiding from?"

She shook her head apathetically, then got up and began to walk towards the playground.

He caught up with her. "Okay, consolation prize. What's pulling you back?"

"Tell me something," she turned back to him after a brief pause, "it's been how many, eight, years since your life fell apart. What's your secret?"

"Secret for what? How to keep nailing days like rivets in the hull?" Rick shrugged his shoulders affably since he didn't consider himself an expert on surviving the unexpected death of a loved one. "I don't know. You just go through it. Well, actually you run away from it...'til you get through it." He knew he sounded preposterous. He then qualified, "And then, after all that, you figure out you're still running, but you're gotten farther than where you were."

While he wore a quizzical expression on his face, Kelly inherently understood. He could have quoted Shakespeare and it might not have been as effective to her. "Hence my rut."

He assumed it must have been about her first boyfriend, who she said 'left' her about ten years ago. It certainly explained why she chose to be on her own since then, and why she considered herself jinxed.

They sat on a platform deck of a wooden playground ship, next to a fat steel slide. "Rick, how's your dad?"

"He's fine, why?"

"I've noticed you don't talk to him when your mom calls."

"We talk," he claimed resistively, "occasionally." Before she could censure his lackadaisical response, he added, "We don't see eye to eye on most things."

"You're not fooling anyone." Kelly then retracted, "But you don't need me to tell you that."

"Maybe I do." He brushed wisps of her hair out of her eyes with his fingers.

"Still waiting for your planets to align?" She was amused by her growing audacity. "Of course, I'm the last one to talk. Apathy is not a virtue. I have no energy to even look at Wendy right now, let alone deal with her."

"Exactly," he laughed, "you understand."

"it's unacceptable: to give up on someone before you have the chance to tell them what you need to…even if it's just in time to say goodbye…to lose anyone you love and not let them know how you really feel…" Inconveniently, the run-on half-sentences had returned. She looked directly at him, "When did this division begin?"

"When I was twelve or so."

Kelly had no idea their strained relationship extended as far back as twenty years. "So early on?"

"He became unavailable. It started when he was gunning for a promotion. When he got it, it was a step up for him, a senior management position and I don't think he adapted. Way too much pressure from higher up, sales type stuff, he used to come home stressed out and frustrated most nights. My mom really noticed it, we all did. His promotion meant more money, but it didn't feel worth it, not to us. Kevin was still pretty young, and too busy being a piss-ant to notice, but as he got older, it affected him too. He jokes about it now. All he remembers is being told to stay quiet and not to bug dad for anything. As he got older, he hung out a lot with his friends out of the house. They'd work his bands in other kids' basements, making racket to their parents' chagrin."

"What about you?"

"What about me," he shrugged.

"How did you handle it?"

"I stayed out of the way." Rick got up to wander and hopped atop the highest platform, where the ship's play steering wheel was. He whizzed it around a few times then halted its spin.

"Is that when your guitar became your voice?"

"Yep. I could spend hours in my room playing but it never drowned out my parents' fighting. Kevin's electric equipment was better for that. He rebelled after a few years and brought his friends home to practice in our basement and that's when I thought he and dad were going to have it out once and for all. But dad never really bit like I thought he would. Mom intervened and only let Kev and his friends practice at our house on Saturday afternoons, when dad was catching up work at the bank."

"So your dad's work never really relaxed after that?"

"Didn't seem to. He kept accepting more work." Rick hopped over a railing and landed back on the platform Kelly was seated on and nestled himself around her. "The subliminal insanity of capitalism. The only time he ever had anything to say to me was when report cards came around."

"You mentioned that," Kelly rested her head back on his shoulder.

"And while I was at it, pull up Kevin's socks, too. Ridiculous perfectionism. Passing the buck, really."

"Let me guess, a lot of pressure school-wise, and no support from him music-wise."

"My mom tried to understand me growing up. She encouraged music for us, it was her saving grace, and she was the bridge between my dad and I, for what it was worth."

"Had you wanted to make music your choice of study?"

"I would have loved to," Rick admitted joyfully.

"Ah. But engineering was a career you could rely on. Music was for layabouts who would do no better than eke out a living." Kelly sensed the nature of the discourse between him and his father.

"Hey, were you hiding in my closet? Man, I think dad actually said that, word for word. And more than once."

"My dad told me there was no such thing as a career in skating. Skating was recreation, a hobby. Competition life was for rich kids, shows were for Ice Princess divas, and he made sure I never copped an attitude. And there was no making a guaranteed living at coaching, around here that's essentially true. Talk to me about having your dreams dashed."

"The things we have to do to survive versus the things we do to live."

"I'm glad your music is still very much in your life and that you just didn't let it fall away. I'm glad I didn't let skating go altogether."

"I can thank Mike for that. He told me the day we registered for university to commit to a profession, not for my dad, but for me. That if I picked something I could like, my music will always be there."'

"Mike basically gave you the same advice as your dad did, but Mike's approach was more open. Naturally, you'd be more receptive to that. So in the end, do you like engineering?" Kelly asked based on his father's pressured workaholic situation.

"I hit some kind of wall after Rebecca died, and I just threw myself into my work, and that's when I discovered I actually liked it enough to commit to a PhD. Just between you and me, research proved to be a legit hideout. More than that, it wasn't about pleasing or appeasing my dad anymore. I had grown enough that his approval was a non-issue."

"That's a moment of enlightenment, isn't it?" Kelly's hands grasped his arms and wrapped them tighter around her waist, holding him closer to her. The dampness of the night air seemed to clarify her thoughts. "Has your dad ever heard you play?"

"Not really."

"That's crazy. God, you play so incredibly."

"You're biased, Kel." He nuzzled her cheek. The waning moonlight cast a ghostlike rainbow glow through the diaphanous scattered clouds that had rolled in over the course of the evening. "He's heard Kev play, he had no choice."

Rick switched topics to speak no further of his family, "Tell me about your poetry."

"Other than the very pitiful fact that it doesn't rhyme?"

"Someone highly evolved told me that poetry doesn't have to rhyme. This radical concept could very well influence how I compose music from here on in."

"You have no idea how lucky you are. Syllables are a pain in the ass, even with non-rhyming couplets and free meter. You can communicate with a means of expression that isn't bounded by the sore limitations of the spoken word."

Evolved, he thought again. "I just think my music could really use some lyrics."

"Then write some."

"But you're the writer here."

"You've got to be kidding."

"No, I'm not. The concept of the 'song' strikes you as outlandish?"

"Hey, in my book, words speak for the mind, and rarely does well for anything else unless you're divinely inspired. Music speaks for the soul. What you do – just the way you do it - stirs the unreachable. Why do you want to mess with a thing of perfection? Don't diminish it, Doctor."

"Why not both means of expression, together? How can you say poetry wouldn't enhance it? Imagine, Kel, imagine." To him, the sky was just the beginning.

"I elect to end this discussion here and now. You haven't even read my poetry."

"Well, maybe I need to," he offered seriously.

"I wrote a poem about your cat," her tone lightened. "I might let you read that one."

"Really? Better not tell Rudy, his little lion heart might burst out of his orange fur, if he knew he was the subject of your poetic efforts."

"That's funny you should say that." Kelly chuckled as she recalled her poem.

"Well in that case, I want to read it," Rick insisted, "and anything else you might permit me to read."

"Yeah. Don't count on it."

"Why not? I promise I won't laugh, I swear," he said, remembering the last time he said that.

"Ever heard of Pandora's Box? Trust me, the last thing you need is a window to nowhere," she said with a diminished tone.

"May I be given the privilege to make that choice?"

"No," Kelly answered forcefully.

He had reached yet another stalemate with her. He expected her to get up and walk away from him. When she didn't, his curiosity became confusion. He wondered whether it was his presence, his approach or the topic of conversation that was causing her withdrawal. He pulled himself away from her. "What am I doing wrong here? What do you want me to do?"

"Nothing." She felt chilled inside. "I'm cold."

The emptiness in her voice was breaking his heart. Without knowing any details of her life, he knew she said exactly what she meant. He leaned nearer to her and only rested his chin on her shoulder. Inexplicably, she wanted to collapse into him, even though she knew her silence was pushing him away. In frustrated determination he tried to hold her once again, hoping she would eventually trust him enough to let him know her. Ironically, for the first time since they had met, he noticed she had her hair completely down that evening; and it shimmered in the hazy moonlight. "Do you know how to play chess?"

"I used to play with my dad when I was growing up," Kelly fondly recalled. "I think he let me win most of the time."

"Remember how to play?"

"I think so. Bishops move on the diagonals, rooks go horizontal and vertical, and knights move in this wacky L-shape, right?" Kelly's finger drew the directions in the air.

Rick saw she was smiling again. "Queens have the most freedom and Kings have virtually none, they can only move one square in any direction."

"The way it should be."

"You wish. We'll play sometime, but unlike your dad, I'm not going to just let you win. Not that easily anyway."

"Good, I might actually learn something about real strategy for a change."

"You already know too much about strategy, baby. You'll kick my ass at this game, I already know."

"You don't know that, we've never played before."

"I just know. You'll have a deceiving offense.... you'll make it appear casually open for invitation... you'll set it up so that it's impossible for your opponent not to bite. Then you lure him in and before he knows what hit him, you'll have him surrounded, powerless and.... Check...Mate." His hands manipulated hers as he demonstrated her redoubtable strategy.

She discovered the game of hands playing hands was deceivingly dangerous. "You realize you're making me out to be smarter than I really am," she whispered.

"But here's the kicker." He closed himself around her and had her lean back on him. "You're far more deviously clever than that." He was speaking methodically into her right ear, filling her head, then her entire being. "Kel, the secret's not in your trick bait offense, it's in your impenetrable defense."

The resonating sound of his voice sent an inundating surge of want that re-awakened in her belly. Her heart rate shot up suddenly and a rush of heat overtook her. She sat upright. She knew she couldn't have it both ways. Her fingers brushed her hair away from her face. "I know exactly what you're trying to say to me. Why don't you just say it??"

For the accusation he acknowledged as partly deserved, he spoke gently back to her, "What do you want me to do, Kel? Disappear? Vanish, once and for all?" He waited only briefly for an answer then started to stand up.

She bounded up and away from the playground platform. She felt the familiar instinctive terror building inside her. Tears stung her eyes as they welled up.

"Be careful what you wish for. Left up to you, we're like two pawns permanently walled up against each other, with nowhere to hide, until one of us is finally killed off by useless strategy?"

"Please don't say that!" she pleaded as his words took on reality inside her. "Nobody wishes for something like that." She walked away from him.

He proceeded to follow her, "Well, I for one would like to know what this pathetic thing with you is really about!"

She kept walking away.

He then stopped and said in an elevated voice, "You got my attention. You got me cornered. Don't you know? Or do you not care? I am at a total loss with you. You want something you don't have anymore, then you don't want what you could have. You actually don't know what you want, or do you?"

Kelly stopped walking away. She held her forehead as she worked her fingers through her hair. "Everything in my life I have handled badly. This wasn't supposed to happen. My life is a mistake, one big joke. On me."

Rick stepped toward her.

"You can never understand how hopeless I've felt since the day I was old enough to understand," she interjected before he reached her.

"What are you talking about?? Make me understand, Kel. Since Rebecca, I never wanted to feel this powerless again. Just tell me what you want. I need to know what to do."

"If you know what's good for you, stay away from me. I'm a bad disease."

"Cut that out!" Rick said angrily. He wanted answers, details, something to work with. "Heartbreak is not like a cold, it's not something you just catch and wait for a week for it to go away on its own, Kel. Heartbreak happens, to you, to me, to everyone. What makes you so special, like your god-given pain is worse than everyone else's?" Nobody could possibly derive this much meaning from their pain, he couldn't comprehend how nuts she was.

She had never heard his voice sound so angry. She knew she was pushing him over the edge, "Why do you even care? You have all your own answers, like you've got the perfect life!" she shouted angrily. **You're stupid…you'll never be smart enough to beat this game…no one will save you, they're all gone….** she kept hearing the demon Agramon's voice scream at her again and again.

"Bullshit," Rick muttered to himself, but it was audible enough for her to hear.

You're a little girl…a stupid little girl. You weren't even wanted, so they left you… Refueled, she cried loudly, "You don't get it, do you? Let me spell it out for you. I am broken, cracked, empty…" She counted with her fingers as her voice continued to escalate with each bitter utterance.

He glanced nervously around the deserted park, "Quiet, Kel." His voice stepped up a notch.

"I'm not finished!" Kelly tested as she persisted in her self-degrading rant, "Fragile, weak, damaged, inexperienced …" She was screaming and crying as she stumbled away from him.

She had succeeded in breaking him down. "Enough, Kel, I mean it." Rick had to turn away from her as worked to quell the pain in his throat. He wiped a tear from his eye.

She stopped long enough to see his back was to her. She hoped he would finally walk away. "How many more reasons do you need to stay the hell away from me, Rick?" She persisted like nausea, "Perhaps you need to see the lovely assortment of anti-depressants, the pills for anxiety and how about the tranquilizers, the anti-psychotics? Or do you want me to tell you in complete detail this secret hell I'm trapped in." The emotional explosion brought on a whirling queasiness and extreme dizziness. She bent over and held her stomach. She was shaking, yet not fully aware of the explosive intensity of the anger she had kept permanently suppressed. Reaching the final intensity of her breakdown, she didn't want to live one more moment like this, grieving for security she never had, as now she fully felt it: there was nothing in her memory left to grieve for except the imaginary life she wanted as much as the grief. In the vacuum of emptiness, the ground fell away from beneath her feet and she tumbled to the ground.

He was still looking back at the playground. Unsure of how to snap her out of this madness and unaware of her collapse, he said with his voice resolutely suppressed, "You've given me a million reasons you think matter." He rubbed his left eyebrow with the flesh of his palm. When he turned back toward her, Rick saw her down on the grassy ground in fetal position. He ran to her and saw she was fighting for air. He could do nothing but partially lift her up off the ground. For the first time, he could see how fragile she was as she struggled to breathe. It was like an asthma attack, but this was different. He thought back to that night in his kitchen, was her anxiety attack just the tip of the iceberg? The choking sensation began to ease and he watched as she caught her breath enough to cry. Now there didn't seem to be an end to her sobbing.

The depth of her pain seemed unimaginable to him. To witness this kind of self-destruction, to see this suppressed battle that occupied her was near intolerable to him. "Okay, okay," he comforted her. "let it all out, so it won't do this to you anymore." Unable to find any other words, he kept reassuring her it would be okay; he hoped this much-needed release would purge some of the toxicity from her system. Thankfully, her crying stopped.

She could hardly speak. "I hate who I've become. I never wanted anyone to know who I really am. I'm so ashamed because there is *so* much I'm afraid for you to see. I know that once you know, you won't want to have anything to do with me. No one would."

"Nonsense, friend. Do you have that little faith in me?" He swept tears from her soaked, reddened cheeks. "I don't know any details about your history and you know what? Doesn't even matter. The stuff you think matters just doesn't. Not to me. I want to know who you are, broken, cracked and all. Did I ever tell you, we found a cat under our car once, he had a torn ear and looked like hell. But we took care of him and he got better. That's all that matters." He spoke softly to her. "It will get better."

And it was working. Agramon's voice yielded. Once again, she was amazed at the cleansing power of his voice.

"Find me anyone without baggage. Nobody's life is perfect. Nobody's life is pain-free. Essentially, you and I, we're no different from the rest of the world because of what we've been through. The last time our slates were completely clean was the day we were born, and you know, there are mystics who'd even argue that." He held her as they sat on the grass under the night sky. "You tell me your life history and I'll tell you mine, I triple-dog dare ya. We'll let go the floodgates and hang on for dear life."

She looked up at him and offered a hint of a smile.

He looked down at her and smiled back. In the patches of clear night sky between clouds, they could see stars. He pointed at a spot of sky to fix her heart upon, "See them? They've been around forever. That's what we'll hang onto."

Kelly secured her sight on a twinkle point, "Arcturus," she identified.

"Hey, you know your stars."

"I have to." It was all she had left of her parents.

They continued to stargaze until the cloud cover masked them. Rick walked Kelly home, never releasing her hand from his. Kelly chose to enter the Old Victorian from the back door. As they stood on the deck, she fiddled for her keys.

"Better way around Den Mother?" Rick queried.

"She may be elderly, but she has ears like a watchdog." Kelly warned as she unlocked the back door, "She hears everything."

"Want some company?"

"No, that's okay, I'll be fine." Kelly's defenses resurfaced. "I've troubled you more than enough."

Rick wanted to kiss her but resisted the urge. Romantic conflict might only propel her confusion and increase the tension between them. "I'll see you tomorrow evening, after nine or so. I'm meeting Mike to play squash. Our usual Wednesday night deal."

She looked down at her keys in her hand. "If not tomorrow, then later on...or whenever." She sounded non-committal, and her eyes could not confront him.

His fingers stroked her hair. "I can stay for a little while, if you want."

She looked at him guardedly, "No. Don't give me that option." The ongoing battle inside her waged on. She immediately looked away again.

"I need to know if you're going to be alright."

"You should go," Kelly whispered.

May 18

Abandonment;
leaves soul seclusion,
first by force
and then by choice.

Joy;
leads to loss and grief
purposeless equation
solved by foolish logic

Reliance;
waters fertile ground of suffering
fearing love yields sickness
allowing love yields sorrow

Fear;
instills hopelessness and distrust
to love and let love
gnaws insidiously at my soul.

Could I be the falling star that you catch in your hands?

Protected Kingdom

Thou shall stand guard, king of thy domain,
Thou shall sleep, O happy creature of comfort
Art thou entrapped within thy peripheral shell?

Thou shall play, master of thy destiny,
Thou shall bathe, feline Narcissus
Dost thou imagine wild universes beyond?

Thy world complete, sight and sound
Art thou sovereign?
Thy needs replete, body and soul
Or art thou enslaved?

Be there no disquiet in thy territorial heart?

Watching Rudy over the last several days, I have come to realize what an
illuminating blessing his little kitten soul / lion heart is to my shelled
existence. His realm may be infinitesimal yet he is always true to his
nature. An original, at all times and in all places. Like royalty, he seats
himself in the very center of the bed, or rests atop the back of the couch or the
telephone table, the highest platform in the room. From these vantages, his
throne-seat gives him full survey of his kingdom, and of his subject. Rick
hates when I call him that, but he reminds me that while dogs have masters,
cats have staff.

"A heavy heart, Belovèd, have I borne" – Elizabeth Barrett Browning

I relate too eerily to EBB.

Following their death, the asphyxiating absence left me incapable of feeling natural joy. People can become attached to grief. But to anchor the heart in the depth of desolation is not heroic. Its meritorious recognition is validated only in its surrender. The freedom to laugh, in genuine joy with a lightened heart, is something we take for granted, until it is stolen and slips beyond our grasp. Having been given the gift of a friend who can make me laugh, over nothing, especially through my tears, I can rest and regenerate, knowing that they watch over me, that I am not completely forsaken.

The Gift

His gift lightens my weighty load
As my Comrade on this winding road
How music sings his soul's insight
And wraps me in his heart's delight

With feeble words, I fail in kind
His melody within me finds
Unbridled pleasure, such saddled woe
How his music speaks for me so!

He weaves perspective in perfect harmony, in fine balance. It crumbles me
without a moment's notice, and fortifies me where I need to exist, right here,
at home.

May 20

Uncondition

I have known times
Blessed, I knew true security
Of unconditionally loving arms
When youthfully, I felt protected
Through trouble, tense and turbulent
Ancestral voices speak wisdom

I have lived times
Forsaken, I craved to feel the touch
Of unreservedly loving hands
When desperately, I longed to hear words
From a voice, calm and comforting
Celestial guardians keep watch

If there would come a time
Bravely, I could know you as you are
That fearlessly you might know me as I am
Then irrevocably, there could come a time
In unity, we would know peace
Heavenly angels hold vigil

The longer you keep a secret, the stronger you believe the secret must remain kept at all costs. This dangerous gamble has shackled me from the power, depth and resolve of the human heart. I fear it was too high a price to pay.

Nine

WEDNESDAY, MAY 21

"Kelly, Dr. Hutchinson is here to see you," Linda informed kindly. Kelly hung up her phone and began to shove several oversize design sheets into a folio she kept beside her drafting table. She hurriedly gathered up assorted Conte crayons, watercolor pencils and gel pens that were strewn around her workspace and tossed them indiscriminately into a tray. She removed the sanguine Conte hue from her fingertips with lanolin.

Still working the leftover cream into her fingertips, Kelly opened her office door and peeked out only far enough to call Rick in, "Hey, aren't you supposed to be at work?"

"Yep." He was astounded by the production that was taking place in such a small space. Her seating lounge was laden with designs, copy arrangements and photo layouts, and the coffee table was lost under stacks of open files. "Wow. Who let the dogs out?"

"Randall Brothers." Frustrated and wanting to make a place for him to sit, a knock came at her already open door.

"Miss Pearson," Paul called out with an exaggerated business-like formality. He entered, shuffling through a series of designs, then noticed she wasn't alone, "Forgive me. I didn't realize you were in a meeting." Paul looked directly at Rick and didn't recognize him as a current client. "Sorry to interrupt."

"Not at all," Kelly responded, "I'd like you to meet Rick Hutchinson." She introduced her boss to him, "Rick, Paul Jameson, creative breath and firm foundation of Graphix Alive. Firm, not necessarily sane."

The two men shook hands amiably before Paul resumed, "Kelly, I need a word with you regarding these autumn panel layouts."

Rick motioned to Kelly that he could step outside while she met with her boss but she directed him to sit at her drafting table.

Paul consulted her, "Kelly, do these backgrounds signify 'bold' to you?"

"As bold as you can get using such muted tints," Kelly answered. "They said they don't want boldness from hue. What, you don't like their 'colonial' palette?"

They rattled on: Paul conveyed their client's complaint and Kelly complained about their client's vacillation. Rick picked at her jammed stapler.

"What about splashes of something, say, red?" Paul suggested randomly.

This provoked a negative reaction from her. She had done everything in her power to keep her equanimity under control all day but too many designs were being handed back for inane changes. "Here, look." Kelly picked up a cel of a dashing male model in a sporty two-piece suit and layered it upon the background design in question. "By the time you get the photo in place, splashes of red anywhere in the background would be disconnected from the focus, the model."

"Maybe if his nose was red. They need a model with a cold."

"That says autumn bold." Kelly rubbed her temples.

"This guy needs to be wearing a red tie," Paul declared decisively.

"YOU tell their fashion design team that!" Kelly ordered brazenly. She sighed, "What is it they think they want now?"

"Something more, Pearson. It needs something." Paul's mind was spinning circles around hers, "Texturize these tints, warm these up, cool those down. I agree with your clash of warm and cool, very autumn. Put in some kind of unified pattern, something subtle, pour your creative wizardry in it, Kelly," her boss encouraged swiftly, "and do it by dinner so I can get the printers on it. Thai tonight?"

"Whatever," Kelly waved her hand, as her face frowned and furrowed concern, "and pour some Jamaican one-fifty-one in with that creativity while you're at it Kelly. Better yet, I'll take it straight up, Paul, right up their -" She realized she wasn't retorting silently to herself. She had truly lost control of her mind.

Paul placed his hand on her shoulder laughing louder than he should have, "Thanks, Kelly, they said what they want, you know what they think they want, give them more." As he exited her office, he called to Rick, who was industriously sampling colored gel pens on a post-it note pad, "Nice to meet you. Let us know if there's anything we can do for you. Preferably after next week."

"Already have. Thanks. Good luck with all this," Rick replied energetically.

She now had to rework an entire set of background layouts in less than two hours. Kelly tossed the file on top of the growing stack on her coffee table. "I don't even know which ones are the rejects anymore," she muttered as she shut her office door. She rested the side of her head against the doorjamb as Rick walked towards her.

"Does it lock?" he asked devilishly.

"Both Paul and Linda have keys, so there's no point."

He gently tugged her away from the door and embraced her in a waltz hold. She looked nerve-racked and this project was draining her.

She let herself be held by him behind her closed office door. A stolen moment's liberty permitted her to feel the strongest sense of emotional clarity she had experienced all day. Ironically, she discovered, her intelligibility surfaced only when she stopped driving her racing thoughts with licensed fear.

Rick suggested they get some air. On the front steps of Graphix Alive, he asked, "Have you talked to Wendy lately?"

It wasn't the topic she preferred to open with; she waffled about answering his question. She nodded a no. "There's no point. We're not talking. There's nothing to say, nothing to talk about. Nobody's listening, so why bother talking." She was curt and straightforward.

"When was the last time you two were this much at odds?"

"When we were little, I guess. Always little tiffs here and there. Joys of being exact opposites. We just got used to each other, I guess, we never really fought as such. Not until now, anyway. It's like a last kick at the can. The resiliency in our relationship is gone, we're too different."

She didn't signal that she wanted to be reassured, nor did she seem beset by the situation. All he knew was that fighting was a strong sign that things did still matter, perhaps now more than ever. "Just a phase, you'll ride it through. Don't give up."

"So, why aren't you at work?" Kelly enquired about his truancy again.

"Doesn't matter."

Knowing his nonchalance usually hid far more beneath it, Kelly asked him reluctantly, "Did you get fired?"

"Such confidence you have in me. I worked through lunch and needed a break. So here I am."

The cool air stimulated her dulled senses. She leaned against the railing next to him. The dark cloud cover was beginning to break. Perhaps it wouldn't rain any more this evening, not that it would matter, she'd be tied up with revisions well into night. "Are you meeting Mike for your squash game tonight?"

"Indeed. He plans to kick my ass." Rick humored with dubious reserve, "But he plans to kick my ass every week."

"And do you let him?"

"Sometimes," he nodded in a neither here nor there manner. "Your boss seems like a good guy."

"He is, when he's not a lunatic under the influence, like this week." Kelly sighed. "Must be great to be your own boss."

"Hell no. Don't be fooled. I have many bosses. Be glad you only have one," he acknowledged. "Too many captains destroy the well-oiled machine. No chain of command."

"Talk to Paul about that. He insists we're under the unfamiliar grip of new bosses every week, every time we take on a new contract. Just when you get used to one, we're onto another, and they all insist they know exactly what they want," Kelly remarked disconsolately, "that is, until I give it to them."

"Your boss thinks the world of you, regardless of the fickleness of clients," Rick encouraged, "That's obvious from what I just saw."

"Just because he hasn't fired me in the six years I've been here doesn't mean he thinks that," Kelly argued. "It means I'll do until he finds someone who's qualified, who belongs in this business."

"Then he would have done it by now." Rick wasn't buying it. "He's doing his job. He's pushing you. He strives for excellence and he sees it in you."

"Evidently, he's striving up the wrong employee." Kelly stretched her neck from side to side and it didn't appear to relieve her.

"Excellence isn't an outcome, based on one single result, it's a process. He knows that and so do you. You're both supremely dedicated. Come on, Kel, perspective," he insisted as he benignly shoved her arm with his. He let up when he saw her fade out. "How are you doing, right now?"

"You know better than to ask me that."

"Still, I want to know."

Kelly smacked her palms on the rail, "Empty." She then pushed herself away from the railing and headed down the front steps, defeated by her dissatisfaction in regard to every aspect of her life. She didn't want him near her should she spontaneously burst into tears but his footsteps were close behind her. A car drove past them sprinkling a white-noise spray from its tires. She stood still. "Ever feel like you just want to disappear?" Her voice faded before she finished her utterance. Her eyes gazed skyward, praying for faith that someone was listening.

The tightness in his gut got him, "A long time ago. Time goes on but it's a feeling you never forget." He weaved his fingers through hers and turned her around to face him; he saw tears stalled at the corners of her eyes. "Talk to me."

She couldn't look at him. "There's nothing here," she whispered to the air, looking vacantly toward the outline created by the dark mansard ridge of her workplace against the afternoon's mundane sky. "People keep pushing me for something that just isn't there. I can't even explain it to you. Nobody understands."

Rick placed his forearms on her shoulders and his hands wrapped around the back of her neck. "I think the most important catalysts in our lives, whether they're people or situations, push us in ways we can't even grasp." He needed her to look at him and he waited until she did. "We don't get it right away, at the time we resist it, we deny it and sometimes we flat-out hate it. It's not until you've pushed through and look back that you realize how absolutely vital it was to go through it, in exactly the way that it happened. That's nature. It's zigzag. The complete solutions are never given to us when we need them, that would be too easy."

Kelly listened.

"Hints come, bit by bit, when we least expect it. And sometimes they're not the answers we thought they would be."

"You don't understand. I've spent ten years pushing through, I'm tired of searching. I don't even want answers anymore." The tears began to roll down her cheeks. She was slowly receding from him again as she pushed her tears aside with the palms of her hands. "Nothing matters. This emptiness makes me want to just fade away."

"Do you want to know what I think?" He asked for her attention and her eyes responded. "Perspective. You think feeling empty is a bad thing. Being in total emptiness means that you're now ready to be filled. So stop fighting it, empty it all the way, let it go, and accept it. Then it's ready to be filled right. It has to be that way. That's the beauty of emptiness, Kel. Because of its nothingness, it holds so much potential. Anything is possible now. Do you see?"

Her mind was wandering away from him as she tried to coerce herself to believe what he was expressing to her. *No one will miss you; they're all gone*, Agramon cruelly reminded. "I just want to disappear."

A force of purpose coalesced from nowhere and squarely met his uncertainty that he could make a difference, "If you want to disappear, plan to go someplace amazing. Have you ever been to Madagascar? The Azores? Or Fiji? Heaven on earth. These places have awesome power to transform you, and trust me, you won't come back the same as when you left."

Her soul hadn't belonged to this world for a decade, and by circumstance had shrunk so terribly miniscule, like a shriveled bud whose infinitesimal breadth was all she believed she would ever know. His dark brown eyes looked far into hers and danced with a wanderlust enthusiasm. He enticed her. But she was progressively losing this battle. She couldn't imagine feeling more feeble in his presence but her instincts were taking over. She had trusted him enough to reveal her true self thus far, "I don't even know where on earth Fiji is." She began to laugh at her shamefully limited knowledge of world geography as tears fell once more.

Rick laughed with her as he wiped tears from her cheeks, "Then let's find out. I hear it's exquisite there. I'll pick you up here around nine or so. I'll call first so you won't have to walk home in the dark."

"The main door will be locked, so ring the bell and I'll let you in." She checked the time, "You need to get going."

"And you have to go make red splashes." He smiled as he waved his hand with artistic flair. He called back to her as he headed off to the Engineering Complex, "Smile. Takes less muscles."

By nine pm, she had changed into her casual attire for the evening. Paul had left to go home only minutes earlier. Her office had been tidied sufficiently, with two more sections of the project having reached the next stage of completion. She surfed the Internet trying to locate Fiji. The sound of a doorbell rang repeatedly in her distant consciousness. Her view of the computer screen darkened and tunneled, momentarily. The two-note ring rebounded and echoed inside her mind; autonomically, adrenalin was dispatched to high alert. *It's too late. There's nothing you can do.* She grabbed the edge of her desk until the rush settled. In her fleeting terror hearing the voice, she had forgotten to breathe.

She walked to the front door, telling herself to calm down, that it was only Rick. She reminded herself that he had just called to say he was on his way. She was expecting him. Upon his arrival, she invited him in to see the changes she had made to the autumn background layouts. The geometric tinted washes were now textured with subtle, random leaf patterns, in varying reduced tones of burnt umber, rust red and deep ochre. Paul had approved the new look and was certain Randall's reps would love it. Rust red wasn't in their original color scheme, but it could be, Rick remarked knowing nothing about graphic design, he only knew what he liked, and she had hit the nail on the head.

Kelly asked Rick on the drive home, "So, how did your squash match go? Did Mike kick your ass?"

"Never mind."

"Two for three or three for three?"

"Enough, you."

"You let him win?" Kelly continued to poke at him.

"I'll say yes." Rick looked to her when he was supposed to be driving. "Or I could give you the very legitimate excuse that I was suitably distracted."

"Hey. Watch the road, Doctor," Kelly ordered with a smile. "Give your opponent a weakness for them to capitalize on, they will." She advised him like a seasoned coach.

They had stopped at an intersection. When the light finally switched to green, Rick didn't proceed. They could see an emergency vehicle heading toward them with its headlamps and warning lights flashing. The ambulance approached, siren blaring. Unsure where it would proceed, Rick chose to wait until it had passed well by. Within seconds, it had sped through the intersection and passed them. He was struck to see her shrunk back in her seat, her fists clenched at her ears and her eyes forced shut. "Hey, are you okay?" he asked her as he gently touched her arm.

Kelly shuddered 'no', refusing to open her eyes.

Rick proceeded through the intersection and pulled over to the side of the street. "Was it the ambulance? It's gone now." He saw that she had released her breath and her fists. "What is it? Are you okay?"

She opened her eyes and warily scanned the neighborhood surroundings. "I don't know." Her eyes darted in various directions, anxiously. "I don't know what happened, it freaked me out, that's all."

He turned his flashers on and waited until he was sure she felt comfortable again, still wondering what prompted her terrified reaction.

"I'm okay. Keep going," she insisted through shallow breaths.

Arriving at her flat, Rick parked his SUV on Walton Street and before stepping out, he handed Kelly a few small booklets.

"What's this?" she asked as she fiddled to undo her seatbelt. She always had trouble locating the buckle receptacle in his car.

"You'll see when we get inside," he stated matter-of-factly.

Once in her flat, she flipped on the light switch that lit the hanging globe over her bistro table. What he had handed her were travel-style brochures: one featured The Azores, a group of islands far off the coast of Portugal, and the other two, Fiji and French Polynesia. "Oh cool. Where did you get these? Did you just pick these up now?"

"Oh no, they live on my shelf. I picked them up a while ago," he said. "Top three on my short list of places to disappear to right now."

Kelly leafed through the booklets, her eyes uninterested in any printed words. The photos were glorious and depicted images she couldn't even conjure up in her dreams of heaven. The concept that paradise could exist on earth wasn't entirely inconceivable to her; it just seemed so remote. These photographs brought her heaven a step closer to tangible reality.

Rick set her stovetop kettle to boil. The evening's dampness and Kelly's weariness warranted a pot of hot tea. "When was the last time you took a vacation?"

Kelly's attention had already sailed to the other side of Earth, in particular to the archipelagos of the mid-Atlantic and the South Pacific. "Clarify. Had days off or took a vacation?"

"Either." Rick was leaning up against her kitchen island. He looked at how she had eagerly seated herself at the bistro table, with one leg folded on the chair, the other foot resting on the floor.

"I took part of my vacation time off last spring, but I didn't go anywhere. I don't think I've ever taken the full two weeks at once. I usually spread it around over the year, so that I don't leave work for too long. Wendy's family had planned a trip to San Diego over spring break and I went with them. That was seven years ago. We stayed in Coronado and it was incredible. The beaches were awesome." Just then, she flipped a page to reveal a stunning Fijian beach. "But nothing like this. This is the heaven I long for."

The kettle came to a boil and Kelly bounced up from her chair to fish out her teapot from the cupboard below, knowing Rick wouldn't have a clue as to where she kept it. "Things only go in here one way. If you want a loaf pan, ask me a week in advance." She deftly retrieved the teapot from out of a stack of mixing bowls.

Rick bent down to see the Tetris conglomeration of kitchen items stacked and close-packed inside the island's cupboard. She had managed to fit most kitchen items well inside a space nearly one-tenth the volume of his kitchen cupboards.

"Not everything is in here, I have some stuff over in those cupboards over there." She pointed to the base of the built-in bookcases by the Larch Street bay window.

"Three weeks in Fiji."

"What?" Kelly said as she prepared Moroccan Mint tea.

"Three weeks in Fiji, Kel, and none of this will matter." Rick's voice grew dreamy.

She had set the tea and covered the pot with a quilted cozy pulled from a drawer. "Three weeks? That's it? Remember, I'm looking at nothing but permanent disappearance." Kelly sat down and lost herself in the photographs of azure waters, pristine beaches, colorful temples and species of fish, flowers and trees she'd never seen before. She would quit her job for this, she silently deliberated; she would leave everything behind, her schedule, her claustrophobic flat, her few treasured possessions, wholly submitting herself to the promises of these pictures. Her mind drifted in meditative delight as she imagined the sight and sound of moonlit waves washing and breaking at midnight, the sensation of delicate breezes kissing her skin as she slept under the stars. But, they wouldn't be her stars, she realized. They would be strange stars. She would make them her stars. She imagined looking up to the Southern Cross as the distant compatriot of Cygnus.

He sat across the bistro table from her, and shifted the brochure to his direction. "Sell everything and go. Just like that." His eyes never left the picture.

"I wonder how much a hut on the seaside would cost," Kelly wondered aloud.

"Pray not as much as a partly paid-off condo, an SUV and the sorely diminished return from a ridiculous garage sale."

She glanced around her congested little flat that had been her hovel for her entire adult life thus far. "Don't you dare sell your guitar or I'll kill you personally."

"No one else would value its worth other than me."

"I know, my skates only fit my feet, they're my treasure and my escape here, but I wouldn't need them there." Kelly's mind was opening to truths that heaven could exist on Earth in many forms. "Somehow, I don't see a snorkel, mask and flippers being a fair equipment trade." She sat back and contemplated for a moment, watching him look at the photos with what she recognized as the same aching need for a promise of hope to be fulfilled. Without thinking, Kelly elucidated the bare necessities of her dream, "Your guitar, music paper, my journals, pencils and Rudy." She glanced across the table to the photos he was perusing. They even looked stunning upside down.

Rick got up to pour the tea, "Told you the kind of effect places like these can have. And we haven't even been there yet."

"You're right."

"Think we could sell our songs to anyone?" He handed her a steaming cup of mint tea.

"Think they'd be worth buying?" She didn't want to sound pessimistic.

"Definitely worth writing. That's where we have to start." He returned to his seat. "Sting used to write in Monserrat. Worked for him…until the volcano… I say Fiji."

Kelly got up, walked to her bookshelf and pulled the last of her seven-volume journal collection and began to flip through the pages. One page was marked with a folded sheet of paper, loosely inset, which she retrieved and handed to him.

He unfolded the paper and recognized it as a sheet from his telephone message pad. "Protected Kingdom, great title." He began to read her words with a thoughtful expression.

She sipped her tea and patiently studied his reaction while he read her poem a few times, actively reading more deeply between her lines each time.

He looked up at her and smiled. "Did I ever tell you I got a C in English Lit?"

"No. Don't be surprised if it doesn't make sense, very little of what I write makes sense. Good poets, on the other hand, make sense to me. Their insights are far more valuable to me than my own."

"I think I get it. Even in his fishbowl existence, Rudy's Rudy. He'd be Rudy no matter where you put him." Rick stopped to consider Kelly's possibly intended message, "Rudy needs a yard. He's never known a world beyond what he has. Can you imagine his reaction?"

Kelly said regretfully as she poured more tea, "Yeah, until he wanders off, gets lost and then we'd really be sorry,"

"Yeah, but he might not be. What else have you got for me to read?"

She picked up her journal to show him. "Total of seven of these thus far. Stay tuned, volume eight will be upon me before long." She handed the leather bound book to him. Their eyes met. He timidly accepted it as though he had just been appointed the bearer of precious parchment scrolls inscribed with testament truths of the ages. A gold satin ribbon was tucked near the end of the book. Seated sideways in his chair, he watched her walk across the flat to her bay window. She stopped in front of it and stared absently beyond the panes to the other side of Larch Street. Her hands were perched at her hips, with only her fingertips in the pockets of her drawstring pants. Her eyes couldn't focus past the glass.

He wondered if her reflection blocked her view. Feeling the weight of her book in his hands, he pondered its symbolic burden. Had he been chosen? Inquisitively, he fingered through the pages, his eyes scanned superficially. The nature of her handwriting looked neat, almost over-controlled, but there were pages where the control had escaped her. There were passages written in poetic form, others in prose, all varying in length. He was afraid to read her words on any particular page. Had she just entrusted her heart to him? He would never presume to enter her private world without her full permission; already, he sensed he occupied a foreign territory within her, and not by her choice. He deemed it a miracle that she had let him in as much as she had. Once again, it struck him that the hidden details of her history, whatever had been the compelling impetus for her to fervently fill seven of these books with her soul, didn't matter to him. But every nuance of how she felt in all its shades of gray, whatever she had written and would endeavor to write, very much did. He set the book down on the bistro table and pensively patted its cover before getting up. Switching on the small table lamp next to her sofa, he switched off the hanging lamp.

"I go to a psychiatrist," she spoke imperceptibly.

He took her hand and led her to the sofa next to him. "Does it help?"

"I think she's very good. But if you read those books, you'll see that I haven't let her do her job."

"When was the last time you saw her?"

"A couple of years ago. I don't see her regularly. We worked for about three years in the beginning after my breakdown. When she figured I was okay, we took a break for a couple of years. When things got complicated again, I went back for another year or two. And then things settled into pretty much as it is now, how I make it appear now."

"Things getting unsettled again?"

"It's never really been settled," Kelly admitted irritably.

"How do you mean?"

"She trusts I can handle life this way. She has this misconception that I suppose I've allowed her to maintain."

"That you're doing okay?" Rick attempted to follow her trail. He stroked her hair back from her ear. "You haven't been totally up front with her?"

"She can't do her job, I really haven't let her." Kelly hesitated for a moment. "I don't want her to see what's become of me. She'll never understand the pain of this derelict grief. It's beyond me."

Rick massaged her shoulder and the base of her neck.

"I can't let her do what she's been trying to do for all these years. She wants to separate me from my only out. She doesn't understand I can't survive day after day, the way she wants me to, without the only security she's trying to steal from me."

"Your security that if it ever gets too much, you can always disappear."

Kelly nodded slowly, with her eyes closed.

Rick probed further in an effort to understand her current conflicts. "Right now, you're feeling immense pressures from work, but there's far more going on. I'm just not sure whether my presence is helping or hindering you right now. I find evidence is mounting for both sides." He conveyed his confusion of her mixed signals honestly. Rick decided to ask outright, "What caused this? Who are you grieving for, Kel?"

Tears burst forth spontaneously.

Rick wanted to earnestly believe that he could be of some comfort to her, as a friend. But he began to understand that this was much too painful for her to express verbally.

"Just tell me when you're going to leave," Kelly blurted out through her tears.

"Leave? For where? Fiji?" They could leave tomorrow as far as he was concerned.

"To leave me. When is it going to happen? It's going to happen." Her voice fluttered her paranoia, fully conveying her belief that she's been cursed.

He had no idea how to ease her cynical mind. "You know, I could ask you the same thing." There, he thought, he would try to challenge her dispirited perspective, rather than enable it. "Don't you understand how senseless this train of thought is?"

"Tell me what to do, tell me how to get through this," she pleaded quietly, forcing her tears to stop.

He turned toward her and kissed her lips delicately. "Talk to me." He said as the tip of his thumb followed the line of her brow. "If talking to me proves to be of no help whatsoever, I'll live with that. I can handle it and I promise, I won't be hurt. In any case, let's work with someone who can help. Let's let your doctor do her job. Let her understand where you're at, where you've been. I'll admit, I'm not qualified here. You need to know I'm the last person to be objective right now..." He kissed her once more and then forced himself to stop.

She sat up on her sofa. How unforeseen this scenario appeared to her, that she would be engaged in this very conversation with him this particular night. The greater she estimated to be in resounding discord with herself in regard to him, the deeper she continued to delve. She rested her right arm on the back of the sofa and her fingers instinctively caressed his left earlobe. She could see by the faint lamplight that he was graying slightly at the temples. It was the first time she had noticed the gray. Studying the gentleness of the laugh lines around his eyes, she couldn't imagine living peaceably like this, feeling blameworthy for the strain that would cause every gray hair on his head and each furrow on his brow. His eyes were still so luminous.

Rick saw her complexion ashen suddenly.

Her expression had fallen away with the onslaught of Agramon. She would never survive this slow poisoning. Her stomach began to twinge and ache and she could feel the bitter sting in her eyes. The debilitating attack had begun again, *You can never win. He would never wait long enough. No one would wait long enough. You will never be cleansed. You're damaged and broken...* Kelly pulled herself up onto the sofa and huddled in a ball against him. "Talk to me," she begged desperately. "About anything. Please, now."

He held her close to him and stroked her hair. What was going through her mind, he asked himself. Was it a distraction she required? He suspected she was headed toward that dark place again. Quickly, he decided to tell her about the Sargasso Sea, a calm body of water in the central mid-Atlantic ocean, and how the temperature of this watery span was mysteriously higher than that of the circumferential ocean. He explained to her how the Sargasso plays a major role in regulating the earth's weather patterns and the flow of jet streams...that any imbalance in Sargasso's temperature and flow, due to widespread environmental changes, could result in extreme weather conditions around the planet.

She struggled to concentrate on the sound of his voice until the monster in her mind had fallen back. She hadn't processed anything he'd said. It didn't matter. She reached up to him and kissed him. His arms enfolded her, lifted her and held her tightly to him. They kissed with their whole selves as they fell back onto her sofa. Every kiss grew in its desperate search, each more powerful and more passionate than the last. His hands left her hair to love the athletically toned shape of her back and slender hips. She melted deeply into him. Her breath had deserted her and had stolen away with her heart, or maybe he had stolen it, she couldn't tell. Or perhaps her heart might have still been there but stopped beating altogether. Her rationality fully evaporated. Besieged by unrelenting twinges of tension that tightened, released then radiated deliciously through her, she no longer cared; given her choice, she preferred to die this way, in his arms rather than anywhere else.

Altogether heightened to the point of blackout by this extremely close encounter, he halted them both before he found himself incapable of controlling this evocatively accelerating passion. He cupped her face and held it just far enough away from his that he could see her clearly. Her eyes looked fiery, wild, and crazed. He drew his breaths deeply, petitioning mind strength; she will not be taken advantage of, he assertively thought, thankfully remembering those harsh yet astute and exactly chosen words of Wendy's that night at the Mercury Club. He kissed her deeply and longingly one last time and then bounded up from beneath her.

Tease of a bitch. Try again. It won't work. He won't wait... "Don't leave me. Tell me what to do if I'm doing it wrong," she pleaded, ashamed, as she watched him walk away from her. ***Baby Bitch...you'll never grow up...***

This angst was insufferable to both of them. His emotions for her were no longer in check. "This isn't right, Kel."

She heard him unlock her door to leave when she pounded her fists against her sofa cushions. "Get the hell out!" she ordered vehemently, her eyes lost in the direction of her bay window.

His voice dropped, "Give this time, we need time, we'll figure this out. But it's not gonna happen tonight."

"Get the hell out of me!" she wailed faithlessly at the ceiling. ***Little girl, Mommy's gone. Daddy's gone, little girl...little girl...say***

goodbye….   Her face was now buried in her hands, her highlighted hair hung forward in clumps. "Get the hell out of me, you asshole! Leave me once and for all!"

In a critical spark of insight, it clicked; she wasn't talking to him. He feared whom she was talking to; he was gravely concerned. All he knew was that he had to find a way to get her to her doctor, and as soon as possible. "Kel, I want your doctor's name and number, now."

"She can't help me, nobody can help me, it's too late," she mumbled through her hands, "it's too late."

"No it's not, I think she can help." Rick relocked her door. He knelt on the floor in front of her. "Look at me," Rick directed pointedly, "I think she can. But, Kel, you need to let her."

Kelly didn't respond.

"Kel, listen to me. Whatever's doing this to you, it has to stop. Don't you care what I think?"

"I want more than anything to believe what you believe," her eyes implored him more desperately than her words. "You see me."

"Yes I do," Rick stated firmly. Who he saw was a scared, haunted, innocent girl with untapped, invisibly powerful strength.

"You see me," she uttered for assurance once more as tears streamed down her cheeks.

"Whatever's troubling you, I don't understand how it operates. But I see its power. I see what it's doing to you."

"I'm so tired of this. I can't fight any more."

"I see you." He embraced her tense body, "I'm not going to leave. Go get ready for bed." He felt a surge of frustration through his veins again as she shuffled to her bathroom. He needed her psychiatrist's name. He could look up the phone number. He was keenly aware he was in no position to help her - she had stopped honestly communicating with everyone God only knows how many years ago… she admitted she hadn't been open with her doctor - he was keenly aware he was in no position to leave her. What if something happened while she was alone? Two one-way tickets to Fiji, his mind flashed, he could liquidate four thousand dollars in the morning. An additional two thousand and he could bring her psychiatrist. His mind was spinning and intuitively, he gained an understanding of how an uncountable number of hours of her life must have been spent like this, tormented, alone, hiding, tortured. Her hell was very much on this earth, spreading inside her, she was enslaved by it, no wonder she longed for heaven. How long would it take him to read her seven books to figure this out? He could read while she slept....

He awoke as dawn broke. She had spent the night closely nestled in his arms, and her sleep was less fitful than he expected. The emotional exhaustion and the accumulated effect of several sleepless nights had finally overcome her, mercifully offering with it blessed rest. He hadn't left her side the entire night, with the exception of one trip to the bathroom. He didn't want to leave her even then, especially when he saw how his momentary departure seemed to disrupt her, when she had awakened enough to realize he wasn't there. The seven books would have to wait until she expressly gave them to him. Rick rolled over to check the time on her bedside clock. It read five-thirty. He looked at her as she continued to sleep with her head resting against his ribcage, despite his rustling. He brushed her hair back from her face with his fingers. Her eyes opened partially.

"Good morning," he greeted. "How'd you sleep?"

She reflected and said with surprise, "I slept." She sat up and looked at him. His t-shirt and track pants were wrinkled and he was lying on top of her bedcovers. "I'm sorry, you didn't." She felt an immediate shame.

"I slept fine," he told her, better than he would have had he left her, "but your bed's too short, though."

"I used to love this bed when I was a kid." Kelly sounded baffled. "Now I hate it."

"I should get going. Rudy's probably in the middle of a kitty-hissy-fit, not because I'm not home, he wouldn't care about that, just worried about who'll feed him."

Kelly got out of bed and straightened her t-shirt and pyjama pants. "Have some juice or coffee, it'll just take me a minute." She headed to her kitchen.

"Kel, hey," he called to her quietly; he didn't want her to go through the trouble. She was still rooting in her cupboards when he called to her again, "Kel, don't worry." He was brushing his hair with his hands and attempted to press the obvious wrinkles out of his clothes, a wasted effort.

She poured a glass of orange juice and brought it to him.

"Thank you." He drank it down in two gulps and hugged her. "Until tonight. It's nearing the end of this hell-week of yours."

She rubbed her eyes to feel more awake. "Last day for this project, everything's got to get done today." There were probably going to be many last minute meetings scattered throughout the day.

"You'll work late tonight?"

"Don't see a way around it. Maybe it will mean I won't have a chance to think, about anything. I'll call you, at some point, I just don't know when."

"Before any of it, call your doctor," Rick enforced.

"I'll see, if there's time."

"No. That won't do. You'll call her today. Right away. I'll check in with you later this morning." He firmly kissed her cheek and made his way out the door.

May 21

Amidst the ruins

How has he found
Me
Misplaced in this murky mess?

Perched precariously
on fractured foundation,
How has he recognized
The endless tower of my soul?

How has he uncovered
Me?
Sifted through shards of fractured heart
layers of litter...
How did he find
Me
Buried so long
amidst these ruins.

Tainted

Death

Hangs on my back
Instinct commands me
To recede into

Black

stain of contagion
Hold deadly clutch
To spread wildfire
Through your innocent

Touch

not, so tainted by sorrow
Thick fusty breath
Renders me untouchable
More cruel than ...

You call out to me when it's quiet, shaking me to awaken. I will not live locked in the past, You will not die locked in the past.

I wait for sleep to come, but it won't gratify me. I can't sleep like this. But neither can I wake when my heart has sunken beneath the rusty bedsprings...

It echoes in the hollow inside me…

…because I didn't have the courage to carry out the task that I should have seen through to completion ten years ago.

…because I didn't have the courage to sever that all-important artery, because I couldn't come up with a plan for which building to jump off, or which tree to hang from.

…because I didn't have the courage to face the real pain of hell.

…because of my weakness, Wendy has suffered, now he suffers today. All who touch me will suffer the same way, if not now, then eventually. It is inevitable. Because I am weak to confront it — face to face.

Ten

THURSDAY, MAY 22

Just after eight thirty pm, the phone rang. Rick predicted it might be Kelly calling from work; he would be happy to pick her up. "Hello?" The voice on the other end was hers, but she sounded incoherent. "Kelly, where are you?" Her voice kept calling his name, slowly and weakly, and she didn't answer his question. She sounded drunk, not like herself. He immediately checked his phone display; she was calling from her flat. "Are you okay? What's wrong?" He kept asking her but all he could make out from her increasingly slurred speech was "I don't know," and what sounded like "something's wrong." He checked the time on his watch, "I'll be right there. Wait for me." He grabbed his keys and wallet and headed out the door. For the life of him, he couldn't figure out what was going on. He had left three messages for her at work, but she never returned his calls. He would risk a ticket to get there sooner, but knew all too horribly well the dangers of speeding. He pulled up on the opposite side of Larch Street. He headed to the front door of the Old Victorian and rang Kelly's buzzer. No response. He waited past another ring. Nothing. He pounded on the main door, hoping Mrs. Wiles, or another tenant might hear it through the interior vestibule door. He stepped back from the front door to see which flats had lights on. Rick then studied the panel of buzzers near the door and found the one for Mrs. Wiles. He rang it. He rang it again.

He simply wouldn't wait any longer and thought to try the back door. Just then, Mrs. Wiles opened the front door.

"Where's the fire, young man?" Her manner was controlled and matronly.

"No fire, M'am," Rick told her respectfully, "but I think there might be an emergency, I'm not sure."

"What's this all about, what's your name?"

"Rick Hutchinson, I need to get into Kelly's, the flat above you. She's in trouble." He spoke with great urgency.

"What's wrong, dear?"

"I need you to help me find out. She just phoned me and she wasn't okay. You have a key to her flat?" He encouraged her to hurry back inside and help him.

"Why, yes, I have keys for all the tenants' apartments, but I never use them...unless they mean for me to. I would never intrude on anyone's privacy..." the elderly lady justified nervously.

"Of course, I understand, but this is an emergency, please get her key, now." He pushed her to do as he said.

Rick pounded on Kelly's door while he waited for what felt like an eternity, continuing to beat loudly with his fist. She still wasn't answering. He grew scared that she couldn't get to her door. Another tenant emerged from his flat, hearing the disturbance.

"Hey! What are you trying to do, break the door down?" the young man asked.

"Exactly. Get over here," Rick ordered the boy from across the hall along side him. "What's your name?"

"Howie," the boy answered dutifully.

The two of them lined up and in one synchronized blow, the door would be out of the way.

"Wait, wait!" Mrs. Wiles called out. "I have it, I have it. These old knees just don't do it for me anymore," she flustered as she hobbled up the stairs.

Rick ran down the main stairs and grabbed the key right from the dear old lady's hand. And he was into her flat. Mrs. Wiles and Howie waited anxiously in the hall. Rick found Kelly unconscious on the floor, her journal fallen from her limp hand. The wood floor of her living room and around her bay window was carpeted in hundreds of photographs. Pictures were strewn everywhere, no less than five photo albums lay emptied around her sofa. He couldn't imagine how all this happened. He ran to her, lifted her head and shoulders up and purposefully slapped her cheek in an attempt to wake her. "Call nine-one-one!" he hollered out to the hallway. "Now! We need an ambulance." He swept her up in his arms, photos flitting down to the floor. While holding her limp weight, he deftly shoved the empty photo albums off the sofa with his foot and laid her there. Photo pocket sheets fell out as the albums hit the floor. He felt for her pulse. He couldn't find it. He could never find anyone's pulse. "God damn it, Kelly, breathe!!" He laid his ear on her chest to hear if her heart was beating. Through her t-shirt and bra, he could detect a barely audible beat. He got up to take a quick look around. On her kitchen island, he spotted a small medical prescription bottle, and several tiny tablets scattered across the counter. He picked up the bottle and read the label, "Take one tablet orally PRN – for panic. Not to exceed three tablets per 24 hours." The medication had been ordered by a Doctor Karen Lake and it was dated approximately one year prior. There were about eight tablets that he counted on the island. How many had she taken? How many would it take? He clutched the bottle in his right fist, nearly crushing it, and screamed at Howie, "Where's the goddamn ambulance?"

"It'll be here, we called, they said they'd be here!" the boy stammered, worried that his pretty neighbor, whom he noticed from the day he moved in, was dead and that the ambulance wouldn't matter. His tears fell, "Mrs. Wiles is waiting outside for them, they'll be here!" He was too afraid to step into Kelly's flat.

Rick went back to the sofa and held her motionless body in his arms. He couldn't tell, other than the faint heartbeat, that she was alive. She didn't feel warm. She felt like she was getting colder. Rick questioned the presence of mind his mother had always proudly touted he had been born with. "Hey," he called out to Howie, "do me a favor, get her blanket off her bed and bring it over here!"

Stumbling over his own feet and slipping on loose pictures, the young boy brought Kelly's bedcover and helped Rick wrap it around her. He gave Rick a look of sheer terror and ran back out into the hall.

Another minute of wait would kill him, Rick thought, if it didn't kill her first. He rocked her and spoke into her ear, "Kel, don't you do this to me. Is this your idea of a solution? Making sure you leave me before I could leave you? Please don't do this to me." Her head lay heavy in his arms. He cried puncturing tears and looking upward he said, "Take it up with me, You have got one hell of a fight on your hands." His fierce words exploded and flew heavenward. Just then, the sound of a siren approached.

There was a coordinated commotion upon the paramedics' arrival. Two medics entered, leaving the stretcher in the hallway. Mrs. Wiles and Howie clutched each other as they stood stiffly waiting for word of Kelly's condition.

One medic attended to Kelly and took her vitals after attempting to bring her around, while another asked Rick for information. He handed the paramedic the empty prescription vial and said, "When she called me, she was conscious… semi-conscious, that was around eight forty. I think she's taken these, I don't know how many, there's more on the counter."

The medic collected the remaining tablets and placed them back in the bottle; then, he made a note of it.

"By the time I got here and got in, she wasn't conscious anymore. I have no idea how many she'd have taken, if this is what did it."

"She's alive," the attending medic reported to Health Science Center, "her BP's ninety-two over fifty-seven, we have a pulse, weak but steady." He secured an oxygen mask to her face.

The medic asked Rick for Kelly's information, her name, age, Next of Kin, and about other medications she was taking. Other than her name and workplace, he couldn't supply any further information. The reality of his place in her life registered mentally, like a shot: he knew nothing about her; he only knew of her what his heart knew. And that if she were to disappear as she said she wanted to, the rest of the world would never have the chance to know the wonders of this extraordinary girl in hiding. He spied her knapsack on the floor by the door and pulled her wallet out to find an ID card in its designated place. For Next of Kin, Kelly had written the name Wendy Kaine, stating her relationship as sister next to her phone number; there was no Pearson parent listed where it should have been. His gut wrenched, the knots already there were being mercilessly tightened. He then found her health card and offered it to the medic who then questioned Rick, "Are you a relative, sir?"

"Yes. She's my cousin." His answer caught him by surprise. Presence of mind hadn't eluded him entirely.

"You found her?"

"She called me for help before she passed out."

"Okay. We need to notify next of kin."

"May I? If it's not outside protocol."

"No, go ahead" the medic surveyed his paperwork, "...tell Wendy Kaine that we're bringing her to Health Science. She can find her in emergency, they'll take it from there."

Before leaving, he grabbed Kelly's wallet, keys and journal, and placed them in her knapsack. "I'm right behind you," Rick announced as he slung the sack over his shoulder and headed down the stairs and out of the Old Victorian.

The last person Wendy ever expected to receive a phone call from was Rick. He called her from the hospital and did his best to sound calm on the line, so she wouldn't launch into hysteria. She listened carefully once he got her attention and assured her that Kelly was being taken care of, although she was currently unconscious. Wendy wrestled with the same unanswered questions that plagued him; she grew frenzied when Rick couldn't provide answers as to Kelly's condition, or what had brought on the overdose. Rick never mentioned the word overdose to her, he hadn't told her about the spilled vial of panic medication. They ended their harrowing conversation with the conclusion that Kelly would likely remain hospitalized until the doctors determined what happened and they could successfully treat her, and that she would probably need a small suitcase containing toiletries and some clothes. Wendy was already on top of it. She had a key; she would stop at Kelly's flat on the way, pick up some things for her and head directly to the hospital.

During the short drive from her apartment to Kelly's place, her guilt-ridden worry swelled to anger as she deliberated the grounds of her best friend's desperate action. Already on the verge of emotionally crumbling as she made her way to Kelly's flat, upon entering, she staggered when she saw hundreds of photographs strewn across the hardwood floor. She stumbled to the floor sobbing as her hands sifted through pictures, years and years of a history that was as close to being her own. Through her tears, she could see some photos had been partially torn, and others bent and crumpled. It seemed that every photo the Pearson family had cherished, old sienna prints of her grandparents, from her parents' youth and wedding, through Kelly's infancy and childhood, photos from their schooldays, family vacations, up to their last summer together, lay scattered on the floor. Evicted. Homeless. Each photo had been meticulously pulled from its secure place in its album. Wendy wiped her tears from her eyes with the backs of her hands. She gathered the photos into a disheveled pile to ensure that not another memory be ruined. The family picture in the silver frame lay face down on the floor beneath the window seat. She picked it up. It was intact, but the protective glass had cracked. She placed it back on the shelf by the CD player, where it belonged. Next, she closed the photo albums, five in all that she collected from around and underneath the sofa, and laid them on the window seat.

Riddled with intermingled feelings of guilt, anger, and worry, Wendy pulled out whatever comfortable clothes she could find from Kelly's chest of drawers. Finding a duffel bag under her bed, she hastily shoved the clothes and a pair of sneakers into it, and then organized needful toiletries and medications from her bathroom. Holding Kelly's bottle of anti-psychotics, she sickened herself wondering whether they would release Kelly from the hospital, or would she be committed straightaway once they learned of her previous suicide attempt. Would they commit her forever, now? What if she succeeded this time and the doctors couldn't save her? She had heard of cases where suicide victims died later while under treatment, if they didn't die right away. Why had she been so selfishly resistant to better care for her fragile friend? Why hadn't she grown up enough to pick up the phone and call Kelly, despite their differences, knowing tomorrow was a crucial day, likely the most psychologically critical day of her life? Why hadn't she done more to protect Kelly from people and situations she simply didn't have the experience to handle?

Wendy let out a grunting scream in response to her dismally evident failure as a best friend. She had to make it to the hospital before it was too late. She feared it was already too late.

At ten pm, Wendy stormed through the revolving door entrance to Health Science emergency. She headed straight through the waiting area to the admitting desk and demanded forcefully to see Kelly Pearson. She insisted to know her condition immediately, that she was the patient's sister. The admitting nurse did her best to calmly respond to Wendy's corporate-like orders, as she looked over the paperwork. The nurse explained that the patient in question was currently being treated, and there was no word as to her condition as yet. She calmly asked Wendy to have a seat.

Wendy huffed. She was scared. How could they not know how Kelly was? They were with her, weren't they? She wandered into the waiting area, securing herself with the thought that if Kelly were dead already, the nurse would have told her. Or maybe that was the attending physician's job. There was an empty seating area down a side hall, so she went in that direction. The last place she ever wanted to be was a hospital. The sight of apprehensive, drawn faces in the waiting area made her feel even more miserable, and helpless. She felt a hand on her shoulder. Wendy asked Rick impatiently, "Do you know how she is? Have they told you anything? Who's the doctor looking after her?"

He could see she could barely manage herself, let alone the gravity of this situation. "No, not yet, they're with her. That's all I know." He spoke quietly. They sat down then he asked, "You brought her stuff?"

"Yes." Wendy unzipped the sports bag and clumsily displayed the clothes and personal effects she had packed in her tizzy. "I hope I remembered everything…"

Rick put his arm around her neck and kissed the side of her head. As he made space in the sports bag for her knapsack, he said, "I have no idea what happened. She was supposed to work late tonight, but for some reason, she was already home. It looked like she had been there for a while."

"Have they called Dr. Lake? They need to call her." Wendy began to get up from her seat.

He guided her back down to her chair. "They have her name on their paperwork, so I assume they'll get in touch with her answering service right now."

"She has a pager, and she'll respond right away, she's good that way." Wendy remembered from years ago.

"Kelly has to regain consciousness before her doctor can do anything for her," Rick noted pragmatically. He had never classified himself as an impatient person. He decided that as of today, he was impatient. "Did she call you tonight?"

"No. Why were all her family photos all over the floor? Did you know she was going to flip out?"

"I don't know. And no." Her question made him remember the sight of her little living room, and finding her on the floor. "Goddamn it." His impatience was prime breeding ground for his angry frustration, "I was worried about her, but I didn't really have anything to go on."

"Did you pressure her?" Wendy asked provokingly.

"To what?" Rick's voice grew alarmingly harsh. "What's your point, Wendy?"

She stood up amidst a rising inferno inside her. He stood up after her.

"She was fine until she met you, you know," Wendy commenced. "We both were. She doesn't want you in her life. She never did, you're pushy and she isn't in any position to handle you. After everything she's been through…. But do you care? No!"

She was doing it again, he thought, creating a messy scene in a public place. "Wendy, shhh. Quiet, get a grip," Rick urged strictly.

"I will not shhh." Wendy retorted impertinently. "Did she ever tell you how her parents died? Did she ever tell you how they were killed in a high speed, head-on collision by a bastard drunk driver on Highway 3? That it happened ten years ago as of tomorrow, to the day? Did she ever tell you how she found out? She was home, alone. The cops came to her door at midnight. She was a kid. She was seventeen…." Wendy's eyes glowered. Her face was livid with rage and her expression showed an acrid pain.

The admitting nurse approached them, on a mission. "Excuse me. This is a hospital. Or need I remind you of that?" She crossly invited them both to step outdoors if they needed to.

Rick stormed through the waiting area with the sports bag in one hand, dragging Wendy by the arm with the other, and they headed out of the building. They didn't make it twenty feet past the entrance before Wendy re-ignited, "Let me guess, while we're at it, she never told you how she tried to kill herself three weeks later! I found her!" she wailed her horrifying memories at him. "She's done this before! She tried to OD, just like tonight. Her life became hell because of that bastard! As a result, my life is hell! So just who do you think you are, Doctor Big Shot? Pushing your way into her life! Toying with her like she's some kind of plaything to you? Some next conquest?"

Wendy was crying and beating on his chest and arms with her fists. "I should have known it was just a matter of time..."

He didn't even try to stop her from pounding him. People were walking by, glaring curiously at the scene. He just grabbed her around her shoulders and pulled her into him. She remained against him for several minutes, crying. There was nothing he could say or do. His own tears flowed, and he let them fall so he wouldn't have to let her go. His only comforting thought was that in what might have been her final moments of desperation, Kelly had called him for help. She had called him.

Within the hour, Arthur and Marilyn Kaine arrived. Wendy introduced Rick to her parents as Kelly's new friend. While Wendy sat, comforted by her parents' presence, Rick checked at the nurse's station to see if there was any update on Kelly. Without any new information, he felt at a loss as to what to do with himself. He began to restlessly walk the hospital hallways, from the emergency ward to the main lobby. The aroma of coffee had subconsciously led him in that direction. He located the Tim Horton's and purchased a large black coffee. He stood there, absent and inert, for several minutes, subconsciously taking in the warmth of the coffee cup. His hands still felt the way she felt before they took her.

"Rick?" He heard his name being called. He turned around to see Mike, who was on duty that night. His best friend was clad in typical hospital attire with a stethoscope in the pocket of his white overcoat. "What are you doing here? Are you okay?"

"No," Rick answered flatly. "A friend of mine's been admitted, I have no idea how she is. She's in the ER."

"Which friend? The cute one you told me about?"

"Yep."

"What's she in for?"

"Don't know. Detox? Possible OD," he answered blankly. "I haven't got a clue what they do in a situation like this."

"Good Lord, she's on drugs?"

"No, prescription, panic meds," Rick began. "Except, I don't think she OD'd, I think it might have been an accident."

"Why do you say that?"

"Because she called me right before she passed out and all I could make out was 'Something's wrong' and 'I don't know'. By the time I got there, she was unconscious."

"Previous episodes of panic?" Mike thought aloud, "Obviously, if she has meds for it," he logically concluded. "What's her history overall?"

"Tragic."

"Medically," Mike clarified.

Rick shook his head and sipped his coffee, which had cooled enough to drink. "Just found out. Suicide attempt ten years ago when she was seventeen." He took another sip of coffee. "She told me a couple of days ago that she's on anti-depressants, anti-psycho stuff and something about tranquilizers, which I assume the panic meds were."

"Possibly." Mike thought for a moment. "There could have been an unexpected contraindication, with all the medications she's taking. Is she in therapy?"

"Off and on. Another thing I just found out is that her parents were killed, no warning, car collision, and that's what's been heading all this up. She was seventeen, that was ten years ago." It occurred to him that he might have said that already.

"Post-trauma. Makes sense," Mike stated his professional opinion. "Does she ever have flashbacks?"

"Panic attacks, nightmares…times when she zones out, like something's abducted her."

Mike reassured, "PTSD-like symptoms, post-traumatic stress disorder, is treatable. Takes work, but with meds and therapy, very treatable, high success rate, good prognosis."

"Patient needs to be on board, though, right?"

"Very much so. Most therapies, especially cognitive-based ones need full patient cooperation, belief in the therapy, belief in themselves and their safety."

Rick's heavy sigh brought with it only a small fraction of relief. A very large piece of Kelly's puzzle had been missing all along. He didn't understand why she staunchly refused to cooperate with her doctor. But she was just a kid when it happened, he thought; she likely had lost trust in everything and everyone because of the very nature of the accident. "Could a ten-year anniversary date trigger it all over again?"

"Sure. Just about anything, practically speaking, has the capability to be a trigger for post-trauma, depends on the case and the circumstances, but just so you know, anniversary dates of the trauma are near top on the list."

Mike escorted Rick back to emergency and agreed to check on Kelly's status, to ease his friend's mind. They parted ways when Mike proceeded through to the restricted care unit to seek out the attending doctor, and Rick returned to the main waiting area where the Kaines were seated. He felt awkward being there with them, but social discomfort paled in comparison to everything else he was feeling. Rick spoke briefly yet congenially with Arthur, mostly about their respective careers, while Wendy and her mother talked. But Rick didn't feel like engaging in any form of conversation. He didn't even feel like listening but found himself a hapless witness to the dynamics between Wendy and her mother, who were both seated across from him. He observed both women to be too highly charged; to him, it appeared that each fueled the other's fire. He couldn't assess whether this mother and her daughter were each other's emotional accelerants unwittingly or purposely. To him, what could have remained a restrained, controlled discussion grew into a heated, argumentative debate about Kelly's deteriorating state of mind that led up to today. Wendy proceeded to justify to her mother that Kelly had been losing it for several weeks now, that there were circumstances beyond her control and influence at play that she was certain contributed to it. Her mother tried make it all better by expressing that Wendy clearly could have done more to help had Kelly been more open and communicative, had she asked for help, but it was too late now. Rick noticed how carefully Marilyn chose her words, and how she never really looked directly in the eyes of any person she was speaking to.

He had heard enough. He was ready to get up and walk away. Dr. Ezat Manka appeared from the care unit with a brief update. He first confirmed that the Kaines were Kelly's family, as listed. Then he began to explain that Kelly was under his care and although she was still unconscious, a preliminary blood chemistry screen indicated that what she did have in her bloodstream at elevated levels was the panic medication from the vial identified in her apartment. It didn't appear that she had ingested a dangerous dosage, just one high enough to put her out. She had taken more than a patient of her size, and considering her other medications, should have taken at once, pharmacologically. They determined this with the aid of her attending psychiatrists records. There appeared to be no signs of toxic contraindications with other medications she was currently taking. They had placed her on intravenous saline and she would be kept indefinitely. They would need to await further tests that would take place through the night, which would reveal the status of her liver and kidney functions, and her electrolyte balance, and how the excess medication was being expelled from her system. In short, her vitals were stable and she would need to basically sleep off the meds. He didn't offer a time estimate as to when she would wake up.

Rick and the Kaines weren't sure whether this report meant they could relax or not. Dr. Manka had spoken calmly and clearly; he seemed to be very much in knowledgeable control of Kelly's condition. After he left, they discussed and re-hashed what the doctor had explained, careful to restate his words exactly, for fear that they not misinterpret what they had just been told. Arthur and Marilyn speculated the report thus far signified good news, overall, and that Kelly wasn't in any immediate danger. After all, as Wendy cogently pointed out, she was being treated with saline, and that she would probably sleep through the night; heaven knows when she last had a good night's sleep. On this point, all the Kaines were willing to rest.

Rick slouched silently in his chair, lost in a vortex of thoughts. He had mentally vacated the discussion shortly after it began. Pharmacology and toxicology might be Mike's and this doctor's areas of expertise, but they weren't his, they never would be. The medical details of how the doctors were treating Kelly escaped him; there was no urgent need for him to know what tests were being done and the various chemical processes involved. He could barely think a straight line. He had no intention of assigning blame or judgment in this vastly convoluted situation he was only on the verge of understanding. He wanted her to wake up. He wanted to hear from her, and her only, what exactly had been going through her mind, what had brought her to this. If he was even in part the cause of this horror, then he needed to hear it from her. His mind waffled between imagining his life with her in Fiji, and imagining his life anywhere without her. He felt nauseous, and needed to get some air. He walked behind Wendy who headed to the front entrance to see her parents off. Rick carried Kelly's bag wondering if they would ever admit visitors.

Wendy spoke directly to him for the first time since her accusation. "Are you going to stick around?"

Rick nodded. "Will you call her work tomorrow and let them know she won't be coming in?"

"What do I tell them?" Wendy asked surreptitiously.

"Tell them she has the flu and she'll be in when she'll be in." Rick watched mist droplets fall around a mercury street lamp. It was difficult for them to look at each other, let alone try to speak as friends.

"I'll stop in tomorrow morning before work to see how she is," Wendy announced her plan.

"Call first, make sure she's here."

Wendy gasped.

He clarified upon her horror-struck expression, "I mean, in case they release her, or move her, or something."

"Oh, yeah, good point." Wendy paused before she headed to her car, "None of us know who you are. Who are you to her, anyway?"

Rick looked back at the mercury lamp across the driveway; he didn't answer her question. She was the last person he wanted to be talking to.

"I mean, what role do you think you play in her life?" She assumed he didn't understand what she meant.

"Whoever she needs me to be. No conditions." He went back inside.

Rick returned to the waiting area along the side hallway, where he sat for what felt like hours. He remembered he had Kelly's journal, the one she was clutching when he found her. He contemplated digging it out of her knapsack, permission or not. He hadn't felt this indecisive in years. He realized he had forgotten what hopelessness and confusion felt like, and how daunting even the most minor decision could be. He kicked the bag, which had been by his feet, underneath his chair.

Mike returned between rounds and sat down next to him. "I just checked on your friend. They're going to be moving her to a room on the third floor for the night."

"Will they release her in the morning?"

"Can't say. That will depend mainly on what her psychiatrist orders, and those things can't be determined until she wakes up and they can evaluate her," Mike informed. "But, you can see her briefly once they get her moved. It will still be a few minutes yet. She'll probably be out like a light."

Rick processed Mike's words slowly. "I'm in trouble." He sounded heavily burdened.

"Why?"

Rick stared at the geometric pattern on the linoleum floor. It blurred into shifting overlapping diamonds when he crossed his eyes. "I might be responsible for this."

"Doubt it, from what you've told me thus far."

"I can't be sure. Something I said. Something I did. Something I didn't do. I don't know." He rubbed his eyes.

"Are you involved with her?"

"No," he answered with conviction, "yes," he continued ambiguously as he looked at his best friend, "but not exactly in that way." Rick was silently relieved Mike was still on duty.

"Okay." Mike was truly perplexed by Rick's two-sided answer. When Rick was in love, it was definite, obvious to himself and to any casual bystander. His approach with women was very no holds barred, right from the onset. At least, that's what Mike remembered about the way it was with Rebecca.

"Tell me something," Rick was hoping for sage advice from his friend who had been married for eight years. "When you met Tasha, how well did you know each other before you were sure?"

"I knew the chances were good when we met, it was worth the risk. Ask Natasha and she'll tell you something very different. I think I need to meet this girl. And you say you're not romantically involved with her?"

"This isn't about that," Rick mumbled as he repeatedly tapped his heel on the floor.

"You sure?"

"Shut up already. Can you be something other than an idiot right now?" He shut his eyes for a moment then blurted, "It's beyond that." Rick no longer recognized himself. "I'm making no sense."

"You're right. This is definitely not your prescribed M.O. when it comes to women," Mike said lightly as he leaned back in his chair.

"Thank God," Rick sighed with his forehead in his hands. He pressed his fists against the arms of the chair then stood up to pace the geometric diamonds. "Explain this to me."

"What's to explain? So it's different with her. Don't waste your energy fighting it. Work with it," Mike advised.

He felt like tearing at his hair. "If she wanted to kill herself, she wouldn't have left eight freakin' pills behind, right? Wouldn't she have taken them all?"

"You think she was trying to kill herself?" Mike probed.

Rick stopped and turned, and his fist gently met the hallway wall in a slow, well-controlled manner. "Don't know what she was thinking." He rested his back against the wall.

"From what I could tell of her tox report, there wasn't enough in her to do it. So either this was a freak accident, a mistake, or at most a call for help. I'd say that before I'd say a genuine attempt at suicide. Delete that from the record. Not my department, all that's up to her psych assessment. But you know what I think, if it helps."

Rick peered around the door to room thirty-one forty-seven. The night nurse had given him permission to visit quietly. There were four beds in the room and Kelly's was closest to the door. There appeared to be only one other patient in the room, at the opposite corner. He stepped in silence and placed her sports bag next to the bedside table. As Mike predicted, she was still in a deep sleep; she still looked like an angel to him in the orange glow of the stats monitor. He tenderly kissed her forehead and observed her peaceful countenance. There was an oxygen saturation monitor on her finger that sent a signal to screen; it read ninety-eight percent. Her heart rate was up to fifty-nine beats per minute, which was fine for an athlete of her caliber, he surmised, and her blood pressure read one hundred-one over sixty. These seemed to be satisfactory statistics, given how weak her heartbeat was when he found her. He made a mental note to ask the nurse when she came by on her next round.

He picked up a high-backed chair located against the wall near the bedside table and gingerly placed it near her bed, orienting it so that he could look upon her. He sat down and rested his right arm on her bedside. His hand supported his head; he studied her face again. Would she dream under the influence of that much medication? He assumed that if the drugs were designed to quell her recurring nightmares, they must also prohibit any dreams of hope, of happiness, of bliss. But she told him the nightmares kept coming. He reached into her bag, and from the knapsack, he retrieved her journal. He laid it on his lap, and held her hand. It still felt cold. He lifted her blanket and tucked her arm underneath, and from the edge of the bed, he reached within to warm her hand. His fingers instinctively stroked hers; he sought her tacit permission, he needed to let her know she wasn't alone. There was no way for him to know how far away she was at that moment.

With his left hand, Rick followed the feel of the satin ribbon bookmark and opened her journal to that page. The golden glow from the stats monitor combined with the ambient hallway night lighting provided barely enough for him to read by. Suspecting he needed reading glasses anyway, he decided that understanding her was very much worth the additional strain.

Over a period of three hours, he read. He couldn't identify what prompted him to begin at the last entry of her book and read back to the beginning; it just made sense for him to do so. His hand never released hers for longer than it took him to turn a page. Her hand had warmed significantly over the night.

Somewhere between three and four am, he must have slept. Rick felt a slight tug on his hand. His eyes opened without delay and he sat up on the edge of the chair. He squeezed her hand in response, "Kel? Hey, Kel." He stood up to look at her eyes. There was activity beneath her lids and he wondered if he should alert the nurse. He placed his hand on her cheek and she responded with a mournful moan. A wincing expression appeared on her face and she was squeezing her eyelids as if to will them to close tighter. He kissed her cheek and whispered in her ear, "Kel, it's okay, you're safe. It's me, Rick. You're okay." Her expression relaxed. "Nothing to worry about," he whispered.

She squirmed and her eyes began to flutter, as though trying to open. He continued to bring her around, "Kel, I'm here, you're safe, you're in the hospital…"

Her eyes opened. She tensed up when she took her first look around, in the darkness. There was little she could discriminate, but she felt the intravenous needle in her left arm; confirming its presence upset her. Rick sat at her side and kept her from tugging at the I-V by caressing her right hand. "It's okay, it's only saline, no truth serum."

Kelly smiled. Her hands reached up to his face and he bent to kiss her. "I'm so sorry," she stammered. Her head felt swelled like a balloon, floating high above her. Her thoughts felt distant and suppressed, her mind felt shrouded in a thick veil of fog.

"Nothing to be sorry for. I'm the one who needs to apologize to you."

"Why?" Kelly asked breathily. She struggled to keep her eyes open.

"Too many reasons."

"No…no. No reasons," she muttered as she fell asleep again. When her eyes reopened, she continued, "I remember." Teardrops began to stream down her cheeks, landing in her hair and on the flattened pillow beneath her head. "They're gone. They're gone."

"I know, Kel." Her arms wrapped around his neck and he pulled her upright enough to hold her. "I know." His hands rubbed the bare skin of her back, trying to soothe her heartache. She clutched him as she cried. He noticed that her hospital gown had never been properly tied behind her, so he remedied that as he held her in the early morning's beckoning twilight. "Your mom and dad are gone. But, you're not, and neither am I."

"Are they going to put me away?" Kelly asked apprehensively, like a frightened child in his arms.

He pulled back far enough to see her face. "Why would they do that?"

"They can, you know." Kelly grew agitated.

"No, they can't," he argued pragmatically.

"They know my history. They'll think I did this on purpose."

"You didn't do this on purpose. I know that."

She began to cry again, "I never meant…"

"I know," he pacified her. "Dr. Lake's going to see you, probably today, and you tell her that. Tell her everything."

"She won't believe me. What if they don't believe me?" Kelly trembled.

Rick picked up her journal and went through the pages with her, "The proof is in here, in your handwriting, and in the sincerity of your own words. They can't ask for more honesty than that." He handed her the journal.

Her expression became downcast. "What's in here could put me away."

"No, Kel. What's in there tells the story of your strength."

May 22

"My future will not copy fair my past" – Elizabeth Barrett Browning

Not if I have anything to say about it.
I have looked upon this sonnet I don't know how many times in the past
decade. I discovered EBB while I was still in the hospital after I tried to
free myself, the summer of my seventeenth year. This one in particular
spoke such hope for me when I was trapped, expected to carry out this
testing life sentence. That one need only will the dream, and the dream will
be. Let it be that the motivated act of writing, applying words to paper
invokes the dream, justifies it, and promotes its materialization.

"Lo! I have seen the eyes of my angel," and he looks upon me with hope for
my future.

Memories' Revenge…

Images Alive
Sounds Too Familiar
Apparitions Flash
Buried Memories…

Waking Dreams
Of Madness Rape
And Assail My Mind
In the Blink of an Eye…

Not one day more. The time has come. I have no choice, yet I choose my freedom. I will face it all no matter what the cost. I intend to walk on imbued with fortitude and the certain knowledge that I no longer enabled this oppression, but that I chose the road of freedom. I want for her to see that I am not weak. I need for him to know.

Flashing red and blue lights in our driveway　　　and on our street
The reverberating ring of our two-note doorbell
Ominously secured, plastic faces　　　their static, porous eyes

Crushing
Freezing
Choking

The smell of the funeral home
sickening perfume   stinking lilies carpet deodorizer   candle wax

Captive
brown stained oak caskets   brass handles, brass hinges

Swarms of them
                mingling bodies
prattling chattering babbling   they wouldn't shut up.
for hours on end

hollow and metallic
They wouldn't stop smothering me their fingertips burnt like ice
asphyxiation

                                No breath
gray latex
                                eyelids closed to the world
no expression
            no motion
                    no emotion
I didn't know who they were
Don't cry, baby, don't cry

                            that is not my mother
                            that is not my father

My walls are closing in…
warping and enveloping.…
blackness all around
I'm suffocating
            Choking on
            billowy white satin

Eleven

FRIDAY, MAY 23

"I don't want to see anyone, no more doctors, interns, residents or whatever the hell they are." Kelly rubbed her temples; the blurry vision still hadn't gone away.

Seated at the edge of her bed, Rick reminded her she still had to wait for test results and a visit from Dr. Lake, but now that the I-V was removed, she was one step closer to freedom. And that Wendy was planning to stop by on her way to work. "When she gets here, I'll head home to check on Rudy and take a shower..."

"And shave." Kelly stroked the prickly stubble on his cheek. She was tired of waiting.

"And then I'll be back," he smiled.

"To get me out of here, right?"

"To take you home." Rick observed her attention shift to the door of her hospital room.

Wendy entered tentatively. "Hey," she greeted quietly, with a half-smile.

Kelly shifted in her bed nervously while adjusting her bedcovers and hospital gown, "Can you give us just another minute?"

Beset, Kelly then groaned quietly to Rick, "I don't want to see her."

Wendy saw Kelly's eyes meet Rick's. "Um, sure, whatever," she hesitated at first then promptly left the room.

"Nonsense. She's worried sick about you, let her see you're okay."

"I don't want her to see me like this." She tugged the neckline of the faded, institutional cotton gown.

He reached into her sports bag and pulled out a stretch-knit black top, matching pants and some fresh underwear. "Here. No reason you have to make that kind of fashion statement," he said as he pointed to her gown, "Not if you don't want to."

"I can't talk to her, she won't listen anyways."

Rick pulled the privacy drape around her bed so she could get changed. With his back turned to her, he searched in the sports bag for her hairbrush. She dressed carefully, occasionally catching her balance against the bedrail.

"You don't have to talk to her about anything you don't want to." He fished out her brush and her lipstick and handed them to her.

"Easy for you to say." There was no mirror nearby.

"Kel, she just needs to know that you're okay, chances are she won't stay that long. Besides, Dr. Lake is supposed to arrive pretty soon for your evaluation. So get over it, she's the one you do have to talk to."

If today was to be the start of the rest of her life, she wasn't looking forward to it. And she hated putting on lipstick blind. "And what am I supposed to tell her?" Kelly sat upon her bed cross-legged, resting her head in her hands.

"Everything." Rick checked his watch. It was eight forty-five am.

Kelly anxiously looked away from him, toward the window. "Everything?"

"Yep, and don't leave anything out."

She massaged the balls of her feet, utilizing nervous energy. "What if your name comes up?"

"Good." He sat with her once again and rubbed her feet.

"But there are things I haven't even told you ... yet." Her voice faded.

"You're lucky, I don't charge by the hour. But, she does."

Kelly looked at him and smiled, then looked away again.

"Wendy's waiting," he reminded as he pointed at the door.

"Is my lipstick okay?"

"Yes," he looked at her flirtatiously, "but it won't be if I don't go." He made her smile again briefly. "You have my number, right?"

She picked up her journal and flipped it open to the last page. Stuck upon it was the little yellow square of notepaper. "Thank you," Kelly said.

"For what?"

"For…" She shrugged her shoulders and exhaled her sense of futility. Looking down at her feet again, tears began to fall. Within a minute, he would be gone, and she would be left alone to deal with the looming trials she knew she wasn't prepared to handle. She still felt dead to the world, in so many ways.

Wendy had been growing impatient in the hallway, unable to hear their conversation clearly past the orderlies' clatter of breakfast trays. She wondered what they could possibly be talking about, and when they'd be finished; all she knew is that ever since Rick showed up, Kelly had withdrawn from her. She peered into the room to see the drape partially pulled open and Rick walking away from Kelly who was resolutely wiping tears from her cheeks. Wendy speculated as to what he'd said or done to make her cry.

Rick walked right past Wendy without looking at her.

She turned to watch as he left the room; he didn't look back to her. Wendy stared at the floor for a moment, recalling the vehemence of her accusation the previous night.

Kelly noticed that neither Rick nor Wendy made eye contact with each other, let alone exchanged a greeting; this caused her a fleeting concern that her mind was unable to tenaciously grasp for any longer than a second or two.

Wendy set the small houseplant she was holding on the bedside table. From her shoulder bag, she pulled out a new leather-bound and gold-embossed journal, identical in style to Kelly's collection, except this one was deep red in color. "They didn't have any brown ones left at our bookstore this morning, I hope that's okay."

"Red is great, thanks." Kelly leafed through the book of pristine, untouched pages that would read the beginning of the rest of her life. Volume eight.

"Mom and dad plan to stop by this morning too."

Kelly nodded uncomfortably, sensing Wendy's eyes scan her with disparagement.

"So, are you going to be okay, now?"

It was her way of asking whether she did this on purpose. "I'm fine, a bit groggy, though." Kelly reached behind her for her pillow and placed it on her lap.

Wendy stood next to the bed. "I called Paul and told him you had the flu." She sat upon the bed facing her and yanked the pillow out from under Kelly's hands and began to fluff it, "And that you'd be in sometime next week when you were better. I called the arena, too, but I guess sessions there are over pretty soon." She occupied her attention by glancing around the hospital room and at the other sleeping patient. "You know, Franklin's been calling me nearly every day now for the past week. He's been leaving messages on my machine that he wants to see me. The guy's persistent."

"Have you called him back?"

"No. He's perpetually heartbroken by his past. He doesn't know what he wants."

"Do you know what you want?"

"I want call-block."

Kelly shook her head solemnly. Even through the fog, Wendy horned through loud and clear.

"Seriously. I don't want to have to deal with him now, on top of everything else." Wendy fixed her sight on the bandage that covered Kelly's arm, where the I-V had been inserted. "Anyway, all men seem to do is make women's lives miserable."

Kelly stole her pillow back, repositioned it behind her and reclined. She closed her eyes for a moment and took in a deep, slow breath. Her thoughts floated amidst echoes of Rick's gentle voice to the ice surface. She could feel her body hovering ever so slightly above the bed. Her mind began to swirl away until Wendy's voice broke the ephemeral peace.

"I think we should dispense with them altogether. What do you say? You and me, we'll go on a cruise, or we'll go to Europe and kick around for a little while, just us girls," Wendy suggested enthusiastically. "No hassles, no worries, no men," she waved her hands decisively. "It'll do us good."

"I'm not going on a cruise. I'm not going anywhere." Kelly slurred as she forced her eyes to stay open.

"Come on, Kelly. We haven't been on a trip in ages," Wendy egged on.

"I'm not going anywhere."

She watched Kelly look away from her. "Okay, forget the trip. Forget Franklin, forget Rick. It will be just you and me, from here on in. That way, I can keep my eye on you," Wendy pledged possessively.

"Forget it!" Kelly shouted as Wendy's distrustful tone caused her to sit upright. "I have no intention of going anywhere." She spoke with purpose, determined to get through Wendy's stubborn mindset. "As far as you're concerned, as far as I'm concerned, you are off the hook, once and for all. From today on, you don't have to watch over me anymore, I don't want you to keep an eye on me, protect me, worry about me, care about me anymore, not from this moment on. You are off the hook."

It took some time for Wendy to process all that Kelly said. "You're still stoned from the overdose, obviously," Wendy pointed out as she stood up, "this isn't you talking."

"For the first time, Wendy, I am talking." Kelly rested her forehead in her hands. "Damn it! Why don't you listen when I'm telling it to you straight? You certainly can't read between the lines. You've waited ten years to be let off the hook, so I'm doing it. You're free from this. I am deeply sorry for ruining every single minute of everyday of your life of these last ten years." Her voice dwindled.

"Kelly, for Christ's sake, look at you. You're in the hospital, you tried to kill yourself again. You're clearly not well. You're not being rational. You haven't been since...."

"That's right, I'm your irrational, fragile, helpless friend you just can't seem to get rid of. You just can't wait to get rid of. Think whatever you want. I don't want this guilt anymore. I can't live another day with it."

Wendy's face reddened as she stared back into Kelly's distant eyes. She couldn't believe what she was hearing; was this what Kelly and Rick were discussing when she arrived? Was that why they made her wait outside, so they could privately plan this brash dismissal of hers? "I'm going to call the nurse." Wendy turned toward the door.

"Call the nurse, call the doctor. Call Dr. Lake, in fact, don't bother, she's already on her way. However I manage from this day forward, I'll do on my own, with advice from professionals."

"Like Doctor Ricky?" Wendy charged.

"Whatever is between Rick and me is between us and us alone."

"You can't even see it. He's manipulating you...you're under his power, you have been ever since..." Wendy threw up her hands.

"Think whatever you're capable of," Kelly grew tired, "this is beyond you, way beyond your immature concepts of...." her sentence stopped short when her psychiatrist entered the room.

Dr. Lake sensed the tension immediately. "Sorry, Kelly, I seem to have interrupted your visit with Wendy."

"No, Dr. Lake," Wendy responded curtly, "you didn't interrupt, we're finished." Defeated, Wendy looked back to Kelly, "Clearly, it's beyond me."

Wendy marched coldly past Dr. Lake looking to exit the building as quickly as her feet would move her. As she awaited the elevator with her arms folded and her right foot tapping out her accelerating heart rate, she insistently reminded herself that Kelly was still under the influence of the overdose, that once it wore off, she'd be back under the influence of Rick. For ten years, she had been looking to throw her life away; eventually, Kelly would succeed. Wendy congratulated herself over the fact that she would no longer have to be a party to it when it happened again. After everything she had done for Kelly in the last decade, year in and year out, in fact it was Kelly's level of immaturity, her callous ungratefulness that was the real issue. As far as she was concerned, Kelly was someone else's problem now. She was officially off the hook. A teardrop fell to the elevator floor as she stepped in. She pressed the button for the hospital lobby.

"Plenty of rest, fluids and I'm to remain calm," Kelly broadcasted to Rick her doctors' parting orders as the elevator doors sealed behind them on Oakton Gate Tower's tenth floor.

Rick shook the excess water from the retracted umbrella before unlocking his door. "Very do-able. Someone else is waiting to check on you, but I guarantee you, he's no doctor."

Rudy meowed when Kelly entered, and promptly abandoned all intentions of escaping the front door boundary to explore the main hallway. She picked him up and cuddled him warmly, offering a simulated purr to get him going. "I've missed you. Yes, I have." She let the cat jump to the floor. "I have to start therapy next week," she redirected to Rick. "Two sessions a week for the next while."

"You got off easy. How long was Dr. Lake there?"

"Over two hours, with me doing most of the talking."

"The way it should be." Rick smiled as he took her knapsack and sports bag into the bedroom.

She met him in the kitchen. "I wasn't sure they'd release me."

"I was." He began to select sandwich items from his fridge, "Chicken or ham?"

"Ham, only if you have that amazing mustard. Just after I had called you to come get me, Wendy's parents showed up."

"I know, they were with you when I arrived. I waited out in the hall."

"How long were you waiting?" Kelly began to separate leaves of lettuce and wash them. She would slice the tomatoes next.

"Until they left. How'd that go?" Rick cut Swiss cheese into sandwich size widths.

"Hmm, fine, I guess. It was nice that they came by, but they didn't have to." She filched a chunk of cheese.

"You're not close to them, I take it."

"Not really, I mean, they've been great all these years, I wouldn't have managed without them, but. . .I'm not their daughter." She noticed the mustard didn't have the kind of tasty zing it did the last time she tasted it.

Rick wondered who she was close to. "What about grandparents, aunts, uncles? I just assumed you had relatives around here that you see."

"My grandparents have all passed on. We lost my grandmother on my father's side when I was little, I don't even remember her. Then grandpa died when I was in junior high school. Ever since grandma died, grandpa just went downhill. It was a wonder he lived as long as he did without her." She carried the sandwiches to the dining table.

Rick brought glasses of orange juice. "What about your grandparents on your mom's side?"

"I lost them both in the last five years. They had to live through my mom's death. They were in Alberta with my aunt and uncle. I don't really know them either, or my cousins. They all came for the funeral but it wasn't like I was close to them."

Rick wondered what the point of family was as he picked at lettuce that had fallen out of his sandwich onto his plate. Wasn't it your family that was to be of support at times like these, independent of time or space or circumstance; especially for a newly orphaned teen? His thoughts then gravitated toward his father.

"Right after my parents died, I had gone to stay with my aunt and uncle in Edmonton. I was there for a week and then I left. I couldn't take it. They couldn't take it, either. My younger cousins were oblivious to everything and all I remember was being forced to listen to heavy metal music. I hated it."

"Careful. You're dating yourself, honey."

Kelly laughed, "I know. Bad decade, all around. They're probably great cousins, great people. I was spaced at the time. Everything was out of control, nothing was real."

"Did you come back and finish grade twelve, or was it grade eleven?"

"I came back. Grade twelve. And no, I didn't finish." Kelly shoved her chair back and excused herself from the lunch table to get a glass of water. "Gosh, I am so thirsty."

"Keep drinking lots of fluids to flush out your system. Then what?"

"Wendy's family took me in and I began grief counseling. I couldn't go back to classes. My high school graduated me anyway, but I never went to graduation. They pro-rated my marks I had earned up till this day, May twenty-third, ten years ago, and exempted me from the exams I missed. I think I had a ninety-three average, or was it ninety-one?" Kelly shrugged her shoulders, "Who cares." She rested her forehead on her hand. She was done talking for now.

"You need to go back to bed."

"I feel zonked."

"You looked zonked. In a good way." Rick grinned.

Rudy approached Kelly's chair and meowed to her. She picked him up and placed him in her lap. He was intrigued by her unusual scent as he began to sniff her t-shirt. Kelly smelled her forearm, then she extended it to Rick, "Do I smell like hospital?"

"Yeah. A bit," he cringed, "but in a good way."

"Shut up," she smirked. "Could I go for a bath?"

"Of course. Your lavender oil should still be in the drawer, somewhere. That should drown out any institutional aroma."

"Can I give you these clothes to run through the dryer to get this horrible smell out of them?"

"Tell you what, I'll do a whole wash load. Go ahead and put what you've got on now in the washer. You can wear something of mine if you need to." He was worried she might fall asleep in the tub.

Lavender, like sandalwood, had an immediate effect on her. The hot bathwater relaxed her and her hair felt washed clean of institutional toxicity. She hadn't been in a hospital in over nine years. She intended to never be in one again, not if she could help it, unless it was for life-giving purposes. She heard the door squeak open and from just beyond the bath curtain, she could hear a chirping purr. She slid the curtain over and Rudy's pink nostrils picked up the steamy scent of lavender as he adroitly jumped upon the tub ledge and crouched comfortably. Kelly sunk deeper into her bath.

"You're not passed out and drowning in there, are you?"

She heard his voice from the hall. "No, still awake. But not for long."

He knocked before stepping in to leave her fresh towels, a clean t-shirt and a pair of drawstring shorts he knew would be entirely too big for her.

"I'll be out in a second." Kelly peered out from behind the bath curtain.

"If you take your time, I can check in on you again." He watched the beads of water on her face roll down to her shoulders, and how she swept her wet hair back and pulled and twisted it into a side ponytail to wring out the water. He needed her to be safe. "Off to make the bed for you."

"Oh, the couch is fine for me."

"No couch, no arguments."

"Rick, seriously, you haven't slept for the last couple nights either, you need to rest and that couch is long enough for me."

"Anything else?" He tossed the towel toward her.

"Yes. Got a hair dryer?" She heard him fiddling around in the cupboard, then the door closing. She lifted the drain stop and the bath water began to murmur and gurgle out of the tub.

The rain fell off and on all afternoon and evening. When Kelly awakened, she could hear the faint tapping of computer keys in the living room. His bedside clock read seven-twenty; she had slept for over six hours. She shuffled down the hall to where he was working.

"Hey there, any nightmares?" Rick rotated around on his office chair.

"No. I don't even think I rolled over." She sat on the edge of the couch and faced his workstation. "I slept solid. What are you doing? Didn't you rest?"

"I did, for a good long while. I kept the bedroom door shut so Rudy wouldn't crawl all over you. Now, I'm dealing with work…the wonders of telecommuting. I made some phone calls, got all sorts of things done." He whirled around in his chair as his computer system powered down.

"Are you going to take me back now?"

"No. You're staying here."

"Oh." Her thoughts crawled at a snail's pace, "Why?"

"Because."

She continued to look at him, pressing for more explanation. "Because," he drawled with professorial expression, "I talked to Dr. Lake as she was leaving from your evaluation."

"Really? I didn't know she talked to you. How did she know who you were?"

"Wendy's folks were in visiting with you, and when she was done signing your release at the nurses' station, I introduced myself."

Kelly raised her eyebrows. "Brave boy."

Rick laughed. "She didn't slap me or order me arrested, so I know you haven't told her everything. Anyway, I asked her if it would be okay to bring you here, and she said you shouldn't be alone for the next little while."

Kelly leafed through the TV Guide movie section, "Do we get HBO?"

"Yep. And I told her that I figured your flat wouldn't be the best place for you right now."

Without emotion, she recalled the events of her last evening in her flat. They spoke no more of it, or her morning meetings at the hospital.

Her eyes opened. Her senses seemed sharper yet she couldn't assess where exactly she was, in the blackness of night. But she knew her heart was being smothered from inside even though she couldn't really feel it. The anxiety had returned, as she knew it would, it was only a matter of time. She lay awake in his darkened bedroom, with only the red glow of his LCD clock on the bedside table. Her hand reached out to the far side of his bed and skimmed between the sheets. It felt cool and crisp where the covers were hardly disturbed. As her eyes adjusted, she could see the corners of the family photo frames on his dresser reflecting the city lights that filtered through the bedroom window blinds onto them. She thought about Rebecca, imagining how a woman she'd never met, no longer alive, would feel about her being in his bed. She sat up and put her feet on the floor. Her hair hung over her forehead; habitually, she brushed her fingers over her crown. She sat there for what seemed like an hour, concentrating on her breathing, but the clock read only seven minutes later. It was one forty-one am. Perhaps a drink of water would settle her. As she made her way to his kitchen, she saw him asleep on a bed pulled out from the sofa. She brought her glass of water into the living room and curled upon the armchair. He lay facing her direction on his side diagonally on the warped mattress, sound asleep. She watched him as he slept. Rudy, nestled in a ball by his feet, awoke to her presence. He stood up, arched his back round and high, yawned then delicately stepped across the sofa bed toward her. He rested with her in the armchair and his soft, rhythmic purr encouraged her to doze off once again. Curled together there the two of them slept.

She heard Rick call her name twice and she awoke.

"What are you doing out of bed?" Rick faced her with his hand on her shoulder. "It's three in the morning."

She was confused; she realized she had fallen asleep again. "Oh. I couldn't sleep. Not now, before."

"Before when? How long have you been out here?"

"Not that long." She felt chilled. It had been nearly an hour and a half. "Did I wake you?"

"No, nature's call did. Come back to bed."

"I can't."

"Why not?

"I just can't."

Rudy vacated Kelly's lap for the quiet of the bedroom.

Rick sat upon the drooping edge of the sofa bed. "Tell me why."

She took a breath. "I had a nightmare earlier. I don't want to go back to bed."

"Same nightmare you used to have before?"

"No, different. Well, kind of the same, scarier in some ways." She wrapped her hands around her shoulders to calm herself.

"Talk to me," he held out his hands toward her.

She took his hands as he pulled her up from the armchair. He was pleased to accept the duty of warming her. He tucked her in beside him and held her close as she began to relay the details of what frightened her this time.

"It started out kind of the same way it always does. I was walking through a forest, sometime in late afternoon…when the sun gets really steamy through the mist, through the trees," her fingers twinkled life in the air. "It's warm and balmy and so lush and fragrant. Peaceful. I'm walking and walking, in no particular direction and then suddenly, my feet go out from under me. The earth gives way and I start to fall. Like Alice, I keep falling, it feels like forever. I can hear my mom and my dad calling me, wanting me to return to them. I'm little, I'm lost….I keep falling….falling away from them, away from the light. I'm looking up to the light as it's flying away. And I can't stop it…"

He pulled her closer to him as her rendition took on an ethereal quality. Her frail voice conveyed well her wondrous fear all at once to him.

"Then the dream changes. Out of nowhere, my fall is halted… hands, grabbing me and holding onto me, to keep me from falling. I'm falling downward, but these hands are holding me tight and I'm being pulled so hard, that I can't hang on. But those hands were so strong, determined…"

"Your parents?"

"No." She paused. "It wasn't my parents' hands. When I've had this sort of dream before, I only felt their hands when they were walking with me through the forest. My hands felt small and safe in theirs." Her breathing grew shallow.

"Then whose hands grabbed you?"

She reached for his hands to ascertain the feeling. Her fingers wove into his tightly. "Yours."

"Then what?" He kissed her cheek.

"I don't know, I let go," she released his hands, "and I'm falling again, forever into the blackness, and I'm screaming, I'm calling out and nobody hears me. It just gets blacker, and the perfect afternoon misty light of the forest is so long gone…." It was everything she could do to keep from breaking down. "What's wrong with me? Am I ever going to be normal again?"

"Nothing's wrong with you," he whispered. "Nothing. For once, everything is right. You're not alone this time." He held her. No wonder sleep has become her enemy, he finally understood. "Have you told Dr. Lake about these nightmares?"

"No."

"I want you to."

"I'm telling you."

"Thank you, and keep telling me, but tell her too, it's an integral part of this whole thing, if you're going to let her help you. It's about feeling safe. Once these nightmares figure out they have no power over you, they'll go away. But, I think they still have power over you."

She rested silently with him until Rudy returned from the bedroom. With no announcement, he jumped upon them and curled up between their legs.

"Tell me about your folks." He caressed her hair down to her cheek.

"What do you want to know?"

"Tell me about who they were. If you want to."

"My mom's name was Bridget and my dad's name was Ian. They were killed in a head-on collision with a drunk driver on the highway. I don't know exactly what happened, but the police said the other driver had jumped the median...they were all killed. Nobody survived. My parents were coming back from a dinner party at one of my dad's colleague's homes when it happened. That's why I wasn't with them, I was home."

"And the police came to your house?"

She nodded silently.

"Tell me about who your mom and your dad were."

"My mom has two younger sisters and an older brother, all in Alberta, and my dad was an only child. Their backgrounds were very different, mom grew up in a bigger family out west, just outside of Edmonton, and dad grew up here."

"I have an uncle in Calgary. How did your parents meet?"

"My dad had taken an assistant professor position at the education department of University of Alberta, and he had been there for a few years, that's when he met my mom, my uncle introduced them. My mom was just getting into real estate at that time and she was working full-time as an agent, concentrating on building a clientele and expanding her region. I think she was around twenty-five or twenty-six when they met, so dad must have been thirty-two or so."

"Not much younger than us. What brought them out here?"

"Much to everyone's shame, I was already on the way...they got married when Dad accepted a better faculty position out here. They needed someone specialized in Educational Psychology and I think he wanted to come back home, more than anything, and he had gotten his chance."

"Home for your dad, but not your mom. What did she think about having to leave?"

"She didn't want to. But with the way things were with her family over her unplanned pregnancy, she just did what she had to do. She didn't mind living here, but she always missed home, her parents and everyone."

"You want to be able to share a new baby with family. When did she start working again?"

"She stayed home with me until I went to school. She had to get re-licensed out here, and she went back to work, part-time, probably when I was six or so. My mom was independent. She enjoyed her career, I think it gave her a lot of fulfillment, not that being a mom, and a wife didn't, but she seemed to be so much happier when she started working again. That's what I remember. Dad kept fairly long hours, with his teaching, his writing and his research. She had to have her own outlets."

"Your mom was stunning, from what I can tell from that picture in your apartment."

"You've looked at that photo?"

"Of course, closely. You look like both your parents, but there's something about your mom's look that you definitely inherited...coloring, complexion, cheekbones," Rick spoke sincerely.

"I always thought my mom was the most beautiful woman I had ever seen. I know my dad felt the same way. I only hope to look that amazing when I'm forty-five."

"Don't doubt it. They say to look at a girl's mom if you want to know what she'll look like in the future."

"I miss her." She wiped tears from the corners of her eyes. "I miss them both so much. People say it's supposed to get better with time, not if it means forgetting. I have forgotten so much. There are times I wonder what they'd think of me, today. They wouldn't be so proud." At least she wasn't unmarried and pregnant, she imagined her mother's shame and regret.

"They would be amazed by you." He kissed her lips. "I am so glad you're here. With me."

She reached for him as her fingers ran through his hair and he kissed her again, soundly, yet gently. She fought against the familiar fear that always accompanied his elevating her, and she regained her breath. "I wish you could have known them." She spoke softly in his ear. "My mom would have liked you."

"Nope, she wouldn't have."

"What? Why would you say that?" Her whisper bumped up to normal volume as she propped herself up to look at him.

"Because. Think about it, any mother would have been incensed at a nearly twenty-three year old man knocking at her door asking for her sixteen year old daughter. She would have chased me through the neighborhood with a rolling pin, your dad would have threatened me with a shotgun, whoever got to me first."

Kelly rolled back onto the bed and laughed loudly. She promptly covered her mouth when she realized it was nearly four in the morning. She relaxed on her back and imagined the comical pell-mell neighborhood scenario complete with garbage bins being upturned by cars being run off the road trying to avoid crazy folks with frying pans in high chase… fit for the big screen. "I see your point." She stared at the ceiling with her hand supporting the back of her head. "Let me rephrase. If she were alive today," she qualified, "I think she would like you."

He rolled over and wrapped himself around her, his wayward hands embarking on journeys of their own. "Oh no, she wouldn't. . . ."

Twelve

SATURDAY, MAY 24

Kitchen clatter caused her to stir just before eight am. Sunbeams streamed in between the patio drapes. Kelly rubbed a kink in her back just above her hip; she attributed it to the uneven support rails of the sofa bed.

When Rick appeared from the kitchen, he saw that Kelly had folded the bed linens and was resetting the sofa bed frame back into place. "Thought I heard you up," he said cheerfully.

She grabbed for the sofa cushions on the floor. "What on earth are you doing at this ungodly hour?"

"It's eight. The day's nearly over." He was out of his pyjamas, showered and dressed in a tank shirt and shorts. "Or did you not sleep enough?" He could have sounded less suggestive.

"No fault of yours, I'm sure. I used to think you were a gent."

He stood by the telephone table blushing the color of guilt, "Every man's job to try."

"My job to resist. The real you has finally surfaced. Behave yourself." She slipped past him patting him preciously on the cheek, and disappeared into the bathroom.

Within minutes, she entered the kitchen, dressed in her freshly laundered casual cottons. She sidled up to him and wrapped her arms around his hips and buried her nose in his black tank shirt. She took in a concentrated, deep breath and directed it deep down into her lungs.

He turned to face her, wasting no time, and began to kiss her eagerly on her neck. "Good morning, officially."

"That's not behaving yourself. I thought we were friends," she reminded frankly.

"We're the best of friends, or haven't you noticed?"

"Here we go again. Man on a mission. Give up already, you're wasting your time on me."

He was flattered by her continued frank honesty. It was clear to him they were friends, at every level. "I don't give up that easy…"

"You're scaring me," she continued, in a serious tone.

"Be very afraid," Rick warned with a maniacal slant. He began to resume his breakfast preparations when Kelly noticed two picnic coolers on the kitchen floor.

"What's all this?"

"Surprise."

"Was last night not enough of a hint for you? I don't like surprises."

"Not that kind of surprise. We're going out. It's a beautiful day."

"Great! Where are we going?"

"Can't tell you." He looked back to her as he handed over a toasted bagel layered thick with cream cheese and topped with blackberry jam. "Surprise."

His charm was annoying, in an endearing way, she thought; and he looked incredibly good in a tank shirt. Rudy nervously sniffed at the cat carrier on the floor. "Is Rudy coming along?"

"Yep. He's a seasoned traveler," Rick paused, "mostly. As long as the road isn't too bumpy… or curvy…." he motioned with his hands. He recommended she repack her sports bag.

Kelly worried aloud, "Why is the cat coming? Where exactly are we going? And how long are we going to be gone?" All legit questions as she gathered this might not be a brief outing.

"Can't tell you…it's a - "

By now she was ready to throttle him with her own surprise but he was holding two full mugs of hot coffee before him, innocently, as his best defense.

They sat down to breakfast. "Okay, Doctor. You run the show. Feed your ego, big boy."

"Thank you," he said with a mouthful of bagel.

They pulled jackets from the closet and began to load the SUV bringing along his guitar and lastly, Rudy, captive in his carrier with his ears pinned well back displaying his displeasure. By ten o'clock, they were on the road, the compass pointing directly toward the sunshine, breezing away from the city along the Eastern Shore Marine Drive. She took in the sights of sheltered sapphire coves, the passing trees against the watercolor wash sky, she paid no attention to where Rick had driven in the hour they were on the highway. They rolled onto a long dirt drive that met a dark clapboard cottage at its end. Behind it shimmered a lovely lake. Rendered speechless by the setting, she simply exited the vehicle and walked to the rear of the cabin, which really was the front, to take in the lake view.

Rick unloaded the SUV. Once safely inside the cottage, he set Rudy free from his carrier and set up his litter box. He then found Kelly standing silently at the water's edge, near a small wharf that extended from a shed on the shoreline. "Mosquitoes will get you if you stand still too long."

"This place is incredible. It's so quiet here."

"Glad you like it."

"You own this place, too?" She swatted at a happy humming mosquito hovering by her ear.

"Nope. It's Mike's parents' property. It's been in their family for a while now, since we were in university anyways."

"They don't mind that we're here?"

"They don't know." He pulled a brass ring from his pocket and dangled it in front of her, "Just kidding, got my own key."

More mosquitoes gathered excitedly upon discovery of their presence. "So nobody lives here year round?"

"No, we all just hang out off and on, and whoever shows up…it's always a party. But nobody's using it this weekend. I made some calls."

"When you were supposed to be resting? Or was it working…"

Rick smiled and watched a loon fly low across the lake. "Thought you might like a change of scenery."

"Thank you. Thank Mike. Thank his parents…thank God for this," she whispered in finality. "Am I ever going to meet this famous Mike of yours?"

"Definitely, and soon. Dinner plans are already in the works. Trick is when they can schedule a time when everyone can actually make it."

"Is he married?"

"Nearly nine years now. Natasha is exceptional. You'll love her. Her parents are from India, but she was born here and she's the most amazing cook."

"What does she do?"

"She's a doctor. Figures, it seems medical doctors can only marry other doctors," Rick hypothesized. "At least that's my observation. Must be a status thing."

"I think it's more a pragmatic thing. They have such ridiculous hours that only another doctor could understand enough to make a marriage work. Career dedication and call to vocation can be a hard thing to understand, and live with. If you can't relate, it can end up being too big a sacrifice."

"Voice of experience?" He took her hand, kissed her fingers, and led her up the steps to the cottage deck. A picnic table overlooked the lake and across the deck stood the barbecue. Several citronella candles in terra cotta pots were evenly spaced around the deck rail. A rickety screen door with a partially torn mesh led into the kitchen. There were dated ochre appliances and a table in a central space. Kelly began to laugh when she spied a plaque on the wall next to the sink that read, "Worry is like a rocking chair. It may keep you busy, but it gets you nowhere." Separated from the kitchen by a speckled peninsular countertop, the main living area appeared spacious and open, brightened by several windows. A stone hearth fireplace was its focal point, a large plaid sofa and two opposing dark green armchairs were arranged in front of the hearth. Set between them was a bulky walnut coffee table on a heavy wool rug. Off the far side of the living area was a bathroom and nearby, a bedroom. Kelly peeked in and found Rudy rubbing his face against the foot of the bed. "I think the cat's claimed his room."

"He's just getting reacquainted," Rick called back from the kitchen as he was placing groceries from the cooler into the fridge. "He hasn't been here since last fall."

Kelly ambled to the back wall of the living room to find an eclectic library collection enclosed behind glass doors. Among the literary selections was a shelf-worn, faded hardcover copy of Edgar Allan Poe's Tales of Mystery and Imagination and Mary Shelley's Frankenstein. Stacked beneath the bookcase were open shelves holding various odds and ends including tools, fishing supplies and hardware items, some board games, and several rustic-styled toys and decorative items. She picked up one that caught her attention. Upon a small, finished wooden square were pitched three twigs tied at the top, like the frame of a teepee. From the apex hung a rock on a string. She read the printing on the wooden square, "Nova Scotia Weather Forecaster – One Hundred Percent Accurate: If rock is wet, it's raining. If rock is white, it's snowing. If rock hangs to one side, it's windy. If rock is coated with ice, it's slippery. If rock is dry, you don't need an umbrella. Have a wonderful day. Hint: Place outdoors." Never having met Mike or his parents, she decided she liked his family, or at the very least, their provincially quirky sense of humor.

Kelly rejoined Rick in the kitchen. "When exactly did you plan this getaway?"

"I figured Fiji would be too much of a hassle at this point, travel agents, passports, paperwork, so this was the next best thing."

"I hear there's political and cultural instability in Fiji."

"Not unlike Australia or New Zealand where there are permanent tensions between the aboriginal peoples and the relatively modern intruders."

"Maybe we should look into Madagascar instead. Are there sandalwood trees there?"

"Couldn't tell you. Hissing cockroaches, definitely. And I can tell you about ring-tailed lemurs," Rick waved his finger assertively. "Unlike the cockroaches, they're cute, very cat-like, even though they're primates. Rudy sometimes gets the same expression on his face when he's been into catnip. His eyes get big and round and paranoid and he gets all twitchy."

"Can't wait. Do we have any catnip?" She scanned around the room for Rudy, who was likely marking furniture elsewhere.

Rick handed her some mosquito-repellent lotion and suggested they go for a walk as he finished up in the kitchen. Rick donned a thin long-sleeve jersey when he saw that Kelly had done so.

The country air was thickly fragrant and the day was shaping up to be a triple-H: hot, humid and hazy. They hoped that if the temperature soared, it might discourage the biting flies until evening. They walked slowly along the dirt road, hand in hand, for the better part of a mile and then took a narrow footpath through dense woods, which led to a clearing that spread out to the lake.

"Local swimming hole?" Kelly asked as she wiped her brow of what felt like a spider web.

"It may not be the white sands of Madagascar, but it is the white granite of Nova Scotia."

They sat along the rocks that stumbled into the lake. Guppies swam in the water next them. "Good fishin' here." Kelly chuckled.

"Yeah, just watch out for the leeches." He rested back on his palms, content to just watch her as she sat silently; as she surveyed her surroundings. He knew if he left her to her thoughts long enough, she might talk.

Her breathing grew uneven as her eyes darted unsurely between the lines of trees on the far side of the lake to the ripples of water near her feet. "Wendy thinks I tried to kill myself."

"Did you enlighten her?"

"I couldn't be bothered. It took every ounce of mental energy I had to just handle her being there."

"Should I have stayed?"

Kelly watched a small school of fish and wiggled her finger in the chilly water, causing them to scatter. "Better that you weren't there."

Rick didn't comment; he reclined on his elbows.

"Do you think I'm crazy?"

"No." He sat up immediately.

"I'm serious."

"So am I."

"I could be schizophrenic, for all you know… for all I know."

"You're not schizophrenic," Rick droned, in a patronizing tone.

"How do you know? Do you know someone who is?"

"No."

She returned her line of sight to the spruce trees on the far side of the water.

"Does Dr. Lake think you're schizophrenic?"

"No."

"Then why are you worried?"

"I don't know," she waffled, "the voices, the dreams, the nightmares, the apathy, the disinterest, suicidal tendencies, this feeling of not belonging, to myself, to this world, to anyone or anything, the flashes…" her voice wavered as she forced her fingers to weave together to keep her hands from shaking. She hoped he didn't notice.

"Flashes?" This was a new symptom he'd never heard her mention before. "Like flashes of light?"

"No, memory flashes, flashbacks…."

"Is that what happened on Thursday?"

"It didn't start on Thursday," Kelly choked on her own voice.

He repositioned himself around her and held her. She felt stiff and tense. "Then when?"

"I'm not sure when, exactly. But I noticed the nightmares were coming back, and they were changing bit by bit, getting more intense. They were different enough to let me know that something was happening that I couldn't control. So I stopped sleeping."

"Go on." He rocked gently with her.

"Then they started in the daytime."

"The nightmares?"

"The flashes. At first they were just pictures," she held her hand at arms length, with her palms facing her, "at a distance." Her tone then relaxed, as though she'd experienced a revelation, "you know, those started to come when I met you."

"Is it because I remind of you someone?" The question of his presence in her life had never been answered.

"There are times I think about you and it's normal, the way it should be." She smiled shyly. "Then there are times that I think about you and I remember my dad, there's definitely something about you that makes me think of him. Your eyes…and your tenacity." She looked to him in confirmation. She wiped a tear when it tickled the corner of her nose. "My dad kept me grounded and other than him, I haven't had a relationship with any man, paternal or otherwise."

"What about your boyfriend? He was still in the picture after your parents were killed."

"Briefly. He was just a boy. And he wasn't mine, he never was." She shook her head, ashamed, "Because I was never his."

"I thought he loved you, and you loved him."

"I thought so at the time. Now I'm not sure it was ever the way I thought it was. I don't know that we ever really had anything. We had been best friends for so long, probably I equated that to love. And I thought that was enough, that it was everything, that it could be everything. He didn't feel the same way."

"Did you ever see him again, after he left you?"

"Once when I was twenty-three. He had come home on a break between jobs, and I had gone over to his parents' home for dinner. That was the last time I'd been back to my old neighborhood, in his house, with them, like when we were kids."

"How'd it go?"

"It went. It was obvious he had no feelings for me. I was long dead inside, so it's not like I had any feelings either. I would look at him, and my soul registered nothing, it felt like a vacuum within me. No connection despite what I was sure we used to have. I considered that a pivotal point in my life…my first true moment of non-existence. In their presence, in his presence, I felt transparent, invisible, untouchable, unreachable. And that's when I realized I had disconnected from myself, who I was, my past, my future, my presence, my pain. I felt strangely safe, like I had finally won."

"The same kind of disconnection you feel from Wendy, now?"

"The same disconnection I feel from her, from everything, everyone, every day. Call it apathy, a brick wall, the official term's dissociation. I'm so out of touch, it's not even funny."

"You're far from out of touch right now. I think you're the most in touch I've ever seen you. Tell me more about the flashes."

She wiped her eyes with her sleeve. "First the pictures came, then the voices. I can't explain the voices. That's why I wondered if I'm schitzo. A normal voice in your head is to go through your grocery list, or to remind yourself to pick up your dry cleaning, or to ask yourself questions, or to hear the words or voice of a loved one, your conscience guiding you along. It's not normal when the voice in your mind wants to stop you from being...or tries to keep you from your world by locking you inside yourself. It's not normal when the voice says horrible, hateful, awful things to you... you have no choice but to believe it, because it's stronger than you are."

"Flashes, pictures, voices, the nightmares, it must all stem from the same source. What exactly are the pictures of?"

"Sounds."

"A picture of a sound? I don't get it. Did I tell you I failed art too?"

"Pictures and sounds. They go together, when I hear a doorbell, I see police officers. When see red and blue flashing lights, I hear chatter, noisy, cold chatter. When I hear a siren, I see candles, I can smell the wax...I hear the voice telling me things...making me remember..." she was flying away from him as she spoke. Her eyes blinked slowly.

"Candle wax?"

She whispered flatly, "Funeral home." She looked and sounded as though she had fallen into a mild trance. "It's a smell I can't wash off, no matter how hard I try. Sandalwood. Lavender. Burning. Hospital."

Strangely, her associations all began to make sense to him as he recalled the incident with the ambulance. "What do you smell now?"

"Candle flame. Flickering... heat up my nostrils." Her eyes were closed as she rocked gently in his arms. "Chatter... stupid, pointless chatter."

"Can you make it stop?"

"Sometimes. It's hard."

He kept repeating the words, "Ask it to stop." He caressed her cheek.

A moment passed then her eyes opened. She had returned to him. "Thursday. I wanted it to stop, once and for all. It was going to be the last day. No more flashbacks. I'd had enough."

"Tell me what happened. Leave nothing out."

"I was in my office, working on the Randall layouts, we were scheduled for a meeting later in the afternoon. The flashes had been coming all week, all day, stronger, louder and more often. I tried to block them out, but I couldn't. I had so many deadlines and I was running out of time. I remember surfing the web for Fiji, I just wanted to get away and go there, praying for a miracle transport out of that office to that beach, our beach. I wanted you to just come and take me away to Fiji. I wanted you so badly ..."

"I left messages for you. All you had to do was call," he insisted, "I would have come. Did you call Dr. Lake?"

"I didn't have time to call," she flustered. "Paul was after me for this, for that, for something else, all this crap, and I was forced to listen to their insensitive chatter through the flashes to the point that I couldn't take it. I couldn't think. I couldn't even hear myself screaming. I kept screaming and the voice was suffocating me so no one would know."

"You should have called Dr. Lake." Rick grew frustrated.

Her tone retreated, "Then I remember being in my flat. I don't remember the time in between, how I got there from work."

"Had you taken your medication?"

"In the morning. I know I took it again when I got home, I took twice as much as I had taken in the morning because I couldn't make it stop."

"What do you mean?"

"I wanted the flashes to stop, I needed the voices to stop. I must have been having a panic attack. I remember writing, hoping to give it the attention it was screaming for, to distract it at the same time....but it wasn't working." Her breathing accelerated as she recalled the turbulence. "The meds still weren't working. So I took more. I don't know how long exactly I had been writing, off and on, up and down. I don't even know how much more I took. I waited and wrote more, I waited. I took one more...that would do it. But the flashes kept coming...they kept coming...." She began to feel dizzy. "Flooding me... I couldn't even see. I must have been in total panic by that time, I couldn't breathe. I can't breathe." She gasped for air.

"Kel, you're hyperventilating. I need you to stop." The point of their getaway was for her to remain calm.

She stopped recounting long enough to resume regular breaths. "I know now I can't do this alone."

He continued to rock her. "And yet you tried to on Thursday, why? Why did you do this alone?"

"I had to handle this once and for all."

He wasn't sure whether the anger he felt within was self-directed for not being there for her when she needed him most, or directed at her, for irresponsibly trying to deal with this on her own. In either case, this wasn't a time for anger, he kept reminding himself. Yet, when he remembered her flaccid body in his arms, he grew fearful once more. These must have been the things she had never told him about that she referred to in the hospital; they definitely weren't in her journal. He felt way in over his head again.

"Pictures. I needed to see pictures," Kelly continued steadfastly. "I needed to remember. It was going to make me do it one way or another. I needed to win. I wanted the good memories to take precedence. I wanted May twenty-third to be a day of freedom, the day of release for me so I wouldn't have the flashes anymore. So they wouldn't be just lost and longed for memories, I'd have my life again, my whole life. I took out the photo albums and I started flipping through them but I couldn't see the pictures clearly. I couldn't make out the details through the plastic sheets, things got so blurry that I pulled them out to look at them up close…so I could feel them, touch their faces, stroke her hair… everything went fuzzy, even the memories started fading into black and finally, the voice was falling away, I couldn't even make out the words anymore. I finally felt at peace. I just wanted to be at peace…."

When his tears burst forth, he knew he had absorbed her experience. "All those meds in you, you could have died!"

She turned herself around to face him. She looked lost. "You…somewhere in there, I called you, didn't I? I knew something was wrong, because it wasn't working the way I wanted it to."

"I'm trying to understand why you did something so reckless, so out of control."

Seeing his tears fall, she cried, "Someone as good, as kind as you deserves so much more than this. You don't get it. You don't understand."

"Then make me," an aggravated breath rushed from him. "What the hell were you thinking, Kelly?" His anger finally broke through.

"I wanted to show you that I could be strong for you, that I could be more than what's left of me. Who would want someone already dead inside? That's what I was trying to tell you last night and again this morning. You're wasting your time, I can't ever give you what you need, not this way. I had to do what I had to do."

"That's what this was about?? You're the one who doesn't get it." His words accelerated. "Admit it, this was some stupid stunt you wanted to do alone. You just can't admit that there are still people on the planet who might actually care about you and that you're not as alone as you think you deserve to be. But you had to do this your way, like some kind of show of strength, without the protection or guidance from Dr. Lake, or anyone else in your life!"

She screamed back, "You mean everyone I've disappointed!!"

"This sounds like some kind of sick poetic self-punishment…death wish…" he didn't know what he was trying to say. "No, you don't get it! You could have died!! This whole goddamn thing should never have happened!!" he hollered.

Her brown eyes welled up with tears again. She promptly stood up, stumbled then ran across the grassy clearing away from the lake, toward the dense woods. Near the forest edge, she tripped upon a large root embedded in the ground, and slammed hard upon the earth. She got up, staggered into the woods, in acute pain clutching her side, but she couldn't find the footpath amidst the thick brush. She stood facing the haunting congregation of spruces and ferns, unable to go forward.

It didn't matter. There was no escaping herself no matter what she did. She refused to look back to the lake. Day two of freedom was proving to be less forgiving than day one. She knelt and cried, realizing she had made yet another grave error in judgment in an effort to be strong, and irrevocably hurt someone else she cared about. Just another in a long line of mistakes she made, each time she desperately summoned strength to force freedom, to conjure any form of faith in a life that in her eyes just wasn't meant to be, the chain had formed the destiny of her own self-sabotage.

The branch of an emerald fern reached out toward her. She tried to clear her vision from the lens effect of her tears. Mesmerized by its growth pattern, she saw how the whole branch grew in the exact shape of every individual leaf, and how the scalloped edge of each leaf took on the identical, overall fern branch shape, over and over again. Level upon level of nature's recurring way, cycling again and again through myriad generations of shapes and details, her fingers touched the delicate leaves and on the underside, she could feel small bumps. She looked to find a multitude of black spores beneath, each precisely the same size and shape perfectly spaced for their own independence in relation to their togetherness. In perfect balance.

He helped her to her feet. By only his hand and without a spoken word, he guided her to the footpath through the dense forest and they walked back down the dirt road.

They passed the afternoon quietly on the deck, with a light lunch of sandwiches, corn chips and fruit, followed by a meditative serenade of Rick's guitar compositions. Kelly wrote in her new journal at the picnic table that looked out over the lake. Rick worked his creative magic on an uneven three-legged stool. He re-played a melodic section that he had been working on, giving her the choice of two options.

"I like the new one. The first one is...expected." Her dad always taught her that tact would get a person far in life.

"Do you think the second one flows okay? It's kind of a bizarre tangent, mixing up majors and minors."

"Follow the tangent. It will take you someplace unpredictable."

"Is that a good thing?"

"Answers aren't always the ones you expected them to be."

He pondered. "I hope those are lyrics you're writing over there."

She looked up in surprise then smirked in embarrassment.

"Great. So I'm over here playing for nothing?"

"Definitely not, your music is awakening, it's unlocking all kinds of things. You never said today's assignment was to write lyrics."

"Get going, you. We have our first million to make."

"Since when were we in this for the money?"

"What are you writing?"

"Journal stuff," she dawdled, fiddling with her pen, "you know, life's messy, write it down."

He said apologetically, "I have a lot to learn, especially when ego gets in the way. Hope you've got the patience."

"It's me who's got a lot to learn." Kelly felt ashamed. Her stomach began to ache again.

Rick set his guitar down. "I'm not saying the flashes would never have happened, had I shown up or not." He sat next to her, took the pen from her hand and began to tap it on the table. "But I can't help feeling guilty for what happened. As your friend, I think I should have done more to help you through this, and find a better way to deal with the flashbacks. More controlled, rather than one flat-out hit."

"You can't help what you don't understand. I've learned that. You have every right to be angry with me. So does Wendy."

"Did you tell her about the flashes?"

"I didn't tell anyone. I especially needed to leave her out of this. There's no way she could handle it, not again. I've wasted so much of others' time and energy, I ruin people's lives. I needed to handle it on my own." She observed the hurt in his eyes.

Rick set the pen down in the crease of her open journal. He didn't respond. He looked back to his guitar and quickly looked away from it. He patted the tabletop, stood up and walked off the deck. His self-confidence had spent the day dwindling away; he realized she might never be able to let anyone in her life.

She felt neither scared nor upset that he had walked away; she expected it. She saw he had seated himself on the edge of the wharf. She knew nothing about writing song lyrics. She wouldn't even know where or how to begin. How could anything that she would write support, let alone enhance, his musical creative genius; she felt defeated, without having even begun. She went inside and found Rudy tending to his paws on the plaid sofa. She picked him up and then reclined along the sofa. She stared at the overhead rafters and studied the shape of the roof support trusses. She knew nothing about writing music, or about science or mathematics... she knew nothing about anything, except grief, and graphic design. There was no such thing as a qualified expert on grief; proficiency in her career was prosaic. Did she even have a career left to return to? The ache in her stomach came again; perhaps it emanated from her dead end trains of thought or from Rudy suddenly springing off her belly and onto the coffee table before landing on the floor. She rolled over toward the back of the sofa and buried her head in the cushion. The upholstery smelled of classic cottage, firewood smoke and the primordial earthiness of mildew. This would never work, she reasoned: an inexperienced girl with barely more than a high school diploma with a man who had traveled the world, been practically married, had a doctorate in engineering. What was she thinking? What was he thinking? Clearly, the problem was that nobody was thinking in this ridiculous web of lives. Any energy he still possessed would soon be drained as well, and she was in position to watch it happen if she were to let this friendship go on any further. Her feelings for him had been growing, now they had reached uncontainable. But she could never be of any meaningful, sustaining value to him. Kelly Lynn Pearson, past, present or future, would never match what he needed, or wanted, in any way she could imagine. Growing up, her mother repeatedly warned her sternly against two danger paths: premarital sex and hitchhiking. She was too far away from home to walk. For Christ's sake, this was only day two. Nausea waved up her chest to her throat and she bounded up to the bathroom.

He knocked on the bathroom door several minutes later. "Kel, are you in there?"

"I'll be out in a minute."

He waited much longer than that. "You sure you're okay?"

"No," her faint voice swayed.

"Are you sick?"

"Kind of." She opened the door slowly. Her complexion looked gray and her dampened face still dripped the splashes of cold water. The rims of her eyes were red.

"Come here, you." He hugged her. "What's wrong?"

She shoved him away. "Take me home. Now."

"Kel, come and sit down, I'll make us some tea."

"No. It's too hot for tea, just take me back...and leave me. Let this go. That's all."

"Don't be ridiculous. I'm not going to leave you anywhere."

She gave the idea of locking herself in the bathroom a second thought. "Fine." And in she went, bolting the pine door behind her.

"Kel, come out here, please," he called to her firmly.

"I want to be alone," cried her tiny voice through the door.

"Fine. Let me know when you want dinner, I'll slide it under the crack in the door." Pancakes would be thin enough, he thought.

Moments later, she opened the bathroom door and stood glumly in the doorway. She knew she was behaving like a kindergartener. "Have you really thought about this? This will never work."

"Yeah, you've said that, enough, already. Come here." He was seated in the corner of the plaid sofa with one leg up on the cushions. He held his hand toward her. She walked over to him, reluctantly took his hand and he let her fall onto him.

"Take me home."

"I will. Tomorrow." He wrapped his arms around her. "Take a nap. You'll feel better." He was not going to let this defeat them so easily. His hand cupped her face and she was lulled into peace by his steady heartbeat.

Rick barbequed hamburgers for supper and Kelly prepared a garden salad. She admitted to herself that she felt better after her short sleep, as she contemplated Rick's evening theory that everything you ever needed to know about life, you did learn in kindergarten. She caught herself in a bittersweet memory of herself and Wendy in Mrs. Larssen's grade primary classroom talking to each other in their version of sign language, when they were supposed to be napping. She remembered the cool, plastic feel of the blue vinyl mats that Mrs. Larssen laid out for her students every day at the same time. They always warmed up after a minute or two, but those first moments were always a shock. She remembered staring sideways into Wendy's olive green eyes that had orange flecks around the centers, wishing hers were green too. She thought of the animal crackers handed around for snacks afterwards along with the fifteen-cent quarter-pint cartons of milk, and how Wendy always wanted the elephant cookie, probably because it was the biggest. Her afternoon nausea had relented and she was looking forward to hot hamburgers with onions off the grill, as the barbeque aroma wafted in the kitchen window.

With the biting flies planning to make their resurgence in the twilight hours, they chose to eat indoors, and Rudy was happy for the company. The cat ate with them and Kelly supplemented his kitty kibble with a few morsels of hamburger. She noticed he didn't eat the pieces that had the slightest traces of mustard on them. Rick had remembered to pack the cat's favorite tail-less mouse, which Rudy had rescued courageously from his carrier, taking the odds-on chance they weren't leaving for a while. Kelly enticed Rudy into a game of fetch while Rick organized firewood in the hearth for a late evening fire.

"Did you guys have a cottage when you were growing up?" Kelly asked him.

"Yeah, we did. But dad sold it a while ago. We hadn't used it for so many years, so there was no point in keeping it."

"Wendy's family tried renting a cottage on Prince Edward Island for a few summers, only for Arthur to realize that neither his wife nor his daughter were cottage-types. They both refused to go outdoors. Heck, with all these flies, I could see why. All I know is that Marilyn was not, nor would she ever be a cottage wife."

"I can hear the constant complaining now. The bugspray probably clashed with her Chanel." He sympathized with Arthur. "How about your family?"

"We never had a cottage, but we did have this wacky pop-up trailer that we used to take camping. It was this old dinner-mint green and white thing that basically looked like your picnic cooler on mini-wheels. Dad bought it used and we towed it behind the old blue Ford. That was fun. Dad used to crack his head every time he went in there. Even hoisted up, the ceiling couldn't have been higher than a few feet. It was great, as long as you didn't mind crouching. Come to think of it, it wasn't all that waterproof, either." She laughed heartily. "I remember the nighttime campfires most of all, with mom, dad and I roasting marshmallows and looking at the stars. Do we have any marshmallows?"

Rick offered to check in the recesses of cupboards, certain that any morsels of what used to be confectionary sponge would be no better than rocks. "Next time," he promised. "But, if it's clear later on, we can offer you stars."

"Perfect."

It was after ten o'clock that they made their way outdoors to stargaze. The night was clear and cool, with only a few scattered clouds. They walked to the wharf. Rick had brought an old wool blanket and their waterfront vantage point proved to be an ideal stargazing location. Kelly absorbed the spectacular wonder of the infinite speckles of light scattered throughout the night's canopy. She hadn't witnessed such a glitter of stars as this night in the country provided, and the nebulous ribbon of light that was the Milky Way spun like powder blue candy silk off toward the horizon. "I wonder if I could have been an astronomer had I actually had a normal life and gone to university."

"You can be whatever you want to be, at any time." He lay on his back beside her. "I wonder if I could have been a race-car driver had I not gone to university."

Kelly giggled. "You don't strike me as the need-for-speed type."

"There's a lot about me you don't know."

"What was Rebecca's field?"

"Pharmacy."

Kelly waited until she worked up enough nerve to ask, "So, what was she like?"

"Why do you want to know?"

She backed off, "Never mind, I don't have to know." She sat up and rested on her palms.

The chorus of crickets offered an insincere solace against the obvious wall of silence between them. Kelly wondered how deep the water was at the edge of the wharf. Her nausea had returned.

He sat up. "Well, let me think..." he began.

"You know what, it's okay. Forget I asked." Kelly's voice dropped.

"Petite, with luscious brown hair, greenish eyes, very extroverted, brilliant, ambitious, competitive, social butterfly..."

Kelly nodded dutifully at his description of a persona nothing like her own, and too uncannily like Wendy's, "Sounds just like someone I know."

"What can I say, it's what I've always been attracted to, right from the beginning."

Was he telling her in a back door way that someone like Wendy was characteristically his attractor type? Or worse yet, that he was attracted to Wendy? Kelly figured she might make it home by morning's light if she started walking now; however, she would first need to stop at the bathroom, she felt the need to vomit again. Thank heavens for pitch darkness, she looked upward for guidance.

"You know, when you're born an introvert, you live your life believing that the only people in the world that are right for you are extroverts. Folks tell you that all the time, that you need someone to bring you out of your shell, someone who'll show you the world, someone who'll take the lead and never give you the chance to look back."

Kelly studied the constellations. She hated this conversation but couldn't generate the nerve to abandon it. Nevertheless, she had things to say.

"There's something to be said for like-mindedness."

She would continue to bite her tongue, except that he had concluded his brief essay on personality matchmaking. "So, what? That's your conclusion? Like-mindedness?" she asked, trying not to sound irritated.

"Yep. One thing an introvert can well do without is someone to take them over, drown them out, overshadow them, and the last thing an extrovert wants is someone who holds them back."

She knew all too well and hated being reminded.

"All the girls I've been attracted to since I was ten have fit that pattern. I recently arrived at the conclusion that it's a bad fit. For me, anyway."

She decided to risk it, "So you're not attracted to Wendy?"

"What? No! Odd though, there used to be a time when I might have pursued her, or should I say, someone like her."

One good thing she had learned from Wendy was to never impulsively blurt out a comment when sweltering in confusion. She bit her tongue again and let him talk.

"Funny thing is," he continued, "my father could see the bad fit and I couldn't. The closer we got to our wedding, the further apart dad and I got."

"You mean he didn't want you to marry Rebecca?"

"Nope. He never liked her, right from the beginning."

"Why? He must have told you his reasons."

"Never really talked to him about it, so I can't say for sure."

"You didn't try to talk to him?"

"Just made things worse. It finally got to the point where I wasn't sure anymore if I was trying to convince him that she was right for me, or convince myself."

"You had doubts yourself?"

"There were things she wanted, she had made up her mind pretty early on that she wanted them from me."

"What kinds of things?"

"Money, social status, prestige, lifestyle, you name it. I don't fault her for wanting what anyone else would want, a home, a life, a career, kids…but it was starting to feel like maybe she wanted those things for her life more than she wanted me in it."

"Means to an end?"

"I never said that. Neither did dad for that matter."

"Hey," Kelly insisted, "I'm just trying to figure it out. We don't have to talk about this." She was irritated now. "Look, I'm sorry I brought it up, it's none of my business."

They headed indoors before being eaten alive by mosquitoes. He began to build the fire in the hearth, and was impatiently shoving Rudy aside every time he curiously meandered in his way. Kelly picked the cat up and brought him to the sofa. Once the kindling had caught, Kelly set off to make herbal tea that she had found in the cupboard. Upon her return, Rick was on the sofa tuning his guitar. The first logs had caught alight and the room basked in a golden glow. She set the mugs of tea on the table and without hesitation she removed the guitar from his grasp and laid it next to the sofa. She sat next to him and handed him his tea. "Change the subject?"

"Not necessarily."

"So, things weren't great with your fiancée."

Rick shook his head and tried to laugh. "I didn't want things the way she did. Half the things, I just didn't care about."

"Like what?"

"Money, status, stuff that puts you in line with a certain category of folks, out of line with others...things for show, for talk, how it looks on the outside."

"I can see your point."

"It's not right when you compromise who you are, what you value, when you learn to hate where you've come from."

"She altered your path?"

"Mostly my perspective." His eyes stared vacantly at the flames that licked upwards from the kindling. She could see the reflection in his eyes and she felt troubled for him. He darted up to set another dry log on the fire. When he returned, he embraced her as he seated himself. "It all comes down to values."

Kelly curled up against him. Her apprehension faded the more they talked. "I just assumed you had common values, given that she was from your home town."

"Big city dreams grow from a small town. She wanted more, I suppose there's nothing wrong with that. She got the dreamer instinct from her dad. He was a psychiatrist, and he set up his practice in the rural area, the city was saturated. He was always looking to move up and out west, into the wide world, and have a big metro practice, with a downtown fancy office."

"So tell me again why you went into engineering?"

Rick laughed. "Don't look at me. It's what everyone else seemed to want for me at the time, family, friends, Rebecca. By the time I graduated, it was becoming clear I had the aptitude... I wanted to do a masters."

"So then, why didn't you?"

He looked at her knowing she already had the answer.

"Let me guess, a high-tech industry job in Ontario would generate a healthy cash flow right away, enough in time for a wedding."

Rick wanted her intuitive postulating to go forward.

"Did you not know what you wanted, if not out of your career, then out of your relationship?"

"Funny how it was never up for discussion. An industry job was practical for the time, not a hard sell."

She remembered his advice about the dangers of not standing up for one's self before it's too late. She wondered if this was a common trait among all introverts.

His guitar music stirred her writing. She wrote upon the hearth by the firelight as he played. Rudy curled up in a ball on the rug next to her feet and slept. The crackling fire radiated as the night grew colder; the burning softwood warmly exuded a comforting scent in a cozy blush of light. In her mind's eye, a lakeside woodland cottage seemed a diametric setting to the dreamed-of azure seaside hut. So the wishful-thinking sound of breaking ocean waves swapped fascination with her serendipitous captivation of the amber waves of firelight lapping upon the cabin's timbered walls. She knew deep down the triviality of geographical setting when real inspiration was close at hand.

Thirteen

May 25

Free spirit restrained
A bird in a shrine
For them she remained
Dutifully confined

Compelled she sang
Her songs they relished
Ringing such sadness
They heard what they wished

Everything was taken away…an accident minimized what had been our life to stacks of corrugated moving boxes, an accident reduced my mother and my father to pieces of notarized paper locked in safe-deposit boxes. Fate encapsulated their humanity and put their bodies in brass urns. Only I remained.

In their years, they wore the marks of human frailty, and as their creation, I preserved them in my mind's rightful image – one remarkably like sainthood.

***

Can a soul that has faced death purchase the meaning of life?

The flashbacks began when I met him. Then, my nightmares grew in intensity and frequency. For the first time in ten years, their imagery began to morph - when I met him. The flashbacks didn't start because he bumped into my life, I gave permission for them to manifest because he broke through their barrier.

Dr. Lake said that a breakdown can eventually happen not when a person feels they're in unrecoverable danger, but when they feel finally safe.

***

The dream of our hearts is the world we envision to live in. Neither Heaven nor Hell shares a place upon this planet unless we dream it into existence.

***

Rolling Stone Magazine - Many songwriters admit they never considered themselves musicians, but always regarded themselves as writers, first and above all. They say even if you don't know how to start, because you're without inspiration, you have to show up at your instrument (or in a writer's case, at the page), you must start, and in any way you can. Because the merit of miniscule progress, no matter how it came about, exceeds not trying.

***

Something had to happen when May 23 arrived, intuitively I knew — like the eerie calm before the storm — when I experienced an unnerving contentment to be that flower fading from his vase. I sensed where I was headed. The timing amazes me, as though he just knew, or I just knew. Maybe we both knew.

Then it began…

… surreptitiously seeped with an imperceptible trickle of memory flashes, sparks…
… slowly summoned a steady, core-quaking rumble of nightmares, indefatigable anxiety and panic attacks…
… exponentially exploded to a monumentally devouring wash of memories, visions and emotions that held no mercy but to sweep me away in its path.

Memory avalanche…

No amount of medication could protect me or rid me of myself, my fate, the asphyxiation…as if I could audaciously defy the destructively cleansing forces of nature.

***

Wisdom is born not from facing death, but from living, it cannot be purchased. It cannot be bargained.

I grieved for so long, I don't think this is grief anymore. It's the pathogenic residue of the painful memories I shoved away. Because I could not look upon them in acceptance when it mattered, and for the last time, I was unable to fully remember who my mother dreamed to be, who my father was, unable to remember their strengths, virtues, weaknesses, transgressions, I locked myself in my idea of them. Time only speaks truth.

I meant to rouse Agramon by looking at the pictures. I kept stabbing at the beast repeatedly with fire-hot irons until I brought forth its caged rage. And then I crossed the threshold, sealed the door behind me and threw far away the key. I wanted to be consumed by it, to offer the automaton self I had become as the final sacrifice, and then be free.

May 26

Rick talks about Beginners Mind, a Zen concept. It isn't as easy as one might think, to develop in your consciousness a blank slate at all times to see things as they truly are, as if for the first time, without judgment like a newborn or a young child. What does green mean to the baby crawling in the grasses of spring? Impressions of our world fill us like vibrant color when we're young. But as we grow, colors are washed of their hue… imagination grows faded… Hearts grow jaded.

I keep thinking of my cup of barren emptiness…

… Light shines through the emptiness where the wall isn't…it's called a window.

Let it go.

Dewdrops

Sun risen dewdrops dancing
Billowing breeze through canopied trees
Soul Light glimmering, gleaming
Dappling dancing dewdrops streaming

Shimmering leaves whispering
Tales untold as shadows unfold
Soul Light blanketing, beaming
Swirling mists from dewdrops steaming

Sun fallen shadows sneaking
Through mossy brush brings with a hush
Soul Light drifting, dreaming
'Til dewdrops dance come dawn.

Walking through the woodland near Mike's family cabin, as we did today, hastens me to a pleasant reality of the surreal state of that dream world... before the fall into the void.

***

Neither of us feels like talking. We've pushed enough boundaries for the time being. Trying to test any further at this point feels like jack-rabbiting forward so you can slam on the brakes and beat everyone else to the red light.

May 27

Dr. Lake's advice is to live my life on my own terms and no one else's. Any limits I push past must be only as far as I'm ready to go. I have to be resolute in respecting my own needs. Only then will true confidence stay.

I hate skating on thin ice. Even though I'm getting somewhere, I can feel and hear the ice cracking beneath me — a constant fear that the delicate, crystalline surface separating frigidity from freedom will give way the moment I let go.

June 2

He asked me if I had heard from Wendy. When I told him no, he asked my why. He asked me when I last spoke to her — I answered him honestly. He just raised his eyebrows and didn't comment.

When I told her I wanted her out of my life, I meant it. I felt cornered and she had closed herself off to my reality, even more than I had. I only did what she was afraid to do.

My heart makes it clear to me what he really thinks. And the part of me that adores him questions my actions.

June 4

Karen wants me to write in detail everything I want for myself out of life, to describe the settings, meanings, philosophy and activities that define and characterize the vision of my role in this world. And I am to keep writing until I have excavated my core motivation for living. One of two things will happen: The page will remain blank, or I'll need a separate journal just for this week's exercise.

Rick and Wendy don't seem to have problems imagining past their status quo. Why is everything so all or nothing with me? Why have I learned to look at life centrifugally from my limits?

I know why. I'm always scaling the boundary walls... looking for a way out.

June 7

Psychologizing...Karen's annoying habit.

My paradigm, according to her, is of the helpless victim - everything I look back at in my life has happened to me, leading me towards a telegraphed, fatalistic end that I have deductively conjured — patterns consistent with victimization. Karen says I have allowed this to happen, by the choices I have made and in perspectives that I have held onto since their death.

What it means to be a Victim — when the past matters more to you than the present.

Hence our last discussion on self-empowerment - I alone hold the power to make new choices, here and now, to consciously redirect the bearing of my life, with me and only me steering the helm.

But how do you purge yourself of the poisons that have infected every cell, every fibre of your being? I am bloated with the pernicious polluted bilge that I have consumed and stored to stagnation... Grief, the very life liquid I have been drinking to quench my thirst is what has been poisoning me all along.

June 14

Next Assignment - She wants me to talk more about what I want for my future, incidentally, so does he. Instead of discussions and writing assignments, he tries to romance it out of me. This is so pointless - my imagination of my future is as abstract as spilled puddles of muddy watercolor... sensations, impressions that are only sketches of feelings that can't be framed or hung on the fridge.

June 22

Lust is pushing me closer to the precipice. I need for us to talk, but like a nervous zoo cat, I keep pacing my cell, stalking any worthy distraction. The murmuring vibration of his voice, his hot chocolate eyes, his ash brown brows and mmm... the dark hairs in the center of his chest, the long, purposeful lines on his palms, and the delicate ones around his eyes... stimulate physical sensations I can't describe (oh I don't even want to go there) from a man I know will flutter flirtatiously through my life. Over the last little while, I have found myself lost in love of his hands, but deeper so now, the uniformity of his cuticles and the evenly shaped half-moons at the base of his fingernails. He granted me a delectable view of him in the hall just out of the shower on the way to his bedroom. Instead of stealing swiftly to either base, he mumbled something about needing to buy shampoo and coffee cream next time we were out – then he just went about the business of getting dressed. Wendy would educate me about guys' habits based on her experiences – universal tendencies that she's observed - when they make up their mind you belong to them, they'll parade around in all their naturalness and not give it a second thought.

From that, I can't conclude anything. Rudy either feels I belong to him or he really can't tell me apart from the telephone table. Which leads headlong to my inability to respond the way Rick encourages me to when I'm with him – like the hall table, we both are made of wood. Things get intense and I feel myself clawing for solid ground, and the gripping NO of my body is acute and sudden, a form of strangulation by my neurotic phobias of sin, rejection and desertion. Such desolate failure fills me once he has penetrated into my skin, the way it always does when I let him, when I breathe him deep into my lungs. Then the softening and arousing ceases and freezes.

In my sauna of frigidity (ridiculous metaphor), I am burning, flushed, yet emotionally arctic. Then when I'm alone and temperate, I stroke with my mind's eyes the gentle curve of his back, muscular and beautiful, descending the linear valley of his spine to where it meets and unifies with that perfect curve…

I'm still troubled by the time Chris forced himself on me and I charlie-horsed him when he wouldn't stop. A gut reaction that embarrassed me, I never told anyone about that night, not my mom, certainly not Wendy. His confidential drift away from me began following that incident. No surprise.

June 28

> *Fool's Valentine*
>
> *Pleasant appeal can be*
> *The prettily packaged container*
> *Enclosing what can't be seen.*
>
> *Confined in colorful box and bows,*
> *Stale, discolored, lain to waste*
> *Vacuum sealed for a decade.*
>
> *Once opened with glee,*
> *Faced such a degree*
> *Of disappointment that it must*
>
> *Be thrown out with disgust.*

This dinner party tonight at Mike and Natasha's has been planned for
nearly two weeks now and I don't have the courage to tell Rick I'm afraid
to go. I'm tired from all these Kaine project extensions. I don't want to face
a formidable front of doctors and engineers and high achievement
professionals. I'm ambitionless by comparison.

Fourteen

SATURDAY, JUNE 28

"Could I get you to restack those boxes for me?" Kelly asked Rick as she fidgeted to get her left earring in. "The ones on the bottom need to be put on top, and the ones on top…" she motioned like a screen director urging his actors to pick up the pace.

"Yes, dear." Rick obliged cheerfully, careful not to brush his trousers up against the dusty corrugate boxes. "Anything else, m' lady?"

"Could you…?" she continued nervously, suspending a gold serpentine chain from her fingertips.

He took a long look at her in her midnight blue silk sheath dress. "You look stunning. Done any modeling?"

"Never."

"Ever think about it?"

"No." She didn't have to hold her hair up from her neck as he secured the necklace clasp. Her new haircut initiated a refreshing transformation to her life. She surprised Betty, her long-time stylist at Milo's Salon, when she requested a look that was modern, sleek and sexy. Her locks shone brighter with a full coloring rather than only highlights. The long side-swept bangs and tresses near her chin framed her face distinctly. The haircut angled up to the nape of her neck, was designed to highlight her jaw line and show off her shoulders.

Her neck was too silky to not kiss, Rick thought; but now, a serpentine necklace lay in his way. He missed not having the longer lengths of her hair to run his fingers through, but found this enticing advantage was well worth the change. He loved her new look.

She fiddled with her hands, concerned that she had absently smudged her newly glossed nails. Nibbling kisses under her earlobe only intensified her agitation.

"Relax. Tonight will be fine," he tried to assure her.

She stepped away from him and reached for the paddle brush on her dresser. "And what am I supposed to tell them when they ask?"

"The truth."

Kelly stood motionless in front of her mirror's dazzling image with a hallmark expression of internal disappointment. She checked her fingernails again.

"Of course they'll be interested in what you do," he pressed on. "I don't think any guest there will know about the wide world of graphic design or ice dance, for that matter, and I bet none of them have ever written a lick of anything creative. I'm fascinated by who you are, they will be too." He concluded with matter-of-fact certainty.

She nodded predictably.

He cupped his hands on her shoulders as he looked to her reflection, "Attitude, Kel, attitude!"

"Attitude, my ass," she grumbled back to the mirror.

"And yes, what a fine one it is."

She swatted his mischievous hands and sent the clear signal it was time to leave.

Upon the Wedgwood neighborhood property of Dr. Mike Hartfort and Dr. Natasha Khanna neatly stood a middle-class, two-story pepper brick colonial. No fewer than a half-dozen cars lined the avenue in front of their home; by her estimation, she would have to socialize confidently with no less than twelve other professional elites.

Rick came around to escort her out of the SUV. "Kel, relax."

"I don't know if I can do this." She felt uneasy until she detected the exotic aroma of North Indian cuisine.

"It's dinner with friends, that's all. There's no royalty, no press.... It will be fine."

"Do Mike and Natasha know about me? What have you told them?"

"That you're *oh* so cute," he emphasized, "and I'm thinking of keeping you." He failed to convince her out of the car. "Kel," he leaned toward her, "we're here. Let's go in, have dinner, meet some other nice, hopeful, good citizens. You're here with me, I'm here with you. We're here together."

This is not Kelly versus Rick, she thought to herself. "We're here together," she repeated out loud. She then answered him definitively, "Okay."

Low-level landscape lanterns lit the walk from the driveway to the front step. Rick pushed open the front door, called a hello, and they both walked in. Their foyer felt degrees warmer than the out of doors in the wave of aromatic heat that emanated from the kitchen. How much trouble had they gone to for this dinner party, she worried.

Mike's appearance was neat and clean-shaven with short dark brown hair. He turned out to be much shorter and heavier set than Kelly imagined; perhaps that's not unusual given that he's an over-scheduled doctor and probably had to get most of his meals on the go, in between on-call hours, referrals and hospital meetings. He greeted her with a firm, enthusiastic hug. It was an embrace of acceptance, not of social nicety.

Natasha was petite and svelte with long wavy black hair and energetic, convivial dark brown eyes. She waited patiently for her turn to welcome them. Kelly found herself sincerely embraced again, this time with a relaxed joviality that placed her at greater ease. Natasha postured nothing of the expected look of a tired doctor, but more the confident appearance of a lady who knew how to throw dinner parties. She led them into the living room where an ethnic mix of young to middle-aged friends chatted amiably. Kelly couldn't determine right away who was paired with whom, from a couples' standpoint.

Natasha and Mike offered an evening of modern blended society in their lovely home featuring an East meets West décor. There were unique metal and wood sculptures on the living room end tables, and the bulbous narrow-shade lamps were Indian brass. The framed wall hangings looked like sidewalk Batiks she had seen at summer multi-cultural festivals, but these were smaller, far more detailed and elegant, distinctly the real thing. Kelly was quickly overwhelmed following the casual introductions with all the other guests. She graciously accepted from Natasha an appetizer plate of stuffed pastry samosas with tangy tamarind ginger chutney. Already, the new term 'samosas' had abandoned her, along with the name of nearly every guest. Tasting her appetizers, she predicted she would enjoy dinner and even confided this revelation to Rick when he brought her a glass of red wine. Rick sat next to her as they began to get involved in conversations with those around them. Within the hour, Natasha summoned the group for a buffet dinner.

Kelly was in awe at the display of tantalizing dishes that lay before them on the dining table. She immediately recognized a tray of Tandoori Chicken and spiced yogurt raita next to the flatbreads. Mike handed her a plate and offered to be her personal dinner concierge. He took her on a tour of the table and explained each and every dish to her, as though he had prepared them himself, as other guests followed along eagerly.

Rick loaded up his plate as though he hadn't eaten in a week. As Kelly sampled her selections, she understood why Rick couldn't be bothered with Indian restaurants. No restaurant could match this.

The evening progressed comfortably and as the gathering thinned towards midnight, conversations became more concentrated, and took on greater depth and focus, as opinions on world issues, career choices, family pressures and various life challenges were openly exchanged. Throughout the conversations, Kelly found Natasha to be strongly intuitive, with world philosophy being of focal interest to her. Kelly and Rick lingered on after the other guests had headed home, intending to stay and help clean up. Rick and Mike chatted companionably while collecting glassware and dishes while Natasha explained to Kelly that mundane kitchen duties were always a time of quality bonding in her family and culture, the time when women could talk freely, and not be heard by their husbands over the din of clattering dishes and running water. She pointed out her culture's relentless attachment to the significance of stellar and planetary alignments, and the perceived will of the deities, miscellaneous forms of superstition, religious or otherwise. Natasha expressed a genuine interest in Kelly, her interests and her thoughts on life in general. Kelly thought it ironic that at no point did Natasha focus on career as a topic, she insisted there were far more important things to discuss, including how she and Rick had met. Kelly humorously recounted the coffee collision at Faders and shyly mentioned that anything from that point onward was strictly natural fallout and that she hadn't been looking to meet anyone. Natasha responded, cultural conditioning ingrained, that nothing ever happened purely by accident, that fate played a hand in every person's life…that their lives had crossed paths for a very important reason.

SUNDAY, JUNE 29

In her free time, Kelly continued to sift through the boxes Rick helped her retrieve from storage two Sundays ago. It was a task she had taken on reluctantly following Dr. Lake's advice to reconnect with her family's past in a more material way. Fueled these days by the kind of penchant that an archeologist or historian might experience while digging up clues out of the ground, she went about the process of investigation with a remote, curious interest, rather than with an urgent emotional attachment that initially terrified her. The boxes contained smaller personal effects and bank papers, stuff the movers had packed from her parents' dresser, nightstands, and home office filing cabinet.

In the four hours they spent rummaging at the storage facility, she and Rick located boxes labeled "educational psychology references and research", as well as "real estate, architecture, interior design." Rick figured that perhaps all her parents' clothing had already been donated to Goodwill or the Salvation Army, likely after the funeral. Kelly knew that her mother's jewelry, along with the hefty bundle of estate documents were stored in the bank. At no time after their final estate settlement had she needed to open that safety deposit box.

In the past decade, Kelly had ventured only once to the storage facility, over eight years ago. Accompanied by Arthur and Marilyn and Wendy, she came to retrieve her family photos and whatever items that she could utilize in her new flat. In addition to furniture and kitchen gadgets, she chose also to bring out books of poetry.

Rick was astonished at how little of her parents' life and their home remained in storage upon their deaths; it was a dose of hard reality.

Kelly remembered only vaguely some of the things that had been sold. Glimpses of her past pin-balled in her mind from the moment they raised the overhead door to that storage room. Selected pieces of furniture that held ancestral significance were stacked around and beneath several boxes containing her family's treasured collected decorative items, dishes and silverware. With reverence and awareness, Arthur and Marilyn had carefully set them aside for Kelly's future. There was a dining room set consisting of the cherry table and leaf, eight chairs and hutch, and a living room suite. The remaining unmatched pieces were inherited antiques from her grandparents' time, including a mahogany hall table, a curio cabinet, and the old Willard upright grand piano of Bridget's, all wrapped in foam paper and plastic. A vision of Christopher in a decorated, conical party hat flashed in her mind's eye. The dining room table she remembered having her birthday parties at appeared much smaller now.

The piano hooked Rick's interest and he worried that a long untended instrument might be of little value now. The fact that it had been carefully wrapped and stored in a humidity controlled environment would be its only redeeming hope until a certified piano re-builder could take a closer look at it. Rick promised to arrange this, if Kelly wanted to incorporate the piano back into her life. She hadn't a clue. It was as large and as daunting as she remembered it being during the four years she took lessons and practiced the way her mom did at about the same age. She hadn't played a piano since she was eleven. She could barely remember how to read music from her teen years in school choir. But the experience of seeing the instrument again and caressing its dark-stained, crackled wood cabinet, even through the airtight wrapping, filled her with a flood of memories that very much connected her to her mom and brought back to life the atmosphere of her former home. She couldn't test the keys to see if they still worked. The key cover was shut tight and bundled with wrapping, but likely not locked. She recalled that nobody in the family knew where the key was. Bridget was sure her parents lost it back in the nineteen-forties.

A real place to call home crossed her mind yet again. Maybe she wouldn't remain in her congested flat that much longer, she thought; her lease was month-to-month. She would look for a new place for next spring, perhaps; one thing at a time.

That afternoon, they loaded what they could fit in Rick's SUV, and boxes now cluttered her living room floor in front of the window seat. Next to them lay a catchall box of five empty photo albums and disorganized piles of photographs. She figured she'd deal with those in the same, controlled way she would everything else from here on in, when it was the right time, when she was ready, and certainly not all at once; both Dr. Lake and Rick reminded her of the cliché therapeutic guidelines. This path to healing was overwhelming at times, but to her surprise, her emotions swelled in more manageable surges. She concluded that time was the only consistent factor she could rely upon; the familiarity of her flat was a factor in how she responded emotionally. She knew the time would soon arrive to revisit her old neighborhood and relive aspects of her childhood: to walk the old, familiar streets from her house to school, the way she, Wendy and Chris did together daily for years, and anything else she felt compelled to do. She wondered whether Rick would still be around to accompany her.

It was around the time that she decided to confront her past with a more hands-on approach that Rick told her the consortium would be forced to dissolve due to funding cuts. He spoke as though this was expected news. She understood when he said he had seen the writing on the wall for some time. He had approximately three months to wind up any loose ends of his current projects and cancel plans for near-future research goals and that he needed to secure new work. He always knew the post-doctoral portion of his career was temporary and it would be either a natural, convenient transition, or a forced one, that would push him the next step forward. That job-hunting would hog his free time. Kelly knew he grew up in small-town New Brunswick, lived in big-city Ontario, then in end-of-the-line Nova Scotia, and he had traveled around the world every chance he got in between. For rovers like Rick, the planet was the playground of choice. No borders. No boundaries. With the exception of gravity, he saw no reason to remain confined anywhere.

Whatever smatterings of time came his way, he gave to her. And she took it. The drudgery of her daily life had fallen back into its well-worn pattern, with ongoing deadlines at work, but with no place to skate during the summer. They made it a point to meet for morning coffee at Faders Café and have dinner together as often as circumstances would permit. Conversations revolved around updates on their daily lives: hopes, disappointments and possibilities surrounding work prospects on his side, family memories and personal discoveries on hers, all interspersed with stolen moments of his flirtatious initiations, to which she nervously granted limited latitude on occasion. Like rules-of-engagement experiments, their attempts to satisfy a growing need for intimacy met with unexpected, invisible and incomprehensible obstacles. Over time, it proved to be more frustrating than either of them could openly confess to each other.

Neither she nor Wendy made any contact with each other whatsoever. For the first time in twenty-two years, they lived separate lives. Kelly felt stronger without Wendy breathing down her neck. For the first time, she was learning to own her entire history and literally bring it home, as she sorted through her parents' belongings. It was the conception of a new way of living she couldn't deny. Perhaps she and freedom would eventually find each other during the gestation of shifting perspective. All she knew was that something inside her had suddenly sparked to life.

Rick's music experienced several reincarnations. When he played for her, she sensed his voice clawing deeper into her psyche than perhaps even he realized. Or maybe he did. For someone who didn't seem to have much time to play, wondrous things were happening musically and Kelly couldn't be sure if Rick just knew how to take advantage of creative serendipity, if he had the omnipotent capability to summon it on command…or if he was naturally uttering what mattered to him the only way he truly knew how. She knew that her soul skated subconsciously every hour she wasn't on the ice; it longed for it. Music must be the same for him, she contemplated, such transcendental energy was his life force, forever inciting and bubbling into formation, always developing, continually honing, even when he was on the phone, the computer, cooking supper, or - she awakened to the possibility - eternally trying to connect to her. What was his true motivation? He only played for her. His music spoke to her, this she knew inherently. Did he fully understand in himself this beckoning? Her confusion ascended to paradoxical heights, a catch-twenty-two, of sorts, and she was still trying to figure him out. Had the steamy tension of their emergent sexual attraction been fueling his music, or had he designed his music to inflame the tension, only to commission its energy toward the turbine of intimacy?

SUNDAY, JULY 13

"Rick, I need you to take a look at these. Tell me what you think they are." Kelly handed him a mottled brown, expanding file folder, which she found buried at the bottom of one of the dusty file boxes that belonged to her parents. He planted himself on the muslin sofa after tossing a plump cushion onto the floor next to a pile of her parents' personal possessions that she had been sorting: cassette tapes without covers, two eyeglass cases, several business cards, pens and pencils, some notebooks, an odd-shaped perfume bottle, and a rather eclectic collection of unused, unsent greeting cards. Rick had just returned the bronzed baby shoes that once fit Kelly's infant feet back to the stash, after studying them closely with delight. If he had time later that evening, he planned to sift through the stacks of photographs in the catchall box, hoping to learn more about her childhood. He unhooked the string clasp of the file folder and pulled out several stacks of legal-sized documents, stapled and bound in an orderly fashion. Two sets of papers looked to be initial drafts of her mom's and her dad's last will and testament. Next was a package relating to the home mortgage and home equity secured credit line. Near the bottom of the stack were documents he was uncertain about. "Were these the ones?"

She curled up on the sofa next to him, "Yes," she flipped through the papers again, "I need to know if you think they are what I think they are."

He took his time perusing the pages, one by one. "What do you think they are?"

Kelly took the first set of documents that Rick handed to her. "An application for legal separation, granted seven years before they were killed and here, filing papers for divorce, incomplete. Not filed?"

"Unsigned," he qualified as he handed her the page in question to check for herself, "by your dad."

"But signed by my mom." She looked again more closely. "Rick, she signed and dated it long before they died, over three years before."

"Guess she turned them back over to your dad to sign and he never did. They couldn't be filed without both signatures. Did you know anything about this?"

"No. If my parents had gotten divorced, they would have told me, right?"

"I would think so."

"Unless these are unsigned duplicates and the originals were filed." Kelly became agitated.

"What? And they neglected to inform you about any of it in the span of x years? No way. Kel, my guess is that your parents may have considered divorce, then decided to pitch the idea and chose not to tell you. Maybe they wanted to protect you, didn't want you to worry. To me, it looks like nothing was filed, except for a separation agreement, because it's been stamped. Had they ever separated?"

"No. Dad would go away for a while off and on, mostly for research. But I was always told that it was because of work."

"Do you think that was true?"

"Dad was away a lot when I was growing up. I just figured it was his work. It's what mom always said, that it was what he did." She remembered her mom stolidly brushing off her questions about her father's periodic absences.

Rick studied the papers again. "Reason for divorce listed here is 'irreconcilable differences'."

Kelly sat silently next to him. Her eyes remained transfixed on the array of greeting cards on the floor. Time passed. She picked up the bottle of perfume and tried opening it. The top wouldn't come undone. The liquid inside looked dark and discolored. She walked to her kitchen island and threw it in the trash.

Rick got up and followed her to the bed. She lay with her fingers interwoven behind her head. Her heart felt vacant as she stared at the white mushroom cap light fixture smack dab in the center of the blank stucco ceiling. He sat next to her. She wouldn't look to him, although he couldn't take his eyes off her. He watched a lone tear roll onto her pillow. "Kel, when did you find these papers?"

"Last week, after you had moved the boxes for me. I finally got to them. When I found the folder, I looked at the papers and I figured what you said they were. Guess you don't need a university degree to know that."

"Why didn't you tell me?"

"What's the point? It's not like anyone could do anything about it. Just like the rest of my life."

"You kept this to yourself for a week."

"There's a lot I keep. Don't tell me you're angry at me for this now too."

"Kel," he began compassionately, but she cut him off.

"There's no point."

"Why can't we talk about this?"

"Talking is the last thing you want to do. Admit it. You haven't wanted to talk since I don't know when. It's not like there aren't a zillion things you refuse to discuss and creatively avoid."

"Not true…maybe a half a zillion." Better not to set this full ablaze, he thought. Things had already grown strained enough over the last month or so. "You know words get lost on me."

"I know. Don't think I haven't noticed." She rolled over on her side, away from him. "Words obviously get lost on a lot of people."

"Kel, I don't know what all went on with your folks, what their problems were. All I can say is you have to deal with the here and now, not about the past and what can't be undone."

"Works for you, does it?" she mumbled.

Her chilly, indignant tone upset him, there was no point pursuing any discussion with her like this. He got up and headed for the door.

"Or I guess sex was always the better cure for you and Rebecca than talking," she called out icily.

He stopped dead in his tracks. Her acerbic words ate deeper into him than he intended to reveal. "Nah, Nyquil. Cure for whatever ails you," he muttered sarcastically as he walked out the door.

WEDNESDAY, JULY 16

She walked with trepidation down the long hallway of the Engineering Complex toward his lab. When she got to the door, space hung deathly silent. She peered in and saw the darkened room was empty of Rick and his cohorts. All the equipment was turned off. Could they have closed up shop already, she wondered; how long does it take to shut a lab down? She thought of the government and how entire programs, lives, careers and structured services end with the lock of a deadbolt, when faced with more month at the end of the money. His office was further down the hall, a small hovel no bigger than a closet, arrayed with a bunch of similar closets belonging to other techs and post-docs. But this shoebox had his name on it and for the tentative duration, it was still his. So she hoped.

She set one cup of coffee on the floor so she could knock upon his office door. As she bent down to retrieve the warm cup, she saw the base of the door swing open in front of her. "Oh, hi," she greeted looking far up to him.

He bent down and balanced on the balls of his feet. He met her greeting at eye-level, "Hi, yourself."

"Peace offering." She handed him his coffee.

He helped her up, relieved to see she had come by to smooth things over. And hopefully not to directly accuse him of being hypocritical, one-track minded, selfish, for statistically thinking of sex every seven seconds and in general, for being a guy. Over the last couple of days, he had reflected upon her point of view. He invited her into his cramped quarters, "Warning: only big enough to come in and change your mind."

Kelly smiled affably. His shoebox was stacked high and wall-to-wall on one side with textbooks, journals, papers that were falling out of other papers and several upright cardboard journal organizers, nearly empty, save but a few publications. To keep the books and random papers company, there was one wooden chair, a built-in desk fitted into a width no more than three feet, and one overhead light. Behind the door was a coat hook. "First time I've even really been in here. Homey. Efficient. Deceivingly much more spacious than it looks from outside."

He wanted to remind her not to breathe too much, for oxygen was a rationed consumable commodity. Instead, he made a trite joke about claustrophobia. He offered his swivel chair to her, but she declined.

Shoving a series of journals and his lab notebook to the back of the workspace, she leaned upon the edge of his desk and sipped her coffee. "I managed to slip away from work without anyone noticing. I'd give them about a half hour before they even notice I've vanished. But at that point, they won't know when exactly I left, so that might buy me a half hour more."

"Well done. Sneaky. Turning a new leaf, I see?" He stood close in front of her and positioned his coffee cup onto the ledge behind her. His eyes smiled up close to hers as he spoke.

She no longer felt like drinking her tepid coffee. She handed it to him and he set it down next to his.

"Thanks for coming to visit me. I like surprises," he whispered to her neck without letting his lips touch her skin.

She let him absorb her and they kissed single-mindedly as though they hadn't seen each other in a week. It had been three days. Realizing the benefits of small spaces, she giggled out loud.

"What's so funny?"

"Nothing." She licked her lips innocently. "Everything." She kissed him again then buried her nose into his chest, just above the shirt button that she considered unbuttoning. His dark chest hair gently tickled her lips. "So, why can't we talk?"

"We can talk."

"No, we used to talk."

"We kiss now. And not just because you're supremely hot in spandex."

"So why can't we talk and kiss?"

"Well, for obvious reasons, they're mutually exclusive. Unless...."

She sensed his testosterone gears grinding. His raised eyebrow gave him away. "You are one naughty boy."

He kissed her again, "Now then, how are you?"

"Coping," she offered, "badly. I saw Karen yesterday and told her about the papers I found, and I told her that I told you about it." She began to explore inside his shirt again.

"And?"

"She was impressed that I managed to tell you after only a week, and she was more impressed that I told you before I told her."

Rick smiled. Battles may be lost on occasion, but the war was as yet hers to win. "Any brilliant insights from the good doctor for handling this glut of new knowledge?"

"Yep." She didn't elaborate.

"Industry secrets, of course."

"I'm stuck in the past."

"Expert analysis?"

"Doctorate in psychiatry."

"Doctorate in engineering, what difference does it make?"

"Chronologically and mentally more stuck than I realize. More than she realized."

"Really." He stepped back and tried to absorb this at a level deeper than he currently understood it to be. "Solution strategies?"

"Time. Awareness. Honesty. Work. More talking. More writing. More faith."

"And for say, someone like me?"

"To be an infinite wellspring of patience and understanding of the reverse black hole variety."

Rick nodded at the magnitude and uncertainty of it all, the majority beyond his puerile comprehension. "I'm looking at Calgary."

"What?" Kelly responded blankly to the sudden change of topic.

"Calgary," he repeated. "Best known as NHL home of the Flames. Lesser known as home of CA Technologies." He handed her a fax listing. "My uncle sent it out the other day. He submitted my name to them."

"Your dad's brother?"

"Yeah. Well-established Cowtown resident, and expert petrochem engineer."

She surveyed the page and read the corporate listing aloud, "offices and testing laboratories in Cleveland, Ohio and Calgary, Alberta… seeking experienced material scientist/engineer.…. electrochemical test instrumentation, metallography lab, coating and polymer lab, SEM, TEM, AFM… Rick, I don't know what any of this means." She handed the page back to him.

"Scanning Electron Microscope, Transmission Electron Microscope, Atomic Force Microscope…"

"Karen was right. You and I do live on different planets. You gonna work for this jargon outfit?"

"Don't know."

"I knew it wouldn't be long before you'd find a good job perfectly tailored to your alien ways."

"Don't have a job yet. For all I know, I'm probably over-qualified."

You're obviously under-qualified, Miss, the voice whispered subliminally to her. She squeezed her eyes shut and willed Agramon away.

Rick saw her momentary distraction, and waited until it passed. "They're going to have me come out next month and meet with them."

She stood up from the edge of the desk and maneuvered around him in what began to feel like something fitfully smaller than a broom closet and was getting smaller. She grabbed her coffee cup from the ledge. "Three quarters of the way across the continent. Nothing around here, I guess. Of course not, how could there be. Hole-in-the-wall-Halifax…" she garbled incoherently, as she guzzled her coffee.

He observed her discomfort every time he spoke of moving on and their recent inability to communicate only made it worse. "Let's get some chow. I know a nice place up the road." And they headed off to the European Deli across from the Public Library.

June 29

Karen's file on me has spilled over to a new carton. My now documented fear of 'in situ' sexual intimacy, like the 'in situ' social anxiety is just one more manifestation of my generalized disorder.

On the bright side, I went to a dinner party last night and actually had fun. I loved meeting Natasha and Mike and I can see why Rick adores them so much. He feels completely comfortable with them. I always felt at ease with him and just assumed that he felt the same way with me. It's not true at all - honest comfort isn't what I've been seeing. He's different with me, just as I'm sure he's different at work with his colleagues. Comfort is what I witnessed last night after everyone else had left. He and Mike exist in the same reality, even though they're so different. They talk, but they don't have to. They don't talk and they don't need to. It's like they occupy the same space somehow. Same with Mike and Natasha — they understand each other, they belong to each other. I noticed how they never collided in the kitchen...

Mike made me feel welcome in their home and with their friends, and Natasha made me feel welcome in this world. (No wonder Rick considers them his family — maybe more than his own blood relations.) I admire Natasha for her bottomless reserve of faith and enthusiasm for life. I was thrilled to meet someone who has discovered her own brand of spiritual harmony as I have been striving to do. She showed me her favorite sandalwood statue of the Hindu Goddess Saraswati (gorgeous ornate carving), the deity of wisdom, knowledge, music, the arts, and higher understanding. It was the first time I've ever touched or smelled real sandalwood - the scent aroused me. Natasha believes that higher states of being can be arrived at through scent. She has been involved in hormone chemistry research and how pheromones are the fount of human physical relationships, familial bonding and romantic attraction. She wants to identify how pheromone compatibility influences sibling relational harmony. I had no idea that was possible! I confided to her that I had always felt immediately comforted by my dad's presence, he always smelled so good to me, and that I missed it. She reassured me that the influences of scent are very real and that specific scents and odorless pheromones vitally stimulate primal forces within us and some can be extremely nurturing and healing. I loved what she said - that the scent of the ones you love draws you into a unique invisible magical realm that modern fad aromatherapy marketers only dream about.

July 1

He definitely knows more than he's letting on. He listens attentively, with tenacity to every word I say as though his life depends on it. Or mine. But he hardly responds, like he's waiting for me to admit more. I feel like I'm disappointing him. Every day feels like one long therapy session now.

Outside my window, a lone cirrus cloud drifts in the infinite surround of blue sky, gossamer rime only to be known from afar… and silently pondered. How heavy would it be, if you could hold it in your hand?

Lighter than air…

I want to float like that above the history and tragedy that has defined my life. Wendy has shown it is possible to move on. She always complained that all these serious contemplations kept me from living in the here and now. I don't want to deal with the psychologizing anymore. I just want to live.

July 5

Tension is mounting by degrees now between us - there is no real communication - only meaningless surface small talk. He is restless, irritated, aggravated and frustrated to the point that he's taking it out on me. For his own protection, he has resolved to treat me like he would one of

*the guys, because he knows I won't ever be one of the girls — One of his
girls... how many, he's never told me.*

*Misty imagination
Miasmic me,
Perception his only truth*

*Such I can never be
As much as I want to be,
I can never come close.*

*I long to reach the horizon
Where the blue of his sky
Meets the blues of my sea*

July 6

*Iniquitous Intuition, you have never failed me
My reasons, I resist to do what I fear to do.
Love me virgin-white naïve
Cherish with me what I have always known,
Let me dream only what I believe,*

And nothing more.

*Ignorance forever be my bliss
Come back this day, make this all go away.
Singeing my fingertips,
Knowledge of truth now fused to my soul
Explodes with bitterness and falsity.*

And nothing more.

I defied my Intuition, She has slapped me back to my rightful place. Search and retrieval of my past was a mistake. Why did I think I deserved to heal?

July 13

(I just found it crumpled up at the bottom of my closet).

I have a few minutes before he gets here. While he was washing the car yesterday, I went into his bedroom to look for a tank shirt that I thought I left behind, the dark blue spaghetti strap one that might have ended up in his laundry. As I rooted through his dresser drawer, I came across my journals that I had given him. He had stacked them in two piles at the back of the drawer, behind his t-shirts. Where did I get the notion that baring my written body to him could magically release me and take us to the next level? I saw he had marked a page in my third journal with a card. There, I found a single-panel white linen wedding invitation. I didn't know who Hannah Etter or Charles LaCroix were - their wedding ceremony was set for August 23rd in Hampton. He never mentioned to me he was planning on going home for it. Maybe he has no plans to go. The invitation happened to mark the page where I had written anniversary goodbye letters to my parents.

***

He stormed out because I shut down — again. So many nagging questions about my parents' marriage and his relationship with Rebecca, ones that can neither be asked nor answered. By putting them on the page, I offer them up to the cosmos.

Why does anyone bother to make a life with someone else? Why did my parents make the choices they made? Why was their marriage so unhappy?

Because I was born? Would they have not gotten married at all if it weren't for me? Does that mean their being dead is better than having been unhappily married alive? Do I go along with Rick to believe that sex really does unite understanding? In my parents' case, sex caused the reason for the division. Why won't he confront his past? Why did he make the sacrifices he did and stay engaged if he didn't feel truly loved by her? Pattern: Why does he willingly give himself up to women who can't love him the way he needs to be loved? Did he genuinely love her despite how she treated him or was everything about their relationship for show? He lives a rivets-in-a-hull philosophy of life, nailing one day after the other, a path that only walks him further away from his truth. He's not a virgin. Is he happier than me? He told me at Mike's cabin that his relationship with Rebecca was physically intense, her initiations right from the beginning. He joked about it being a "youthful" kind of love - an opportunity to answer curiosity's call with each other. He never actually said that he didn't want to marry her - that with as bad as things were getting, he still had no intention of calling off their engagement. My parents didn't dissolve their marriage and maybe they should have but didn't because of me. Do these circumstances verify cowardice as a virtue?

July 16

I had to get all this crap off my chest to Karen yesterday. All she could do was stand back and play outfield to the volleys of my immature understanding of "mature" relationships, all my own childish, self-righteous, virtuous judgments of people who don't deserve shallow criticism from an inexperienced little girl who masquerades through life beneath a veil of womanhood.

I'm starting to catch onto Karen's diagnosis drift — simply put, I'm like a little girl, emotionally stalled at a very virginal 17 — so here I lie in my bed, still technically pure as snow at 27, lagging at least ten years behind my chronology. By calculation at 34, mentally and experientially, that puts Rick a full seventeen years ahead of me - twice my "emotional age". Shades of a cradle robber behind the romantic smoke and mirrors… someone who considers himself mature, honorable and sensitive might be horribly ashamed by this. I know I am and I don't want to be the one to explain it to him. I wonder what kind of ego-twisting damage this minor theoretical detail would do to his masculinity.

***

For the first time, he talked to me about real things today over lunch, mostly his job situation and his family. He wasn't comfortable. I continue to jump to conclusions about his life and who he is because all I have to go on are unanswerable questions. So I tried to encourage him to speak more, but I think my desperation just got in the way and rallied his defenses even more until he clammed up.

He also told me he contacted a piano restorer who would come out to the storage facility and take a look at the piano there. I know what he's trying to do…He wants to tie up what loose ends he can before he moves away.

July 19

Even the grocery store isn't safe.

We crossed paths with Wendy in the produce section. She was with Franklin and Timothey. I was cornered the instant I saw them. I wanted to dash past them, but I was struck motionless, next to the melons. (Even now, I can see, feel and smell those cantaloupes with a level of intimate detail I've never previously known with fruit.) No use, she came rushing towards me leading Timothey joyfully by the hand. She introduced this bright-eyed ten-year-old boy to me and I shook his hand. It felt so tiny and limp - I grabbed it so tightly in my nervousness. Before I could fabricate an excuse to get away, Franklin came and stood next to her and I finally got to meet him. He took my hand and greeted me as though he knew me. He said he was sure he had met me before. I insisted that he and I had never met. He wouldn't let go of my hand and babbled on at how familiar I seemed to him, but he just couldn't place how he knew me. Of course he couldn't. We had never met before. Wendy rattled on about something or other and I felt awkward, out of place, next to those damn cantaloupes. It hadn't even been two months, yet it felt like several years had passed by, and she was introducing me to her growing family that I knew nothing about.

About an hour later, it hit me how surreal that eclipse of a meeting was, like moons orbiting the same planet, communal not coincident. She couldn't conceal her obvious discouragement when she saw Rick join me. I don't even know how I responded, outwardly. I think I nodded and smiled as Wendy blathered on...

Franklin still remained curiously fixed on me...

It creeped me out.

Fifteen

SATURDAY, JULY 19

They headed out for what locals call a tourist day. Rick had been looking forward to stealing a day to do nothing - with the way things had been going with Kelly, better that time arrive sooner rather than later. The day was set aside for her, no phone calls, emails, faxes, no discussion relating to unemployment or relocation. He planned their day off together carefully: after completing needful errands after work on Friday, they would spend a quiet evening enjoying dinner and a movie at home with the plan of hitting the road early the next morning to head out for a day along the South Shore.

Weeks ago, Kelly expressed a desire to revisit the historic seaside town of Chester. It had been several years since she had puttered around this picturesque Maritime resort setting. She remembered a weekend there seven years ago when they all went up for Wendy's sailing club's participation in the province's annual regatta. Kelly took every opportunity to be near the water. She could swim, but knew little about sailing; nevertheless, she remained satisfied on the shore's sidelines to observe the action of lasers, ketches and sloops sharply tacking, looking to gain a competitive edge from the shy, shifting breezes. Wendy placed second in a solo race that weekend, beating a rival from the Royal Yacht Squadron. Kelly remembered the vermilion red ribbon with gold stitching Wendy received and how she pinned it on the corkboard above her desk in her room. Arthur Kaine grew up in a family of recreational seafaring folk, owners of a variety of inboard sailboats. He concluded that while his wife and daughter were not ideal cottagers, perhaps they'd enjoy the more preferred activity of upscale Maritime aristocrats, sailing. The province-wide sailing and yacht club community was visibly populated by upper-class socialites, although the membership profiles dipped into middle-class territory as well. His family's jovial participation proved Arthur to be right on the money this time. They proudly wore the emblem of Halifax's esteemed Waegwoltic Yacht Club, as did their Roue 30 schooner, Adelaide, who wore a plated brass version on her stern. She hadn't made the coastal journey from the Northwest Arm to Chester Basin for the events that weekend, so a family outing on the waters of the Bluenose Route would have to wait for another weekend. Around that time, talk around Halifax was that several Hollywood movie stars had purchased summer properties in Chester, opting for the seclusion, simplicity and social privacy of Nova Scotia over the more hoidy-toidy resort locales like Martha's Vineyard and Cape Cod. In time, even the province's best-kept secret would be out, as Hollywood movies began to be filmed in Halifax and all along the Lighthouse Route. The capital city was the film production hub, with local filming in Chester, Mahone Bay and Lunenburg. Kelly always giggled that Lunenburg would play Nantucket in made-for-TV movies, and Mahone Bay acted as any non-descript town on the coast of Maine; the other reliable favorite was to film at Halifax's Historic Properties waterfront region when Boston was written in the screenplay. No doubt, filming in Canada was cheaper than in the States, and Hollywood relied upon the fact that viewers would be pleasantly fooled, provided locations were chosen smartly. Wendy always hoped that an A-level film producer would spot her on Spring Garden Road, doing so much as dropping a lone envelope into a mailbox in front of City Centre with such an alluring mystique, and then approach her to be an on-camera extra. And it would be the perfect dream beginning of her famed big-screen career. Just the kind of story Wendy could itch to tell when being interviewed on entertainment magazines shown on second-tier cable networks.

How she could recall certain details of her past so lucidly, when ones she wanted to remember hid in the curtains. Memories of Wendy seemed to hog center stage. "I don't know, Rick, it was just weird. All of it."

"What was?" He looked back at her, wearing his metro style shades. The wind blew his hair in all directions. He returned his attention to the twisting road.

She noticed the way his sunglasses concealed the major Hollywood attraction, his eyes, but not the edges of his laugh lines at the temples. The teasing appeal made him look intensely and mysteriously beautiful to her. 'Metro Shades. Lingerie for men.' There was a twist tag line for Wendy, she thought. "Movie Star," she poked at him, still very much on the thought train to LaLaLand.

"Only if you're my groupie."

"You need a haircut."

"I know." His fingers swept his crown to confirm the unruly length. "What was weird?"

"Running into them yesterday."

It was the first time in several weeks that Kelly mentioned Wendy. He decided take her bait. "Everything to do with Wendy is tinted a tinge of odd, wouldn't you say?"

"Did she seem normal to you?"

Rick grinned his refusal to state the obvious.

"You know what I mean," she shook her head to the clouds.

He wanted to hear her version more. "Oh do tell, Madame Mahalia," he thought the off-cliché name suited her well, "all-knowing seer of everything incomprehensible."

"You mock me, Doctor? You dare mock my intuition?"

"Hell no," he attempted at serious. "A Real Man knows better than to do that. Should you be able to predict the future, which I'm not prepared to dispute, you would already know exactly in what tantalizing manner you would have me fall prey to you."

"Remember that, Doctor." She surveyed the high hillside homes situated on her side of the road. "She seemed over the top to me."

"Three ninety-five a minute for that, Mahalia?"

"More pushy than usual. Before you joined us, she'd already been nattering at me for I don't know how long. It was like she didn't care I was there. She could have been yammering on like that to anyone, the checkout girl even."

"She looked happy to me."

"Just what she'd want you think, like a well-rehearsed courtroom defense lawyer to a jury box listing off the overwhelming evidence displaying how perfect her life is now."

"She's not happy? God! And I thought I was getting better at this. They seemed very together, like a happy little agglomeration," his fingers wiggled over the steering wheel.

"Dramatic Fiction acting, her unfulfilled life's dream. She's never fooled me. It's all about show with her."

"The kid seemed cute. Cast him."

"Timothey. Yes." A pause followed. "So was Franklin, for that matter."

"Hey. I heard that," Rick begrudged. "Thinking out loud again, are we?"

"Fragile ego, big boy?"

"Very," he drawled then flashed a flirtatious smile at her. He rounded a tight curve with more speed than he meant to. The tires let out a gripping squeal as the white-capped ocean whizzed by in a blur.

"Like I said, overcompensating."

"What are you aiming to say about me, Mahalia?"

"Not you, Mr. Spotlight. There goes that bipolar ego again," she commented with girlish tease. "Wendy," she reiterated, "overcompensating. That's the feeling I got the entire time. It wasn't a conversation," she announced. "She didn't want a response, she wasn't interested in a discourse, with me, you or anyone. Never mind it was the first time we'd seen each other in nearly two months." Her rhythm of speech sped up another notch.

Rick felt the need to brake. Town was approaching.

"There was no conversation," Kelly railed on. "She was delivering a news broadcast, about her born-again life of freedom as the all-important epicenter of this new instant-just-add-water family." Her pitch dropped an octave for news-radio, "These are the headlines. Now the Details."

Rick thought quickly about Kelly's perception of Wendy's newly landed lead role. "Kel, nothing moves that quickly, no matter how many soap queens she's chosen to identify with."

"So you agree. You don't just maneuver into someone's life like that and fit that seamlessly. For that matter, tell Franklin that! Did you notice him? Cornered speechless the whole time she was prattling on about her new promotion to the very central wifely-maternal figure they'd all been sorely missing. If you ask me, he looked smothered."

"The kid or Franklin?"

Kelly still was convinced that there was something Franklin needed to say when they met, other than bumble around at how he was sure he had met her before. "Rendered mute," she exemplified his plight further, "as Wendy nagged him about the softness of the tomatoes he had just picked out. He's a grown man, for Christ's sake," she loosely tossed to the wind and road noise. "Did you hear him pipe up for his independence and sense of boundary, personal freedom?"

"A Real Man should always have firm tomatoes," Rick felt obliged to stand up for self-aggrandized machismo, especially if Wendy's fella couldn't seem to. All things had to balance out in the universe in the end.

"Shut up, Ricky, or make your point," she delivered impatiently.

"Ask any lonely man with a knife," Rick laughed with a pained look. He turned to see that Kelly wasn't laughing with him. "Maybe he knew she was right, did you think of that? Maybe Franklin has always picked out loser tomatoes his whole life, forever disappointed at the proverbial cutting board. Maybe it's the way it's always been for him until he met Wendy. Maybe he recognized the void in his life that's always been there. And it drives him wild his tomatoes are firm when she's around." He paused to consider the absolute value of his argument, and knew he had fallen short of his mark. "Girls will never guess what all turns a guy on..." He glanced in her direction to see if he had generated any kind of entertained reaction.

It was Wendy's newspaper thesis again. "Dammit," she barked, glaring at him over yet another absurd meaningless discussion.

Startled by her steely stare, he clarified with some seriousness, "A successful flight maneuver is always gimbaled with high-factor precision."

She looked at him with further incredulity and sneered, "Gimbaled?"

"Gimbals, rockets." Surely she knew what he meant. Okay, maybe she didn't. "Every general course needs accurate fine tuning all along the way. A man may try to program his own vector, but it's the smart woman he relies on who controls his maneuvering thrusters."

Kelly couldn't tell if he was kidding or not. What did rockets have to do with Wendy? Or tomatoes?

"You sure you're not just pissed that she didn't ask how you were doing?"...

"My life is going just fine thanks." She wished she were a smart woman.

"Well, I'm pissed she didn't ask how my life was going..." Rick said dryly.

"It was just weird, that's all," Kelly reiterated.

Chester stood like a grand matriarch against the choppy Prussian-blue waves, every detail as charming as she remembered it. The welcoming atmosphere did what it could to appease her, but unanswered questions of her parents' secretly failed marriage nagged at her and got her insecurities all riled up. She knew she would never be the kind of smart woman to know about relationships, or men in general, but deeply wanted to know and experience this man in particular. She wanted to drive Wendy's crooked railroad perceptions of men over a cliff.

Over the last month, the fading connection between her and Rick had risen to the apex of her concern, to the point of becoming insurmountable, knowing his new job would steal him from her. Her inability to respond to his romantic efforts arose around the same time, although outwardly, she continued to appear in control and committed. A lump in her throat swelled. Barbs of ice had been crystallizing within her for her own protection, her internal defense against such regrettable timing of his appearance in her life. Her belly tightened into knots. He mattered to her. Time was growing short, but to succumb now would be disastrous to her heart, no matter how she imagined his departure. Was he really trying to tell her something in the car, the stuff about the tomatoes? Hope, when she needed it most, couldn't make up its mind – was it surging or receding?

They ambled the narrow sidewalks of the town's shopping district. He made the first move to hold her hand as they window-gazed together. She then stepped into an old-fashioned quilt shop.

While he waited for her in the sun's warmth outside the shop's door, pacing the sidewalk, an elderly gentleman carried coffee from a nearby coffee shop. As he passed by, Rick offered a casual acknowledgment.

"Fair day," the old man stopped to chat. His shore accent was thick.

"Seems you know the goods around here. Care to let the secret out?"

"Tell all the honeymooners like you, son, not a damn thing a man can do about his wife's call to shop. And the sooner a man learned that without bickering, the better."

Rick laughed never thinking he'd be mistaken for a newlywed. He was just a single guy who wanted to know where to get decent coffee. Yet there he was, dawdling impatiently in a resort town on a summer day checking the time outside a shop window opposite an eye-catching blond casting eyes on him. Rick smiled genuinely and told the man he'd remember his advice.

The sun gleamed brightly overhead and Kelly found him playing with his watch when she emerged from the shop.

"Find anything?" His watch beeped unceremoniously.

"Yes. Lots."

"Let's go in and see."

"Nothing to buy."

"Show me."

She wouldn't. Instead they walked down Main Street away from the shops; he floundered a mere step ahead of his confusion. They ducked into a deli across the green where they picked up chicken-salad Kaiser sandwiches and iced tea. They took lunch to go and seated themselves in the shade of a plain, whitewashed gazebo overlooking the water.

"I would have gone in with you, you know," he began again as they ate.

She nodded nonchalantly and made her first dent in her Kaiser. Her grandmother kept a handmade quilt bearing the traditional Celtic wedding ring pattern on her old walnut sleigh bed. One of her earliest memories was her index finger following the round, intersecting loops and tracing out the pattern in unbroken continuity from any point she picked, back to that very same start. Such amusement kept a three-year old in her grandparents' bed when she couldn't sleep at steamy twilight. All her life, sleep had eluded her. Her Dad's voice echoed back to her in wave-washes, those times when he'd put her down for the night at her grandparents home, 'Scraps and swatches…bits of fabric…' Distant memories revolved then coalesced. She could feel once again the puffy swatches of gingham and chintz and pilled broadcloth as her fingers stroked the sesame seeds on the surface of her Kaiser bun. 'She had saved every bit of cloth in her hope chest since she was a little girl, Grandma made this in the first year of their marriage, when times were tough in the depression. Each bit, every patch, she sewed together to make this whole thing. Down here, in the corner, you can see Grandma stitched with a needle and thread Ethel and William Pearson.' He would read the stitching to her as her tiny fingers felt and followed the lettering, like Braille. Grandpa didn't live long after Grandma passed. Kelly needed to cling to the memory. She wondered where that quilt was now… she had spotted a wedding ring quilt in the shop, but this one was made from decorator-coordinated sections of fabric in lemon yellow and pale blue. Brand new, devoid of a history and wishfully waiting for one, it felt stiff and smelled of dye-fixative. She fidgeted with the garnet ring on her left ring finger.

"Tell me about it," he asked, pointing to her ring.

She didn't answer him. "Do your parents get along?"

"They manage, yeah."

"Are they happy?"

"They're married."

"Married. Yes. As opposed to. . .?"

"Not." Rick saved a clump of chicken salad from falling out of his sandwich.

"Great." Enthusiasm and the topic of marriage just didn't go together in anyone's mind these days. "What are they like? As people?"

"Polar opposites. Go figure."

"Opposites do attract, you know, Doctor."

He remembered her stand on his theories of like-mindedness. "Mom's mom. She does her mom-things, church choir, baking, visiting with neighbors, her friends, and that keeps her going. Dad's, well. . .there. They have it worked out. Well-oiled machine. Don't get in the way."

"Worked out? You make it sound like a math problem."

"They share deductibles for prescription plans. Mom lives in her world, dad lives in his. He reads a lot."

"You said that before. Is that all he does? Read alone all the time?"

"Oh, no, not at all. Crown Royal keeps him company."

"Scotch?"

"Whisky Blend, actually. Get it right if you're gonna bring it up. In which case, be prepared to duck. Devil's drink."

Maybe Rick came by his evasive, escapist tendencies honestly, she thought. If alcoholism might be hereditary, better that he's chosen music over a bottle. "I've never really seen you drink, just wine with dinner or when you're trying to get a girl you like to give in. Does Kevin drink?"

"Probably."

"To me, good music is as intoxicating as fine wine."

"Really good music is like strong gin. Sorrows drown more deadly in gin. Piercing. Bitter. Makes more the statement."

She noticed the whiplash of his tone. "Your music is beautiful, it isn't bitter," she whispered.

"It's not? Wonderful," he fell backwards defeated. "Guess I'll have to start all over again."

"Ricky," she felt that familiar sharp pang in her throat.

"What," he avoided looking at her.

She forced the golf ball wedged in her throat down into her stomach where the knots insisted on squatting. "You don't know your own music, do you? You have no idea. You spend so much time and energy making it, pouring your silence and pain into it, but have you ever really listened to it?"

He crumpled his sandwich paper looking for a bin to aim for.

"I have. It's not bitter…quite the opposite. There's a vulnerability to it. It's honest. Listen to it sometime, will you? With your whole heart."

He had no choice but to listen.

"Allowing your music inside is challenging because there's something aching in it… a lament that we all need to let out but don't want to face."

There were many things he didn't want to face.

"Rick, your music isn't just sound. Just as paintings aren't just visual, and sculptures aren't only form." She thought for long moment. She wanted to tell him what his music really did to her, how it exposed her heart and awakened her sensibility. What touched her inside were the confessions of quivering strings and undulating tones coaxed from the gentleness of his fingers. Secretly, it was always about the textured ways his sound touched her, urgently and with immediacy, its want as potently enticing as a feather stroking her body. "To me, your music is like the relief of final recognition, of letting go. A primeval release, like being heavenly drunk on fragrant wine with a secret lover at sunrise… after spending the whole night talking, crying, laughing, reminiscing, breaking through to the real and the true until the outside world beckons…and you know you can't ever return to who you used to be, because going back means hiding…again."

He watched her gaze shift from him to the ocean. He knew she was entering the realm where the true Kelly dwelled. Phrases began to flow from her…

> "Music, your intangible connection,
> Between you and your ancestral voices.
> Generations of hopes, hurts, and dreams,
> Both dashed and delightful,
> What coursed through their veins and now yours,

Is the legacy that is yours alone to speak
You are humanity's presence,
To fulfill the reality the seed dreamt,
You make eternity tangible."

There was a moment of peace. He secretly wanted her to keep speaking, not simply for the validation of his soul, but because he loved her words. When she didn't continue and instead stood up, he felt a sudden emptiness. He promptly rose to his feet as though he were mystically tied to her being. Then she walked away to the shoreline. And like the poem, upon its closure, she was gone. He stood, penetrated by her words. Like a river's flow, she filled him...

Kelly leaned forward pressing her fingers against the balcony railing. Her eyes struggled to peer straight downward in an attempt to conquer her fear of heights and the unavoidable vertigo. She convinced herself it was safe to look down for an instant from ten stories' height, to Oakton Gate's tennis courts below. Everything started to spin in a counter-clockwise direction. She quickly turned around. She could see no greater fallacy in human society than the institution of marriage. And with modern times, society was still conditioned to rely on it. She knew her parents' marriage failed because they were too different. Her dad passionately pursued the only avenue of life he wanted to engage in, one that brought them to the other side of the country, and her mother agreed to let herself be dragged there, away from her roots, for the promise of something more. She raised a daughter as well as she knew how, and conformed herself to be the kind of wife she needed to be. The truth might very well be that her mother had no passion in her life. Modern times indeed, women were still the ones making all the sacrifices.

As her thoughts wandered, she considered that Rick might never agree to show his father how much his music means to him. Was it wrong for her to want to understand why he entered a field of study he wasn't sure he wanted to be in, why he got engaged to a woman he wasn't certain he wanted to marry, why he had to run away to the Peruvian Mountains after she died? Was it to deal with his own sense of failure for his inactions? Surely his mother must have worried the very same things. She thought of his family estrangement, his aging parents in a small town and his stalwart choice neither to interfere nor resume a role in their lives, especially when it came to his dad's drinking. She knew he had tried once, as a teenager with limited tools, and failed. Why would he risk trying again? Maybe it was easier to go about nailing in his rivets, away from the condemning pain of his father's rejection, knowing he was never good enough as a boy. Perhaps he feared the same now as a man. What would it take for his father to quit drinking? From what Rick had told her, his father never sewed a stitch for him in his youth. Instead, he seam-ripped his younger son to the point of rebellion out of a sorely belated sense of fatherly duty. She couldn't guess Kevin's plight well enough, she barely knew him. Would it have ever dawned on his dad that his eldest son just ached to be accepted? That his futile search for companionship thus far left him only to wonder what acceptance would feel like?

That must have been why he went on about the fine-tuned guidance of a smart woman... to steer a man toward true happiness, as parents ideally would do for their young ones – a form of unconditional love and sure, it is all in the details. No wonder his mom calls so often and gets after him about settling down.... to try and replace what he never got from his dad. Fine–tuned guidance from loved ones. Add the necessity of sex to a man's equation and that precludes the company of relatives. That would explain why he resists phoning back, going home, visiting on a whim out of sheer delight, because he needs to prove to them he's just fine on his own with his cat, and his guitar, and his lab equipment. His dad could very well die from liver failure in the near future if he drinks as much as Rick says he does. That means he'd be dying today, right now; socially isolated and emotionally decayed from the self-administered anesthesia of royal blended Crown whatever, his father's time was running out. Not five hours drive away sat an old man with a bottle waiting for the last days of a lifetime to do him a favor and just end already. And he might never hear the truth strummed from his first-born son's fingers and heart, the sound of his music that would break the silence of apathy for everyone's benefit.

Yes, time was running out, she told herself again, he would be moving away. She had succeeded enough in locking him out, in every way he tried to enter her, spiritually, emotionally, sexually, she kept restrained, and any concession now was unthinkable.

Rick stepped out from his living room carrying two glasses of lemonade on the rocks. He set them on the patio table and invited her to sit with him on the bench. There was more than enough room for two.

She sipped from her glass, in love with the sensation of the frosty tartness on a late afternoon. "What do you know?" she asked him out of the blue.

"About what?"

"What do you know, for sure? That you would bet your life on."

He gulped his lemonade and thought quickly. "Salt on grapefruit makes it taste sweeter. Just don't ask me to tell you why. Doesn't make a lick of sense. What do you know for sure?"

"Goose-egg. Can a person really get away with that?"

He thought of the dolt at the Queensland gas station they stopped at on the way home from Chester. He couldn't make change for a twenty without a calculator. "Many do, somehow."

"I mean, can you really live life to its fullest, really be happy?"

"With kindness and pity from others, someone said innocence is bliss." He smiled wistfully.

Every time he smiled at her, or touched her, she couldn't guarantee her reaction. "No it's not. Besides, that's ignorance, and trust me, it ain't either."

"I'm getting a hint you're not blissful."

"How can I feel blissful? I feel angry because life is speeding by in overdrive while I'm trying to get out of first gear popping clutches everywhere. Don't tell me you'd feel blissful if you still felt like a stupid seventeen year old."

He was going to mention something blissful he experienced when he was stupid and seventeen. "Never mind. No comment."

"See this?" She took off her garnet ring and handed it to him.

He set his glass down to receive it. "Noticed it from the very beginning."

"Wendy used to make fun of me, saying that I wore it on my ring finger to purposely keep guys away from me, until Chris gave me one with a diamond in it."

"Was she taking wagers?"

"I knew I'd never get a diamond ring from him." She sipped her drink. "But it has fulfilled Wendy's role pretty well."

"Neat. Just like Flash Gordon's ring, the power to perform the impossible!"

"Is that a compliment?"

"Complaint, actually." He smirked as he leaned his back against the bench, studying the dark red gemstone. He tried to recall his courses in physical chemistry to identify the compositional difference between a garnet and a ruby.

"Maybe it never had any power. Only what I willed it to have."

"Okay, it was a compliment. Hell, I noticed the ring the first day. I wondered about the ring. I worried about the ring. Then you know what? Decided to ignore the ring. I asked you out moons ago, and you said yes. If you ask me, it wasn't as powerful a repellent as you thought."

"Would you have gone out with a girl if you knew she were married?"

"Only if she were married to me."

She adored his genius Jack-be-nimble-and-quick humor. Only Rick Hutchinson would say something so sweet and tuck it unflappably beneath a witty veil. "A guy with integrity."

"Just a game I play with innocent girls who fall for it. So why do you wear it on that finger?"

"I used to wear it on my right hand but it never really fit that well."

"Yeah, yeah. Promise ring of eternal first love, admit it."

She laughed. "Is that what you think it is? It was my sixteenth birthday gift from my parents. Garnet is my birthstone."

"Ah." An enlightening statement all around, he thought. "Your birthday's when?" He handed her back the ring and she slipped it back on her finger where it settled back into its furrow.

"January the fourteenth."

He took her hand and looked again at the ring. "Sweet Sixteen, I've seen pictures of you." The thought of the old high school saying 'Sweet sixteen, never been kissed' popped in his mind, but he didn't want her to know his true mentality when he automatically replaced the 'kissed' with 'laid'. He was ashamed he permitted that thought through to completion since the ring was a gift from loving parents to their cherished girl on a milestone occasion. The guilt passed quickly. "And what did you get from them for your seventeenth birthday?"

"I was supposed to get a car. A used something-or-other that we hunted around for well into the spring. They wanted me to have my own transportation in time for university, no matter where I chose to attend."

"And?"

"Story ends."

They both hated uncomfortable silence.

"And...you don't drive." He kissed her hand, unable to veer around the broad brick wall he just crashed them into.

"I don't, even though I got my license when I was sixteen, and I keep getting it updated. I used to drive the Buick all the time. I even drove it the morning of the day they were killed."

"And not since then?"

"No. The Buick died with them," she chuckled aloud.

Her uncharacteristically black humor caught him off guard. "That's not what I meant, Kel," he said contritely, "I meant about you not driving in general."

"I know what you meant, Rick, I'm beginning to understand how you think - I'm a single girl living on her own, earning a decent salary. And you're wondering why I don't own a car, why you haven't seen me get behind a wheel and if this is yet another irrational neurosis far down the long list of problems stemming from my tragic past."

Oh boy, he thought, so he kept quiet. Rudy meowed anxiously at the screen door because he hated closed doors and other physical barriers. Rick stepped forward to slide the door open enough for him to hop out onto the balcony.

"I'm sure it is." Kelly picked up the cat when he trotted to her. "But Karen says it can be helped, if not cured altogether. I'll get there when I get there."

"Let me know when you want to start driving again, we'll take a whirl at it."

She took a long look at her ring as she stroked Rudy's back. "This was the very last birthday gift I got from them, it means everything to me," she whispered to the cat's ear in a childlike voice.

TUESDAY, JULY 22

Rick breezed out Faders' door with an Ethiopian dark roast as he headed to his office to continue his job search. He noticed Wendy was just coming in so he adroitly bounced back two steps to catch the door open for her as it was swinging shut.

"Oh, thanks." Wendy caught the door halfway then stopped in the entry as she saw him.

He noticed she was alone and her eyes were red. "Hey, what's up?"

"Nothing." She smiled wistfully.

"Are you okay?"

"Fine. Couldn't be better." She began to head inside, then turned back before letting the door go, "You?"

Rick grabbed the door again. "Fine. Good." He went inside with her and bought her a French Roast. The call to CA Technologies in Calgary could wait.

She didn't say anymore as they waited in line, but once they sat down, Wendy asked how Kelly was doing. Rick informed her she was working hard, she was still going to therapy and, all things considered, she seemed to be getting better. Wendy began to rattle on about her life moving forward with Franklin, and most of it was a rerun from the meeting at the grocery store. At least she knew her lines well, Rick thought. He updated Wendy that his consortium funding had been cut and that he was in the process of looking for new work. Wendy unsubtly fished for information on where he was concentrating his search. Rick assumed she was attempting to ascertain when exactly he was leaving Halifax. He decided to play along and told her that his current best chance was in Alberta and he was hoping to start work in the fall, perhaps September or October. That would give him enough time to move and get settled in a new place.

"Does Kelly know?"

"Yep." Although he really knew nothing was definite.

"Hope she can handle it."

"Excuse me?"

"Don't be surprised if she tries it again after you go."

Little surprised him when it came to Wendy, and he was prepared to just follow her lead. "You're scared she'll do it again?"

"I don't care anymore. I was forced to live through it once before and it was one time too many. Just wanted to warn you."

"What happened, exactly?"

"When? The night her parents were killed or the night I found her when I came into my room to go bed?"

"The latter. You said at the hospital parking lot that it was you who found her ten years ago. You were so upset, you could barely talk. I didn't know what to do or say."

"Don't tell me you were worried about me."

"As a matter of fact, yes. I have been ever since."

"Forget about me. It was Kelly's call for attention. Kelly was the one everyone cared about."

"Tell me what happened."

"Well, what don't you already know? Her parents died, she stayed with us right afterward. She was out of it all of the time. None of us knew what to do, even my parents. She wouldn't eat, she couldn't go back to school, nobody expected her to, not with only a few weeks left until graduation. She wouldn't do anything, talk to anyone, not even me. My parents were flipping out over her, all the time, because nobody could get through to her. Mom and Dad finally forced her into an intense counseling program. I don't know what all was said, what all went on, because I wasn't there, I still had to go to school. I still had to get my stuff done. I still was expected to graduate. One night, I had a grad committee meeting and I didn't get home until pretty late. My parents had gone to bed and the lights were out everywhere in the house."

"So you assumed Kelly had gone to bed too?"

"Yeah. She stayed in our guest room, next to my room. Anyway, I come home, I go up to my room to get ready for bed and I open the door and flip on the light and. . . ."

"And?"

"There she is." Her eyes stopped blinking.

"Where?"

"There," she pointed to a spot on the bistro table. She continued in a hushed voice, "Laying on the floor, in her pyjamas. She was asleep on my floor, next to my bed, in front of the night table. . .but she didn't have a blanket."

"What did you do?" Rick asked quietly.

"I went to her, bent down, and tried to wake her up, so I could ask her what she was doing on the floor. I figured she must have fallen, or gotten sick suddenly, and ended up there, because she didn't look normal. She didn't look right." Wendy whispered, staring at the same indeterminate spot on the bistro table.

"Not right, how?"

"Pale, almost blue, kind of cold. Not like pink and warm when you're asleep. I couldn't wake her up. I shook her and shook her and called out to her, Kelly, Kelly! She wouldn't wake up. That was it, she was dead. I ran to the hall and screamed for my parents until they came. Then I don't remember. Dad called the hospital then he put her up on my bed and mom kept screaming at him when she couldn't get her to wake up. I stood in the hall telling them she was dead. She was dead on my bed, dead, I knew it." Wendy began to cry uncontrollably out loud. "She killed herself in my room, she hated me that much."

Rick touched her arm and tried to get her attention away from the images that troubled her.

"She was dead on my bed. I could never sleep in my bed ever again. I never did anything to her. I loved her. She was like my sister. I never did anything to her!" She began to wail.

It was no use. Rick had to get her out of the café. He had no idea she had been this close to breaking. Rick helped her up from the table.

"She was dead on my bed, in my room…" she pointed back toward the table spot, tears rushing down her cheeks, pulling runs of mascara and dark brown eyeliner down with them. A hush came over the café. A group of customers grew alarmed. He huddled her out, away from that table. Rick took her outdoors into the fresh air, with Cindy closely behind, carrying a jug of ice water and a glass and some napkins. Rick sat her down at the nearest patio table and poured her some water. Cindy knelt down beside Rick on the sidewalk and held Wendy's hand as he talked to her. Faders' young employees gathered at the door to see what was going on and Cindy shooed them back to work.

"I loved her and she hated me. She still hates me."

"She never hated you," Rick spoke steadily, "she was lost, she was traumatized."

"She hated me because I still had my parents and this was the way she wanted to show me. To this day, I have my life and she hates me for it. It wasn't my fault!" She kept repeating that it wasn't her fault.

"Of course it wasn't your fault. Wendy, listen to me, she was grieving, in shock, and needed professional help, you all did everything you could. You did a lot for her, didn't you?"

"Ever since then, I've been like her guardian angel. I found her and she lived, it meant I was responsible to make sure she would always be okay."

"Who told you that?"

"No one. I just knew. I just did it."

"Did your parents tell you to watch out for her?"

"Yes. They had to watch too. We all had to watch out for her, that was what the doctors said. So that's what I kept doing, up until she kicked me out of her life, she had been everything in my life."

"She never kicked you out of her life, Wendy."

"Oh yes, she did. She ordered me to get out of her life just before she got out of the hospital this last time."

Rick was startled by this information, but he'd have to come back to it later. "When Kelly went for grief counseling, did you see a therapist too?"

"No."

"Did anyone let you know that you could, if you needed to?"

"No."

"Your parents didn't realize what you were going through?"

"No."

"Did you explain to them how upsetting it all was for you?"

"No. What did I have to be upset about? I still had my life. It was Kelly's life that was ruined. We had to think about her. She had no one. I still had my parents."

Wendy had calmed down enough for Cindy to return to work inside. Rick thanked her for her assistance. He then pulled up a chair and sat next to Wendy. Cindy brought out hot tea for both of them.

"After you found Kelly in your room, how did you deal with it, when you knew she was okay, when she was in the hospital and being cared for?"

"What do you mean?"

"Did you sleep in your room, in your bed?"

"I was terrified to."

"But did you?"

"I had to. My parents told me to go to bed, to stop being a baby, to stop worrying, Kelly would be okay."

"I'm sure you could have slept in another place. There was the guest room, a couch somewhere."

"My parents were so tired. Fed up, we all were. They just wanted everything back to normal. Like nothing had happened. They kept telling me to forget what happened, to erase what I saw, to remember that Kelly was fine and that everything was fine now. That everything I saw was just a memory, and I could just as well forget a memory as I could remember one."

"Your parents said that?"

"Yes."

"Did it work for you?"

"It was the only thing I knew to do. So that's what I tried to help Kelly do when she got out of the hospital, so that she could forget too. It was working. I got her a job, we found her a place of her own and I figured that things were okay."

"When did it dawn on you that she wasn't okay?"

"I always knew. She was never the same after her parents died. To me, she wasn't Kelly anymore. Not like when we were little. She was never okay again. But we all were just supposed to keep going, living our lives, like nothing had happened."

"Wendy, tell me honestly, were you okay?"

"I had to be. I was supposed to be strong for her. I was okay. I've always been fine. That's me. Always okay."

"Honestly?"

"Yeah."

Rick brushed a tear from her cheek and held her hand.

She squeezed his hand as she squeezed her eyes shut. "No. I'm sorry, no." More make-up stained tears fell as she stood up tall. "My best friend, the only person who liked me the way I was, the only friend I've ever had, had died. In my room, on my bed."

Rick stood up also.

"She never woke up after that. She was dead and they took her away. Even when they told us she was alive, and they brought her back, she was gone. All I could do was get on with my own life, and look out for hers. I got so busy taking care of her that I never had to think about me. I was fine with that. Until you called me and told me she was in the hospital again."

"What happened then?"

"I flipped out. It all came back. When I went to her flat, to get the stuff you asked me to, I saw all the pictures, everywhere, all over the floor, torn, crumpled, everywhere. It was everything all over again, it's never going to go away!" She covered her mouth.

"You felt like you had found her all over again, like she was right there in front of you, even though she had already been taken to hospital?"

She nodded with her trembling hand covering her lips. "Right there. On the floor," Wendy nodded and fell into his arms. "I saw the same pyjamas, same blue cold."

"Same blue cold. Oh God, I know." He cried but he held her tightly to him so she wouldn't see. "Wendy, listen to me, this last time was an accident. She never meant for it to happen. Tenth anniversary came and all the trauma came back the same way it did for you, she panicked. You know what that's like, Wendy, every bit as much as her."

"It all comes back just like you were there again...like it was happening all over again...when all you wanted was for it to go away," she admitted holding her hands to her temples.

"Wendy, listen to me." He softly touched the side of her face, "You need to know she was trying to calm herself and she took too many meds by mistake. Wendy, I believe her. She told me she never meant to kill herself that day, she wanted to live, but she got scared and something went real wrong, by mistake. Do you understand? Do you believe me? She never hated you. In fact, she's the only one who really understood how hard all this has been on you. She just wants to live again. She wants the same thing for you too."

Wendy nodded slowly. Her insides shivered until she calmed down, in his arms, in the summer air.

July 17

It happened almost a month ago and I still haven't gotten up the courage to tell Karen. I'll be damned if I have to admit to anyone that the only form of natural feminine delight I've experienced was born in a dream and died in a nightmare. God has never created anyone so base - I can't stand to look at myself in the mirror. I will have to burn these pages once written, but in order to save my soul, better to burden paper with this shame confession. Did I really have one? Can you have one while sleeping, unaware of everything around you? How can images in your mind create such a visceral state of being?? How sick does your mind have to be? How desperate do you have to be? God help me. Maybe I just dreamt it. But my body still quakes at the thought and it's impossible to keep from thinking about it when I'm with him. To love him so strongly, invite him so deeply into my

*being only to have him vanish from my clutch at the crisis? To feel
something for the first time in myself, to feel so alive with him, then as I
climax, to watch him dematerialize like some sick kind of B-movie CG
effect.*

*He's leaving. Oh my God. He's leaving. He's really leaving…for a new
and better life.*

July 20

*Looks of Longing…paralyzed at the precipice.
He electrocutes me with his touch. When he looks in my eyes, he doubles the
voltage. Standing in line at the grocery store, he looks at me in a way I can't
handle or encourage. At dinner, he looks at me with yearning eyes. I don't
want my eyes to engage his for fear that he notices me searching into him,
past his safe zone from beneath one veil too deep in me. Temptation is too
powerful and I need it to stop. When he talks to me with pedestrian
enthusiasm about the goings on of his day, as if I can really listen, I am tied,
anchored beneath his skin, trapped there. I don't want to leave a place that
surrounds me with the only feeling I have delighted in since they died. He
wants me to stay longer each night. I know he's leaving. This has to stop.*

Falling Away

*I can't say if you were there or not.
But you were present, if lost in thought*

*Maybe it was just inside of me
That you became free*

*To fall away
From me*

(God, I can't even tell him, I feel so broken inside.)

July 25

What's the four letter word for "Eureka!!"? I've located the fountainhead of Agramon.

I'm terrified. I'm beginning to see who I really am, how stuck I am, not just in time but in the infantile mindset of a Pollyanna-sweet-sixteen-and- never-put-out mentality. My childhood concept of Bridget and Ian keeps me the way they left me. The mistake that shouldn't have happened. Trapped under glass.

This volume is becoming my very own Book of Revelations - I just figured out why I could never tell mom about what Chris did to me that night they were out of town. The fact was I brought it on myself, naively by secretly inviting him over to keep me company. Even though he apologized, I innocently accepted that the matter was settled, there was no reason to bring it up — to anyone. But he would have been just as embarrassed as I was because his long-time investment of a public girlfriend had refused him in private.

I need someone to blame other than myself. I want to blame Bridget and Ian for lying to me about how life really was for them. Their lies and rose-colored views colored mine.

July 29

There is too much inside that still isn't finding its way out. My writing fails me, my words skim over my deepest reality. Maybe it's because I haven't been able to feel for so long. Maybe that's why I resist physical union with him. Just like Agramon and my hidden memories, I won't let myself feel at all, for fear I will feel too much. I'm still afraid to say what needs to be said. Words aren't enough.
I can see that.

It frustrates me.
I feel so limited.

August 3

RICK – MOVE AWAY NOW!! THIS HAS TO STOP!!

I almost didn't come home last night – again. It's that God-Kill-Me-Now ringing of that hormonal alarm, like clockwork – that urgent drive, deadly desire that would have succeeded in keeping me there longer, in his arms, in his bed, in this molasses guilt, had I not gathered my senses and my pathetic virtue and left. We had finally reached the breaking point between us – every time we're together, it happens no matter how hard we try to control it. The looks, a touch of understanding, of tenderness, feelings of helplessness, one kiss. Nearer to each other. Another kiss... Seduction goes on autopilot. Wrapped in each other, he ignites my love for him again. He wanted me to stay the night with him, he quietly and lovingly asked me not to leave him again. All I could tell him was that I couldn't, that it would be a regrettable mistake for both of us. He frowned his eyes shut. The instant his hands met his forehead, I knew. I think rubbing his feverish brow deflected the aggravation of what he really wanted to say to me – something along the lines of "fucking tease of a bitch". So I said it for him as I rushed to dress because I loathe myself enough for the both of us.

So much loathing now that I told him I wanted it over, once and for all. I told him we will not see each other anymore if his plan was to break me down, so that out of my defeat, he would get what he wanted, because that's the way it's been feeling like to me every time we're together more than a few hours. We haven't been able to relax with each other in so long. What he wants reduces at its base to sex and I am incapable of that kind of intimacy. I don't even think I apologized to him. I wouldn't know how. This shame of my sexual dysfunction overcomes everything now. I ran out of his bedroom and nearly tripped over the cat. I wanted to get out of there as fast as I could, so I wouldn't have to see that look on his face again. He called me by full name from his room (he's never done that before, he sounded like my father) and ordered me not to walk out the door. Again, I asked for it. Why don't I learn from my mistakes? Me, the little girl with no experience, believing it's okay to test the temperature of my waters with him. Even though he has invited me to, I feel like I've strung him along like Rudy's fluff toy attached to the braid of yarn. It is my own fault for consciously craving him without any concept or understanding of being able or belong to him - I don't know how to be anyone's companion or partner...I suffer the indignity that I couldn't even be his pet. Before he made it into the living room after me, I was out the door. I ran down the long carpeted hallway past endless apartment doors (through my tears, the carpet pattern undulated like a psychedelic trip — I've gotten good at seeing at the world through my own tears) and once out of the long hall, I remember not being able to get on the elevator when it finally arrived. I didn't even have a dignified way to get home on my own, ending up on unlit streets in the middle of the night, knowing it would agonize and betray him in the worst possible way, even more than I was already responsible for doing. Perfect shame overcame me, to realize that I could never successfully run away from myself. Time slowed somehow - he found me curled up in the corner under the window by the elevator door. All I know is that as my heart drummed, it hurt and I could feel it pounding, beat by beat, I grew more nauseous. If only my heart would just explode in a mass of heat and flames that would immolate me, incinerate me in his sight, that he could watch this sickening mutation freak of a woman that I am burn before him. All I remember was wishing I had died the first time.

Getting back home was the longest ten minutes of my life. I fled his car toward this lonely flat that would surround me in silence. He said nothing to me the whole drive back. Nothing, until the moment I reached the upper step of the Old Victorian. I was shaking worse than before because he had gotten out of the car and followed me to the main door. Please just let me die alone, I wanted to tell him, but I couldn't speak. By the time I had found my keys, he had caught up to me. He stood right behind me. There was nothing I could do to get away quickly enough. He took the keys from my hand and unlocked the main door for me. Abject fear kept me from looking at him, so I stayed focused through these tears on the sinewy agility of his hands, all I could see were the same hands that awakened me, through his sensuous music and his sensual touch, as he precisely selected the key, penetrated the lock, turned it then withdrew the key out of the spring deadbolt. His left hand pushed the door open for me — he offered me the last invitation to walk back into my world.

And out of his life.

I remember not being able to move past the doorway, then he handed me my keys and escorted me into the vestibule. A swirl of dizziness nearly caused me to puke right there because I knew that in a matter of seconds, whether he said anything or not, he would go away. And that would be it. What I had asked for. Everything I asked for.

I felt stone-dead inside. Nothing he said registered. It still hasn't yet. I won't let it. I remember staring through the etched glass of the vestibule door toward the blurry, warped form of the staircase as he spoke his last words to me. I remember catching the cold worn iron of the antique oval doorknob. I want him back, right now.

***

I woke up here on my sofa, it's past 4 am and I wonder if it was only in a dream that he said he loved me, he always had and we would make it through this. I heard the waves of his voice gently lapping in my ear, peacefully washing over me…I can't remember everything he said. I want to. I need to.

August 4

I am fully awake, no longer in that altered state. Please, God, protect me from what was not a dream. The faintly swaying memory of his whispering words are only penetrating like his touch into me now. The subtle tingling sensation that has returned to my fingers enables me to write what I cannot believe, incredulously, hours later and I must keep writing what he said to me in the vestibule…

I love you,
I always have,
I always will.
We'll make it, Kel
Whatever time it requires,
Whatever work it takes.
I need you every bit as much as you need me,
No matter what you think at this moment.
The music I make means nothing - it will be forever incomplete without your words.

I love you,
I always have,
I always will.
We'll make it, Kel
Whatever time it requires,
Whatever work it takes.
I need you every bit as much as you need me,
No matter what you think at this moment.
The music I make means nothing — it will be forever incomplete without your words.

I love you,
I always have,
I always will.
We'll make it, Kel
Whatever time it requires,
Whatever work it takes.
I need you every bit as much as you need me,
No matter what you think at this moment.
The music I make means nothing - it will be forever incomplete without your words.

Sixteen

TUESDAY, AUGUST 5

The overhead door jerked then rumbled open. Kelly found the switch that flooded the storage facility in a greenish fluorescent light. "The piano is over there on the side wall," she pointed in the general direction. "It hasn't been touched in over a decade."

"We'll take a look and see what shape she's in, no promises." Terry Howe was Halifax's most respected piano technician, with a reputation solidly built from twenty-five years of tuning, restoring and reconditioning. He had been the University's Music Department caretaker and rescuer for all their pianos for more than a decade, He came with the highest recommendation from those whom Rick made an inquiry.

While Kelly quietly hoped her mother's dark-stain piano would still be in satisfactory condition, she prepared herself to ditch it if it couldn't be saved. The piano was not her mother, she reminded herself. She poked through some unsealed boxes as Mr. Howe unwrapped the instrument. She helped him wheel the piano away from the wall and then he surveyed the soundboard and bracing from behind with a large flashlight. Impatiently, Kelly tested several keys. What emanated was without substance, like a rusted bell, and bore no resemblance to the musical notes she expected to hear, what she remembered hearing when her mother had played it so many years ago. The hollow dissonance of her key strikes sounded like the moaning of invisible ghosts in the night; these lost, disconnected spirits called out, grief-stricken, begging to finally be let go. Flashes of the funeral home setting filled her mind; she prayed there would be no voices anymore. "Diagnosis isn't good, right?"

Mr. Howe continued to look inside the dusty cabinet, and at the harp which hung firmly in place, he knocked on a panel or two, floated his fingers across the surface of the crusty strings, then tugged on several of the pins in the pin block. Completing his initial examination he concluded, "The soundboard's cracked in three places that I can see, this part here is starting to visibly warp out of shape. Strings are shot."

"That's what I figured."

"Hate being the bearer of bad news. The harp structure is the only thing left. Bracing's pulling away in several places, hammers are all hard as stone, they would need to be rebuilt from scratch, the whole action is like molasses. Wood's broken under there." He fiddled with the motion of one of the keys as a demonstration.

"Not worth anyone's trouble, I can see that."

"Humidity's gotten to it, spells slow death for pianos. They need to be climate controlled, played, cared for."

Kelly imagined the pictures of show homes in ads of her mom's real estate magazines she had found in one of the boxes. Glossy black grands perfectly angled in Palladian window alcoves next to dark mahogany library shelves lined with leather-bound collections. She did not touch any more keys on her mother's corpse of a piano.

Mr. Howe knelt in front of the piano and applied pressure to the pedals with the palm of his hand. "Well, Miss, you say it was your mother's? It's up to you. If you want to keep her for sentimental reasons, history or whatever, put in your dining room, she's got the Willard look and name. Still has the original ivory on the keys. Outer cabinet could use some refinishing in places, but overall, she looks fine. Not a playing instrument though, I'm afraid. Do you play?"

"Used to. Not now. No." She held the flashlight near where Mr. Howe knelt when something white caught her eye from behind the harp, at the base of the cabinet, just above the footplate. "What's that, Mr. Howe?"

"What's what?" he replied looking up to her from just above floor level.

"Behind that," she pointed, "shoved in behind."

He reached far back in between the harp and the bracing and found what Kelly was referring to. "Hope it's not a dead rat, that happens sometimes. Feels like paper." He groped around until he dislodged the tightly wedged bundle out of place, scraping his knuckles on the harp. "What's that doing in here?" He handed the wad of paper to Kelly then quickly examined the back of his hand.

Several envelopes, and their contents, were folded over and rolled into a bundle. The tension of being wedged in place forced the bundle to hold its shape, even though she tried to flatten it. She set the curved stack down on a box and thanked Mr. Howe for coming to check the instrument. She retrieved her purse and pulled out her payment. She dusted off the envelope bundle then stuffed it into her purse, pulled the overhead door down, locked it and walked back to Graphix Alive.

WEDNESDAY, AUGUST 6

The weekly administration meeting that brought all the employees of Graphix Alive together in the same conference room, had just concluded. Paul distributed the new round of orders and schedules and handed Kelly three new files. Surely that would keep them all off the streets and out of trouble, Paul joked. She returned to her office and set the new files upon her credenza. Spring-cleaning came later than usual this year. As days passed in a blur, she was getting older, and feeling more behind. The monitor screen on her desk flashed a little envelope icon, alerting her that she had new e-mail. She shut her office door and logged onto her personal account. She rarely ever got e-mail anymore. Wendy used to clutter her inbox with nuisances, cutesy chain letters promising 'wishes granted if you sent it out to everyone on your list within ten minutes', silly trivia or pop-quizzes to 'help you determine your pet's zodiac sign'. Without Wendy's mouse indiscriminately hitting the 'send' button to her address anymore, the status of her personal inbox hardly varied, except for the occasional concise message from Rick. She smiled when she read the note:

I haven't changed my mind. I don't plan to. I meant what I said. Call me - we need to talk.
Love, R

PS: imagine red rose here.

This note was his second attempt to call her on the noticeable avoidance to discuss recent events and undoubtedly, the nearest future. She had no idea where she was going with her life. Her therapy with Karen Lake was beginning to build breakthrough momentum and her job was here. He would be moving in a couple of months, and sure, people pack up and move all the time. A certain amount of undiluted nonchalance is just the cure for that hang-up. It must feel great to be able to sing the song of the open road at the top of your lungs. Realistically, if she could see herself leaving Halifax, then she would have to talk to him about her future, possibly their future together, or just as likely not together. She fired back a quick response, "Talk Only – Dinner tonight". She logged out of her e-mail account and fetched her purse. Pulling out the bundle of rolled envelopes, she tried to separate one from another, there were at least at half dozen, some of which had stuck together and resealed themselves, perhaps from the years of humidity getting at the envelope glue. Or maybe they had never been opened in the first place. She had no way to really tell. It wasn't until she pulled one envelope apart from its neighbor and took a closer look that she saw it was addressed to her mother, as B. Pearson. There was no return address, no identification of the sender, just a Halifax postmark on the stamp. The date was faded and imperceptible. Kelly peeled the yellowed paper of the envelope tab open. She could see by the way it separated that it had been opened before. Only in certain places where the original glue remained is where it resealed itself. Inside was a handwritten letter. Perhaps it was from her father. As she unfolded the page, she knew it was not of her father's hand. Reading the contents of the letter, she grew troubled. No reference to specific circumstances was mentioned in the letter, there was no date on the page, and it was clear to her that the content was of a highly personal nature. The salutation read, "My Love," and was signed as "only yours" followed by two initials, likely the sender's first and last name. She couldn't be sure if the initials were JT or FT, JF was another possibility. The penmanship was difficult to read, the letter was written in block capitals, and quizzically, the f's, t's and j's all looked the same. The letter focused on the sender's heartfelt feelings… phrases were gloomy, laden with a heavy aura of disappointment regarding something that her mother hadn't done, the letter concluded with a vague but dignified apology. As she studied the handwriting, the author's u's, m's and n's were also hard to tell apart, so she relied upon the context to figure out certain words. She began to open the other envelopes. All the letters were written by the same person on the same plain notepaper, all the envelopes looked to be identical, and addressed in exactly the same way. She quickly perused each note and by the time she made it through the stack, she was convinced her mother had purposely hidden these letters in the piano, away from prying eyes. Great hiding place, she thought, who would ever think to look inside an upright piano? She would have something else to talk about with Rick that evening over dinner. A knock upon her office door forced her to set aside her current interests in order to confer with Paul and a new walk-in client.

Rick would wait in the SUV in front of Graphix Alive until she came out. He didn't want to be the one to again bring up what happened three nights ago. He had no idea it would be this difficult. The pain behind his eyes radiated, as he tried to convince himself that things with her would sort themselves out, in time. After all, she had agreed to dinnertime talk with him, it wasn't as though she had called it quits outright. He knew his timing was terrible. But time was flying away. Relationships were never his forte. He had spent a chunk of the afternoon designing circles around the many obstacles, seeing if he could organize life for them together with time galloping headlong the way it was. He had been thinking about his grandfather a lot the last several days, remembering his lifelong adage that good planning was what took a person far in life. Of all he had faced thus far, and would yet confront, Rick could imagine no test more worthy than this one, whose lasting effects would weigh solidly and most valuably in his life. To do this right and not screw up again, would require smarts. More smarts than he had. Rushing things with her was his biggest mistake and he found himself praying to an unknown higher source for a way to make it right again.

She startled him when she opened the car door. As she began to tell him about her day from the passenger's side, he lost himself in her brown eyes. The thought of making out in the car in the empty parking lot next-door leapt into his mind. An answer to his prayers hadn't come. But everything else about this relationship with her continued to manifest differently than with anyone he'd cared about in his past. Something told him to go with her flow, no matter how zigzag it seemed. He remembered dangling from a rock face somewhere in the Andes during a shotgun climbing getaway after Rebecca was killed. He had wondered a while ago whether Kelly needed something more definite to go on, something more secure than the shortest distance between two points. He thought romantic reassurance would help her. Now he fastened his hope upon his clear statement of his feelings for her, that it would make the difference this time, because he simply and courageously expressed it to her in words. A form of communication she cherishes, he hoped it wasn't too late; surely it would have to be more effective than his previous attempts to seduce her into feeling safe with him.

Kelly voted for Szechuan take-out, knowing that Rick preferred spicy food. While waiting for their order in the restaurant lounge, he asked her about her morning session with Karen, then she told him of her lunchtime meeting with Mr. Howe at the storage facility. She said while Karen predicted hope for her future, Mr. Howe diagnosed the piano as terminal. Rick shared her disappointment for the instrument, thinking that music was just what Kelly needs to have in her life…maybe she still could.

Once home at Rick's, Kelly curled up on the living room carpet and laid out the take-away boxes on the coffee table. The spicy chicken dish smelled heavenly. Rick went to the kitchen to bring wine and extra napkins. Rudy faced moral and ethical dilemmas about sticking to the rule of staying off the coffee table. He stood up on his hind toes to get a better look. Kelly could see his front paws reaching from the edge of the table toward the food. He considered once more a reconnaissance mission. "It's all too spicy for you," Kelly said to the curious cat. The look of dejection in Rudy's eyes as he sniffed at the air was too much for her to bear. "Rick, what can he have? Rice?"

"Kitty Kibble," Rick said as he returned to the living room. Setting the wine glasses down, he picked up the cat and relocated him away from their supper. As they began to eat, he asked her, "Are you upset about the piano?"

"No. I expected it."

"You know, if you really want to play, we can always go shopping for another one, a used one if you want or maybe a compact digital."

"If I didn't have so much to do at work, I might actually have time for lessons and practice. It's not so easy to start again when you were never a maestro to begin with. The thought of going back to the beginning musically…"

"Quit it baby, you talk like you're old. See these?" He pointed to his graying temples then to his knuckles, "I'll get arthritis before you and then we'll see who has the last laugh."

After they ate, Kelly reached behind her for her purse and pulled out the envelope bundle. "Remember I told you how I hate surprises? Here's the latest. Found it today."

"In a box at home?"

"No, in the last place you'd think you'd find anything. In the piano."

"In the bench?"

"No, Rick, in the piano, right inside, shoved in there behind the strings."

He fingered through the stack of envelopes. "They're all addressed to your mom but it doesn't say who they're from."

"Exactly. Can you make out the postmarks?"

"Not really." He retrieved a magnifying glass from his desk drawer and looked at the envelopes up close. He seated himself on the sofa next to the end table where the lamplight was brighter. "This one looks like 77, or maybe 71. Definitely in the 1970's." He checked another one, which also looked like 77.

Then Kelly found one postmark that looked like 76. She crawled upon the sofa with him and told him what was in the first few letters she had time to read. "I don't know who this person was, but I think they're love letters."

"You know that for sure?"

"Well, would you sign a business letter 'only yours'?"

"Depends." He grinned.

"And some of them start 'My Love'."

"Ah."

She opened up the letters and together, they looked at each of them and compared notes. Rick said he thought the block capitals handwriting looked masculine. They both agreed there was nothing to indicate a feminine tone of voice in any of the letters. Most of the statements were short, abrupt and quite focused, no expression seemed embellished or flowery or overly emotional. Having read the entire collection, they came to the conclusion that the letters had been written and sent over a period of anywhere between six months to as long as a one year, maybe longer, spanning 1976 and 1977.

Rick stated, "Whoever JT was, or FJ…I think it's FT personally because there's two slashes on this first initial, but then again, I could be wrong. Your mom continues to be a mystery. I dare say she's almost as intriguing as you."

"Thanks. First unfinished divorce papers that only she's signed, but not my dad, and now these letters from some secret admirer?"

"Sounds like it was more than just a remote admiration, Kel. Hate to be the bearer of bad news, but this person was intimately connected to your mom." Rick picked up the notes once again and sorted through them. "Here he's written… and I remain on the assumption that it's a he…"

Kelly grew exhausted and felt a pain in her stomach. What if it wasn't a 'he', the thought precipitated a sudden nausea.

"…that he's 'saddened and disappointed by her last minute decision.' Looks like he's trying to be big about it.. Sounds like he's whining, if you ask me."

"In one of them, he wrote about 'plans that we made'" Kelly searched for the note in question, "and also goes on to talk about 'fulfilling her dreams'." Kelly thought long. "Maybe this person was a friend to my mother, trying to help her through something, some kind of conflict. Maybe about whether to get a divorce?"

"'Plans that we made', 'My Love'? Nope. Sorry. Broken-hearted lover. Definitely."

Kelly picked up the notes from Rick's lap and began to put them back in their envelopes. She quickly numbered each one in pencil so that they didn't get mixed up. "Do you think that's why my mom wanted a divorce?"

"And your dad wouldn't grant her one? Outta spite, heck yeah," he duly launched his machismo opinion outright. "If it were my wife thinking of leaving me for another man, I wouldn't be so quick to oblige." Then he thought twice. "I don't know. This mystery lover spends his ink reminiscing about the time that they spent together, how life meant something with her in it…and how he didn't want to have to go on without her… They obviously had a relationship."

"Kinda sounds like he's trying to talk her out of suicide… I don't remember my mom being suicidal. I knew she was unhappy at times, but… I don't know what to think. Was my mom in love with this person? Was this man a friend trying to help her in a rough time in her marriage? These letters are only one side of the story."

Rick slouched back on the sofa. "Broken-hearted lover, pouring his heart out to her because she didn't intend to follow through. This guy's obviously hurtin' for her and he didn't get the response he hoped he would." Rick now felt honored to carry the torch for all lovesick men.

"Great. My mom loved a man other than my dad."

"What do you remember about those years?" he asked her.

"Disco was in."

"I mean with your folks, your mom."

"She had gone back to work in real estate and started to work full time once I was settled in grade school. I'd say around that time she was working almost full-time and my dad was teaching at the University."

"Was your dad away a lot?"

"For longer stretches at different times."

"You don't remember your mom meeting with anyone while your dad was away?"

"What? You mean like bringing other men home while my dad was gone?" Kelly resented his question, "No. Of course not!" she emphasized. "My mom was there for me, when dad was home, when dad was away, she was there, always there."

"Okay, okay. She was there. But you were in school all day…"

She really would have been too young to know if her mom were depressed to the point of suicidal, Kelly thought, or if she were seeing someone during the day. She began to resent his genius tendencies once again.

He took the bundle of envelopes from her and placed it on the end table, out of sight, then handed her the TV remote. "HBO. At your fingertips."

She took the remote from him and threw it toward the armchair across the room. Without speaking, she let him know she needed to be held; she wanted nothing more, and nothing less would suffice.

He switched off the lamp.

"I don't like surprises, Rick."

"I know. You've told me."

She settled into his arms.

"Some surprises can bring good, Kel, but you have to be open."

"Warn me in advance."

"Life doesn't always sound distant early warning."

FRIDAY, AUGUST 8

"I've been thinking," Rick opened, as he drove them away from Graphix Alive, "I know it's safer to let sleeping dogs lie. But I'm thinking about rebelling."

"Rebellion can be healthy."

"Interested in going to a wedding?"

"Depends," Kelly responded with a cool delay.

"On?"

"Whose wedding." If it were her own, Kelly might understand the obligation to show up. "And when? And where?"

"A friend's. Neighbor actually, from back home."

Kelly waited for details, eager to learn if it was Hannah or Charles, as was written on the invitation hidden inside her journal in his drawer. She would even accept Chuck.

"Girl down the road."

Hannah it is, then. "Old girlfriend you couldn't let go?"

"Maybe." He winked at her. "You jealous?"

"When's the wedding?"

Rick filled her in on the details and how his mom has been a close friend of Hannah Etter's mom since the beginning of time and that he was struggling to think of a unique wedding gift.

Kelly wondered if he was struggling at the thought going home. "Are they registered?"

"To get married? I would imagine. They need a license."

"No, you dope. Gift registry, you know, for china patterns, silverware. Or was that the thing about getting married that didn't sit right with you?"

Rick found her becoming more and more brutal with her honesty. Was this the pinnacle purpose of her therapy sessions, the art of prickly bold confrontation? "Nothing on the invitation specified."

"It's probably not going to say right on the invitation."

Her tone was definitely cactus. "So are you going to help me out or not? Are you making me go to this wedding alone, or are you going to keep beating up on me until the move?"

"I have to pick?"

"Can't have it both ways, sorry."

"Your preference then." She wasn't going to make it easy for him.

"Wait till I get you home, baby. You're gonna get it."

"Home here, or home Hampton?"

"Your preference then, baby."

"I have to pick?" She waited before answering. "Hampton," she chose nervously. "What am I saying, I can't get time off from work."

"So would you actually enjoy the idea of accompanying me home?"

"Really I just want to put off whatever it is you're threatening."

She was cute whenever she got insecure about them, he thought. "You'd have to meet my family."

"Worse, Doctor. They'll have to meet me. Although it might be your best defense, you know, to bring a perfect stranger along and everyone will have to behave…"

"Exactly."

"So it's your plan to mess them up by bringing a girl home…purposely giving them the wrong impression. Are you sure you want to do that?"

"Hey, maybe the rumors about me and my cat will stop."

"Noble cause, for Rudy anyway."

He spoke softly as he glanced in the rear-view mirror, "Actually, I think you should meet them."

"Why would you say that?" She grew nervous. The entire scenario began to seem like a bad idea.

"I don't know. Call it men's intuition." It was all grasping at straws when it came to her.

"Is there such a thing as male intuition? I thought they called it reasoning, to me it always looks more like denial. You'd know about that."

Pots and kettles, certainly he had a thing or two to say about Kelly and denial being acquainted. Wendy, too. But now wouldn't be a good time to bring any of that up either. He had risked her fury asking her to come to

Hampton knowing how much the discovery of her mother's secret had upset her. One day at a time, he heard his grandfather's voice echo with gentleness.

THURSDAY AUGUST 21

Her former conventional prudence may have gone permanently AWOL when she told him yesterday she would come with him. Now, she had less than two hours to pack for the trip to Hampton. She planned to leave work at lunch hour leaving plenty of time to get organized. Her life was morphing beyond her comprehension like a spinning optical illusion. Nothing this important should have been left till the last minute. She had a routine once. And not that long ago, days were predictable, everything operated on a punch card. She spilled coffee on some guy by accident. Then he told her he loved her. Everything had changed. Life rushed straight at her. She tried to keep the image of blinding headlights out of her mind's eye. She dug out a suitcase from the back of her closet. For God's sake, she was attending a matrimonial ceremony with a man whose heart would undoubtedly be pinned on his suit lapel like a big fat red cabbage, she rattled to herself. They would be seated alongside his family no less. Would she need attire for various social events surrounding the ceremony? What do Hamptoners wear? Or are they called Hamptonians? She quickly shuffled through the items still on hangers barely clinging for dear life. Should she aim for formal or informal? Would black be considered gauche or fashionably understated, like Queen Street West? She didn't own anything country floral. She did have a spaghetti strap top that winked Milan runway, according to Wendy. Damn it, what would Wendy wear to a wedding in Hampton? She still needed to hunt down hosiery and jewelry and she nearly forgot about shoes, but thank goodness, she wouldn't have to worry about her hair. No pins, clips, curling irons, nothing. Her hair was now just hair, cut to be. God bless Betty and her no-name scissors from Japan. Once she hauled the valise out, she flung it onto her bed, then she got down on all fours checking to see if her strapless bra had been sucked into the black hole of winter wear at the base of her closet in case she decided to bring the slinky fashion parade top.

She didn't have any gifts to bring for Rick's mom and dad. It was something she had meant to do, but never got around to shopping. Rick had purchased the wedding gift one evening when she had to work late.

Resourcefully, chores had gone the way of divide and conquer in the last couple of weeks. Reluctantly, they were doing less and less together and became more concerned with crossing tasks off joint to-do lists. Rick's agenda was several times longer than hers, so she combined some of his chores with her own, namely laundry and running errands downtown over lunch hours and spending quality fetch time with Rudy. Anything she could to do to help as a friend, she offered; she had even cooked suppers, wholeheartedly accepting the challenge to strive toward the heaven high standards Rick's cooking had set for her. The irony of her selflessness struck her, she had been helping him leave her.

She knew all that remained on his short list now was Calgary's CA Technologies and there was no news. He informed her that one company he interviewed with had already hired from within, and another company that had advertised had retracted their ad due to immediate downsizing. More choices might have been available but he limited his search to positions within Canada. The last thing he wanted to add to was the national brain-drain. So many of the country's educated specialists crossed the border the first chance they got, to take up work in America or across the globe, citing more varied employment opportunities and better pay as chief reasons for leaving.

She knew he would reconsider the States if no suitable job opportunity arose in Canada within a reasonable time frame. He would have to. She helped him sort through closets, forming piles in the dining room, one for donation, one for keeps, another for trash. She still didn't know whether he was going take his furniture with him, or sell it with the condo. Perhaps that would depend on what kind of moving allowance the new company would offer him. That would be discussed at his interview and she knew he was waiting for the date.

She packed hastily. Why was she going with him to his family home, she questioned herself once more? Over the previous weeks, she consistently shoved aside thoughts about his moving to Calgary, or the States, or anywhere away from her. Not once had he suggested that she accompany him. He wouldn't ask her to leave the only home she's ever known. He'd know better than to ask, she told herself. The survival structure of her life was in Halifax. From the beginning, the future was a taboo topic that ended up being the silent bone of contention in their relationship. Leaving Halifax to go to Hampton for four days was scary enough. She had never been away with a man before. She had never gone specifically to meet parents of anyone that mattered since she was seven. Would his mother like her? Would his father care? Why would it matter knowing they would go their separate ways? She waffled about going on this trip ever since he invited her. But she could not ignore an unrelenting call that only her going there could answer. She needed to meet his family and witness his home life with her very eyes. She couldn't dismiss it: the core of Richard Allan Hutchinson would otherwise remain permanently unfathomable to her in all her years to come. She prayed for gracious closure.

She heard him toot the horn. She zipped her suitcase shut and not without a fight. She threw her manicure kit into her shoulder bag; she could do her nails on the way. Before she headed out the door, she quickly pulled out a small photo album from her nightstand, one that she always kept there. It held special photographs of her parents and grandparents, a few podium pictures from skating competitions and random snapshots from her youth. It was the only photo album still intact since the incident of May 23. She didn't know why she grabbed it at the last second, she just did.

"Five hours to Hampton," Rick announced once they were on the road. The weather was partly sunny and slightly cool. He rolled the windows down a crack.

She heard Rudy caterwaul pathetically through the mesh of his carrier in the back seat. He'd lived through this drive before and would once again, thanks to kitty dramamine.

Rick had booked off time until Monday and was prepared to cut the trip short, immediately after the wedding if necessary, for possible eventualities too many to list. "Five hours. Just the prologue. Hope you're up for it."

The prologue? Of what, she dared not address. Agreeing to this emotionally precarious situation to satisfy a curiosity made no sense. She pulled out her manicure kit from the bag at her feet. The upcoming week loomed to overwhelm. Should this be 'just the prologue', what kind of novel could possibly unfold? The leading man was scheduled to exit the plot somewhere in Chapter Two. Epilogue: Emotional destruction. Not much of a tale, unless you live for fatalistic, depressing extra-short stories. Filing her nails would take her mind off the worn debates, but only for the time being. To maintain composure for five hours with him seated only a foot and a half away from her, she'd have to file off her fingers to the knuckles. So much for playing the piano again.

Time lapsed consciously and luckily, Rudy was unconscious. They listened to music and took in the rural sights. Not even an hour passed before she catapulted her first confrontational serve, "So, how do you intend to introduce me to your family?"

"How would you like me to?" He sounded amenable.

"I asked how you intend to." Her voice was flat as a pancake.

He chose not to toe the line of what he was sure was a trick question from a woman in no mood to joke.

Fine, she thought. Wearing her shades meant that she could look at him without really looking. It still might not be too late to renege on the trip. "Mind telling me the real reason why you need me to come with you to this wedding?"

"Bodyguard incognito."

"Can't you be serious for one minute?" Everything with him bore the sting of irony lately; it was she that needed protection right now. "No, of course not," she muttered. "That would mean being real and having to take it in unfiltered."

"Official taste-tester, then?" Humor had to have some positive effect; he believed this sincerely.

"You never answered my question."

"You might not like my answer." Yes, he realized, she had the capability to induce fear in him and she knew it. Humor would get him nowhere any longer.

"A little preparation might help, you know." Shit, she thought, what was he planning? People naturally would ask about her. By Twentieth Century Fox rating, their relationship was still very PG, extending occasionally to a nominally rated R. Fact is, they were ever only "just friends"; okay they were close friends. Her belly fluttered, then breath surged out from deep down without permission. She remembered how being in his arms pushed her boundaries: at times she floated, and when her hormones were in sync with her psychology, she felt the uncontrollable pull of the Eros dance. Too often, her time next to him was spent on her side, turned away from him, barricaded inside – a punishing solitary confinement – while her soul was forced to tread water in a limitless cold gray sea. With her love for him first thwarted by defenses she could not overcome, then forced under, she drowned beneath the shapeless waves in the neurosis of non-consummation. She did not want to drag both herself and the man she loved to the dark depths of failed intimacy, but the cement on her feet had set long before she ever met him.

Silence revisited them like a guardian angel until Rudy began to wail. A stop for a sip of water and a walk in the fresh air was exactly what he yowled for. Two more CD's had passed and her nail polish had long dried. Something in her plunged with leaden heaviness down to unknown crevasses inside her, to the dark place where her suicide cravings always stowed away. The motion of the vehicle only spurred on the sick feeling.

"Am I allowed to talk?" he asked furtively.

She hummed a yes as she rolled her window down.

"You sure your relationship with Wendy is over?" He knew there would be no chance of a reunion if they never confronted the issues surrounding their related traumas.

"Why are you bringing this up now?"

"Captive audience. Gotcha all to myself." He had crossed the threshold of safety. "I don't believe it's over. The way you left it, it's just not right, Kel. You're not finished when it comes to her."

"You don't know what you're talking about."

"I do know."

How could he? She knew exactly how much she elected not to tell him when it came to her history, her suicide attempt and subsequent relationship with Wendy, partly out of her growing independence, but mostly out of shame. "I doubt it."

"I had a long talk with her."

"When?"

"A while back. We've actually talked a couple of times, about a lot of things. She confided in me. I never told you about it."

"I'm not discussing this." She cranked up the stereo then looked away from him, angered and insulted by his betrayal. She had long suspected that he knew more about her than he admitted. And he was calling her on it while she sat there, cornered.

"Kelly, you're not done with her. There's more you need to do, more you can try, both of you, with Karen's help," he shouted over the music, wind and road noise.

She was trapped in his car. "Good, so that means you're gonna talk to your dad, then!" she fired back bitterly. "Finally!"

"That's not the topic right now," he barked.

"The hell it isn't!"

He turned the volume back down. "She's not okay, Kel. She's been traumatized too, all this time, but no one ever knew. She hid it well and she was too proud to ever admit it. She's hurting and she needs your support and she won't get through any of it without you. You're the one who can make the real difference because you're the only one that matters to her. She told me you kicked her out of your life? Is that true?"

She cranked the music right back up again.

He hollered back to her, "How can you be so selfish and wash your hands of it? No more convenient omissions." He had flung himself out of the frying pan, he knew her fire could finish him, but he felt satisfied that he said what he needed to without mentioning the word 'suicide'.

"You hypocritical son of a-!" She managed to hold her tongue.

The noise and their raised voices caused Rudy to cower in his carrier behind them. His eyes narrowed as his ears lay far back.

Rick ejected the Brazilian Acoustic CD and tossed it out the window. The stereo system turned off automatically. He kept his eyes fixed on the whizzing persistence of the dotted yellow line of the two-lane highway.

Her anger seethed, and there was no way out. If he would only slow down and head toward the grassy shoulder, she would bail. "Stop the car." She began to gather her things from the floor in front of her seat.

"What?" Alarmed, he applied the brake.

"Stop the fucking car, turn around and take me home."

"Kel, calm down." He kept driving as the car slowed.

She fidgeted with her door lock to see if it was engaged or not then she pulled at the door latch. The door came partly ajar although the safety latch barely held it shut.

"Oh no you don't!" he growled. Her childish provocation pushed him past tolerance; he slammed on the brakes, pulled the steering wheel to the right and rolled onto the dusty shoulder until the hood of the car tipped downward into the shallow ditch. He put the flashers on.

"Screw this," she piped, "all of it. I've had it with your hypocritical... You think I'm the one who has all the problems here and you know what? You're right - I do have problems and yes, I'm frustrated. And you know what else? You're no better. Deal with your problems however you want but don't blame me alone for your frustration. Go ahead, call me frigid, but you're every bit as distant! Unwilling!!" She swung the door wide open to the grassy slope and her breakout was imminent.... but shit, like always, she couldn't find the seat belt receptacle.

His eyes blinked quickly and unevenly behind his metro shades. He forced her to remain where she was as he held tightly her forearm above the belt buckle. He dashed his fingers at her, "I never called you frigid. Not once. Say what you need to me about us and what's not working for you, but don't speak for me, Kel."

"And why not?? You sure as hell won't. You barely speak for yourself and that's one thing that isn't going to change with you. Because you don't talk. To me or to anyone. When it comes right down to it, you won't face anything. All your crap about tomatoes, is that as good as it gets with you? You don't need a smart woman with big gimbals, you want what won't talk back to you."

He couldn't believe what he was hearing from her. He advised her to hold fast her tongue by dashing his fingers at her once again. "You want the truth about men? Or are you really happier living in your walled-up dream world as to what we're all about, impish or selfish, depending on what side-effect mood you're in or what day of the hormonal week it is, and then wonder why you're disappointed all over again?" He was sick of her self-serving righteousness, the iron chastity belt of martyrdom. He got out of the car, slid down the ditch around to her side and slammed her door shut. Once back in the car, he threw his shades onto the dash and leaned into her with a raised voice, "Here's one version of it. Men's lives are condemned disaster zones without women to love them, whether by pity or by passion," he asserted, "we'll take it either way, baby! Yes, for some of us, *it is* that bad. And, here's the kicker for this pathetic lot that we are," his finger waved his scrutiny, "guys don't know they need it. But they reach that point in life when they finally figure it out - by sad n' sorry elimination - that the way it's been without her, until her, it was hell on wheels and all downhill!! Men need smart women, and I really thought you were one of them." He slumped back in his seat, tired. "Should we be so goddamn lucky enough to find her, we won't be wasting energy fighting with her about tomatoes." He sat low in his seat, in the listing car, and rubbed his forehead and temples. He felt no bigger than the cookie crumbs on the floor mat.

Kelly shifted uncomfortably in her seat never having heard such a razor-sharp edge to his voice before. She looked out the rear window past Rudy awkwardly tilted in his carrier in the back seat.

He had never been so blunt with her and his outburst slapped him hard with mixed feelings. The thought of taking her right there and then kept crossing his mind. It ached him to not kiss her, having raised his voice at her, desperate to make her understand. "You won't ever pull a stunt like that *ever* again." He donned his shades, switched off the flashers and reversed back up to the highway.

As he drove onward, she fumed in questioning silence, and lingered upon his tirade that reflected his dark side more acutely than she had ever witnessed: a self-deprecating aggression that was passionately silly even when he got really angry. And she was struck by her love for him, stuck in her love for him. She noticed him flick the right indicator on and the vehicle pulled a sudden, sharp turn onto a narrow country road. The façade between them had crumbled. These were not minor disagreements. She knew he had finally admitted to himself the truth of who she was and everything she failed to be. He would turn around, she was absolutely sure, he'll pull a U at the gravel patch up ahead, drive back to the highway and within hours, this will all be over, once and for all. No matter how much the mystique of interconnectedness drew them together, they were too different. It was evident that his music wouldn't be enough to fill the chasm. Her relationship with her former best friend ended because of the inability to build a bridge under the direst of circumstances. Her parents' marriage failed due to consistent lack of communication. Her future would not be written in the same hand as her past; heartbreak aside, she would face the future and exercise her volition to carry on, as she was, without him. She had done for him what she could. The U-turn never happened. She looked back to watch the main highway recede farther behind them. Rudy's eyes were wide open and staring at her through the carrier mesh with captive confusion.

Rick sensed her puzzlement regarding the turn. "Etter Road," he said sullenly. "Named after Hannah's great-grandfather. Short cut through fields, literally. No facilities on this road so if you have to pee…"

Kelly slunk back in her seat, snowed under by defeat in the heat of the summer. "Something else you could have warned me about sooner and I wouldn't have had that ginger ale."

Neither of them turned the music back on. Time flowed like molasses on her ice floe. They were still a couple of hours from Hampton with the hood of the SUV aligned in that very direction according to the map. There was no getting away. She cried silently as she looked out the window. He hadn't asked her to come to Calgary and now, he had no intention of taking her back to Halifax, no matter how fiercely she fought him. Her tears continued to fall, in useless absence of words.

They reached a junction where they made a left turn then into a service station where Rick pulled in to refuel. Kelly ran straight into the tiny convenience shop to get the key for the restroom. Not even the biological relief of a long-delayed pee would make returning to the SUV easier. The washroom was dank, stark and utilitarian. One of the two overhead fluorescent tube ballasts flickered its last series of mayday calls. There were no windows. The tissue toilet seat cover slipped out of place when she sat down, she didn't care. She sat long after her trickling stream had finished. Her feet barely reached the stained concrete floor. Somber truths she never wanted to face revealed themselves to her: there was never a guardian angel watching over her, watching over them, at any time. Her mother and father, and all her wishful sentinel concepts of them felt galaxies gone from her heart. She could never look at the sky the same way again. She stared at the vacant space on her left ring finger. The pale indentation where her ring used to be told her she was on her own and she knew it, fully and completely, for the very first time. When she stepped out of the restroom, still drying her hands with brown paper towel, she saw Rick standing, waiting for her. The spring tension of the heavy blue iron door shoved her unkindly away from its dark threshold straight toward him. Her feet faltered beneath her and the paper towel fluttered to the ground. Her eyes conveyed her confusion.

He took her and held her close to him, closer than he ever had, and cupped her head firmly, pressing her nose into his flesh. Her hair felt full yet weightless, like silk between his fingers. He had missed holding her. For the last two weeks, she had not let him get anywhere near her.

He held her so tightly she could barely breathe. She didn't care. She let herself feel as much of him through summer sportswear as the layers that separated them would allow, on public asphalt, no less. "Has anyone ever told you what a hassle you are?"

His insides felt caked and hardened; too much was trapped inside him. "My whole life. If you only knew." His voice broke.

The gravity of his tenor hit her. She stepped away from him. She knew he was being pulled back to memories he kept hidden against his will. He was scared and it leveled her; yet, the only footing upon which she felt they were equals was on the emotional plateau of grief and fear. A graceful closure of this relationship would be born of compassion on their only common ground. Whenever he played her his music, it always evoked her own inner sadness, his preludes spread like a pall blanket over her to comfort her private lamentation. Since the day he told her about Rebecca's death, she had longed to feel his suffering, the distinct pain of his loss in place of her own. "Because you'll be going away, I've had to put whatever could have been between us at the bottom of the list. There won't be time left after dealing with our own individual failures. Past that, problems between us are too complicated. Our priorities are just too different."

Rick stood with his hands in the pockets of his shorts looking down at the oil spots on the pavement.

Her voice steadied, "I always knew I wasn't smart enough for you but the only advice I feel I can give you is to get your priorities in order, Rick. I had to, and they were some of the hardest decisions I've ever made. At the top of my list, I wanted to help you, somehow, before you go out West. That's why I agreed to come with you on this trip. I'm supporting you as your friend. There won't be anything further between us after Monday because your life will start again in Calgary."

This was not what he wanted to hear, he thought, anything else, he would prefer that she lay into him about his myriad weaknesses, his lack of courage to face his father, but not the final word that she was breaking up with him and had assigned a day to it. "No."

"What do you mean, no? You've applied for this position there and you're going to get this job. You said all that was left was just the formality of an interview, that's what you're waiting for, isn't it?"

"I retracted my application."

"What? Why? You said this position was a good match for you."

"Maybe not. It doesn't matter now, I withdrew over a week ago."

"Then reapply. Are you nuts?"

"I've thought about it. I'm looking local."

"There's nothing local in your field. Even I know that. Why are you screwing this up for yourself?"

"For the first time, I'm not screwing up." His voice was calm and even.

Kelly turned away from him and thrust her fingers into her hair, gripping them tightly until the ends of her hair stood up like a leaf rake. She whipped around, "You've thought about it? And when did you make this ridiculous decision?" More importantly, she wanted to know how long she'd not known about it, not that it was any of her personal business now.

"You know as well as I do the timing's just bad. All over the place."

"No it isn't. One job is shutting down, another one's opening up!"

"I'm not referring to jobs. It's not about the work. We need more time. You said it yourself just now."

Kelly gasped, not expecting to have her words returned at her this way. "Rick, I've been dying inside, trying to shut down my love for you for so long now and all along you've made it impossible for me." Her voice crumbled, "You're making it impossible for me." She began to cry because she finally came clean with what's been eating at her all this time.

He put his hands on her shoulders and shook her gently. "Then don't shut it down. Listen. It's not about a job. It's not about making money. I don't care about the income, I can manage without work for almost a year, I did the math. Something will come up before then. Thanks to you, I have been getting my priorities in order and right now, work's not my priority anymore. You are."

She couldn't believe her ears. "If I was your priority then how come you never asked me to go with you?" She wiped tears away with her clenched fists. "That only left me one conclusion - that you were moving on, without me."

He needed a cogent explanation and knew he didn't have one. "I looked at everything, over and over again. But I couldn't come up with an acceptable plan, I'm not able to, I can not plan a future without you. I thought I was clear when I told you I loved you and that we'd get through this, no matter what."

She hadn't forgotten what he said, but she had forced herself to not set her heart upon it. "You were leaving…" She stepped further away from him.

"Nothing was ever definite with Calgary, hopeful, but not definite. I haven't ruled out the idea of switching fields. Bottom line was I needed more time. But whenever I brought up the future, it upset you. You weren't ready to think about it. I needed to see how you were doing with Karen, then all this stuff with Wendy's trauma came up…and then the shipwreck of your parents' marriage just turned you off commitment in general… and lost in all that, I still didn't know if you loved me back….you never said one way or the other. Each time you pulled away, I just trusted that maybe somewhere, deep down, you might." His eyes darted back and forth as he looked up to the sky. With pools puddling in the corners of his eyes, emotions seized him. "But if you don't…."

"I always did." She felt too far away from him where she stood. "I was too scared to tell you…all the uncertainty…because…what if I can't…"

He released his breath with force. "Forget all the negative what ifs…if you love me, then that's square one to move forward from."

"Back up. Square zero is I need you to talk to me."

He kissed the crown of her head. "I learned from them it's better to keep it to yourself."

She didn't know to whom he was referring. "This is crazy. Since I met you, I've stopped believing that. God, I started talking because of you! I want to listen. I always have. I need to hear everything you have to say. I'm not your dad, or Mike or Rebecca. I'm not anyone you've ever known." The double entendre wasn't intentional.

"You're the only one who can say it for me. Write it so they'll listen."

She could barely write for herself. In fact, she had stopped writing altogether. Whatever he was holding in, she realized he needed as much protection from the cruelty of life as she did. "If it's about voice, then you need to tell me everything behind the music you make. What good will it do if I just guess? I need to know if I'm to be the one do it. Wait, what am I saying? I don't have the skill. I'm not a real writer."

He embraced her and held her in perfect stillness. From a distance, she'd appear to his family as just another pretty girl who dabbled in her passions.

Without meeting her, they'd never know her depth. "You've always had the constitution it takes." He knew it from day one.

They left the gas station and drove a few kilometers up the road then stopped at a quaint memorial park near the river. They sat under a droopy old willow tree up the riverbank. The water flowed with golden laughter. Rudy curiously explored the nearby ferns, bugs and rocks while Kelly held his leash. She listened intently to every word Rick spoke. He was ten when he stopped after school into the bank where his father worked. He rarely visited his dad at work, he had been told not to. It just wasn't proper. He did as his mother advised him, and understood his dad spent his days in business meetings and attending to clients. His father would always be there for him in the evenings and whatever it was, surely it could wait. But not that day. Reports had been handed out in school and he beamed with delight at the long list of 'Excellents' and 'Very Goods' his grade five teachers assigned him for the end of year report. He was sure that he hadn't worked any harder in spring term than before, just that his teachers miraculously came to their senses and now he had proof on paper. He stood third in his class of thirty kids that June. The sun highlighted his hair as he told her his story and Kelly could easily envision him as a boy the way he described himself at that time: a brown-haired, wiry ten year old bicycling his way down the main avenue of a small town carrying a piece of paper worth to him several times more than its size in platinum. As he continued his story, she pictured an old stone bank building and how this little boy must have marched with pride through the plate glass doors, past the coiffed tellers at the side counter, and around the lineup of waiting customers to the back counter. He had asked an old man permission to see Mr. Howard Hutchinson and when questioned by the lanky administrator behind the tall counter, he proudly announced that it was his eldest son here to see him. He remembered the man's arthritic finger pointing towards offices at the back of the building. When he arrived at the door around the corner labeled with his dad's name, he knocked and waited. He knocked again. But there was no response. The door was locked and the lights were out. He peered into his father's office through the slanted fins of the venetian blinds. At first, it just looked like a solitary figure lying very still atop the desk. Light from the hallway where he stood filtered in faintly. He looked again and watched for a time. He had waited until the outline moved again, until he was able to determine that his father was with a woman whom he couldn't recognize. He knew it wasn't his mother. Rick admitted not knowing much about sex at that age, but he knew enough to gauge the significance of what he saw. And he knew enough about the holy vows of marriage, the Ten Commandments, virtues like fidelity and honesty, everything his mother and church taught him. He pounded upon the office door with his fist clenched like a baseball one last time, a dare for his dad to answer, then ran home. He forgot his bicycle that stood in the rack across the road from the bank. It didn't even dawn on him until his mother asked him where it was. He lied and said the tire was flat when he got out of school. Then he went straight to his room. His bike would stand across from the town fountain all night, three blocks from school. He didn't care if the bike was gone in the morning. What mattered far more was that when he lied about the bike tire to his mother, he knew he would lie to her forever. To this day, he never told her what he saw. When dad arrived home that evening, there was no mention of an unannounced bank visit. Rick was sure the bank officer would have informed his father that his son had been by to see him just at the time the knock came upon his office door. As far as his dad let on, it had been another normal day at work. It was possible that his dad didn't know the knock on the door came from him, in which case there would be no reason to suspect that he was spying in the office window. Regardless, his mom never suspected anything. Rick had brought his term report to the supper table and Kevin, his kid-brother wart of only seven years old, managed to smear butter over one corner of it. His mother proudly regaled the academic achievements of her firstborn son while his father sat silently, picking hither and thither at his supper. Rick recalled roast beef and mashed potatoes. His dad outwardly ignored him during mealtime and made no acknowledgement of his successful report.

Kelly noticed Rick's equanimity strengthen as he told his story. For her, getting her feelings out in the open always made her feel worse, at least initially. It was the reason she found therapy so damn draining. Had she been the one to tell such a story where they sat, she'd have long since fallen to pieces and then pondered the depth and speed of the river. She mulled over his story paying close attention to his nuances. In the past when he confided anything to her, even in jest, had always contributed some vague glimmer of who he really was. Humor and theatrics must have been the only ways he knew how to safely spill, as his approach was often cryptic and satirical, yet purposely pointed all at the same time; it was his nature, his poetic principle. This time, however, he had told her a story, a plain narrative devoid of emotional content, a tale from history that was both coldly objective and distant, like sans serif black print in a textbook. Rick recounted with detail, but said nothing of how the experience made him feel. Karen had taught her over the years to learn how to distinguish between the content of what happened in her past and how she felt about them, that while both aspects were conjoined sides of one coin, heads and tails were very different entities and not to be confused. Both sides were crucial. His unusually rigid composure worried her. She couldn't be sure if this was a natural difference in how men and women reacted to stress, or if he was in emotional denial. "Is there more you want to tell me?"

"Of what happened? No, that's pretty much it."

"Make the leap, Doctor. How did it make you feel? All you said is that you made up your mind not to say anything to your mom and you haven't. But it must have been like the end of the world to you, as you knew it. Your dad cheated on your mom and you saw it with your own eyes."

"I cried when I ran home. Managed to quash the tears before I got there so mom wouldn't see."

"Did your dad ever say anything to you after that, if he suspected you knew?"

"Nothing. But he knew I was there. I could tell from the way he was at supper. Ever since then, nothing's been the same. I thought my parents would divorce and then we'd come from the kind of home that people whispered about. Broken. I didn't want that, but I knew what my dad had done, I don't know how long it had been going on, but it was flat-out wrong. There's no excuse for that."

She saw his emotions begin to surface. "So you decided not to talk to him anymore. To avoid the whole mess just as he wanted to do."

"I can't even look at my dad. It's damn near impossible for me to respect him, as a man, as a person. That wasn't the kind of father I wanted in my life anyway. I was better off without him. It's not that I didn't want to confront him, I've always wanted to ask him why he did what he did, why he betrayed Mom… why he married her if he didn't love her, or how he could just fall out of love with her if he ever did love her. I had wondered why he stayed with

Mom all these years if he loved someone else or at the very least didn't love her."

"How did that make you feel, all that confusion?"

"I felt like shit in a bucket. Still do. I don't want to know why anymore. All I want is to kick his ass, right now, just like back then." His face reddened as he twisted long blades of grass. "He probably was pissed that I knew. Venetian blinds suck, by the way. Don't ever get them. They don't block shit. He hated that he'd been found out. He probably hated even more that I was a ticking time bomb ready to explode with the truth at any moment, whenever I felt like it. So he steered his way through it, tough, insanely defensible, and took on the supreme leader role in the household, lording his power over all of us. Total overcompensation. Everyone had to do what he said, when he said it, and we all had to stay out of his way. So there he was, King of his castle, and us, his pitiable minions."

"Enter the Crown Royal?"

"Yep. He became nasty under the influence of that poison."

"Did he ever hit you?"

"No, but he loved to threaten. He became this big-walking, big-talking threat, strong with a bottle in his fist."

"You know for sure he never hit your mom or Kevin?"

"Not for sure, but I don't think he did. Something about my dad - he's all bark and no bite. Ego the size of Texas as long as he has his precious bottle, vile weapon, but when it comes to dealing at ground level, he retreats. Fear of being found out." His voice shook with incredulity, "Tell me how someone can fall so far out of your life and still manage to burn into your skin like lit cigars? That's how he looked at me that night at supper and ever since."

"Secrets can do that to you. Whether the people involved are still alive with you or dead and gone, there's no getting away from it. It just follows you wherever you go. Did your mom ever learn about the affair?"

"He wouldn't have admitted it to her. I imagine she must have gotten wind of it from someone in town. Walls have ears. Small town party line, it's more effective than direct-dial. Then things at home started to really fall apart. My parents began fighting a lot. I hadn't really remembered them fighting much before that. Loud, tense.... They waited to have it out until after we went to bed. They hadn't done us any favors if they thought they were protecting us.

I always wanted to tell them anyone could hear dad snoring upstairs in their bedroom all the way from downstairs in the rec room. After the rounds of fighting came his drinking, and from his drinking came more fighting, then the distance…all downhill. After about a year or two, the fighting stopped. Separate lives, same house."

"Does Kevin know what happened?"

"I never said anything to him. He's never said anything to me. Your guess is as good as mine."

"Would you talk to your dad about it now?"

"Twenty-four years of being threatened not to talk sends you a message for one thing. Keep your nose clean. It's not my business to talk about it. My dad made it obvious to me that night at supper. My whole life since then, his message for me was that nobody wanted to know what I had to say, didn't matter the topic. Anything I ever tried to do after that rarely met with his approval. Can a father hate his own son?"

"Meaning does your father hate you? No. It's not hatred, that's too simple. This is way more complicated."

Rick found sanctuary in that sense of sureness in her voice.

   "And I hope you don't hate your father even though he's made a mess of his life. Circumstances mask and divert how we really feel about people. It gets so difficult…you just have to clear out all the crap and get back to the core of things. He needed to take charge of a situation he knew he no longer had control over. It's not hatred for you, it was about him trying to keep you and everything else around him in control. You were witness to something he didn't want anyone to know about. And I think it is your business to talk about it – to someone. It's your business because it's your experience, what you saw with your own eyes changed everything inside you. But writhing over your dad's motivations and actions isn't the task at hand for you. It never was. Don't work off assumptions about others, work off what you know to be true. And truth as you take it exists only within yourself. Your task is to be aware how this has affected you. Something like this is supposed to affect you. It propels change, the real kind that emanates from the center of who you are to make things better. You owe it to yourself to work through it, not against it."

As he listened, Rick noticed the increasing lucidity of her analysis of the complex situation. Her ability to reach into the heart of what he had struggled with for years astounded him. "Do you think that could be why I can't stand roast beef and mashed potatoes to this day?"

She laughed because she recognized the man she knew. "Address this. If you don't, it will only take you farther away from your family, emotionally. Either do it with a professional or without, it's your choice, but work to be at peace with it. Staying silent about something you know is wrong cuts you down inside to nothing more than shit in a bucket. Maintaining silence about something that's wrong is insidious, and it sends the wrong message, because not speaking up nullifies your whole existence…denying the truth is never healthy. Take it from me. It can change the course of your life. It's hard enough when you're a kid and you don't know what to do, but when you're an adult and you know better…"

"Truth's a bitch."

"But denial has the power to kill you."

August 5

He just phoned to ask me to seriously consider writing songs with him. I told him I wasn't the right one — for many reasons. I'm afraid that he's looking to me kind of like the way she looked to him to provide her with what she wanted. Our desires have a way of transcending beyond ourselves without our realizing it.

I'm this close to giving up writing altogether. I can't deal with all this and I think the writing is making it worse. Reading is marginally better.

August 9

He mentioned plans of a trip home to Hampton. He finally brought it up last week, but omitted anything of the wedding and I just let it slide. Yesterday, he offered up about the wedding and asked me to go with him. I don't think I even acted surprised. He wants me to meet his family, his grandparents and now he tells me that his uncle's family from Calgary will be there on vacation and he's really looking forward to seeing them again. He's heading up on Thursday and says he'll hang out at home for a few days and wants me to make arrangements with work if I can. He's going to want an answer soon. Going there with him will give everyone the wrong impression. I can't afford any more baggage.

August 19

I took my ring off today.

Seventeen

THURSDAY, AUGUST 21

The rest of the drive to Hampton allowed them to re-establish a sense of equilibrium that had lurched out of whack over the past few months. Even though it pushed their arrival at Rick's home back by almost three hours, what started out as a bathroom break turned out to be the flood wash. Kelly never would have imagined such poignant moments, how truths could be revealed outside a gas station restroom by the side of the road to nowhere. For her, both the gas station lot and the willow tree by the river would be sacred places of alliance. They would be local points of interest holding little value to anyone else passing by, but them.

Rick pulled into a long dusty driveway that ended in a small gravel lot aside of his parents' house. The Hutchinson home was a plain, double-gabled two-storey house, finished in white clapboard with dark green trim. The home stood centrally on a half-acre of land and its features were uncomplicated and looked like a life size version on the LEGO box. In the long shadows and waning coral light of the evening sun, the home looked warm and welcoming.

"Maggie and Hal."

Kelly surveyed her surroundings before getting out of the car. "Huh?"

"Maggie and Hal, or Howard if you insist on being formal."

"You sure I shouldn't refer to your parents as Mister and Mrs. Hutchinson?"

"Definitely not. Could you get Rudy?"

She reached for the kitty carrier and set it down on the gravel next to her feet. She heard the side door squeak as it pushed open and a gray-haired lady with a beautiful smile came rushing from the side steps. His mother's eyes sparkled. She was slightly heavy-set and wore a sleeveless floral print sundress with a square-cut neckline and brown leather sandals that were well worn along the sides.

"Oh you're here! We expected you hours ago!! Did you have car trouble? I figured you'd call if you had trouble..."

"No trouble, Mom. We took the scenic route." He winked at Kelly across the roof of the SUV then scooped up his mother warmly in his arms, without reservation. "Mom, this is my Kelly. And Kel, this is my Mummy... Mom...mmmMaggie."

Kelly's heart lightened at the perfect introduction. "So good to meet you." Maggie's look fit perfectly to the voice she'd heard on the phone at Rick's condo in the spring. Before she knew it, she too was greeted by the irreplaceable comfort of a maternal hug.

"I'm so glad you're here, both of you. Come in and bring the cat. I have something special for him all ready."

"For Rudy?" Kelly asked with interest.

"Yes. He loves kippers."

"We get the leftovers for supper, if Rudy leaves us any," Rick warned sardonically.

The kitchen smelled of pork chops, the kind his mom smothered in a slow-cooked sweet and sour sauce that Rick always mouth-watered over. Rudy chattered nonsensically in his carrier and bolted out onto the kitchen linoleum the instant Kelly opened the carrier flap. Rick pulled Rudy's tail-less mouse from his pocket and threw it on the floor. It slid past the cat and under the round birch kitchen table. And Rudy felt at home. It would be mere moments and he'd have his delight of freshwater packed kippers.

"Where's Dad?" Rick asked congenially.

"Oh he'll be back shortly. He just stepped out to get some wine for dinner. He was waiting for you to get here, then remembered at the last minute we didn't have wine."

"Is Kevin coming for Hannah's wedding?" Kelly asked as she helped Maggie set the table for supper.

Rick gave no response since he didn't know the answer.

"Oh no," Maggie replied to Kelly. "Kevin's not really so close to Hannah, she was closer to Ricky's age and I think you two were friends more so growing up." She looked to Rick for confirmation. "Wouldn't you say?"

"You could say that. Reality is, she's the daughter of your best friend. I just happened to be in the same grade as Hannah. I dated her you know, Mom."

"Yes, dear, I know…." An expression of weariness came over Maggie. "She was never your type. But there was no telling you."

Rick smiled at Kelly, with a look that conveyed, "See? I told you there was nothing to discuss."

Rick took Kelly on a cook's tour of both levels of the house. They ended right where they began, the heart of all Maritime homes, the kitchen. They continued to talk about the weather in Halifax, their day trip drive to Hampton and the so-called scenic route that had no public facilities. Comfortable chitchat occupied them until Hal walked in the side door carrying two paper-bagged bottles. His interruption came with perfect timing, as Rick's inventive but thankfully incomplete explanation of their delay could only account for at most two hours of their time, where they had been nearly an extra hour late. Kelly blushed as Maggie did a noticeable mental calculation of the time.

"Brought red and white. Don't ever know what goes with pork," Hal gruffed. The evening was warmer than he expected and he happily doffed his cardigan and threw it on the back of the chair next to him. Rick's father was tall and walked with an unusually firm carriage. His hair had thoroughly grayed, and hadn't been cut in a while. His cheeks looked flushed and sort of sunken and Kelly wondered if it was because of the drinking. Then she contemplated whether a person who drinks constantly should be out on the roads; perhaps you get used to doing everything, including driving, in that altered state and you can't drive safely sober any more. Country roads wouldn't be as congested with traffic, thank goodness. In any case, his eyes looked clear enough, she observed, his speech wasn't slurred, and he never staggered once. Oddly, she thought, if Rick hadn't told her he were an alcoholic, she might not have known.

"Either goes, dear. Ask the kids what they want."

"Oh," Hal mumbled. Then he looked to the svelte blond, standing between his plump wife and his tall son, whom he hadn't yet outwardly acknowledged, "You must be Kelly….uh…" He fidgeted with the corkscrew in his right hand, shifting it to his left so he could extend a polite greeting.

Kelly shook his hand with confidence and filled in the blank, "Pearson."

"Named after the Toronto airport," Hal chuckled.

"No relation to the Lester B. family, Dad." It was the first thing Rick said to his father.

"Oh…I suppose not. Memory's going, anything helps these days."

Rick extended his hand to greet him. "Good to see you Dad."

"Hope your car didn't conk out on the way. We thought you'd be here hours ago." He stepped to the fridge to put away the white wine.

"Never mind, Hal, as you can see they're just fine. Supper's ready." Maggie diverted attention expertly, a necessary skill in order to raise two boys.

Aside from a few moments of stilted discomfort whenever Rick tried to engage his father in conversation directly, suppertime talk seemed to flow with relative ease. Kelly could see that Rick's obligation to fish for his father's approval on the topic of a possible position in Calgary, where Hal's younger brother's family resided, only seemed to steer Hal toward increased uneasiness. Rick gave up. He had no plan to tell his parents he had retracted his application. Maggie voiced many questions and comments about Rick's employment status and the type of work he might be doing if he gets the job at CA Technologies, and Hal absorbed every word of his son's responses. Kelly sat in quiet observation during this part of the meal, enjoying her smothered pork chops. She had the chance to come out of her shell around dessert and tea when she answered introductory social questions about herself and how she and Rick met.

After supper, Kelly noticed Rick go into the living room with his dad. The supper table reverted to original pristine form once the dishes had been cleared and the surface scrubbed down. The kitchen was bright and remarkably tidy. There was nothing on the counters. While Kelly washed and Maggie dried,

Kelly watched where things in the Hutchinson kitchen belonged. If she were to successfully last out the week there, it might help to know such things. Her mother had always taught her to be alert, useful and if possible, indispensable. It was a surefire way to gain acceptance in new positions, and always helped to break the ice. Maybe it was a real estate career tactic.

"I have a rash of baking and hors d'oeuvres to make for the wedding on Saturday. That's why there's nothing out. I put everything away so there'd be plenty of room for me to mess it all up."

Rick walked quickly and purposefully through the kitchen and out the side door. He didn't utter a word. Rudy nibbled a second helping of kippers.

"So good to have him home. The boys hardly ever get back these days, they're so busy. It's not easy for him," Maggie confided.

"I know, things aren't simple with Rick."

"What you think about the job in Calgary?"

"I thought he said things weren't settled yet." Kelly responded casually.

"Calgary's lovely. Very modern."

"I've never been to Calgary, but I've been to Edmonton. I have relatives there. Not ones I'm close to, though."

"I think you'd like Calgary."

Kelly watched Rick pass right through the kitchen without reaction as he carted suitcases during her comment. She paused at her dishwashing and dropped her shoulders as far down as they would go, remembering his oath in the vestibule that they would make it work no matter what. No matter what really meant no matter where; she felt drained from the day's surprises.

"Oh," Maggie sighed openly. Hopes she might have held for her son's present state of happiness dissipated as he breezed by. "I shouldn't have assumed."

"It's okay. One of the first things he told me when we met is that he'd likely be changing jobs soon that might mean a move on his part. So it's not a surprise."

"Richard talks a great deal about you."

"Oh great," Kelly sang despondently. "How much has he told you about me?"

"Quite a bit. That you're an exquisite skater, a lovely dancer, a visionary writer with a heart of solid gold."

"It's all a lie," she half laughed.

"My son may be a crafty manipulator but he doesn't lie, I assure you. He told me your expressive writing is why he fell in love with you. Or was it your skating? I can't remember now." Maggie's openness was refreshing.

"It wasn't my cooking, that's for sure."

They agreed Rick was adept at methods of buttering up and discovered in more cheerful discussion that they shared some common interests.

Rick had taken the bags upstairs and walked into the kitchen to find his mother and Kelly talking about choral arrangements and the works each of them sang in their respective choirs. "You never told me you were in a choir," he pressed himself against Kelly's back and buried his nose in her hair. He sandwiched her against the kitchen counter then wrapped his arms around her and grabbed the dripping dishcloth from her hands. He began to scrub down the sink. Anyone peering in the kitchen window might think that Kelly was a mutant with four arms and an extra head. "I didn't know that you sing, my love. This changes everything."

Kelly nudged him in the pit of his stomach, "School choir, alto. You never asked." Her curtness prompted him to kiss her lustily just beneath her ear. She watched him walk to where his mother stood near the fridge and he bear-hugged her. Kelly leaned back on the counter and drank in the joy on Maggie's face as her son lifted her well off the ground.

"Mom's a soprano and you're an alto, I'm in heaven. My world is complete."

"Correction, Ricky, I was an alto. From age twelve to sixteen."

"Once an alto…" his index finger waved with optimism.

"Eventually a tenor," Kelly finished wryly. "I need a drink."

"She used to play the piano too, Mom, did she tell you that?"

"Oh brother. Give it up, music-man," Kelly chuckled.

"Did you bring your guitar, Richard?" His mother asked.

"Don't fall over, I did."

His mother lit up like Christmas. "He plays very well, for a boy who taught himself to play, you know, Kelly. But I haven't heard him play since he was living at home. Looks like we're all in for a treat this time around."

That night before drifting off to sleep, alone in Rick's old room, she prayed earnestly that things would be different, for everyone, from this day forward. It was going to be a trying several days. She needed to believe that people could marshal the strength to embark the Ship of Change knowing it would be a one-way journey to fearless acceptance of truth. She needed to believe it more than anyone.

FRIDAY, AUGUST 22

Her sleep was as fitful as Kelly had expected. Being in a different bed in a strange place is the quick recipe for insomnia. An unusual array of nocturnal sounds, which didn't include loose mufflers or emergency sirens, floated in through the open window with the night's breeze. She had no idea crickets could be so loud, and she convinced herself many times during the night that they had crawled inside the house, and camped in the hallway just outside the bedroom door. Nature's hush seemed to descend before twilight ascended and she slept briefly, at long last. When she finally got up, she looked out the window. The sun was peeking up from behind the trees in the distance and the sky took on benevolent rose petal hues of newness. She was about to make the bed when she heard a gentle pattering at the door. Kelly grabbed her silk robe from atop her suitcase and wrapped it around herself. "Come in."

The door inched open and the orange cat chirped a hello, trotted into the room and hopped upon the bed. Kelly reached across the foot of the double bed and induced a sensuous purr from Rudy by rubbing his belly.

"What can I say, you have that effect on us, whether you mean to or not," Rick whispered as he entered his old room. "Like my room?" He gently shut the door and came over to sit next to her, still in his nighttime t-shirt and boxers. "Don't worry, no girls have been in this bed...my old single bed got ditched long ago."

"Great. I feel better. Not much left of 'you' in your room, if you ask me. Just a desk and a bookshelf." Sitting on the bed, she pictured the room filled with records and schoolbooks, his guitar, and clothes heaped on the floor. "Where are the Sports Illustrated swimsuit posters?"

"Mom must have thrown them out. Wonder why." He reclined next to her and breathed in the scent of her skin. "I'd rather sleep in here than on the pullout in the study down the hall. It's too hot in there."

"No problem, I'll take the pullout and you can stay in here."

"But that would defeat my purpose." He snuggled closer, wanting to know if she tasted as good as she smelled.

"And wouldn't your parents be pleased."

They laughed in whispers together at the preposterousness of their plight: two adults who, for their own reasons, still felt like they were kids. For all the problems they grappled with at home in Halifax, parents walking in unannounced wasn't one of them. It placed Kelly's inhibition in perspective. They were grown-ups, she as much as he; and with this revelation, she hoped the issue of bodily consent on her part would take a hike, and fast. It didn't take her long to gear up her feelings for him again.

"One foot on the floor at all times." Rick shared his mom's sage advice to her sons and their friends alike. "Look, there's a lot you can still do…"

"Did you get a chance to talk to your dad last night?"

"A bit. Is that why you jumped ship to go to bed early?"

"Talk, already."

"Hmm…he complimented me."

"What about? Your exceptional taste in women?"

"The walls are thin in this house. He told me that bringing you home was the only sign of intelligence he'd seen on Planet Me thus far."

"Kind of a backhanded compliment if you ask me."

"I lied. It was really a compliment for you. I just wanted first dibs on it. Congrats, Pearson. He likes you."

"Can't imagine why."

"He said you were real."

"As opposed to what, imaginary?" Maybe his father meant 'real' in the context of phoniness, but she couldn't be sure with such limited information. "This is all very bizarre. Is your mom up?"

"Probably. And wondering how long I've been in here."

"She got a kick out of your sorry story for an excuse last night. 'Duh, we took the scenic route so I could show her the river, the dam, and the historical museum'? Please. It would have been 'real' to tell her we had a fight in the car and needed to sort it through."

"Alright. I'll tell her we were late because we made out under a tree. That would easily account for the lost hour or so."

"Don't bother. She probably figured that out on her own. She's a smart cookie, you know."

Rick cuddled up at her side, wrapping his arms and legs tightly around her. "My family's scrambled eggs, can you tell?"

She was ensnared, and she loved it. "Do you want to know what I really think?"

"More than life itself. Hold nothing back. I can take it."

"Your father does respect you, in his own weird way. Except he can't say it or show it in the ways you want him to. I think he's afraid to."

"Don't buy it. He's not afraid of me."

"That's not what I said. Pay attention. He's afraid to change course now, he probably thinks it's too late and there's nothing he can do anymore."

"You think my dad respects me? Has Hell sprouted daisies?"

"They've been known to pop out of the snow. He was nice to me, right from the beginning. If he didn't care about you, who knows how he'd have welcomed me. Maybe not at all."

"He probably wishes he were thirty years younger. In which case, I'd have to kick his ass."

"Enough nonsense from you." She ruffled his hair. "I was happy to meet him and I think he felt the same way."

"Okay, I'll buy that. He never liked Rebecca and it was clear to everyone, right from the get go. He was downright cold to her."

"I never sensed coldness from him. Also, I noticed during supper last night he paid very close attention to everything you told your mom about your life, your work, the job search. I watched him closely, his body language and expression. He wasn't put off, he wasn't flinching out of disgust, he didn't come across as irritated. He was listening, carefully, and I'm confident to say he was interested. He didn't look any differently at me when your mom asked me questions and I answered them."

"Then how come he never talked to me directly? Even when I made the first move? He never even shook my hand when I offered it to him."

"You did the right thing by offering. Like I said, it's hard to make a course change once the groove deepens. You both have grown accustomed to not talking to each other, out of fear more than anything else. And you've hardened, I'm sorry to say, clinging to the belief that he doesn't care about you, so you wouldn't notice a change if it slapped you. Twenty-four years, you said?"

"Twenty-four and mom doing her damnedest to cover it up like nothing ever happened. Scrambled eggs, like I said."

She slithered down the bed to make eye contact with him. "Dysfunctional, yes. But not impossible. Keep trying. You have nothing to be afraid of."

"Beg to differ."

"You're afraid of change for the better? In which case, trust me, I can relate. Rick, he's the one who's lost pretty much everything in his life. Everything worth having, the respect of his son, maybe both his sons, the sanctity of his marriage, the trust of his wife… and out with all that family value glue goes inner peace. Rick, I imagine he became an alcoholic to deaden the grief of all that loss. I know about wanting to anaesthetize grief. Learn from his mistakes."

"Are you saying I'm on the same schedule?"

"No, of course not. You're not your father. I'm saying you're the one who's best off here. Out of everyone, you're in the strongest position, emotionally and experience-wise. You know that when you've suffered and lost everything, hitting rock-bottom means you have everything yet to gain once more….and you're not the one at rock-bottom, he is."

Rick rolled on his back. "Tell Karen she's worth double her hourly rate if this is the kind of stuff she's teaching you."

"Nah. Some wicked Zen concept about emptying out an overflowing teacup… I learned about it from some unemployed musician thespian-wannabe who stole my heart when I wasn't looking. Turned out he saved my life."

He pulled her on top of him and brushed her hair off her face and kissed her, forgetting that his mom had been roaming about the upstairs hallway, likely laying out fresh towels. His hands made their way beneath her silk robe and under her nightshirt. "So what do I do to help my parents marriage?"

"Excuse me, Romeo. Your job isn't to heal their marriage, that's their job. You need to know what your mission is."

"I know what my mission is."

"Do you? Then tell me."

"To make you my wife."

She expected a half-ass comeback from him, with his reliably perfect timing. His answer went in her right ear and straight out her left to the wall, "Oh, enough of your insolence," she laughed. Then it rebounded off the wall and back into her head where it lodged somewhere in her forward cranium. "What did you just say?" They were on top of the bedcovers, her robe had fallen to her side and his hands were firmly on her behind and she feared his mother walking in the room without knocking. It was her house after all. She watched the bedroom door like a hawk while Rick repositioned her robe over her.

"She won't come in. You were asking me what my mission was." His hands worked their way up her back.

"Your mission when it comes to your dad. Rick, stay on task here with me."

"My dad? I don't want him to be my wife."

She sat upright on his belly, resting on her knees, and began to pummel his chest with her fists until he laughed uncontrollably out loud. "She won't come in? You sure??" She began to laugh hysterically as he tickled her feverishly, while managing to hold her down to him so she couldn't get away. They called a tickle treaty and she lay back down on his chest. "The last time I was in this particular position with you, we were so unhappy."

"I remember, yet we were wearing far less...." It would have been a tough concept for any man to rationalize.

"I'm sorry I stormed out. We were just so far away from each other."

He lay quietly, loving her weight upon him. It slowed his breathing. "More often than you'll think, I need you to remind me about everything I've done wrong in my life. Including pressuring you."

"Are you apologizing??" Her eyebrows lifted high.

"Last I checked, I was proposing," he frowned. "I'm not so good at this, huh?"

"It's too early in the morning. Go back to groveling." She rested her forehead on his chin, bewildered by his torturing sense of humor. There was so much about him she might never understand.

"Slap me rosy, sweetheart, but I can't explain it - it makes me feel better when you hit me with feminine wrath without mincing words the advanced high-tech idiot I am."

"You are an idiot."

"And you still love me."

Kelly nodded, marveling at the paradoxical phenomenon.

"Say it again."

"You're a first-class dolt."

"I love you too."

"I love you three."

They were enjoying the visit home. Conversations rolled back and forth at meals and over tea. Rick mowed the lawn while Kelly helped Maggie with the wedding baking. Kelly had offered to help Rick with the outdoor chores, but he suggested she spend time talking with his folks. After all, they needed to get to know her. He insisted that to rob them of the pleasure of her company would be criminal. Later, it occurred to Kelly that she might have a better opportunity to get acquainted with them if he weren't in the room. Several trays of puff pastries, biscuits and rumaki were on the kitchen's agenda. It was to be a simple ceremony tomorrow, in the late afternoon at the Presbyterian church the Hutchinsons and the Etters attended. A dinner and dance reception at the 4H Club would follow the wedding. That would be her chance to see Hampton proper and a good fraction of its residents. Rick had arranged for the two of them to do some family visiting, stopping by to visit grandparents on Sunday and they were scheduled to head back on Monday.

Maggie and Kelly talked a whirlwind while baking. By the time the last trays came out of the oven, Kelly was familiar with Maggie's upbringing, family history and the normal happenings of her days in Hampton. Maggie learned about Kelly's background, some details surrounding her parents' deaths and a wealth more about Kelly's passions in life, and how they helped to buoy her emotional slumps. Rick had told her a fair bit about Kelly during various phone calls home but Maggie preferred to listen to her in person, a far more enlightening encounter. They sat on the bed in Rick's old room and Kelly showed Maggie her bedside photo album and described each photo to her with delight.

"It's good that you brought this with you to show me," Maggie smiled. "It makes me feel that I've known you all your life."

"Rick loves this ice dance podium picture when I was sixteen." She flipped back to the photo in question.

"Boys have a thing for girls in skimpy dresses. And you have beautiful legs. Such a lovely slim figure. Keep it up and when you're my age, you'll still look like a young girl, and not an old frump."

She smiled at his mother, and received a look of whole acceptance and affection in return. "I don't want to look like a young girl." Kelly looked at her chest with disenchantment. It was the first thing her eyes fixed upon. "I wish I was more curvy and voluptuous, like my mom. People always looked at her."

"She was lovely, and you look just like her. Losing your mom at such a young age…such a shame. You've had to grow up on your own. What was that like?"

"Don't know. I haven't grown up yet." She let her frustration show. "I've spent too much of my adult life feeling exactly the same as the day my parents left me. I still feel like I'm seventeen, and I forget I've been fending for myself for so long."

"Don't worry, all things come in due time. There's a time and season to every purpose under heaven."

"Ecclesiastes. And The Byrds."

"You know your scripture. And your lyrics."

"I just wish I had more faith in both."

"To waste time wishing you'll ever have all the faith you need…you've missed the boat, I suppose. What I've learned is no matter how much faith you have, use it and you can always find more."

"For me, it's just hard to know where hope fits in anymore….when you've lost all your dreams and can't afford any expectations. Hope feels dangerous."

"Hope is who you are. You are the living embodiment of hope. It's not something beyond you or outside of you. You are the substance of progress in humanity. Hope is you, what you live. And how you live, with respect for what's true. I think you're doing it already, as well as any of us can be expected to do."

"So here I've been searching outside for something that's always been a part of me? Missing it, grieving for it, wanting it to find me and I'm it…? I can see where your son gets his divine patience from."

"Patience?? He's never had a whit of patience in his life. He's so much like his father."

"You think? He reminds me more of you, now that I'm getting to know you."

"I'll take credit for that." Maggie laughed and the bed jiggled beneath them.

"I keep thinking he'll just run out of patience for me. I would if I were him."

"How do you know he doesn't worry the same thing when he thinks about you?"

"I don't. There's so much I don't know. He has so much faith in me, I think he's making a big mistake by giving up a solid job possibility for me." A solitary tear welled up, rolled down and splatted on her dress. She had let the cat out of the bag.

"Giving up a job? What do you mean?"

"It's too much to get into, but the long and the short of it is that… well…he only just told me about it, so all this is still reverberating like a bell in my brain. He says that the way things have happened, how we met, what's developed, the timing of it all, the job search isn't his first priority right now."

"I know he has no intention of moving on without you."

"He said that? When?"

"I can't remember exactly, around the time when he said they were shutting down his lab."

"He only just told me yesterday. I think he's making a huge mistake, Maggie, to risk a stable life for someone so cracked."

"Cracked? Why do you say that? It's clear you both are so in love with each other. And nothing you've said makes me think you're cracked at all. Where are you getting these ideas? Your feet are very much on the ground and you know who you are, deep inside. You're not a fantasy-chaser. You've had your hard knocks from life in the first half. You've had it much rougher than me. I had a rock-solid youth. My life's knocks came later, but I had my foundation. You never had the chance to know yours."

"I wish I understood my so-called foundation. There are still so many unanswered questions... I'll never know the answers. They're gone." She caressed a photo of her parents in her little album.

"Seasons, dear. You will find your way. You penetrated my son's heart, and that's a feat all of its own."

"I think he's been lonely for a very long time. We both have been. Part of me thinks we gravitated toward each other because we were both feeling lonely at the same time."

"Loneliness is a guise, for all of us, and don't fall for it. Loneliness means we haven't met our real selves yet. I know my son. And he's been in love before, many times, so he says. He thought he was in love when he wasn't. He said he wasn't when I believe he really could have been. He even swore up and down he'd marry his grade ten Drama teacher if she was still single when he graduated high school. I've seen it all from that boy."

Kelly laughed. "This is supposed to be making me feel better? I didn't know about his Drama teacher."

"He's himself with you. He's not someone he genuinely isn't, or shouldn't be when he's around you. He is who he is. With you. Take it from me, I know him. You got the golden egg, missy. More than any other woman he's dated that I've known about."

Kelly grew somber. She felt her stomach wrench in its usual way every time she thought about herself in the context of his life. She leaned forward pressing her arms into her belly wishing the soreness of ineptitude would fade.

"What's wrong?"

"Nothing, I'm fine. Really."

"You look like you're in pain. This could be serious…if you're pregnant."

She put her hand on Maggie's arm. "No chance of that. I'll be fine."

"Are you sure you're okay? You're not…?"

"Definitely not pregnant." She glanced at Maggie with wide eyes of pure embarrassment. "I'm still a virgin." She covered her face with her hands in utter shame. "The very last of the dodo birds the world thought had gone extinct eons ago." The words crept out sheepishly from behind her fingers.

The dramatic irony of this young lady's life was truly compelling, bordering on entertaining. Maggie laughed in the way only an experienced mother could. Before long, Kelly's shoulders were bent over and heaving and Maggie couldn't tell if Kelly was laughing along with her, or crying in sobs. A fumbled hug proved it to be a bit of both. "That's nothing to cry over. There are women who would ask for their virginity back if they knew it was possible. Born Agains, we call them. Some women would say you weren't missing out on a thing and would steer you clear from it. And we'll feel sorry for them, won't we?"

"Yep." She thought of Wendy and did feel genuinely sorry for her, grabbing for love from all the wrong shelves. She thought of her mother and about the likely extramarital affair with JT or whoever he was. She thought of Maggie's situation and looked instantly to her. "I don't really know who my parents were…"

"What? You were adopted? Richard never told me that."

"No, no. My mom gave birth to me and she and my dad raised me, but now that they're gone, I'm finding out I never knew who they really were as people."

"Welcome to life, kiddo. What kids ever truly know their parents?"

"Some do. Don't they?"

"Well, I would say I know my parents. I've heard their stories and I understand them as well as any separate soul who lived in their house could."

"I just found out that my mom loved another man when I was in grade school."

"How'd you come to learn of this? Who told you? A neighbor? Because you can't trust what people say sometimes. They say all kinds of things if they have good enough reason."

"I didn't hear it from anyone. I don't know the man's name, but I found letters that he wrote to her, and I think they were definitely in love with each other from what he said in the letters. I think she loved this man enough to ask my father for a divorce, I found the divorce papers a few weeks ago. And I knew nothing about any of it growing up."

"There's a lot parents don't tell their kids, and rightly so. We parents must protect our kids as much as we can."

"What about commitment, and living based on what's true? Now I feel like I can't believe a thing my parents taught me, or even in how they raised me. If I never had the chance to secure my foundation, where do you go when you're kicked out blind, and now you don't even know what your real starting point was?"

"Heavens, Kelly. These questions can't be answered in two days, I can't even bet on two lifetimes. Mistakes of people around us teach us a great many things, as does God and Nature. It's up to you to find perspective, because each person you talk to will have their own version of what's true. Right and wrong are relative only to each other."

Kelly flopped backward onto the bed and cried out, "I give up. This is all too confusing for my little virginal pea-brained mind. There are days I feel Rudy understands more about life than I do. Rick should marry Rudy."

"Heaven forbid!" Maggie howled.

"You're my first choice, Kel," Rick's voice called in from the hall. He walked into the bedroom following a long shower. "I can say that out loud, Rudy's not here. He'll be crushed, but...who cares. He's a cat."

"We're talking about those letters I found in the piano."

"Those," Rick said in a Film Noire tone. "Whoever the guy was, he had the hots for her mom somethin' terrible."

"Thank you for that synopsis," Kelly said snidely.

"Let's kick his ass."

There was no getting off the boyish vengeance bandwagon, not if Rick had any say. Maggie shook her head reflecting years of weariness.

He curled up around Kelly and felt the wetness of tears. He wiped her chin dry. "So Madre Mahalia," Rick got his mother's attention, "we seek your sage advice. Consider this bed the snowy mountain top we have assiduously ascended in humble faith..."

Kelly groaned. "He must have gotten his A in drama."

Both women giggled like girls at a slumber party. "I don't think so, that might explain at least one heartbreak." Maggie said quickly.

Rick sat ostracized by their coincident bursts of laughter. Rudy climbed atop the family mountain with a running start looking rather disgruntled that he had been left alone downstairs while the social congregation took place upstairs. The giggle fits subsided.

"So Madre Mahalia? Recommendations as to how I go about convincing this nubile goddess that you're ideal madre-in-law material?"

"I thought we were discussing..." Kelly interjected. She couldn't believe he was still making silly jokes. He must be stressed more than she thought.

"Fine. Resume. Make it so." His was a four-star command.

"Well, where were we..." Maggie began. "Don't ask me, I was known around these parts for being naïve. Then I got married and had two boys. Now, I always have an opinion and usually something to back it up."

"Good mother-in-law material, you say?" Kelly asked to Rick's chin that sat upon her shoulder. "You need to shave, Captain."

"Aye, me mate. What's the point in having an opinion unless you know wholeheartedly you're right? Eh? Something I learned from dear ol' Dad."

Maggie chimed in, "As for you and you," she said poking each of them, "life gets figured out as you go along. You can't plan it all in advance, so don't even try. You'll get lost in the plans and forget to live. So work out what you can and face the rest as it comes. About the letters you found, were there any written by your mother?"

"No. Not in that lot. But who's to say I won't dig out another bundle inside an old blender. I'm ready to retire from sorting boxes of stuff that aren't mine."

"And you say you don't know the name of the man who wrote them?"

"No. Whatever the relationship was between him and my mom, I've been letting it bother me. It's been clouding me. I have spent so much of my life permitting other people's experiences and opinions to cover my own inexperience instead of just living my life. Here I am telling this one to tear down the crap and get to the core of things," she patted Rick, "and I need to listen to my own advice. This other man wasn't my father. I wouldn't know how to find him anyway. I don't know if he's still alive or around. I don't even want to know."

"Is it something you can let go?" Maggie knew how to ask relevant questions.

"I hope so. But these days it keeps me up at night. Thinking about what marriage is supposed to be about. Is it worth it in the end? That for everything my mom did for me, for us, she wasn't happy. She was a caged bird. Sure, she had a husband, a home, a family, a career, but still, she must have felt trapped, obligated to her life with my dad and me. It hurts me that for everything she sacrificed for my dad and me, she didn't gain any satisfaction from her life with us. That she had to look to someone else, some stranger, to feel a sense of passion. It kills me to think she was unhappy with her life when she died."

"Yes, I can see your concern. Well, try resting in the knowledge that regardless of your parents' circumstances, your mother did experience passion in her life with the man who wrote the letters."

"I think she did," Rick volunteered. "From what the guy wrote, he was more than an acquaintance. Apparently they had made plans for the future together, probably hinging on her divorce, and I got the feeling it was a difficult decision to call it off. Which likely was your mom's decision, Kel. After all, your parents did stay together. Stands to reason she changed her mind about getting a divorce. In any case, there was evidence of regret on both sides in one of the letters."

Kelly agreed. "Part of me wonders maybe it's my fault that she didn't go through with it because the family shouldn't have been torn apart."

"Your dad didn't concede. He never signed the papers," Rick reminded.

"In which case, my mom was cornered into staying. Back to being trapped and unhappy when she died. See?"

Rick knew her tears were imminent.

"Kelly," Maggie counseled, "whatever your mom's decision was, it was hers to make. And she made it. We can't always be a part of the decisions that affect us so greatly. Sadly, you'll never know the reasons why she chose to do what she did. Unless the person in question talks directly to you about it, you can only infer. And that's not wise. It causes more problems than it solves. You can't force someone to talk to you."

Both Kelly and Rick sat motionless and listened. The focus of Maggie's point had shifted, with the subtlest turn. Kelly nodded her acknowledgment and reached out to hug Maggie for her maternal warmth and heartfelt contribution to her plight.

He noticed they remained clutched to each other longer than he would have expected. It fortified him to see the kind of bonding power that could develop in such a short span of time between two people who had never met before; he had only known Kelly for a few months. He quietly pondered what he missed of their late afternoon's talk; but watching them both, this loving reunion of strangers, he knew bringing her home was the right thing to do.

Eighteen

SATURDAY, AUGUST 23

Wedding mania was upon them all. The baked goods and appetizers were laid out, ready to go, and gifts were wrapped. Pantyhose without runs had been laid out and Maggie had given Kelly her approval on the slip-dress she brought to wear to the wedding. It had simple lines with a soft angled ruffle around the skirt. To Rick, his mom's confidence in their future together as a couple was both bracing and terrifying, the latter being Kelly's current hold as she dressed for the ceremony; she tried not to tear her nylons. Nobody knows a son better than his mother, she reminded herself.

Kelly noticed that Rick's quirky jokes about proposals, marital relations, and in-laws had been left behind. Maybe his stress was abating, she hoped. Certainly, being in his father's presence was enough to have him spouting gibberish without thinking. That's all it was, stress. What else could it be? At least he played the guitar this morning, for nearly two hours and she felt a sense of relief come over her from his music. His mom was in heaven for it. His dad was in and out, so at the very least, he would have heard a phrase here and there, if not entire pieces. Did a feeling of pride fill his heart? Was he touched by his son's music? Was there a feeling of regret inside him for negating a young boy's passion for music? For negating him altogether? The habitual assumptive, judgmental thoughts befitting her patterns signaled a mental alert;

therapy was paying off, she had gotten better at halting herself mid-fixation. Maggie's words secured a strong foothold in her mind: if the person in question doesn't talk to you directly, you're tempted to infer. That only creates more problems than it solves. She knew Maggie's wisdom came from personal experience.

Hannah was an elegant bride, petite with auburn hair and a twinkling smile that hadn't left her heart-shaped face since moment one. Kelly thought she did look a bit like Wendy and she understood the image Rick was describing the night she stayed with him at Mike's cabin after her hospital stay; Hannah's was very much the look that had always appealed to him. Kelly felt on edge long before the ceremony began. It started the moment she entered the church, which was nothing like the one she attended as a child. Her family's church, the grand, hallowed place where her parents' funerals were held was expansive and airy, a masterpiece of classic architecture. With its tripartite gothic stained-glass windows and tall stone pilasters that grew skyward blending into arches over the hall, some might feel more removed from their source than closer to it. Their funeral day marked the last time she had attended a church service. In contrast, this little place of worship in Hampton was humble, clear in purpose, blessed and snug. Perhaps God might hold her closer to Him in this house, if she asked Him. She hadn't felt religious fervor to any degree since her parents left her…another question to add to her long list of whys. Rick held her hand throughout the ceremony, but her tension remained until they passed the receiving line. Whether she still had longstanding issues with God, in particular, or because she suffered increased trepidation of marriages in general, she wasn't ready to address this one.

During the reception dinner of baked chicken and grilled haddock, the band set up in preparation for the evening dance. The wedding couple looked radiant at an intimate round table with their loved ones. An ice sculpture in the shape of two hearts fused into one was set in a pool surrounded by a lighted champagne fountain. The three-tier wedding cake adorned with real red roses stood on a separate table nearby. Guests were seated at round tables in groups of eight. Hal and Maggie consistently presented Kelly as Richard's friend from Halifax. She had been introduced to so many people, there was no point in trying to keep up. So she graciously talked quietly to Maggie, who sat to her right, with Rick to her left. Hal sat next to Maggie and spent much of the evening enthusiastically bantering with the guests around him. Rick promised Kelly that they would dance the night away despite his permanent claim he didn't dance. She had never danced with Rick before. Maggie asked her if she knew how to polka and Kelly was proud to say that she could do the foxtrot, the argentine tango, the quickstep and the rumba, albeit on the ice and not the floor. But she told Maggie they'd make do with a basic waltz. Once the speeches were over, many guests got up to chat and several went outdoors to smoke. The 4H Club had an adjacent outdoor patio that terraced down the sloping hill toward a small pond. Crystal white mini lights lit the outdoor area with magical stars close enough to touch. It made Kelly long for Christmas.

Rick excused himself from the table just as the music began. As Kelly waited for him to return, she sipped champagne and admired an elderly couple on the dance floor, and wondered how many years they had been married. She had grown fatigued of greetings from pleasantly cheerful people with surveying eyes, whose names flew away without ever having touched down. So she continued to drink champagne and the servers just kept bringing more, and she kept tapping her toes, drumming her fingers and looking around the hall for Rick. Despite her tiredness from several sleepless nights, she still felt like dancing. As the evening wore on, a torrent of pain surged from the back of her neck to her frontal lobe. Ladies kept coming to chat with her and asking all sorts of curious questions, some of them could have been construed as prying. In this small town, it wouldn't matter whether his parents told these people that she was Rick's cat sitter, or his cleaning lady, or the woman he planned to abduct on the spaceship he was building to fly to Mars, he was a rocket scientist after all... They all gobbled down her introduction the very same way: 'Richard's brought a girl home. Richard's getting married? Why, Hutchinsons, you never said a word about him deciding to get married again...such a shame about his last wedding, wasn't it? We had the gifts all wrapped and everything. Is he really over Rebecca? No, he couldn't be...such a tragedy. You can't get past something so tragic...we just thought he'd be a bachelor forever. How long has he known this one? My, just four months, oooh...she must be pregnant. Girls from the city, you know.... "Kelly....Kelly." She heard her name being called.

It was Maggie. She was leaning over her shoulder to get her attention, "You were a million miles away."

She rubbed her temples. "Hmmm. Mars, all I could see was red. Where's Rick?"

"I don't know, I thought maybe you knew. I haven't seen Hal either and I've been looking for him."

For Kelly, every minute at this reception without Rick ticked quarter-time.

"We should go search them out. I'll get Constable Davis here to put out an APB," Maggie laughed with yet another guest.

Kelly thought quickly past the cloud of red ash left in the demon's wake, "They might be outside."

"Could you check?" Maggie's ankles were swelling from her dress shoes, having been on her feet for so long.

The fresh air would do her good. Why hadn't she thought to step outside earlier? Meandering through the guests, she walked onto the patio and took a long look around. It was much quieter compared to inside the hall. Outdoors, the crickets sounded muted; her hearing had been numbed from the loud band music. There were steps leading down to a lower terrace on one side so she walked in that direction. From above, looking down one level, she spied Rick talking with his father. They sat adjacent on a white cast iron bench, hunched over, resting elbows on knees. She couldn't hear anything, so they must have been speaking civilly to each other. Much of the time she watched, Rick was looking away from his dad and down to the ground. She could see a highball in Hal's hand, and a cigarette balanced between his fingertips butted up against the rim of his glass. Rick held a drink and a cigarette, too. He doesn't smoke, she thought, he's a health nut. But he took long, experienced drags from the twig between his fingers and didn't hack once. He then took a serious gulp of his tawny drink and winced slightly. She sat at a table by the stairs on the terrace above them. A young man came by, asked her to dance and she politely declined. Several minutes later, she returned inside.

"We were right." She sat down next to Maggie. "They are outside, talking, but I didn't interrupt."

"Should I go out there?"

"Looks okay. Let it be."

Maggie grew nervous but did her best not to show it.

"I think I'm too tired to make it any longer."

"You haven't been sleeping well. You should head home."

"Thanks for understanding."

"The house is open, I'll have Constable Davis drop you there."

"I don't want to trouble anyone. It's still early," Kelly yawned.

"They're heading home now, and it's in the same direction. I'll wait here for Hal and let Rick know you went home to rest."

Kelly stepped through the squeaky screen door and Rudy galloped to meet her. She carried him upstairs and brought him to the bedroom. She undressed, washed up, swallowed her assortment of pills and crawled into bed with her journal. She felt like she would sleep right away, but knew that feeling could quickly extinguish once her head hit the pillow. Her brain ached and her mind raced. All roads to peace were jammed solid in her mind. Awake and writing for longer than she perceived, she switched off the lamp and closed her eyes.

She awakened at the creak of the bedroom door opening, then shutting. In the dark, Rick took off his smoke-filled suit jacket and it landed on the floor. He had missed the chair by more than a foot. He sat on the bed next to her and leaned down and kissed her then began unknotting his tie.

She sat up a bit, "I'm awake. What time is it?"

"It's well after midnight," he whispered. "I'm sorry we never got a chance to dance."

"You'll do anything to get out of dancing, won't you? You smell like a saloon. God."

"I'll go have a shower." And he left, taking all his olfactory offending attire with him. In ten minutes, he was back.

Kelly switched on the lamp. "I got this insane headache, and when I saw you were talking to your dad, I decided to come back."

"Did you sleep?"

"Yeah. Like a log. Not long enough, though." She rubbed her eyes. "You look cooked."

"Do I?"

"Yeah. You've got that permanent frown you always get when you're upset." Her fingers caressed the furrows on his forehead. "Are you okay?"

"No. For the third time in my life, I feel the supreme urge to drink myself into oblivion."

She knew when one of those times was, and could make an educated guess as to the other time. "I think you smoked yourself halfway there. Medicinal effects worth the pollution?"

"Players has no medicinal value. No THC last I checked."

"Since when do you smoke?"

"Since never. Nah. Hate the stuff…. Emergencies," he coughed to clear his throat.

She draped her arms around him and pulled him to her. His damp hair soaked her skin through her nightshirt. "You're stressing me out. You haven't been normal since we got here."

"I've never been normal." He fussed with the bed sheets, trying to get closer to her.

"What happened? Why do you feel you need to drink to make it better? Did you have words with your dad? Did he say something to you?"

"He said plenty."

"And now you're sorry you talked to him."

"I got what I asked for. Shit. More than that."

"You're scaring me. Did you provoke him?"

"No. Yes. After a quarter century, how do you not provoke by bringing it up. I didn't mean to corner him, I just wanted some answers. And they were so damn late coming. I need a drink."

Kelly sat bolt upright. She might need a drink too, if this went as badly as he's intimating. "The last time you drank, you ended up in the Andes on a whim without telling anyone where you were going, and practically fell off the side of a mountain."

Truth crawled up his throat like severe heartburn. A drink would singe it, then wash it back down where it belonged. "I didn't fall, I dangled. I got out of it."

She guided his cheek so that he would look at her. "Remember our dream of Fiji? There was no alcohol on that list. There was music."

"Maybe we better leave now."

"To go to Fiji?"

"To get out of here, this house."

"Rick, it's after midnight. What are we going to do, pack up the car and drive away without saying goodbye?"

"Exactly, you have the MO down pat. You're in."

Rudy jumped up on the bed. He wanted to be in too.

"Is leaving like this necessary? First tell me what happened."

"I can't think straight in this house. I need to get out of here."

"Fine." She got up, whipped off her nightshirt and slipped on her sundress. She set his guitar in the black case that lay under the window and tossed her journal in after it. "Well put something on, then. You can't leave the house like that."

He realized he was in his boxers so he put on his walking shorts and t-shirt that were folded on the desk. He grabbed the covers off the bed before he left the room and Rudy was given no option but to curl up in the center of the unclothed bed and watched them walk out. They stole quietly out of the house and into the SUV. Night in Hampton's outskirts wasn't as black as it could have been thanks to the dome of haloed stars. The air was sticky and warm. Rick began to drive in the direction of the waxing moonlight. They kept up speed until he pulled off the road and across a shallow culvert into what looked like nothing more than open grassland. The SUV bumped and bounced and trampled its way for the better part of a kilometer beyond a stand of trees until it found a small clearing by a dormant tractor and thresher.

"Where are we?" Kelly asked.

"This is my grandparents' property."

"They live here?" She didn't see a house.

"No, it's their land. Make hay when the sun shines, they always say." Rick stopped the car and shut the engine and the headlights.

They got out and Kelly craned her neck in all directions soaking in the magical night. "So we're not going to get arrested for trespassing, are we?"

"Who'll think to look?" He grabbed his guitar case and a mini Maglite torch from the rear hatch, then he spread one of the bed sheets over the tall grass nearby. He sat down and began tuning. "Some have said I do my best work in the dark..."

"I brought you something." She knelt before him and handed him her journal.

"What you wrote?" He set the guitar aside. "Lyrics? To my music?" He felt around for the flashlight that had settled somewhere between them.

"You know better than to count chickens with me, Rick. I have no idea what I'm doing. But what you asked me to do, I've given it so much thought, because really it's about so much more than just songwriting."

"Are you saying yes?"

"So much wasted time, questioning, over-thinking. Throw all the crap out, there's no answer but yes. My heart tells me what little I can do, I want to do it for you. Because with you, it will grow into something so much more."

"When did you start writing again?"

"When I realized this was too important to let fly away."

Stars hovered like jewels in the moonlit velvet above them, each shining their singular piercing grace to the earth below. Music filled the night air and souls danced in harmony, cleansed in a rain of healing tears. The heavens seemed to move closer as they communicated in their own extraordinary way, loving each other, the stars sparkled brighter and more brilliantly than her solitary vantage had ever granted her. She had found Cygnus, her gemstone swan far toward the western horizon, soaring without sound in its infinite flight, forever aligned to heaven. To each of its five jewels that granted her deliverance, and carried her over the threshold of earthly consciousness to the cosmos of freedom, she whispered a prayer, graces of thanks for their eternal watchfulness, surrounded by certitude that she could let her mother and father rest in peace.

SUNDAY, AUGUST 24

They awoke late morning in Rick's old room, having crept back into the house after sunrise, while all within the Hutchinson home still lay quiet. At eleven o'clock, Maggie rapped upon the door, "Are you alive in there?"

"Oh yeah," Rick called back to his mother.

"Do you want breakfast in there or downstairs? Or are we to lunch now?" Her voice sung strongly through the six-panel door. She had just returned from church service, so her larynx was joyfully limber.

"We'll come down," Kelly's voice was light and flowing. She wondered if Hal was around, if he might join them for breakfast. Likely, he had already eaten. While she showered, she cherished the miracles of their night. She wanted to form an indelible memory of the feeling of resting securely in his arms in the covers under their stars. Recalling what Rick recounted to her, he had pushed past his own comfort limits and cast open the doors of communication with his father the previous evening in the relative privacy of the lower terrace at the 4H Club. She was proud of his courage and said a prayer of thanks as the shower draped her in warmth. From Rick's unabridged account to her, Kelly felt he had succeeded in his mission. Discourses this serious and long overdue don't come without some degree of distress. And with the topics on the agenda, the degree was dire. But she had faith that the risk of confrontation would be worth it in the long run, for all of them.

It was under the starry sky that Rick began telling Kelly of the discussion: He told his father on the terrace that he didn't want one more day to go by without talking about that day he came into the bank. Once the valve had loosened, the pipe broke under its own pressure.

Hal admitted to his son the severity of the mistakes he had made in his own life, and how each mistake compounded and complicated his life, lodging firmly and painfully into the previous ones. Rick knew that his father was older when he married, much older than men of that generation would have been. For multiple reasons, the pressure was on him, both personally and career-wise, and he agreed to marry Margaret Scanlon upon the advice and preparation by his parents, Howard Senior and Lorna Hutchinson. Margaret was charming and pleasant and everybody knew she would build a good home; she had come from a highly respected one. Back in those days, it was understood that marital love was a garden to be grown from the ground up and it took nurturing. But Hal's passion never sprouted, not in the way he was told it would. His career at the bank progressed slowly, he put in time, and promotions came when they came. Hal said Maggie applied little pressure and insisted that things would move forward when the time was right. As Hal climbed the bank ladder, and their boys grew like weeds, the guilt began to build to the point that he knew something was wrong in himself. It hadn't occurred to him, but apathy was what it was. A woman had come into the bank looking for a loan. She had ideas, big ones, and she wanted to start her own cosmetic retail company via a new multi-level corporation. Her husband sold insurance in the region, but she insisted it wasn't enough for her, that she wanted more for herself. In those days, Hal confessed to Rick, banks didn't give loans to women for business start-ups, not without her husband to co-sign. She had no intention of allowing her husband to own any control over her, or her new business. This woman was definite on two things, she wanted her independence and she made Hal feel that he could be the one to give it to her. She would come by frequently to visit him during his lunch breaks, full of energetic compliments and dreamy whims. She had this way of bolstering his ego, by flattering him and suggesting his position on the financial ladder would improve if he took her advice on ways to influence his higher-ups. The world needed contemporary vision, and Howard Hutchinson was the one to bring such modernism to an institution that was still living in the business stone age. She simmered in an intoxicating brew of feminine potency, combined with a hard-core business plan and she would stop for nothing. Things happened, so Hal indicated. He explained how invigorating she was, it was clear she didn't want to be married and tied down. She was heady, attractive, and exuded a bold confidence not normally seen in such a small town. She had no intention of remaining in Hampton. Her highest vision would take her to Montreal. But that kind of plan required monetary rocketry, a significant chunk to propel her off the ground. Her notions excited him and his apathy evaporated. He followed her suggestions and got promoted just as she predicted. He had been given increased responsibility and freedom to make large scale lending decisions for the bank; and he had become involved with a client. It fundamentally changed him, and at the time, he was sure it was for the better. This futuristic go-getter gal offered him a zeal that elevated himself both as a man and as a financial officer. With her, there was a synergy, foreign and addictive, that he never experienced with his wife; the paradigms were dichotomous. She got her loan, he had broken his marriage vows. And she high-tailed it to Montreal with another married man who promised her mutual business benefits. He had been used. And he offered himself up for the using. He felt the kind of basic, naked shame he could never admit to anyone, least of all his wife. A person could only be born with that kind of shame already attached, Hal said, like leeches on your belly, the blood in your veins already contaminated by the devil. Just like that woman had been born with the devil's instinct to suck blood from any source, no matter what the cost. Some souls were sold downstairs before they were born. He cried as he spoke words he never imagined he would. He never said what her name was. It never mattered. Hal was mortified at the idea of someone learning about it. He never imagined his son would be the one to discover his secret. Alcohol had naturally become his steadfast confidant.

Later on, when Rick had brought Rebecca home, shortly after they began dating seriously in college, he panicked inside, and even more when they announced their engagement. It would be his due reckoning, his just rewards: having to watch the grave mistakes of his life repeated in the generation after him. He saw shades of 'that woman' all through Rebecca right from moment one. But he couldn't utter a word about it. The old apathy hardened and he pickled himself alive, hoping to numb the pain of the inevitable outcomes. He couldn't offer any kind of warning that Rick would justifiably accept because he could never provide support for his position unless he divulged his own betrayal. So he had to let Rick make his own mistakes without intervention. Hal couldn't do anything. Both his hands and his tongue were tied. He knew Rebecca had a want for the wide world in the very same way as 'that woman'. She had her own mind, her own ideas of what she wanted, and the force behind it was the same. It was the way Rebecca talked every time Rick brought her home, the ways she dreamed out loud with tunneled, fixated determination for what she wanted, and only what she wanted: to get out of Hampton, and far away from it, out into the big wide, ego-flattering world. Hal did find agreement with Rebecca on one thing: Rick's bad choice of music for a career. And as time went on, Hal watched Rebecca romantically manipulate Rick's compliance until he made the switch to engineering. His son was her one-way ticket out of town, all the while the boy was blinded by her charm, fierce independence and triggering beauty. A mechanical or electrical engineer, she informed all of them, was guaranteed work in Toronto or Vancouver. As a pharmacist, she could set up shop in either city, but cost of living was high. But it would be worth it, these were large, socially diverse centers where income potential was limitless. There was nothing of inherent value or interest in New Brunswick, or anywhere in the Maritimes for that matter, Rebecca railed with disgust to Hal and Maggie more times than he could recall. He held such a strong distaste for that girl.

As the night in Rick's grandparents' field drew to a close, Rick concluded his recount to Kelly of the conversation with his father. He explained to his father about how his obvious hatred for Rebecca always troubled him deep down, because he could never figure why her opinions bothered him so much. Kelly listened as Rick admitted to her in resolution that everything his father identified about Rebecca was true, more or less. And blinded by her seductive intelligence and beauty, he was the last one to see it. Physical attraction aside, he must have been in love with her ideas, and got swept away in the flow of her educated enthusiasm for a big-city life. When they moved to Ontario and began to live that very life, he was instantly unhappy and he knew it. During their engagement, she just got more agitated and restless with him, as though her expectations weren't being fulfilled fast enough. He was doing everything he could. He genuinely believed he could give her all she wanted. It would just take time. But she couldn't seem to wait. Nobody could have predicted the ending...

Kelly switched off the water and as she toweled off, she shook her head in wonder, willing to entertain the possibility that maybe some part of Rebecca deep inside knew her life would be cut short. Maybe Rebecca knew... that ultimately, time wasn't hers. No wonder she was in such a hurry, as Rick pointed out.

Hal did join them for brunch, much to his wife and son's surprise and Kelly's delight. Maggie sat with them as they inhaled French toast and bacon strips. Still full from her earlier meal, she nibbled on bacon crumbs. They chattered on noisily about the wedding that took place the day before, sharing tidbits of small town news gleaned from other guests. Hal was downright cheerful and he enjoyed looking at Kelly's little photo album and talking with her about her life. Maggie wished several times out loud that Kevin could have been home with them that weekend. For her, it would have made it all complete.

TUESDAY, AUGUST 26

Kelly's curious impulses couldn't be quelled. In a flash of brilliance during the drive home from New Brunswick, there indeed was someone that Kelly could talk to directly regarding her mother's past. Marilyn Kaine and Bridget had been good friends till the end. A spur-of-the-moment visit with Marilyn first thing after returning from Hampton had yielded more than Kelly was prepared to learn. While Marilyn was overjoyed to see her, she was put off to learn Kelly hadn't popped by for chit-chat.

"I know it's a lot to ask of you, I know there was something going on. My mother was seeing someone for a while." Kelly chose to be up front with Marilyn right from the start.

Bridget's clandestine liaison was the last thing Marilyn expected to discuss so many years after the fact. "Well, Kelly, I must say, I am surprised that you'd come to me with this now."

"I only just learned about it…I found some old love letters written by him. Anything you could share with me would make a difference. To me." She didn't know how to explain her feelings. "I want to know my mother."

"Kelly, now you know as well as I do that I promised to look after you after your parents were killed. My objective was to see you grow into a healthy productive adult. I can see, you're a grown woman now, and apart from you coming and asking me so specifically, it was a secret she asked me to keep. But I feel it's important to tell you."

"Do you know what his name was? Do you know if he's still around? Or where he is?"

"I had only seen them together once, completely by accident, you see. I had run into them at a restaurant downtown one day and your mother introduced him to me. She said his name was James. But she called him Jamie. Oh, it was so obvious." Marilyn edged toward gossipy denigration.

Kelly had no way to know that Marilyn had her own reasons for revealing what she knew. It was as though the chance she had been waiting for had literally shown up on her doorstep.

"Indeed your mother had been very unhappy in her marriage, but I didn't know the reasons for your mother's actions. Suffice it to say, with your father working so much all the time, I expected as much. Lonely women will look. And the men who look for lonely women will find them. And your mother would have been a hard one to miss because of her good looks."

"Did my mom say to you she was lonely?"

"Well, yes, she always went on how much she missed her family and her home back in Alberta. And how little your father was there for her."

"What else can you tell me, Marilyn?"

"This man was a real estate colleague, so she told me. I liken those very men to opportunistic snakes in the grass. Real Estate just crawls with men like that, hardly any of them are in it for the career. I've told Wendy, time and time again, stay away from them. They're professional lookers, crafty salesmen, and it has nothing to do with houses..."

Kelly wanted only the facts, not Marilyn's opinionated editorials. She felt like Dragnet when she interjected, "About this man, Jamie, and his relationship with my mom..."

Marilyn explained to Kelly, "Your mother's mood had changed around that time. She was happier. She had even lost some weight. When I asked if her marriage was improving, Bridget admitted to me that it had nothing to do with her marriage. She had met someone who was over the moon for her, a younger man from work. I guess he told her all kinds of lovey-dovey stories, how he wanted to build his entire life around her. And can you imagine, your mother had fallen for it! Well, my land, I couldn't believe it. It had gone so far she told me she was seriously considering divorce. That she wanted to start again. I just didn't approve."

Astonished by the description of her mother's apparent infatuation, Kelly wondered how a relationship Marilyn was presenting as a superficial affair could have escalated to her mother contemplating divorce. Maybe Marilyn's shock and disapproval colored the relationship as immature. Jamie's letters came across as more serious than that. In any case, her parents decided not to go through with the divorce. Was it because her dad refused to let her go? Or did her mom change her mind on her own?

"Now, dear, I'm only telling you this because you're like a daughter. I had never said a word to anyone about all this, not even Wendy's father, out of respect for your mother. She confided in me after all. But I admonished her for her impropriety, for dreaming such silly castles in the sky, after all, she had a daughter to consider. How people would talk!! And for heaven's sake, to resume her sanity!!" Marilyn grew livid as though she were reliving the moment.

"I guess she listened to you. I found some divorce papers in a pile of her stuff, but they were never signed by my dad. And I gathered from the love letters that she was the one to break it off with this...James. Jamie?" She couldn't imagine her mother being in love with a grown man who had the same boyish name as a surly kid Kelly remembered Christopher getting in a fight with on the playground in fourth grade.

"I suspect your mother just faced reality and put it all aside. Oh," she sighed, "I just wanted him to go away. That boy was just... that! A boy. Now whether your father knew about her liaisons, don't ask me, but honestly, I think he did know," her voice fell to a shameful whisper.

Kelly didn't react outwardly. "Thank you Marilyn. I know you didn't expect me to come to you with all this, so I really appreciate you being so open about it."

"That's all I can tell you. You girls are grown up now," Marilyn sighed sentimentally, "and ready to embark on your own lives. You don't have parents to listen to, but you were always such a good girl that way, well... keep up your search. I hope you learn all you need to about this," she pleaded. "And that you do something good with it."

FRIDAY, AUGUST 29

Kelly waited on pins and needles at Faders Café. The post-workweek rush thickened steadily. She was lucky to claim a window table. Days had flown by since returning from Hampton. Between her own job and helping Rick look for work, she decided to tackle the cleanout of her flat as well. There was so much she felt ready to get rid of. The boxes of her parents' stuff from storage had been whittled down to two small cartons. Even then, she waffled about what she chose to keep; she didn't want to refer to it as junk, she couldn't bear to out of respect. She wanted to talk to Wendy immediately after returning from New Brunswick, with the humble intention of trying to set things straight between them, and at the very least, apologize for the way she treated her that day at the hospital. She wanted to patch up their relationship having considered the details that Rick relayed from Wendy. She had called Wendy's place on Tuesday and left a longwinded, rambling message of apology for her inexcusable behavior earlier in the summer. By the time Wendy called her back on Thursday, new developments had again taken place. Now she wasn't sure what her primary target for their meeting today should be.

A dark green mug of coffee, half decaf sat in front of her, steaming. In her hands, she held a business card whose corners were worn and split. On the back was a phone number along with the initials JT written by hand in the same script as her mother's love letters found in the piano. She could not take her eyes off it.

Wendy breezed in with a lofty demeanor and sat across from Kelly. "Hi," she sang. "I was floored when I got your message, you know. Talk about out of nowhere! Luckily, I like surprises."

"I hope it's okay that I called."

"Sure. Who am I to rebuff a sincere apology? You didn't ask me here to kiss me off again, I hope."

"No, definitely not. I'm still sorry about that. How've you been?" Kelly inquired.

"Good, busy. Work's been picking up and my father is putting together an audio production division in the firm. Can you believe it? A staff to handle audio sales for ads, working in tandem with Solar Studios. So we'll have the capability to move past visual still, into video motion! With sound! TV and radio ads too! Dad says there would be a place for me. I could be producing commercials. A lot of stars got their start that way, you know."

"Wow! You must be really excited. Something new and unexpected to take you in a different direction."

"It's a dream! But," she took on her sovereign air, "I can handle it. It's right up my alley," her eyes danced with delight. "You look great, by the way. I love your haircut! Betty's amazing with a pair of scissors, isn't she?" In fact, Wendy noticed she looked totally different. And it wasn't just the haircut. "So tell me about you," she pushed.

"What do you want to know?"

"Are you still with Doctor Train Man?"

"Yep. He's fine….fantastic." Kelly smiled with poise.

"I ran into him here one afternoon, he bought me coffee."

"Really?" She was interested to hear Wendy's side of it.

"He said something about his lab getting shut down."

"It's happening now. One more month to tie things off, but I'd say it's pretty dead there already. He's still trying to figure out the next step."

"He said he might be moving to Calgary, or was it Medicine Hat? Are you going to go with him? What is there to do in Medicine Hat? The Medicine Hat Dance….HA!"

Wendy always beat everyone else to laugh at her own jokes, Kelly chuckled. "It was Calgary. You know, he never asked me to move there with him."

"Well, fantastic or not, dump his ass."

"Calgary might not happen."

"He doesn't want the job?"

"I think he does. He applied for a second time...long story. Don't ask. We'll see what happens."

"Nothing around here, eh?"

"Jobs for Materials Engineering braniacs don't crawl out of the Maritime woodwork when you need them to. He's open."

"So you're still together then, at least for now."

"Regardless of time or place. Romantic and reticent, a bad combo, write that down for your reference manual. He told me the reason he never brought up Calgary to me at the time is because he knew I wasn't prepared to leave here. He was thinking longer term."

"No way! The sneak! Too smart for me."

"If he were smarter, he should have told me. Might have saved me a lot of unnecessary heartache. I hate surprises."

"So? Explain! Details!!"

"Explain what? How much of an idiot I was? Thinking that because he hadn't asked me to move to Calgary with him that we'd just automatically call it quits when he left. Thinking that he wanted to move anywhere else no matter what....there's something to be said for not talking openly," Kelly appeared incredulous, but still sounded very self-assured. "He told me we'd stay in Halifax for as long as I needed to be here."

"And he'll do what? Flip burgers at McDonalds with all the other PhD's? I hear Shoppers Drug Mart has decent benefits."

Kelly shrugged her shoulders. "I know, it's not practical. Here's the thing, it wasn't until he said he'd stay here for me that I started to feel that I wouldn't mind giving a new place a try, a fresh start...it could be fun."

Wendy excused herself to refill a piping hot French roast. When she returned to the table, Kelly's light expression had gone gray. "Are you alright? You look like you've seen a ghost."

"Change of topic. Tell me something. Was Franklin ever in real estate?" Kelly waited impatiently as Wendy thought.

"Yeah, he was, a long time ago."

"Is his last name Tullig?"

"Yes…" Wendy grew suspicious with an air of gravity. "Where is this coming from?"

Kelly concealed her agitation and showed her the front face of a wrinkled twenty-year old business card. Franklin was not a common name anywhere, Tullig even less.

Wendy read it aloud, "Franklin J. Tullig, Clearwater Real Estate, Halifax Nova Scotia….Clearwater…Wasn't that the agency your mom worked for?"

"The very same. Did he ever talk to you about when he was in real estate?"

"A bit, here and there. It was so long ago, he would have been in his twenties back then. All I remember him saying was that he'd never go back to it because it nearly killed him."

Kelly listened, and thought. "What did he mean by that?"

"I just assumed he meant the workload was hell or he just hated selling houses. I would."

Kelly flipped the card over for Wendy to see what was penned on the back. "Is this his handwriting?"

"Yes. Definitely. Look, an old phone number, let's call it, I bet it's disconnected now. This is so cool!"

Really, it wasn't. She wanted to press Wendy if she knew what the 'J' stood for, as added confirmation, but changed her mind knowing Wendy would start pecking. She had all the verification she needed.

"Where did you get this card, Kelly? This is bizarre."

"It was with my mom's stuff in a pile of other business cards I came across but never really looked at it until a couple of days ago. So there you have it. My mom knew Franklin way back in the seventies."

"Which explains why he was convinced he knew you from somewhere the day we ran into you at the grocery store."

"He must have seen a resemblance to my mom and just assumed he and I had met before."

"So that explains it." Wendy's startled look released a bit.

"Small world, eh." Kelly paused, reviewed her options, recalled Marilyn's perturbation and carefully chosen words. She decided to say nothing more. For now.

Wendy slid the card across the table back to Kelly's hand. When she took it back, Wendy noticed something on her ring finger. It was neutral colored; camouflaged against her skin, she almost would have missed it entirely. She grabbed her hand to get a closer look. It looked like a cord wound around her finger and tied in a sturdy knot underneath. "What is this?"

"I think he said it was an E-string." Kelly heart lifted again as she took a close look at her finger. She smiled.

Wendy tipped her chair back and howled out loud. She practically fell backward but caught the table at the last second sending her mug of coffee crashing to the floor splashing the guests at the table next to them as bursts of audible laughter broke out at Faders Café.

August 23

Cygnus Awakening

groping
*

screaming

clawing

drowning

gasping

receding *

grabbing

hiding

clutching

*

resisting

crawling

mystifying

searching

blossoming

*

emerging

reaching

*

sharing

accepting

loving

ascending

*

Turning Points Lyrics

REMEMBRANCE DAY

Reflections of you
Impressionist dreams
Calling for heaven's delight
To love you is to know you
To know you is to lose you
To know me is to let you go

Love's fascination
Found only fixation
To hold you, preserve you
Though breath is gone
Locks my heart in darkness
Further away from you

If I let you go, must I do it alone
What if I succeed,
will I be all alone

Reflections of you
Fading twilight
Darken my dreams to fly
To have you is to keep you
To see you is to free you
To feel you awakens the pain

Life's contemplation,
Begs transformation,
To admit all that you were
Might reveal me
Fully alone for the first time
Could it bring me back to you

If I let you go, must I do it alone
What if I succeed,
will I be all alone

Need to let you go,
need to do it alone
When I let you go,
I will be all alone

HOME

You know the feeling
I'm forgetting something
Spinning round and round
Trying to believe
There's someone, a place,
somewhere…

You know the feeling
Trapped beneath this icy shell
Wanting to understand
Trying to remember
Knowing, feeling you

Visibility,
Tangibility,
Sensibility
Can't accommodate for a
Distant memory that
Never clarifies
Never confronts me

Do you recognize,
like I recognize
Your voice, your kiss,
Your touch, misty longing
Will your heart remember
Does your soul want to
come back
Home to me… Home to me…

You know this feeling
Indescribable connection
Transcending circumstance
Trying to ignore this link
Through space and time

Your destiny entwined,
Perpetually with mine
Days drawn to eternity
Devoted to fulfill
(Devoted to fulfill)
This silent, driving force

You call me home

Please call me home
Please, call me home

WHO I AM

You've got it all wrong
As right as you think
This might be
I've been going along
With what you need
To see
In me

You've chained who I am
To what you imagined of me
Windowless walls of your mind
I can't break free
Let me be

You keep telling yourself
Just who I am
Now I'm telling myself
Just who I am

I smolder beneath
Ashes of my dreams,
Smoke's blown away
I never stood on my own
To say that I can't stay
And live
This way

You rearranged who I am
Rebuilt my life for me
What else could I be
Well you won't know
Let it go

It never dawned on me
That by failing you
I could succeed in me

Keep fanning your fears
With what you believe
What remains of me
Won't be deceived
I'm not going wrong
Betting on what you believe
To be
Is me

LIGHT

Northern glow
She needs it slow
She won't move close enough
Orion light
I call tonight
I can't hold her long enough

Passion's flame
Cannot be blamed
When you get lonely enough
Aurora shine
Send me a sign
Crossroad's never bright
enough

She can't trust in the night
Afraid of losing her sight
Waiting only for Light
'Cause love comes in with the
Light

Daybreak near
Wash away her fear
So she'll feel strong enough
Dawn so warm
Please calm her storm
She's evermore than enough

Night got locked in the role:
Demon, stealing passion
She won't give up control
Let night's healing happen

I need to believe in our nights
While love comes in with the
Light
Let her know that I'm right
Love grows all through the
night

There's nothing to fight
Love comes in with the Light
Love lives on through the night

QUIET LOVE

We forged beyond
Our own frontier
Our hearts have cried
All that we have tried

Now this Quiet Love
Can forever shine

Together one
My breath, your fire
Kept warm so long,
Undying ember

Of this Quiet Love
Was never wrong

Will we remember
Darkened words
Mercy has shone
Over rough terrain

This Quiet Love's
Bitter ache is gone

Evolving frames of
Reliant reference,
Loyal alliance,
Our trust in us grew

Through Quiet Love
We could become
What we always knew

We stayed the course
Through tossing nights
Ebb and flowing faith
Abiding Quiet Love
Golden glow surrounds
A wider dimension
You and I have been crowned,
On Fortitude's ground

Lay the ashes of our defenses
Through Quiet Love
The truth of us we've found

The truth of us we've found.

FORBIDDEN

My world is watered
Shades of gray without you
You'll just have to go
I'm finding ways
Tending my days

Fantasy…little less than a lie
When you dance with forbidden
Your ego's aiming too high
Just keep me apart
Far from your heart

I wish you hadn't told me
What nourished you all this
time
Reckless Longing for me
Helpless dreaming of me

It took your truth to remind
Me what's been calling so long
I'm open / hopin' to face it
When now I see
What I longed for was me

Why did you have to tell me
What has nourished you all
these days
Reckless Longing for me
Helpless dreaming of me

May your choices in life
Your remaining dreams
Bring you joy and not strife
When you wonder how
I'm doing now

For me, it's easier to cry
Than forcing the lie
Don't make me the drain for
your dreams
When you wonder why
I said goodbye

There are too many literary collections on my bookshelf to list, so I have picked some of my most cherished...I hope you enjoy them.

Complete poems / Emily Dickinson, edited by Thomas H. Johnson, 1st ed. Boston, Little, Brown, 1960.

Sonnets of the Portuguese/ Elizabeth Barrett Browning, 1850.

Poems / Rainer Maria Rilke [translations by J.B. Leishman, and J.B. Leishman and Stephen Spender], New York : A.A. Knopf, 1996.

The glance : songs of soul-meeting / Rumi ; translated by Coleman Barks with Nevit Ergin, New York : Viking/Arkana, 1999.

Waste of timelessness, and other early stories / Anaïs Nin, Weston, Conn. : Magic Circle Press ; New York : distributed by Walker, 1977.

A book of luminous things : an international anthology of poetry / edited by Czeslaw Milosz, 1st Harvest ed. New York : Harcourt Brace & Co., 1998.

These are books that I could suggest to anyone who is ready to break free – they really helped me get started.

You can heal your life / by Louise L. Hay, Santa Monica, CA : Hay House, 1987.

Life after trauma : a workbook for healing / Dena Rosenbloom and Mary Beth Williams, with Barbara E. Watkins, New York : Guilford Press, 1999.

Finding your own North Star / Martha Beck, 1st ed. New York : Crown Publishers, 2001.

Emotional clearing / John Ruskan, lst Broadway Books ed. New York : Broadway Books, 2000.

Losing your parents, finding your self / Victoria Secunda, 1st ed. New York : Hyperion, 2000.

Rick loaned me these treasures from his collection that I refuse to live without now...

A new earth : awakening to your life's purpose / Eckhart Tolle,
New York, N.Y. : Penguin Group, 2005.

The prophet / Kahlil Gibran, New York : Knopf, 1923.

Untrain your parrot : and other no-nonsense instructions on the path of Zen / Elizabeth Hamilton ; [foreword by Rosa Parks], 1st ed. Boston : Shambhala, 2007.

More books that Rick cherishes – he asked me to include them for you.

Zen guitar / Philip Toshio Sudo, 1st ed. New York : Simon & Schuster, 1997.

Leaves of grass / Walt Whitman following the edition of 1891-'2 [Woodcuts by Valenti Angelo], New York : Modern Library, [1933],1982.

Full woman, fleshly apple, hot moon : selected poems of Pablo Neruda / translated by Stephen Mitchell, 1st ed. New York, NY : HarperCollins Publishers, 1997.

ABOUT THE SETTING

http://novascotia.com
http://www.pointpleasantpark.ca/
http://www.new-brunswick.net/new-brunswick/hampton/

Discussion Points

1. The sound of breaking glass is a recurring element in the story. What does the sound of breaking glass connote to you? What does it signify for Kelly in particular?

2. Kelly is fixated with the astronomical heavens: stars, the blackness of space and in particular, the constellation Cygnus. What do each of these symbolize in Kelly's philosophical paradigm?

3. Who is Agramon? Kelly named the entity after the mythical demon Agramon. Why? What is Agramon's role in her life? What does the concept of 'an Agramon within each of us' represent in terms of the human condition?

4. The following favorite poets of Kelly's have distinct influences on her view of life: Elizabeth Barrett Browning, Emily Dickinson, Robert Frost, and Rainer Maria Rilke. Similarly, Rick identifies with the following poets: Walt Whitman, William Blake, Pablo Neruda, and Kahlil Gibran. Choose one or more of these poets to research (their works, poetic style, life history). How does your research further your understanding of Kelly, and of Rick? What do the choices of poets demonstrate about each character?

5. The relationship triangle of Kelly, Wendy and Rick form a subtle, interconnected balance. How do these three distinctly different personalities in this story represent the larger spectrum of human nature? Consider these three characters in the ways he/she deals with one or more of the following: grief, temptation, betrayal, stress, shock/surprise and joy. Highlight similarities and differences.

6. Kelly and Wendy are bound to each other not only by their shared youth, but also by Kelly's tragedy. Why did Kelly try so desperately to break that bond? Would you have done the same in her situation?

7. Most characters in the novel are faced with a unique challenge and his/her personality comes through on many levels. First impressions, just as in real life, make an impact on the reader. Similarly, as the story unfolds, the reader learns more about each character's plight. How did your feelings change by the end of the book as compared to your initial impression for Marilyn? For Hal? For Wendy? For Bridget? Discuss other characters as well.

8. People are affected by their surroundings. Settings offer the reader clues toward Kelly's interaction and perception of her expanding experience, the author describes many places in detail that were not part of Kelly's daily routine: Rick's condo, Point Pleasant Park, the Mercury Club, Mike's cabin, the self-storage facility, Mike and Natasha's home, the town of Chester, the hamlet of Hampton...How does each new setting provoke specific actions Kelly might not have otherwise initiated that helped her actively seek her freedom? What aspect of her personality does each setting reveal in a deeper sense? List the places that seemed to have caused the greatest changes in her. What do you conclude?

9. The cover of the book depicts a fern leaf. Why is this image important? Consider the title of the book. What is Kelly's turning point? Does she experience more than one turning point? What is/are the turning point(s) for Rick? For Wendy?

10. The nature of Kelly's journal entries (content, writing style, mood etc...) changes over the course of the novel and her journey of growth through this phase of her life concludes with her song lyrics. Study the following poems: Freedom (Ch.1), Blackness (Ch.3), Water Under Bridge (Ch.5), Trust (Ch.6), The Gift (Ch.8), Tainted (Ch.9), Dewdrops (Ch.13), Cygnus Awakening (Ch.18). What changes in her writing do you notice? What other excerpts from her journal support your opinion? How has she responded to her rapidly expanding world as reflected in her song lyrics?

11. Compare and contrast Kelly's conceptual understanding of the terms 'freedom' and 'emptiness' with Rick's idea using evidence from the story to support your points.

12. Kelly, Wendy and Rick have differing approaches to handling life's challenges. Which character do you relate to and why?

13. The power of the imagination is undeniable. What are the pros and cons to having a vivid imagination? How does this create tension between the characters in the novel?

14. 'Apathy is the main cause of the destruction of relationships' is one theme of this novel. Discuss the ways this theme is addressed and elucidated in the story using as many characters and examples you can find.

For ***Turning Points*** Book Club and Reader's Guide
information

www.quintessencestudio.com

To order this book from Quintessence

www.lulu.com/quintessence

www.ingramcontent.com/pod-product-compliance
Lightning Source LLC
Chambersburg PA
CBHW060411030726
47495CB00003B/534